Katherine Howell is a former paramedic. Her award-winning and critically acclaimed Detective Ella Marconi series is published in multiple countries and languages. She lives in Queensland with her partner.

www.katherinehowell.com

TELL THE TRUTH

KATHERINE HOWELL

MACMILLAN

Pan Macmillan Australia

First published 2015 in Macmillan by Pan Macmillan Australia Pty Ltd
1 Market Street, Sydney, New South Wales, Australia, 2000

Cataloguing-in-Publication entry is available
from the National Library of Australia
http://catalogue.nla.gov.au

Typeset in 12.5/14 pt Bembo by Post Pre-press Group, Brisbane
Printed by McPherson's Printing Group

The characters in this book are fictitious and any resemblance to real persons, living
or dead, is purely coincidental.

Papers used by Pan Macmillan Australia Pty Ltd are natural, recyclable products
made from wood grown in sustainable forests. The manufacturing processes
conform to the environmental regulations of the country of origin.

For Benette

ONE

Rowan Wylie drove into the Playland car park just after ten on a Monday morning in early April, his granddaughter, Emelia, wriggling with excitement in her car seat in the back.

'We here!'

'We are indeed,' Rowan said.

Playland was two months old and Emelia's favourite place. It was part of a small new development in Homebush, a U-shaped collection of precast concrete buildings facing each other across an asphalt car park. Most of the business spaces were still being finished, so the majority of the ten or so cars were parked outside Playland, the remaining few on the facing side outside the wholesale nut shop and the lighting and electrical store. An array of utes and vans stood parked at angles outside the spaces being fitted out.

Rowan switched off the engine and stepped out of his car into the morning sunlight and the muffled sound of children shouting. Playland's door was firmly closed but it didn't stop the noise. He turned to set Emelia free, then stopped to look twice at a car parked across the way.

Emelia smacked a hand against the window. 'Pa!'

'Coming,' Rowan said, and released Emelia's harness.

He lifted her out, then closed the door, looking again at the car. Silver Astra, paramedic sticker on the back window the same as the one on his own, SD 177 numberplates. Stacey's. He looked around. If she was here, he could talk to her. Apologise.

'Down,' Emelia demanded.

'Just a sec.' He couldn't see Stacey. She might be checking out one of the empty spaces for James, but she had nothing to do with his IT business, so that made no sense. Besides, Simon would've mentioned it if James had any plans for expansion or moving.

Emelia kicked in his arms.

'Hold on.' He crossed the asphalt and went inside the nut shop.

A man in white smiled and offered him and Emelia samples of candied peanuts. Rowan shook his head and looked down the aisles. Stacey wasn't there. He walked outside and into the lighting place. The ceiling was hung with banners advertising opening specials, and a saleswoman was demonstrating something on a light fitting to a couple in their sixties, but Stacey wasn't there either. He went back outside, Emelia complaining and trying to lean out of his grip.

'Okay, okay, we're going inside,' Rowan said.

He had to walk past Stacey's car on the way to Playland's door, and glanced in. There was a big dark stain on the passenger seat and floor. A stain that had spattered and trickled. A stain that looked unnervingly like drying blood.

The cool autumn day got cooler.

He tried the passenger door. Locked.

'Pa,' Emelia whined.

'Just a minute.'

He took out his mobile, scrolled through to Stacey's number, and pressed to call.

Emelia struggled in his grip. 'Go in!'

'I know, buddy. Just hang on.'

Voicemail picked up. '*Stacey here. Leave your deets and I'll bell you back.*'

'Just me,' Rowan said. 'I'm standing by your car outside Playland. Are you here somewhere? Let me know. Thanks.' He hung up, then called her home number. The machine answered and he left the same message there.

'Pa!' Emelia fought his grip. 'Down!'

'Stop it.' Worry made Rowan speak more harshly than he'd intended. 'Be quiet or we'll go back home.'

'Not fair!'

'One more sound and we leave.'

Emelia started to cry. Rowan put her on the ground and grasped her arm while scrolling for James's mobile number.

'Rowan,' James answered. 'How goes it?'

'Do you know where Stacey is?' Rowan said, trying to moderate the tension in his voice.

'It's her day off so she should be at home,' James said.

'Have you talked to her this morning?'

'I texted her earlier to say I was back, but she didn't reply. I figured she was asleep. Why?'

Emelia squirmed. 'You're hurting me.'

Rowan loosened his grip. 'I'm standing by her car and it looks kind of abandoned. I tried to call her and she didn't answer.'

There was a pause. 'What do you mean, abandoned?'

'Maybe not abandoned.' He didn't want to mention the blood. 'It's in the car park next to Playland. I thought you might know why she'd be around here.'

'The only person we know who goes there is you,' James said. 'She probably decided to meet you there.'

That could be it. It was common knowledge at the station that Rowan brought Emelia here on most if not all of his days off, and it was loud enough inside that Stacey might not hear her phone ring. It was best to check inside before he crashed James's world.

'She probably thought it'd be a big surprise for Emmy,' James was saying. 'Speaking of, how is the little munchkin?'

'Dragging me to the door this very second.' Rowan forced a smile into his voice. 'You're right; she'll be in here somewhere. Sorry.'

'No problem.'

Emelia tugged at the heavy door. Rowan put his phone away and helped. The noise inside enveloped them and Rowan smiled at the girl behind the counter. She smiled back, then leaned over to talk to Emelia who had pulled off her shoes and was jumping up and down on the spot.

'How are you today, Emelia?'

'Going in the ballpit,' Emelia shouted.

'Off you go then,' Rowan said.

She thrust her shoes at him, then ran into the centre. Rowan tucked the shoes under his arm and took out his wallet. The girl gave him his change and he walked in. Be sure, he told himself. Despite that sick feeling, make sure.

Emelia was already in the pit and called out as he passed. 'Look where I am, Pa!'

'Yes, right where you said you'd be.'

He looked around. Adults talked and drank coffee and watched their kids from the cafe area. He walked around all the equipment. He lingered outside the female bathroom until a woman came out.

She looked startled for a second, then smiled. 'Rowan, right?'

'Hi.' He couldn't remember her name. 'I'm looking for a friend. Is anyone else in there?'

She shook her head. 'It's empty.'

'Thanks.' He headed off on another lap.

'Pa, I'm up here now. Look, Pa!'

'I see you.'

Stacey wasn't here. He went to the bathroom woman – Sarah, that was it – who was talking to her child through the ballpit net.

4

'Find your friend?' she asked.

'Not yet,' he said. 'I have to nip outside and make a call. Would you mind keeping an eye on Emelia?'

'Love to.' She squeezed his arm, then took the shoes from him. 'I'll mind these too. You take your time.'

He called Emelia down and explained to her, then went out. He looked in the window of Stacey's car again. He walked up and down the rows of business spaces, looking in at the plasterers, the painters, the electricians bent over their work. He went to the street and looked both ways. It was busy with people going about their day in cars and utes. It was all so ordinary.

He took out his phone.

'You find her?' James answered.

'No,' Rowan said.

James cut in before he could go on. 'I called her mobile and got no answer, then I called home and got the machine. I rang Marie, but she hasn't talked to her since yesterday. Her phone has that tracking app on it so I looked it up – it's turned off now so the app can't find her, but the last place it was turned on was near that Bicentennial Park in Homebush, at ten past six last night.'

'Do you have a spare key for her car?' Rowan asked.

'At home. Why?'

'Because there's something else . . . It looks like blood.'

'Say that again?'

'In her car, on the seat and the floor,' Rowan said. 'At least, that's what it looks like.'

There was a pause. 'Like if she got her period?'

'No. It's a big pool,' Rowan said. 'Like something bad happened.'

'Jesus,' James said. 'I'm coming down.' He hung up.

James's shop was in Strathfield, James and Stacey's house in Haberfield. James wouldn't arrive with the key for half an hour or more. Rowan looked inside the car again, then checked on Emelia. She shrieked down the slippery dip. Sarah caught his eye and gave a thumbs up, and he went back to pace beside the car.

When did you make the decision to smash the window? When did you call the police? He thought it was blood, but he couldn't be absolutely certain without getting closer, without smelling it. If he was certain, he'd have been onto the cops already. If he called them and it was something else – though he couldn't think what – he'd feel a total idiot. A paramedic freaking out, ha ha. If he broke the window to find out more before he called them, and it was nothing, he'd feel a fool in front of James, and, even worse, in front of Stacey when she did turn up.

Wait until the key gets here, he thought. Once he smelled it he'd know. A pool of blood that size smelled like nothing else on this green earth. But he couldn't help remembering patients who'd waited before calling for help for one reason or another and got much sicker as a result. He was always telling them to stop worrying and get on the phone. Now here he was, doing the same thing.

Possibly. Don't panic.

The stain was just in the car – no drips outside, none leading anywhere. It could be motor oil. It was that dark, after all. He looked in and tried to make himself believe it. And twenty minutes couldn't make that much difference when he was lucky to even have spotted the car. It could've been here who knew how long otherwise.

You're assuming something bad has happened to her.

He was, and he couldn't stop.

Simon's dinged-up white Camry sped into the car park. James leapt from the passenger side, and Simon, Rowan's son, got out from behind the wheel. He'd worked for James in his computer shop for close to a year.

'Where's Em?'

'Inside,' Rowan said. 'She's okay. A friend's watching her.'

James cupped his hands against the glass of Stacey's car window. 'Jesus.'

'You got the key?' Rowan said. 'I can't be sure what it is from here.'

Simon shook his head. 'We came straight over.'

James looked around the asphalt. 'I need a rock.'

'I've got a tyre lever.' Rowan went to get it from his boot. His hands were clammy on the metal. James's urgency made it real and he wished he'd broken in himself.

'Do the back window,' he said as James grabbed it. There could be evidence in the front, he was thinking, but didn't want to say.

James moved to the rear driver's side without asking why. He struck the glass hard and it shattered into the car. A meaty metallic smell billowed out and he fumbled at the door lock with shaking hands.

Rowan eased him away and looked over his shoulder at his son. 'Call the police.'

TWO

Detective Ella Marconi crouched inside the car's front passenger door to study the pool of blood in the passenger footwell, while Detective Murray Shakespeare looked across from the driver's side. The car's owner was Stacey Durham, paramedic, last heard from yesterday afternoon. No criminal record. No DNA on file. No history of disappearances.

The car smelled like an unventilated butcher's shop. The footwell carpet was soaked with blood, the cracked surface strewn with thick drying clots. Dried blood stained the front of the seat and spatters marked the centre console and the underside of the glove box. The roof lining was clean.

'Anything on the driver's side or in the back?' Ella asked.

The Crime Scene tech shook his head. 'Nor in the boot.'

Behind him, a couple of uniformed officers watched on. Across the car park three men in civvies sat in plastic chairs, one holding a toddler. They were kept apart and silent by a heavy-set constable.

'And it's human?' Murray said.

'Definitely,' the tech said. 'Hard to estimate exact amount, but based on the area it covers and the absorbency of the carpet, I'd say around one and a half litres.'

Murray whistled. 'That's a lot, right?'

'If you lose that much and you're still alive, you sure don't feel good,' the tech said. 'The body only holds about seven.'

'Don't feel good?' Ella asked.

'I don't know the full ins and outs,' the tech said. 'I guess you might be unconscious? Dizzy at least.'

Ella took out her mobile and pressed the first listing in the favourites.

'Hey,' Callum answered, a smile in his voice.

'I'm at work,' she said. 'If a person loses a litre and a half of blood, how do they feel?'

He was immediately serious. 'They'd be pale, sweaty, short of breath, nauseated, anxious and agitated. They'd feel weak and faint. Some people might be close to unconscious, or even already there. They need help, fast.'

'And if they don't get it?'

'If the bleeding keeps up, they die,' he said. 'Even if it's stopped but they don't get help – fluid replacement and/or blood transfusion – they run the risk of dying anyway. Who are we talking about?'

'I'll tell you later,' she said. 'Thanks.'

'See you tonight?'

'I'll let you know.' She ended the call and put her phone away.

Murray winked over the car at the scene tech. 'Doctor boyfriend.'

'Ah,' the tech said.

Ella looked back into the car. 'You ever seen this much blood in a faked disappearance?'

The tech shook his head. 'Not even close.'

Every such case that Ella had read about or dealt with herself had involved small quantities of blood and insignificant wounds. People thought they could cut themselves to make it look like they'd been attacked, but soon found out it hurt. A lot. Cops saw the shallowest cuts and tiny tentative stabs as the would-be 'victim' tried to get up the courage to go deeper. They very rarely managed it.

'Might be a stabbing,' Murray said. 'Carjacker forces her over, she fights back, he goes nuts.'

'But there's no arterial spray,' the tech said. 'You'd almost expect it with a stabbing that left this much blood in one place. And the shape of the spatters indicates sideways movement, which seems odd too.'

'And if that is what happened, then what?' Ella said. 'There're no drag marks, nothing on the sill or the ground, nothing that looks like it's been wiped down. Hard to get out without leaving any marks at all.'

'We'll put it under Luminol later and see if anything like that was cleaned up,' the tech said. 'Lab tests'll show us the rest, including DNA. If you can get some known sample of hers, hairs or whatever, we'll try to put a rush on the match.'

Ella's mind was in high gear. They needed to search the area, speak to everyone in the vicinity, check local CCTV. Everything. If this blood was Stacey Durham's, the situation was urgent. Unlike a murder scene where the person was dead and the task was to identify and find the killer, here they might have a missing and dying woman – a life they might be able to save.

'Call the office,' she said to Murray. 'Tell Dennis what we've got. Tell him to send everyone.'

Murray took out his phone and moved away.

Ella looked across the car park to the three men sitting in plastic chairs. The first, aged about forty with short brown hair, sat back in his chair, his suit coat hanging open and his hands linked over his eyes as if he needed darkness to think. The next was older, in his late forties perhaps, fit-looking, balding, in khaki shorts, blue T-shirt and runners. He leaned forward, his back straight, his elbows on his knees, watching her and the activity around the car. The third and youngest, sandy hair combed sideways like a little boy's, in suit pants and a white shirt with the sleeves rolled up, bounced a giggling little girl on his thigh. The constable behind them stifled a yawn.

'Husband's in the jacket, James Durham, owns a computer shop in Strathfield,' the senior uniformed officer said behind her. 'Middle guy's Rowan Wylie, a frie nd and colleague of the woman. He noticed her car when bringing his granddaughter to the play place there.'

Noticed, Ella thought.

'He saw the blood and called the husband,' the officer went on. 'Young guy is Simon Wylie, Rowan's son, works for James as some kind of computer tech.'

It was all very buddy-buddy. Ella eyed them. James Durham pressed his thumbs into his temples. Simon Wylie and his kid pointed at birds in the sky. Rowan Wylie hadn't moved. His gaze was steady, watching them.

'Anything else in the car?' Ella asked the officer. 'Purse, handbag, phone?'

'Nothing.'

Murray came around the back of the car. 'Troops are on their way.'

'Good.'

Ella looked back at the three men. You always started with those closest to the victim, because closeness meant emotion, and emotion of some kind – hate, love, jealousy, revenge, greed – were behind most violent crimes.

'So which one's the husband?' Murray asked.

'Follow me,' Ella said.

James Durham stood as they approached. His light blue shirt was creased under his coat, his navy tie pulled away from his neck. His eyes were dark and deep-set with reddened rims as if he'd been crying, and he smelled of anxious sweat.

'Stacey's my whole life,' he said, as if by way of introduction.

'Detectives Ella Marconi and Murray Shakespeare,' Ella said.

11

Closer up she could see he was a little older than she'd thought, with lines around his eyes and grey at his temples. 'Can we have a word?'

He followed them a few steps away and leaned against the boot of a parked car as if he couldn't trust his legs. 'So much blood.'

'We don't know that it's hers,' Murray said, taking out his notebook.

James Durham looked at him flatly. 'That guy said it's human.'

Ella took careful note of his response. People tended to hope, even against the odds, when someone they loved was missing. Despondency at this early stage could indicate that he knew Stacey wasn't coming back.

She asked him his date of birth, contact numbers and address, then Stacey's date of birth and mobile number. Murray sent both mobile and landline numbers to their boss, Dennis Orchard, to start the processes of getting their phone records and tracking Stacey's mobile signal in the hope that it might show them where she was.

Ella said, 'When did you last talk to Stacey?'

'Yesterday afternoon, about four,' James said. 'I was in Melbourne for a conference. We talked for five or so minutes. She said she was tired and going to have dinner in front of the TV, a bath, then an early night.'

'Who called who?'

'I rang her mobile from mine,' he said.

'Where were you staying?' Ella asked.

'The Novotel on Collins Street, where the conference was held.'

'When did you leave there?'

'This morning,' he said. 'I texted her from the airport and said I'd go straight to the office when we landed, but she didn't reply.'

'Was that normal for her?' Murray asked.

'It wasn't abnormal enough that I worried,' James said. 'Sometimes she sleeps in. I tried her again later, when Rowan called about her car. Tried home too. Got voicemail on both. I called her sister too, but she hadn't heard from her either.'

'What's her sister's name?' Ella said.

'Marie Kennedy.'

'Is she at work today?'

'Home. It's her RDO.'

'Where does she live?' Murray asked.

James gave them an address in Padstow. 'She's a physio. She told me she talked to Stacey yesterday and she was fine. Her daughter, Paris, is a paramedic too. She works with Rowan there.'

'Stacey's parents?' Ella asked.

'Dead five years. Car accident. There are no other siblings.'

'What about her friends?' Murray said.

'The three she spends most time with are Aimee Russell, Claire Comber and Vicky Page,' James said. 'Claire's a paramedic, the other two are nurses. They all go out for drinks sometimes, dinner, movies. That sort of thing.'

Ella nodded. They'd track them down later. 'Do you know your wife's blood type?'

He glanced past her at the car. 'AB positive.'

'Is she on any medication?'

'Nothing,' he said. 'Oh, the pill. Does that count?'

Ella wrote it down. 'What did you think when Rowan told you Stacey's car was here?'

'First I assumed she was in the kids' place, waiting to surprise Em and Rowan.' He nodded towards Playland. Ella saw a couple of people watching them through the glass door. 'Then when he said he couldn't find her, and I couldn't see where her phone was through that app, and there was blood in the car, I started to worry.'

'What did the tracking app show?' Ella asked.

'That the phone's turned off,' he said. 'Or the battery's flat, or the SIM's been removed. The last time it was working was at Bicentennial Park in Homebush, at ten past six last night.'

'Is that a place she would normally go?' Ella asked.

'She likes the boardwalk-type things there. She's been a couple of times in the past year, but never at that time of day.'

'Did she ever meet anyone there?'

He glanced sideways at Rowan. 'Not that I know of.'

Ella noted his action. 'Have you had any immediate thoughts about what might've happened?'

'All the worst ones, I guess.'

'Like what?'

'What do you think? Kidnapping, abduction, assault – god, you want me to say it? You want me to actually say out loud that someone's taken her? Might've killed her?'

'Okay, Mr Durham,' Murray said. 'Does anyone have any reason to want to hurt her?'

'None,' James said. 'None whatsoever. She's perfect. She's a complete sweetheart.'

'How about wanting to hurt you?' Ella asked.

'No.'

'No other computer shops in your area?' Murray said.

'You're thinking another business owner might've done this?' James shook his head. 'There are always people who'd like to see competition go down, but I can't imagine anyone doing this.'

'So you haven't had any calls or threats?' Ella said.

'Not recently. Three months back somebody told you people that I was running a scam. I wasn't. You people checked it out. The investigating officer said anonymous tips are generally bullcrap anyway.'

'Do you recall the officer's name?' Murray asked.

'DC Elizabeth Libke.'

'You've got a good memory,' Ella said.

'I remember her because she was useless,' James said. 'More or less shrugged and said there was nothing she could do.'

They'd check that later. 'How's your marriage?'

'Better than anyone else's that I know,' James said. 'Five years this year, we hardly fight, she's my entire world.'

'Kids?' Ella said.

James shook his head. 'It's just us.'

'When did you leave for Melbourne?'

'Friday afternoon, 5 pm flight. Simon came with me.' He nodded at the young man with the toddler.

'He works for you, correct?'

He nodded again.

'And you're friends with his dad Rowan?'

'For years,' he said.

Ella chose her words carefully. 'How close are he and Stacey, do you think?'

'They've worked together a lot.' He shrugged, a rather tense shrug in Ella's eyes.

'Do they socialise?' she asked.

'She sometimes meets him and the baby for coffee, or here at the play place.' He glanced over at Rowan again. 'We sometimes get together in a group, though that hasn't happened for a while.'

'Why not?' Murray asked.

James shrugged once more. 'Life's busy, I guess. Between shift work, the business, and the baby, we never have the same time free anymore.'

'When did you last actually see Stacey?' Murray asked.

'Friday afternoon when I left home for the airport.'

'She didn't drop you off?'

He shook his head. 'It was peak hour. She would've spent an hour stuck in traffic. We took a taxi.'

'Was she working over the weekend?' Ella asked.

'No, she was off.'

'So why didn't she go with you?' Murray asked.

'It was a computing conference,' James said. 'She's not into any of that. I said she could come along and spend the days shopping or just wandering about, but she said no.'

15

He could've slipped back into Sydney without anyone knowing, Ella thought. He could've arranged for someone else to deal with Stacey while he was fully alibied. He looked anxious, and she wondered if he was trying to act the scared and worried husband, trying to remember to use the present instead of the past tense: *I love my wife* as opposed to *I loved my wife*, which could slip out if he knew she was dead.

'We're going to need to search your house,' she said.

'Do whatever you need to do. I just want her found.'

★

Rowan watched the detectives talking to James. He knew this was how it worked, that they'd all be interviewed and it was the beginning of a long process of investigation, but it felt wrong to be just sitting like this, in a chair in the sun. Something had happened to Stacey and here they all were practically killing time.

He looked at Simon, blowing raspberries on the back of giggling Emelia's neck, and asked, 'Did James say what he thought might've happened when you were driving here?'

'No conversation, thanks,' the uniformed constable behind them said.

Simon raised his eyebrows at Rowan, then looked back down at Emelia. Rowan stared across the car park. The female detective gave James a card and he kept it in his hand as he walked towards the chairs, his face so full of emotion that Rowan had to look away.

The detectives conferred, then motioned for Rowan and Simon to join them. The woman took Rowan in one direction while Simon followed the male detective in the other, bouncing Emelia on his hip. The woman was around forty, with dark hair blowing across her face in the breeze. Her navy pantsuit and white shirt fitted her well.

'I'm Detective Ella Marconi,' she said.

'Rowan John Wylie.' He recited his address and date of birth without being prompted.

'You've done this before,' she said.

'Paramedics get to be witnesses a lot.'

She nodded. 'How did you come to notice Stacey's car?'

'I glanced across the car park and saw it,' he said. 'I see it parked at work. With the numberplate and the sticker on the back window, it's familiar.'

'What did you do when you saw it?'

He told her about looking in the window, calling Stacey's mobile, checking inside Playland, calling James.

'Why did you look in her window?'

'I've never seen her car here before,' he said. It sounded weak. 'It seemed out of place.'

She studied him, then she said, 'When you called James, how did he respond?'

'The first time he said she was probably around here somewhere. The second time he was worried and came straight over.'

'When did you last see or speak to Stacey?'

'Last Thursday, at eight o'clock in the morning. I was going off duty and she was starting an overtime shift.'

'You're certain?'

He nodded, but Marconi watched him as if she expected more. Unnerved, he glanced away to where Simon was saying something to the male detective about James calling the bank.

'Mr Wylie,' Marconi said, but before she could go on, cars pulled up on the street and people who he guessed were plain-clothes police got out. She excused herself and went to speak to them, leaving him glad of the respite from her stare, but the police rapidly fanned out along the street and through the car park, and too quickly she came back.

He steadied himself. *You know nothing about this, you have nothing to hide.*

'Mr Wylie,' she said again. 'Have you ever been to Bicentennial Park?'

'We took Emelia there last summer.'

'What about recently?'

He felt uncomfortable under her gaze. 'No.'

She made an abrupt note. 'How long have you known Stacey?'

'Eight or nine years,' he said. 'We met on the job. I played soccer with James back then and when my wife turned forty, seven years ago, we had this big party and invited them both. Turns out James and Stacey knew each other as kids – James went out with her sister Marie a couple of times apparently – but they hadn't seen each other for years. They got together, then a couple of years later got married.'

Marconi raised her eyebrows. 'Happily ever after, huh?'

'From what I've seen, yes,' Rowan said.

'So how long have you known James?'

'Ten years, thereabouts.'

'And your son works for him?'

Rowan nodded. 'For the last ten months or so.'

'And Stacey's niece works with you?'

'She's my current trainee, yes.'

'It's quite a little circle, isn't it,' Marconi said.

He couldn't read her tone. 'I guess so.'

She went on without pause. 'Has Stacey ever told you about problems she's been having?'

'We've talked about annoying patients, or issues at work with rosters and so on, but that's it.'

'Nothing personal?'

'Nothing that stands out in my mind.'

That gaze again. 'Would you say you and Stacey are close?'

'Not close exactly. Good friends.'

'Good friends aren't close?'

'To me close means something more.' He felt sweaty. 'Good friends are . . . friendly.'

Marconi nodded. 'Has she seemed normal lately? Happy? Sad? Angry?'

'She's been her normal self,' he said. 'She's cheerful. She's got a black sense of humour, and she's smart and she's funny.' He felt he was babbling, but couldn't stop. 'So when I saw her car I was hoping she was here because she's good to be around. She's one of those people others just like to be with.'

'Including you,' Marconi said.

'Well, yes.'

'You said you were married?'

'I was. My wife, Jennifer, died two years ago. Breast cancer.'

Marconi said, 'I'm sorry.' She glanced at Simon and the other detective.

'He and his girlfriend and Emelia live with me,' Rowan found himself saying. 'Megan's parents threw her out when she got pregnant. We all looked after Jennifer at home. Emelia was six weeks old when she died.' He closed his mouth.

'I'm sorry,' Marconi said again.

'Stacey and I are good friends. That's all.' He could feel the sweat run down his sides.

She looked at him for a long moment. 'Understood.'

'Hi, Pa.' Emelia was waving at him. He waved back, a feeling like a cramp in his chest.

Marconi said, 'Do you know Stacey's sister, Marie?'

'Not well, but we've met a few times.'

'How about Stacey's friends?'

He nodded. 'She's got three that she hangs about with. Claire Comber, Vicky something and Aimee Russell. Claire's a paramedic based at Rockdale. Vicky and Aimee are nurses at Westmead. Surgical ward, I think.'

Marconi wrote in her notebook, then looked directly into his eyes. 'What did you think, deep down, when you saw the stain in the car?'

'About how I've seen less blood in cars when I've pulled out stabbing victims too late to save their lives.'

Saying the words aloud made the skin go tight on his scalp.

★

Murray was still talking to Simon, so Ella took the spare moment to type Stacey's mobile number into her phone then call it.

'*Stacey here. Leave your deets and I'll bell you back.*'

'This is Detective Ella Marconi of the New South Wales Police,' Ella said after the beep. 'Stacey, we need to know where you are and that you're okay. If you need urgent assistance call triple zero. Otherwise please call me back on this number.'

When she hung up, Murray was waiting for her by the boot of the car.

'I think there's something between Stacey and her work pal Rowan,' she said. 'Between the way that James looked over at him when we asked if Stacey ever met anyone at Bicentennial Park, and Rowan himself saying that he just "noticed" the car here, I get the feeling there's something deeper going on.'

'A relationship?' Murray asked.

'I don't think so. But something. He did say he hadn't been to the park recently, though. What'd you get?'

'Simon said that James called his bank on the drive here and asked about any withdrawals by his wife from their accounts,' Murray said. 'He also asked about putting a stop on them.'

'Did he now.' Ella beckoned James Durham back over. 'You phoned your bank?'

He nodded. 'I thought that if she'd been abducted or something she might've been made to give up her cards and PINs, and if the bank could tell me where a withdrawal was made we could start to find her. But the accounts haven't been touched.'

'You wanted to put a stop on them too,' Murray said.

'And an alert, for the same reason. I want to make life hard for some scumbag kidnapper, not easy.'

'You were already thinking that she'd been abducted?' Ella said.

'Rowan said there was blood in the car. What else was I going to think?'

His voice was hard. Ella assessed his face again. He looked

furious. Either he really was, or anger was an easier expression for him to fake than concern.

'Okay,' she said. 'And you were once in a relationship with Stacey's sister, Marie?'

'If you call going to the movies a couple of times at the age of sixteen a relationship. People've sometimes made a big deal about it, like it's a huge joke that once I was with Marie but ended up with Stacey, but it was nothing.'

They let him go.

'That was interesting,' Murray said.

'Fishy's the word I'd use,' Ella said. 'He doesn't ring true to me at all.'

'You always think it's the husband.'

'Yeah, because most of the time it is.' She looked at him. 'I hope the wedding hasn't fried your brain, made you go all pro-husband just because you're going to be one.'

'I refuse to give that statement the dignity of a reply,' he said. 'Besides, you were just saying how something's weird about Rowan.'

'So? The two things aren't mutually exclusive.'

'You're exhausting,' Murray said. 'I'll call Dennis and update him, then how about we do the home visit?'

Before Ella could answer, Detective Sid Lawson came up at a trot. He was new to the team, bright-eyed and keen, with razor burn on his cheeks every morning as if he wasn't yet skilled at shaving and a grin like a schoolboy let out early. He and Detective Marion Pilsiger had been checking CCTV in the businesses across the street.

Breathless with excitement he said, 'We got something.'

THREE

Ella and Murray followed Lawson across the road to a small office-supply company. Inside, a woman in a tight red skirt and blouse hurried to shake Ella's and Murray's hands.

'Margo Grace, proprietor.' Her palm was damp, her eyes bright. 'That poor woman. I'm so glad to be able to help.'

'Margo's brother works for a security firm,' Sid Lawson said. 'He got her a top-of-the-line system and installed it himself.'

'Fantastic,' Ella said, her eyes on the monitor in front of Detective Marion Pilsiger. It showed a paused image of the front of the store, the street and some of Playland's car park.

Pilsiger pressed buttons and the screen jumped to life. It was evening, six forty-two according to the timer in the corner, and Ella watched as Stacey's car slowed and turned into the empty car park.

'Sunday evening, so everything was closed,' Margo Grace said.

Ella nodded. There looked to be only the driver onboard. The car parked in the position in which they'd seen it, the headlights went off, then there was a two-minute delay before the driver got out.

'Wiping off prints?' Murray murmured.

Ella didn't answer.

The driver was thin, dressed in dark jeans and a dark shirt with long sleeves and a collar, and a dark cap pulled down low. The clothes were loose and Ella couldn't tell if the person was male or female. They opened the boot and lifted out something that Ella didn't initially recognise, then after a moment's struggle by the driver she saw it was a folding bicycle. Once it was set up, the driver shut the boot, glanced around while clipping a dark helmet on over the cap, got on the bike and rode a little unsteadily towards the street. The cyclist looked both ways, then turned left, the direction they'd driven from. There was one false start when they wobbled into the gutter, then they seemed to get the hang of it and pedalled out of view.

Maybe not a good bike rider, Ella thought. Not their bike? Or a new bike bought for the occasion? They needed to find out about sales of those things.

'Rewind,' she said.

Pilsiger was already doing it. She slowed the footage and they watched once more from when the person got out of the car to the moment they disappeared off screen. The face wasn't clear enough to see detail except to be sure there was no moustache or beard. The hair was either short or tucked up under the cap and helmet. Ella studied the arms, the build, the way the person moved.

'It's either a woman or a small slim man,' Sid Lawson said happily.

Hey, state the obvious, Ella thought, but she didn't want to discuss it in front of Margo Grace. 'Bring James Durham over here for a look,' she said to Murray.

When Durham arrived, Pilsiger pressed play. He stared at the screen intently. Ella watched his face.

'I have no idea who that is,' he said after the person had ridden out of view.

'Watch it again,' Ella said.

'I don't need to. If I thought that person was at all familiar I'd say so, but I've never seen them before.'

She studied his face, thinking about accomplices. Things could've been arranged so he could truthfully say he didn't know the person. Didn't mean he was innocent.

Murray took Durham back across to Playland, while Ella turned to Margo Grace. 'May we take this footage?'

She beamed. 'Of course.'

When they had it, and Pilsiger had handed her card to Margo with thanks, the three detectives went outside.

'We'll check what we can see at these other places.' Pilsiger motioned along the street to the neighbouring businesses. 'Even if we can't spot the car itself, we might see where the cyclist went.'

'Traffic cameras might show something too,' Lawson said.

Ella nodded. 'We need anything that shows their gender, gives us more of their face, any tattoos, hair colour, whatever, and any encounters with anyone – pedestrians, drivers, other cyclists. When you get back, make copies so we can show other witnesses too. Talk to Dennis, see about putting it out to the media as well.'

Lawson and Pilsiger departed to the next business, a pool supplies shop, and Ella crossed the road back to Playland. Stacey's car was still being examined by the techs. Later it'd be taken on a flatbed truck to the lab where they'd search it in even more detail and try to work out if it'd been the scene of the incident or only used to transport a body. She felt determined, driven. These first few hours were so important, and as Murray came to meet her she nodded in the direction of James Durham.

'Let's go to the house.'

★

Rowan watched the detectives put James in the back of their car. They were going to search his and Stacey's house. It was procedure, Rowan knew, but he still felt sick.

'I'll follow so he's not alone,' Simon said beside him. 'You'll take Em home?'

Emelia didn't want to go, and was still yelling when Rowan fastened her car-seat harness. 'Want Daddy!'

'He has to work.' Rowan kept seeing Stacey's face the last time they'd talked, the tears in her eyes. Em's screams didn't usually bother him too much but he wished she'd shut up now. 'Listen, I'm putting The Wiggles on. Just be quiet and listen.'

It took a while for the shouts to stop, but by the time they reached home she was singing along, though Rowan couldn't muster his usual accompaniment.

Megan's faded Hyundai was in the driveway when he pulled in, and she came out the front door before he'd turned off the engine.

'Simon rang,' she said. 'Are you okay?'

'Mummy!' Emelia called, bouncing in her harness.

Megan opened the back door and lifted her out but kept her eyes on Rowan. 'Simon said James is shattered.'

'He looked it too.' Rowan got out. The sun was warm on his shoulders, the house appeared the same as ever. He'd left here so recently; how could the world have turned upside-down so quickly?

He followed Megan into the house. She put Emelia down and she ran off to get her dinosaurs.

'Tea?' Megan said. 'You sit. I'll get it.'

He sat at the kitchen table and watched her move about, getting out milk and sugar and pouring the water, stepping over Emelia who was roaring T-rexes across the tiles.

Megan glanced at him over her cup. 'Simon said it was bad.'

He nodded. 'It was.'

He'd told plenty of stories before in this kitchen, stories about people who'd lived or died, stories about injuries that made everyone cringe and Jennifer punch his shoulder and tell him to stop. This was different.

Megan looked away, brushed hair out of her eyes. Emelia lay on her stomach and set up dino battle lines.

'How was college?' Rowan asked.

'Great. I got ninety per cent on my assignment.'

'That's fantastic. Congratulations.'

Her smile was broad. 'Thanks.'

'I'm really proud of you,' Rowan said. 'You and Simon both.' It felt important to tell them what they meant to him. 'You're doing a remarkable job with Em, and I'm really glad you all live here.'

'Thanks,' she said again, but a cloud crossed her face.

'What?' he said.

'Did Simon talk to you yet?'

'About what?'

She brushed her hair back again. 'We've been talking about moving out.'

'But you can stay here for as long as you want.'

'It's not that we don't want to be here with you, but we just want to do it on our own,' she said. 'A place of our very own. Simon was going to bring it up. He explains it better than me.'

'I understand the feeling,' Rowan said. 'It's perfectly natural. But rents being so high, and places so hard to get, it'll –'

'No, because James told Simon a few weeks ago he knows someone who has an apartment that'll be empty soon. He said he can put in a good word and he can't see any reason why we wouldn't get it. We didn't want to say anything to you until we worked out the money, but it looks like we'll be able to do it. Simon told James on the weekend.' Her face was bright, her eyes shining. Rowan remembered the first flat he and Jennifer lived in, the tiny rooms, the torn flyscreens, their excitement.

'It sounds great,' he said, but was glad to look down when Emelia stomped a stegosaur over his foot.

'Doesn't it?' Megan took their empty cups to the sink. 'We thought we'd go round the second-hand stores for furniture. I said to Simon it doesn't matter what nick they're in, because we can just paint them and they'll be like new for us, as well as in the exact colours we want.'

The idea of them moving out made him sadder than he'd thought it would. *Because you'd never imagined it happening so soon*. But that wasn't entirely it. For one thing, he'd never lived alone in this house. He and Jennifer had bought it when Angus was four and Simon one, and they'd painted, and done up the garden, and later renovated, putting in an ensuite and a bigger kitchen. They'd often talked about selling it when they retired, buying a unit on the beach and walking there every day at dawn and dusk. But privately he wouldn't have been surprised if they'd stayed here in this house the rest of their lives. *Well, Jennifer achieved that*, he thought wryly.

For another thing, there was Angus.

'But hey,' Megan faced him, 'you're still going on your coffee date this arvo, right?'

That. He shook his head. 'I don't think so.'

'But unless you know where to look for Stacey, there's really nothing you can do.'

'It just doesn't feel right.'

'But Imogen's been looking forward to it so much. At college this morning she looked awesome, she's had her hair like straightened or coloured or something.'

'Plus I'd be terrible company.'

'She was all like sparkly in the eyes when we said goodbye.' Megan squeezed his arm. 'Please go. It'll help take your mind off things. And Stacey would want you to, wouldn't she?'

'Well,' he said, knowing he was giving in just to get her off his case. 'If she was sparkly in the eyes, I guess —'

'Yay!' Megan said.

'Yay!' Emelia echoed under the table.

Megan's phone started ringing and she dashed out of the room to get it, leaving Rowan wondering if the set-up was part of their plan to move. *Dad won't be lonely if he's not alone.*

'I'm not lonely,' he said to Emelia, but Emelia was absorbed in her plastic menagerie and didn't answer.

★

The Durhams' two-storey house stood on the curve of a street in Haberfield, shaded by a massive gum that scattered flowers and leaves as the wind blew through it. Ella and Murray had tried to get conversation going with James Durham on the drive here, but he'd been silent, wiping his eyes now and then – Ella could never see if there were actual tears or not – and answering, monosyllabically, only when he had to.

She opened the car door and he climbed out, gripping the handle as if he felt shaky, then the three of them crossed the lawn to the porch. As they did so a marked car pulled up, the officers there to wait with James while Ella and Murray searched; then a white Camry, out of which stepped Simon Wylie.

'We'll get you to unlock the door then wait out here, thanks,' Ella said to James.

'I have to disarm the alarm,' he said. 'Assuming Stacey set it. It's just inside the door.'

'In then out,' Ella said.

He unlocked the security screen and the solid timber door and a small wire-haired dog leapt barking into his arms. He carried the dog inside, where he pressed buttons on an alarm panel on the wall, then he came back out, the dog licking his neck.

'It was on?' Ella asked him.

He nodded.

Ella and Murray went inside, Murray easing the screen shut behind them. The house was quiet and felt calm. They checked the living room, dining room, the attached and empty garage, the toilet under the stairs. Nothing looked disturbed. No area of flooring looked like it'd been recently replaced, or lifted, or scrubbed to remove a bloodstain. There was sufficient dust that it looked lived in, not cleaned to pass police inspection.

Ella noticed motion detectors high up in the corners of the rooms and alarm stickers on the windows. In the kitchen, Murray tested the back door while Ella looked into the dishwasher.

'Locked,' he said. Another alarm panel on the wall flashed green lights.

'One plate, one knife, one coffee cup,' she said.

Simon tapped on the front door. 'Any chance we can come in? James isn't feeling well.'

Ella could see him sitting on the step behind Simon, his face in the dog's fur. Beyond him the uniforms stood talking together.

'Won't be long,' she said.

Murray gave her a look.

She pushed him up the stairs ahead of her, and on the landing she said, 'Just because he was in Melbourne when it happened doesn't mean he's not involved.'

'You could've let him get a glass of water.'

'I'm sure there's a tap out there somewhere.'

The master bedroom was on the left. Ella stood in the doorway and looked at the neatly made bed, the quilt and pillows in smart shades of grey. A dog-hair-covered folded blanket lay at the foot of the left side. Matching fringed lamps stood on the bedside tables, framed photos of James and the woman she assumed was Stacey lined the lace runner on the chest of drawers, and an open doorway led into the big walk-in robe and the bathroom beyond.

Murray slid back the wardrobe door and looked in.

Ella knelt by the left-hand bedside table. People tended to keep their most personal and private possessions close to where they slept; in the past she'd opened bedside drawers to find diaries, nasal spray, photos of lovers hidden inside books, haemorrhoid cream, lubricant, folded wads of cash, sex toys.

People never thought the day would be their last, never imagined a cop looking through their stuff. It was poignant proof of people's similarities.

Stacey Durham's first drawer held none of these things. Instead Ella found a woman's silver dress watch with engraving on the back that read *With all my love, James.* The strap was delicate, the face small and decorated with diamonds. Underneath were three paperbacks by Jeffrey Deaver and a clean folded white handkerchief. Ella shook the books by the spines and fanned the pages but nothing fell out. She pulled the drawer from the unit, turned it over, checked the sides and back for taped-on letters, notes, money or drugs – all things she'd found in previous searches. Nothing.

From the second drawer she took pink silk pyjamas that smelled like fabric softener, two more Deaver paperbacks, and then there, right at the bottom, saw a small hardcover notebook. She sat back and opened it, hoping for revelations about the miserable truth of Stacey's marriage, her secret lover, her plans to leave or divorce.

The first few pages had been torn out and the rest were blank. She held it to the light and could just make out the slight indentations left by the writing on the missing pages. The lab could work on that, and she put the notebook in an evidence bag to take with them.

She checked the sides and bottom of the second drawer, found nothing, and replaced the drawers and items as they'd been before.

She looked across at Murray. 'Find anything?'

'Nope. They're no hoarders.'

Ella went into the bathroom. A pink toothbrush stood alone in the holder, and she guessed James's was still packed from his trip. She bagged the toothbrush and a red hairbrush for DNA, then searched the drawers and cabinet. Over-the-counter cold and flu medication, mouthwash, most of a packet of Valium a year out of date and in Stacey's name, steroid cream with James's name on the label and instructions about applying daily to the rash, a box of the contraceptive pill prescribed to Stacey. The last tablet had been popped out on Saturday.

She went through James's bedside table, then together she and Murray searched the ornate chest of drawers. Nothing but clean folded clothes. They lifted the quilt and sheets, looked under the bed, felt along the frame, checked behind the chest. Murray found a stepladder in a cupboard along the hall and Ella stood on it to check the surfaces and depths of the high shelves in the wardrobe. No diaries, no photos of lovers, no drugs, no money, no hidden letters, nothing.

'It feels a bit too tidy,' Murray said.

She nodded. 'Like someone knew we'd be looking.'

They went into the other rooms. One was a spare bedroom, the queen bed made up with a blue quilt and valance, the carpet clean and unmarked, the built-in and bedsides empty. The other was a home office with a computer on a desk in the middle of the room, a printer on a shelf underneath, a wheeled chair on a plastic mat, a bookshelf full of folders and manuals on one wall, and three four-drawer metal filing cabinets along the opposite wall by the window. Ella opened each drawer and looked in at files marked 'Staff super', 'Invoices', 'Forms'. Murray moved the mouse and looked at the computer monitor.

'Lots of work stuff,' he said.

Ella went through the few papers in the desk's in tray. Invoices for orders of computer parts, shop electricity and phone bills. The bin by the chair was empty.

Murray pulled folders out of the bookcase and leafed through the contents. 'Nothing of hers that I can see.'

'Let's bring him in and have a chat,' Ella said.

FOUR

James Durham wanted coffee. Simon said he'd make it. Ella and Murray stood in the living room, the dog skittering between them and Simon in the kitchen, while James stared at a shelf of framed photos.

He picked one up and passed it over. 'This is probably the clearest.'

Ella looked at James and Stacey in thick woollen jumpers on a winter beach, dark clouds and white surf behind them, faces lit by smiles. Stacey's grin was wide, her face symmetrical and attractive, her teeth white and small and square. Her dark hair reached her shoulders. It was a good shot. Once James was cut out it'd work well for the media release.

James glanced at the evidence bags in Ella's hand, one containing the hair and toothbrushes, the other the notebook. 'Did you find anything in your search?'

'A few things,' Ella said. If he himself had done the cleaning, he might've seen the notebook, he might've been the one who tore out the pages, he might know what had been written there. If he hadn't seen it, it was good for him to wonder. 'We need a sample of Stacey's handwriting.'

'Oh.' He looked around, then left the room. He brought back a calendar with people's birthdays written on it in a tall narrow hand. 'This is all I've got.'

'Thanks,' she said. 'Why was Stacey prescribed Valium?'

'Because of work. She went through a stage where she couldn't sleep after nightshift. The doctor said to take them when she really had to, but I don't think she took many, in the end. She said they made her feel really dopey.'

She wrote that down. 'Does Stacey use the computer in the office?'

'No, that's mine. She has her own. A nice little laptop.'

'Any idea where it is?' Ella asked.

'It's usually here in the house.' He looked around the room. 'Here on the lounge or in the kitchen.'

'We didn't find it,' Ella said.

'Then I don't know where it is.'

'Might it be at her work?' Murray asked.

'No, she had it here at home on Friday and she's not back on duty until tomorrow. I can't think of any reason she'd go in there with it over the weekend, let alone leave it there.'

'Does she have an address book?' Ella said. They had the details of the three friends, but she wanted to see who else was in it.

He shook his head. 'She stores everything on her phone and her laptop.'

'What about a will?' Murray asked.

James nodded.

'Everything goes to you?'

'Of course. I'm her husband.'

'Life insurance?' Ella asked.

'Yes. We took it out together when we got married.'

'How much?'

'We started at five hundred thousand each, to cover the mortgage. I guess it's gone up since then.'

Half a million, Ella thought. 'Plus she's no doubt got cover through her super?'

33

'I suppose so,' he said.

'How's the business? In any financial trouble?'

He glared at her. 'What are you suggesting?'

Before she could answer, his mobile buzzed and he pulled it out of his pocket. 'It's a text from Stacey's phone but it says . . .' His face filled with thunder. '*You know what this is about and you won't see her again if you don't do the right thing.*'

Ella took the phone out of his hand and scrolled down but there was no more. Murray stepped away to call the office on his own mobile and check the tracking of the mobile signal.

'This is bullshit.' James's hands were in fists by his sides. 'I don't have the first fucking clue what that means.'

Ella typed a message. *Who is this?*

You know what this is about, the next message repeated. *It's time to tell the truth.*

This is Detective Marconi of the NSW Police, Ella typed. *Where is Stacey?*

A moment later an answer arrived. *James knows everything.*

Explain what that means, Ella sent back.

Tell him to tell the truth.

Please explain that to me, she sent. When there was no reply she showed James the exchange.

'I don't know a thing about it,' he said.

Murray was still on his own phone, talking in a low voice.

Simon came in with a tray, the dog at his heels. 'What's happened?'

'Have you had other messages like this?' Ella asked James.

'I'd have told you, wouldn't I?' He took the phone back and started a message.

'I'd suggest you don't send anything right now,' Ella said. 'It could make things worse.'

He kept thumbing then hit send. 'She's missing, there's blood all through her car, and some arsehole's claiming I'm the reason why. I can't see how saying I'm going to make them pay could possibly make anything worse.'

'What happened?' Simon said again.

James screwed up his face. 'Some prick's telling lies.'

'Like with the complaint?' Simon said.

'Exactly,' James said. 'It's just like with the anonymous complaint. I said at the time you lot should've worked a bit harder. That Libke did nothing, and now look what's happened.'

'There's no evidence that the two are linked,' Ella said.

'There's no evidence of anything yet,' he snapped. 'And isn't that what you're doing here? Looking for any proof that I did something to her? I know you always look at the husband first. I can tell you now that there's nothing to find because I had nothing to do with whatever's happened. I love my wife like I love nothing else on this earth, and I'll do anything to find her.'

He headed out of the room and up the stairs.

Ella and Murray followed, Murray saying in a low voice, 'They located Stacey's mobile in Stanmore, then it was turned off.'

In the office James yanked open a filing-cabinet drawer and dug out a manila folder. 'Here.'

Ella looked inside. The couple of stapled pages were print-outs of email correspondence between James and Senior Constable E. Libke about the anonymous complaint. Libke stated that she had looked into the matter and was unable to find any evidence of any wrongdoing, and that the source of the complaint remained unknown.

'I rang and asked her how hard she'd looked before she came up with that "remained unknown",' James said. 'She said she had to move on to other cases, but to get in touch if it happened again. Pathetic.'

Ella knew what it was like to hit an investigative dead-end, but at the same time, and despite her suspicion of James, she couldn't help wondering if a more thorough job back then could in some way have prevented the current situation.

James took back the manila folder and slapped it down onto the desk. 'Whatever's happened to her, I had nothing to do with it. So if you stop looking at me, you can spend more time and effort on whoever really did it.'

★

Outside, the uniforms had left. Ella and Murray locked the calendar and evidence bags in their boot. The wind had dropped and the morning was still and sunlit.

'Those texts are something else,' Murray said. 'Still, they show it can't be James himself sending them. Or his sidekick Simon.'

'It's not like there couldn't be another accomplice,' Ella said. 'How close did the locator get?'

'Somewhere between the railway line and Parramatta Road. A few hundred square metres.'

Stanmore today, and Homebush last night. It didn't take a genius to know that phones could be tracked, so the texter would no doubt keep it turned off, but with a bit of luck over time they'd be able to make out a pattern from where the texts were sent, no matter how vague: locations around a central point suggesting a possible home base.

Next up, though, they'd be talking to the neighbours. James had told them that he and Stacey were friendly with the people on both sides, and on a 'smile and wave' relationship basis with other people in the street.

They started with the house directly to the right of the Durhams'. The garage stood open and a brown EH Holden was parked half in, half out, with the bonnet up.

Ella knocked on the back panel. 'Hello?'

A woman in an old khaki workshirt and cut-off jeans peered around from the engine. Her short hair was grey and her face was deeply lined. Ella guessed her to be in her mid-seventies.

She gave them a loose salute with a spanner. 'Hello to you.'

'Detectives Ella Marconi and Murray Shakespeare,' Ella said. 'Do you have a moment?'

'Absolutely. Come on in.' The woman put down the spanner and wiped her hands on the tail of her shirt. The garage smelled of oil. A washing machine rattled through the spin cycle in the corner. A fluorescent bar lit the grime of the car's engine and the new battery that sat on the concrete floor. 'I'm Esther Cooper. I saw the car out there before, and the constables. I hope nothing's happened to the Durhams?'

'We have a few questions about them,' Ella said. 'Could you tell us when you last saw either James or Stacey?'

Esther Cooper frowned. 'Are they okay or not?'

'James is fine,' Murray said. 'Stacey we're not sure about.'

'What do you mean?'

'She's missing and might be in danger,' Ella said. 'So we need to find out who saw her last, and when.'

'Righto,' Esther said, businesslike. 'I last saw James on Friday, when he came home from work. I was weeding out the front there and he waved as he drove into their garage. I last saw Stacey yesterday evening when she went out in her car.'

'Was she alone?' Ella asked.

'As far as I could see. The driver's window was down and she was playing music. I was watering as she went by. I waved and she smiled.'

'She didn't look upset?'

'No. She looked fine. Big smile.'

'What time was that?'

'Between five and half past,' Esther said.

'Did you see or hear her come home?' Murray asked. 'Either yesterday or today?'

'No.'

Ella asked, 'Would you normally be able to hear if they were home? Or when their cars came and went?'

'Depends. If I was in the garden there, or in the garage or front room, I'd probably hear the cars. Anywhere else in the house, I wouldn't necessarily hear a thing.'

37

'Have you noticed anything unusual happening in the street lately?' Ella said. 'Strange people or cars lurking about?'

Esther shook her head. 'And I do notice things like that. My old Tom used to tell me I was a stickybeak. I called it "interested".'

Ella said, 'How well do you know James and Stacey?'

'We've been friends since they moved in, two or three years ago. They're nice people and we get along. When Tom collapsed last year Stacey did everything she could to save him. They came to the funeral, and have me over to tea at least once a week since then. James fixes my computer when I run into problems, and Stacey and I help each other out if one of us runs out of milk or eggs or whatever when we're cooking. We both like to bake, see. I give her what I make and she takes it to work.'

'Have you ever seen or heard them fight?' Murray asked.

'Not once,' Esther said. 'In fact, they used to make my Tom uncomfortable with all their holding hands and pecks on the cheek. Tom was old school – reckoned that was for the bedroom.'

Old old school, Ella thought. She said, 'What are the other neighbours like? Are there any disputes going on, things like that?'

'Everyone's lovely except the grumpy bastard over the way.' Her face darkened. 'Bill Willetts. Lived there almost as long as Tom and I've been here, close to twenty years. Never got on with anyone, and he doesn't like dogs. When Stacey walks little Gomez and he stops at the trees on the nature strip, Willetts shouts out the window. Says it kills the grass. It's not his grass anyway.' She shook her head. 'Obsessive unpleasant little man.'

'What number is he?' Murray asked.

'Fourteen.' Esther pointed across the street.

Ella saw a house with cream siding, grey roof tiles, and rows of tightly pruned topiary along the front of the house and on the nature strip.

She said, 'Did either Stacey or James confide in you?'

'James didn't, but that's a man thing. Stacey used to come over during the day sometimes, when James was at work, and talk about cases she'd done. She said James could be squeamish, and sometimes she wanted to talk and he'd put his hands over his ears. It'd be more after nightshift that she'd come in. I think being so tired made her dwell on it. She'd bring Gomez – she adores that dog – and we'd sit on the back patio and drink tea with lemon in it and look out over the garden and she'd just talk. Sometimes she'd doze off. I'd just read. Or doze off myself too.'

'It was always just about cases?' Ella said.

'More or less,' Esther said.

'Did she ever talk about problems she was having with anyone at work or anywhere else?' Murray asked.

'We'd sometimes laugh about the bureaucracy in the system,' Esther said. 'I used to be a teacher, and government departments never change. But she never said that anyone in particular was giving her trouble.' She looked at Ella. 'When you said missing, what did you mean?'

'Her car was found this morning and we've not been able to locate her,' Ella said.

'She could be shopping or anything.'

'There was human blood in the car,' Murray said.

'How much?'

'A lot,' he said. 'Around a litre and a half.'

'You're not serious.'

'That's the estimate of our Crime Scene person.'

Esther sagged against the front of the car. 'So something's happened to her. Someone's done something to her.'

'We're not certain it's her blood yet,' Ella said.

'Do you have leads?'

'We've got a lot of people working on it.'

The washing machine shuddered to a stop in the silence, then Esther said, 'How is James?'

'Upset and anxious,' Murray said.

'I should go and see him.' She released the bonnet support and let it fall with a bang. 'See Gomez too. They'll both be heartbroken.'

'Please call us if you remember anything else, or if you see or hear anything that seems suspicious,' Ella said.

Esther took the card she held out. 'You bet I will.'

★

They hadn't had a call from the office to say more messages had been sent from Stacey's phone to James's, but Ella knocked on James's door and asked him anyway. Letting him keep his phone meant the kidnappers could send him demands, and with the numbers being monitored and his records having been requested, they had both the past and future covered.

The neighbours on the Durhams' other side weren't home. Ella made a note to follow them up, then she and Murray crossed the street to number fourteen.

The topiary shivered in the wind as they stepped up to knock on the door. The man who opened it looked about sixty. His thin hand gripped the frame. 'What's going on?'

Ella guessed he'd been watching since the second they'd pulled up. 'I'm Detective Marconi, this is Detective Shakespeare. You're Bill Willetts?'

His pale eyes narrowed further. 'I don't know what that old witch told you but I never did anything to anyone.'

'Can we come in?' Murray said.

Willetts huffed through his nose then unlocked the screen. 'If you must.'

He didn't invite them past the entryway, so they stood on the plastic mat that ran the length of the carpet. A hall table was bare except for a spotless glass vase containing a plastic rose, and the air smelled of chemical cleaners. Willetts wore neatly pressed brown trousers and a white shirt buttoned snugly at his wrists. His face was long, and his iron grey hair, moustache and goatee were all clipped short. The overall impression was narrow and uptight.

Ella said, 'When did you last see James or Stacey Durham?'

'I saw James just now, when you lot arrived, and I saw Stacey yesterday morning. She walked that mutt past and I watched to make sure he didn't pee on my trees. Why she can't walk on her own side of the street I don't know.'

'You didn't see her later in the day, or this morning?' Murray asked.

'If I had, I would've said so.'

'Just checking,' Murray said. 'So you've had words with Stacey in the past?'

'Yes, but I've said the same thing to everyone who walks their filthy mutts past. They say they can't control where they pee, but they damn well can. Just drag the beast further along. It's about the worst thing for trees and grass both. I have to get the hose on it quickly or it burns.'

'You're clearly a keen gardener,' Murray said. 'The topiaries out there look good.'

'Of course they look good,' Willetts said. 'I spend a lot of time taking care of them. You know how much those things are worth when they look that good?'

Ella said, 'Do you have words with James Durham too, or just Stacey?'

'He doesn't walk the mutt,' Willetts said. 'What reason do I have for words?'

'Did you see anything unusual happening at the Durhams' house over the weekend?' Murray asked.

'You think I have nothing better to do than watch what happens over there?'

Ella had heard enough. 'Mind if I use your bathroom?'

She was already moving up the stairs when he said, 'There's one down here,' and cut him off with 'Thanks very much,' as she kept climbing, her shoes crackling the plastic runner on the stair carpet.

Upstairs smelled more strongly of cleaning products. Carpet deodoriser and air freshener, she thought. Pine. She glanced into a bathroom – towel hanging straight on the rack, shining mirror, no dust or hair on the tiled floor – then into the bedroom next to it. Neatly made-up double, pillows in clean crisp slips, matching lamps on matching bedside tables. The tops of both tables were dust-free and bare, except for a paperback that lay aligned to the corners. Ella went closer to read the cover. *Madame Bovary*.

The next bedroom was empty. The bare carpet showed vacuum marks and faint indentations where furniture had once stood.

The last room faced the street. The sun streamed in on a dark leather armchair and matching footrest, and a small table with three books on gardening in a tidy stack. Ella moved past to look out the window and the top book fell from the pile with a thud.

'What are you doing?' Willetts' footsteps started up the stairs.

Ella bent to retrieve the book and saw tucked under the footrest a pair of binoculars.

'You were supposed to use the bathroom.' Willetts scowled in at her.

She dangled the binoculars by the strap. 'Been keeping an eye on the neighbourhood?'

'You have no right to look through my things.' He snatched them off her. 'It's not illegal to use them.'

'It is if you spy into people's houses.' Ella pointed out the window. 'You think that's the Durhams' bedroom there at the front? You see much between those curtains?'

'I watch birds in the trees. I look for dogs. That's all.'

Behind him Murray said, 'If you've seen anything unusual, we need to know about it.'

'I've seen nothing.'

Ella looked at Murray. 'Perhaps we should all go to the station and discuss it further.'

'Good idea,' he said.

'This is stupid,' Willetts said. 'You're going to arrest me for that?'

'Just a chat,' Ella said, happy to let him believe otherwise.

'This is supposed to be a free country.' Willetts' face turned red. 'I never saw any sex or anything like that.'

'What did you see?'

'Stacey sitting in the window downstairs there, holding that dog. Sits for hours sometimes. Staring out at nothing. Ask me, she's touched in the head.'

'So you admit to watching the Durhams in their home,' Ella said.

'I keep an eye on the street. For security reasons.'

'Did you see anything else odd or unusual recently, either at the Durhams' or somewhere else along the road?' Murray said.

'That old woman has a man over sometimes,' Willetts said. 'That the sort of thing you're after?'

'We can still go down to the station,' Ella said.

'I've seen nothing.' Willetts thrust the binoculars under the table.

'Your house is exceedingly fresh and tidy,' Ella said.

'I clean daily, like any normal person.'

'Your garden too,' she said. 'It must be frustrating when somebody messes that up.'

'Like when a dog kills your grass,' Murray said.

Willetts narrowed his eyes. 'And I might get so frustrated that I'd hurt someone? No sirree. Not me.'

'Where were you last afternoon and evening?' Ella said.

'Right here, watching the news and one of those talent shows, then *60 Minutes*.'

'Can anybody confirm that?'

'No. In case you haven't noticed, I live alone.'

'Have you ever been in trouble with the police?' Ella said.

'No,' he said. 'Never. And I think it's time you left.'

He bustled them downstairs and out, then slammed the front door behind them.

'Touchy,' Ella said.

'He couldn't focus when you went upstairs,' Murray said. 'Probably got OCD and hates having people in his house.'

Ella glanced back as they crossed the street and saw Willetts watching them from the window. 'Neat freaks can snap.'

'He's a prospect,' Murray agreed. 'Look him up when we get back to the office.'

The Durhams' front door was open and Ella tapped on the frame. Simon let them in.

James sat on the lounge staring into space with the dog on his lap.

'Have you had any more texts, or a call?' Ella asked him.

He shook his head dully. Simon hovered like an anxious mother.

'No more thoughts about what might be going on?' Murray said.

James shook his head again.

'He's been trying, though,' Simon put in.

'Okay,' Ella said. 'We'll be in touch.'

They got in the car and headed towards Padstow to talk to Stacey's sister, and Ella pondered. James had looked like a man who was thinking hard, but was he thinking about who might've taken his wife and where she might be, or something else?

FIVE

Rowan stood in front of his wardrobe in his underpants. He didn't know why it was so difficult to decide what to wear. He was only really going to the cafe to get Megan off his back, and he figured that after today he'd be safe from future set-ups for a good few months. So he wasn't trying to dress to impress anyone, but at the same time it felt important to dress normally. Act normally. Whatever that meant. Though in one respect it didn't matter – he hadn't been out with anyone in this sort of circumstance for twenty-five years, so nobody would expect him to be normal. Right?

Emelia came in and walked a dinosaur along the edge of the bed. 'Where your pants?'

Jeans would be fine.

'Right here,' he said, pulling them on. 'This shirt, or this shirt?'

She studied them, then pointed to the blue and white checks. 'That one.'

'Done.'

He buttoned it up and looked himself in the eyes in the mirror. Not too nervous. More or less normal. Good.

★

The Merrylands cafe was busy. Rowan looked around and a woman at a small table by the window caught his eye. She half-stood, raising a hand. Megan had described her as forty-five but looking forty, with short red-brown hair and a face like a cherub. He went over.

'Imogen?'

'Rowan.' She smiled. 'It's nice to meet you.'

'And you.' He sat down and a waitress came over.

'Chai tea latte, please,' Imogen said.

'Mugaccino for me, thanks,' Rowan said.

When the waitress had left and they were sitting alone, he couldn't think of anything to say. His palms were damp and he pressed them to his jeans. He felt like he shouldn't have come. He kept thinking about the apology he should've made to Stacey, and the look on her face when he saw her last.

Imogen smiled brightly. 'So Megan told me you're a paramedic.'

He nodded. Yes, work. Talk about work. 'Twenty years, give or take,' he said. 'And you were in accounts?'

'For about the same length of time,' she said. 'I took a redundancy and decided to do what I'd always loved, hence the graphic design course. Where I met Megan.'

They fell silent again. Around them people chattered. The air was cold and Rowan felt awkward and out of place. He missed Jen, and had a flash of her sitting opposite, smiling and swinging her crossed leg under the table to poke him in the knee with the toe of her shoe.

Imogen shifted in her chair. She seemed as uncomfortable, as stuck for conversation, as he felt.

He scratched around in his mind. 'So, do you have kids?'

'Three,' she said. 'Chloe's twenty-two, and Trina and Mark have just turned eighteen. They're twins. Chloe's an architect, works for a big firm in the city, and the others are in Year Twelve. You?'

'Two boys,' he said. 'Simon, who's with Megan. He's

46

twenty and works in a friend's computer business. And Angus, who's twenty-four now.'

Twenty-four and two weeks, to be precise. He never forgot, just like he never forgot the tiny things, like the baby ringlets of wet hair that would curl up his soft neck after a bath, or the same neck tanned and broader as he grew through his teen years.

'And what does he do?' Imogen asked.

'I don't know,' Rowan said. 'He left home five years ago saying he was going to the country to work, and we've only had the odd postcard from him since. No return address, no real message except hello.'

'That would be awful,' Imogen said.

It was, Rowan thought. Angus didn't know that his mother was dead, nor that he was an uncle.

The waitress brought their drinks and left. Imogen kept her gaze fixed on her tea as she stirred it. Rowan felt even more that he should've cancelled. So what if he couldn't have done anything to help find Stacey – he wouldn't be feeling like this.

'So,' she said, 'you live at Homebush?'

Enough, he thought. 'I'm really sorry, but I think this might've been a bad idea.' At the look in her eyes he added quickly, 'It's not you. A friend of mine is missing. I feel distracted. I shouldn't have come. Megan said I'd be fine, but I don't think I am.'

'It's okay.' She looked interested. 'What happened?'

He found himself telling her about it. 'And so I really feel I should be doing something.'

'But what could you do?'

'I've been thinking about that. I could ask her friends if they've seen her or heard from her.'

'Won't the cops do that?'

'Yeah, but every little thing will help. Won't it?'

She looked at him for a moment. 'Do you know where they live?'

'More or less. With a bit of help from Google I can get there.'

'So let's go.' She downed half her drink in a gulp.

'Really?'

'You said yourself, every little bit might help. And Megan wouldn't be happy with either of us if we'd only met for ten minutes.'

He felt better. Action was always the best way to go. 'Okay then.'

*

Marie Kennedy, Stacey's sister, was a tense and angular woman of forty-three, dressed in white three-quarter pants, a silver and black top, black sandals, and large silver hoop earrings that swung against the ends of her black bob. The furniture in the room was in disarray, as if she'd been in the middle of re-arranging it. She sat on a chair pushed into a corner, but within a minute was on her feet again, pacing about, wiping dust from the spines of shelved books with a fingertip, adjusting the position of ceramic ornaments and framed photos by millimetres.

'I'm just glad Mum and Dad aren't here,' she said. 'This anxiety would kill them.'

It'd taken twice as long as normal to get her date of birth and other details because she couldn't keep on track. Ella blinked hard against her growing headache, and said, 'So you had coffee with Stacey at her place on Wednesday, and that was the last time you saw her, but you talked to her yesterday afternoon. What time was that?'

'About three thirty,' Marie said.

'How was she?'

'She was absolutely fine. Cheerful and happy.' Marie looked with distaste at her fingertips, then rubbed them against her thumb.

'Did she call for any particular reason?'

'My daughter's twenty-first is coming up. We're trying to decide whether to have it here or at a restaurant. I went to see a couple of places last week and Stacey wanted to know what they were like. The birthday was what we talked about when I was there on Wednesday too. Because I'm on my own she helps me with things like that. You know? My husband, Paul, was killed in a work accident eleven years ago. He drove a truck, and hit another on the Hume Highway. The other driver died too. The police said they were burned. I hope they were unconscious at least. But anyway, times like this you wish more than ever he was still here.'

Her gaze couldn't stay in one place for more than an instant. Her hands trembled as she tweaked and retweaked the position of a framed photo.

Ella said, 'How about you sit down?'

Marie perched on the edge of the chair, her hands pressed between her knees. Her shoulders were high, her breaths like little sips of air that hardly moved her chest. She bounced her heels on the carpet.

'Are you all right?' Ella said. It felt like anything could happen, like Marie might burst out screaming, or suddenly confess.

'My sister's missing,' Marie said. 'How "all right" am I supposed to be?' She wiped sweat from her forehead with the back of her wrist.

'Would you like a glass of water?' Murray said.

Marie shook her head and held up a hand. 'I'm okay,' she said, then her eyes rolled back and she slumped neatly to the floor.

Murray leapt to his feet. 'I'll call an ambulance.'

'Hold your horses.' Ella had seen people collapse in similar fashion and knew the real ones were never so cautious. She knelt by Marie and saw she was breathing fine. She squeezed her arm. 'Marie.'

Marie didn't respond.

'Now will I call?'

Ella shot him a look. She brushed Marie's hair off her face and saw her flinch. 'Faking,' she mouthed at Murray.

'What?' he said.

She rolled her eyes and looked back at Marie, thinking she was either trying to get away from the questions or hoping to garner sympathy. Ella plumped for the second. She said to Murray, 'Pass me that cushion. She's obviously fainted from the stress, poor thing. I can't imagine how difficult it must be, having lost your husband and now with your sister missing.'

Murray handed her the cushion, looking confused. Ella tucked it gently under Marie's head. She saw Marie's eyes flicker, and laid it on thick. 'The poor, poor thing. Murray, doesn't this job sometimes break your heart? It's just so terrible, what people have to go through.'

Marie whimpered and reached weakly for Ella's hand.

'So sad,' Ella said, thinking *Bingo!*

Marie blinked and looked around. 'Did I pass out?'

'Just for a second,' Ella said. 'Are you feeling better?'

'A little.'

They helped her sit up on the chair. Murray still looked puzzled. 'You're sure you're all right?'

'I'm fine,' Marie said. 'It happens sometimes. I have hypotension. Low blood pressure. At times of great stress it drops even lower and down I go. Could I have a glass of water, please, and perhaps a damp cloth for my forehead?'

Ella fetched them from the kitchen, and Marie smiled weakly as Ella put the glass on the coffee table. 'On the coaster, please. Save the timber.'

Ella lifted the glass and slid the tile coaster underneath without a word, and handed her the tea towel. Marie leaned back and placed it over her forehead and eyes. *Covering up?* Ella thought. *Because she doesn't want to see us?* Perhaps the 'faint' wasn't only about attention after all.

Murray seemed sucked in. 'Would you prefer to do this later?'

'No, no. I can go on. She's my sister.'

Ella re-opened her notebook and got stuck in. 'Stacey's younger than you, correct?'

'Four years. I'm her big sister. Always looked out for her when we were kids.' She pressed the tea towel to her face with one hand.

'There are no other siblings?' Murray asked.

'No.'

'Any cousins or such that she's close to?' Ella said.

'We only have four, and they all live in Hobart. We haven't seen or spoken to them for years.' Marie put down the towel. 'I feel much better now. Thank you.'

'What about her friends?' Ella said. 'Have you met any of them? Do you know who she's closest to?'

'The three she talks about most are Aimee, Claire and Vicky. They're either nurses or paramedics – I can't keep track. I've met them all at one time or another. They're all lovely.' She took a sip of water.

'Do you happen to have their phone numbers or addresses?' Murray asked.

'I don't, I'm sorry. They'd all be in her phone.'

Ella nodded. 'Did Stacey confide in you about any problems she was having?'

'We talked about work issues sometimes,' Marie said. 'Sometimes she'd have an upsetting case, or a bystander would cause problems. She can be easily frustrated and sometimes she stews on these things. A few times she had to work with paramedics she didn't get on with, and that annoys her as well. But she's been pretty happy the last year or so.'

'What about personal things, like her marriage?' Ella said.

'From what I've seen, there's nothing to confide. They hardly argue. They always look happy. And he's often holding her hand. Paul never wanted to hold mine, I can tell you. James is a nice guy. Ask me, she's lucky.'

51

'You sound envious,' Ella said.

'No, I just think she's lucky. How's James doing? I tried to call him a little while ago but he didn't answer.'

'He's upset,' Murray said.

'You and he were in a relationship in your teens, is that right?' Ella said.

'Of a sort.' Marie smiled. 'Like any sixteen-year-old girl, I thought it was much more than it was. Like any sixteen-year-old boy, he thought it was much less.'

'So . . .' Ella said.

'So to me it was serious and to him it was a bit of fun,' she said. 'And fun could be had in many places.'

'Who broke it off?' Murray asked.

'It was never really enough of a thing to be broken off.'

Ella felt she was taking them in circles. 'So he was seeing other people and you thought he shouldn't, then he kept seeing those other people and stopped seeing you.'

'Yes,' Marie said. 'That about sums it up.'

'Did he and Stacey know each other well back then?' Murray said.

'Not particularly. She was only twelve. Still a child. She would've barely been on his radar.'

'So what was it like when they met up again at Rowan Wylie's place?' Ella asked.

Marie shrugged. 'I wasn't there.'

'What did Stacey tell you?'

'She was laughing, she thought it was funny. After so many years, and who'd've thought. They started going out pretty much straight away. Next thing they were engaged, then married. Paris, my daughter, was a bridesmaid.'

'How did that make you feel?' Ella said.

'Happy and proud,' Marie said with a big smile. 'For all of them.'

'So Stacey's good friends with Rowan?' Ella asked.

'They get along well at work, Stacey's told me that much.'

'Do they spend time together outside the job?'

'Sometimes at that kiddies' playground,' Marie said. 'I don't remember her talking about any other time.'

Ella nodded. 'Have you ever felt that Stacey or James might be seeing someone else?'

'Having an affair?' Marie looked horrified. 'No, a million times no. They're the most loving happy couple I've ever seen. It's wrong to even suggest such a thing.'

She was protesting a little too much, Ella thought. 'So you've never seen James flirting with anyone, or –'

'I just said no. Never.' Her eyes were hard. 'Neither of them would even consider it.'

Hmm, Ella thought.

Murray said, 'James was trying to think who might have reason to want to hurt Stacey. Do you have any thoughts on that?'

'There's a neighbour who yells at her from his house when her dog widdles on his trees, but she never sounded frightened when she mentioned him,' Marie said.

'What about someone who might want to hurt James?' Ella asked.

'I know there was that anonymous complaint a while back. Stacey said James was pretty stressed and angry over it. Apparently he thought it was some competitor trying to wreck his business. But that's all that comes to mind.'

Ella said, 'Do you know anyone who owns a folding bicycle?'

'You can get bikes that fold now?'

'Never mind,' Ella said.

There was the sound of a key in the front door and a young woman appeared in the hall. 'Hey, Mum – oh. Hi.'

'Paris, is it?' Ella got to her feet and introduced herself and Murray. 'Can you join us for a few minutes?'

Paris – Stacey's niece, Rowan's paramedic trainee – was dressed in gym pants and shoes and a white Adidas jacket over a black T-shirt, and carried a gym bag.

She eyed them warily. 'What's going on?' She cast a sceptical look at the folded cloth in her mother's hand, a look Ella noted with interest. 'Fainted again, huh?'

Hmm. Scepticism in the voice too.

'I'm fine, darling,' Marie said. 'No need to worry.'

Ella said, 'Paris, when did you last see or talk to your aunt Stacey?'

'Last week, at work. Thursday morning. Rowan and I were finishing nightshift and she was coming in for a dayshift. Why?'

'Has she told you about any problems she's been having?' Murray asked.

'No, nothing.'

'Would you say you're close?' Ella asked.

Marie let out a bark of laughter.

'Mum,' Paris said.

'Paris would say yes, but I doubt Stacey would,' Marie told Ella. 'I myself would call it a severely lopsided relationship.'

Paris looked at the floor, and Ella saw the muscles in her jaw tense.

She cleared her throat and glanced at Murray. 'Marie, if you're sure you're feeling better, could I perhaps trouble you for some water, please? Or maybe even tea?'

'Tea sounds good. I'll give you a hand.' Murray stood and helped Marie to her feet.

When they were out of the room, Murray talking a constant stream in the kitchen, Ella said to Paris, 'No matter what your mother says, you and your aunt are close, aren't you?'

'Yes.' Paris's cheeks were flushed, and she shot an angry look towards the kitchen. 'Sometimes I feel closer to her than I do to Mum. She helps me with work, she's been there all my life. We talk on the phone every other day. Why? Has something happened?'

'Her car was found with blood in it. A lot of blood. And she's missing.'

The colour fell from Paris's face.

'It's really important that you think hard,' Ella said. 'Has she confided in you about trouble she was having with someone?'

Paris shook her head, her eyes brimming over. From the kitchen came the sound of teaspoons in cups and Murray's continued blather.

'Does she get on with everyone at work?'

'Yes,' Paris croaked. 'Everyone loves her.'

'How about with your mother?'

'They bicker a lot,' Paris said. 'Stacey says they always have.'

'Is there anything they bicker about frequently?'

Paris shook her head. 'They just don't seem to agree on things generally.'

'What about your uncle, James? Do he and Stacey argue?'

'Not exactly,' Paris said. 'I mean, I've never seen them. I remember Mum and Dad yelling at each other when I was little, and even the times I used to stay at Stacey and James's place after Dad died and Mum needed a break, I never saw or heard anything like that.' She hesitated.

'But?' Ella said.

'But a couple of times when Stacey and I have been doing stuff, like she's been helping me study or whatever, she was almost crying, and when I asked her what was wrong she said it was nothing major, just a bit of disagreement at home. I don't know what about – she didn't tell me and I felt weird asking. I tried to say that she could talk to me if she wanted, but she just moved on to whatever we were doing.'

'When did that happen?'

'In the last few months,' Paris said. 'Once since I've been working, so in the last six weeks.'

Ella could hear Murray still talking in the kitchen, but knew she didn't have much more time. 'How do you get along with James?'

'All right,' she said. 'He's okay, though if it wasn't for him being with Stacey I wouldn't be his friend, probably.

I sometimes feel like he's laughing at me, you know? I don't know why. I said to Stacey that I don't think he likes me, and she brushed it off. But he rang me last week, and asked me about Rowan.'

Ella sat further forward, one ear on Murray. *Keep Marie out there!* 'What did he say?'

'He wanted to know how he and Stacey got along. I said great, as far as I'd seen, since I hadn't been on the station for long,' Paris said. 'He asked if they worked together much, if they spent nightshifts together. I didn't really believe what he was asking, and must've sounded surprised or shocked or something, because then he laughed and said he was joking, couldn't I tell that? He can make you feel really silly.'

'What day was that?'

'Tuesday,' Paris said.

'Did you tell Stacey?'

Paris shook her head. 'It felt stupid.'

'I have to ask,' Ella said. 'Do you think Stacey could be seeing Rowan? Or anyone else?'

'No,' Paris said. 'I can't imagine that she ever would.'

She sounded certain – as certain as a niece could be about her aunt, at least. Ella nodded. She could hear Marie and Murray coming back. Time to shift to a safer topic. 'So this last weekend, did you talk to Stacey on the phone?'

'I talked to her on Saturday morning. She's been helping me with work stuff, going over treatment procedures and protocols, and I asked if we could get together and do some more. She was busy and said she'd call me back and let me know if she had time. But she didn't call.'

Murray brought in a tray of tea things and placed it on the coffee table.

'She tell you everything you needed to know?' Marie asked.

Paris took an Iced VoVo and bit into it with her head down, avoiding her mother's gaze.

'She did great,' Ella said.

'How wonderful.' Marie reached for the teapot. 'Milk? Sugar?'

'Actually, we need to get going.' Ella put her card on the table. 'Please call any time if you – either of you – think of anything else that might be helpful, even remotely. And thank you.'

Outside, Murray nudged her arm as she unlocked the car. 'What did you get?'

'Paris and Stacey are closer than Paris and her mother.' She told him about Stacey crying and mentioning problems at home, and about James's questions about Rowan. 'Ties in with James eyeing Rowan off when we were at the scene, and the feeling that there was something between them.'

Murray clipped in his seatbelt. 'So has James done her in because he thought she was having an affair?'

'And put the car there for Rowan to find, to set him up somehow? I don't know.' Ella started the car and pulled out.

Murray looked back at the house. 'I thought that passing out thing was a total furphy.'

'Really? So did I, but you looked like you'd swallowed it hook, line and sinker.'

'Nah, I was all over it.' He checked his notebook. 'Next stop the friends?'

'Sounds good.' But Ella was still thinking about James, and Rowan, and what might really be going on.

SIX

Aimee Russell opened her front door with a surprised look that turned into a smile. 'Rowan, right? Wow. How are you? It's been ages.' A girl of about three peered around her leg.

'He nodded at them both, and remembered the child's name was Charlotte. 'Do you have a minute?'

'Well, sure. Come in.'

They sat in the kitchen. Aimee wore jeans and a black T-shirt with a cartoon chicken on the front, and her feet were bare. The little girl ran off, and he could hear *Play School* on in another room. He said, 'This is Imogen.'

The women smiled at each other. 'Can I get you a coffee or something?' Aimee said.

'No, thanks,' Rowan said. 'Have you heard from Stacey today?'

'No, why?'

'I'm sorry to say it like this, but she might be in trouble.'

'How do you mean?'

'He found her car with blood in it, and the police don't know where she is,' Imogen said.

Aimee looked back and forth between them. 'Are you kidding me? Is this for real?'

'When did you last talk to her?' Rowan asked.

'Hang on a minute. You're not joking?'

'I wish I was,' he said.

She bit her lip. 'Last week. Friday. I rang to see if she wanted to go out for coffee. She was busy. We planned to catch up this week.'

'Did she tell you about anyone hassling her, anyone who might want to hurt her?' Rowan asked.

'No. Never anything like that. Why aren't the cops asking me this stuff?'

'The cops start with the family then work out, so I'm trying to find out anything that might help.'

The thought of Stacey's tears and the apology he owed her burned his heart.

Aimee let out a breath. 'Was there a lot of blood in the car?'

'Too much,' Rowan said.

'Let me call Claire and Vicky.' She picked up her phone.

★

Ella and Murray arrived at Aimee Russell's house to find four cars parked outside. Ella swore when she recognised the one in the driveway: a blue Ford sedan with a paramedic sticker on the back window. 'Rowan Wylie's here.'

She banged on the front door with an angry fist, hearing sombre conversation inside, smelling coffee. Murray fumed beside her.

The woman who answered looked about forty, and wore jeans and a T-shirt. 'Yes?'

Ella held up her badge. 'Aimee Russell?'

'Yes.' She looked relieved. 'Has there been any news?'

'Not yet,' Murray said. 'We'd like to talk to Rowan.'

Rowan was sitting in the lounge room drinking coffee

with three other women. He looked a little embarrassed to see them in the doorway. Ella beckoned him out, and they went into the dining room and she shut the door. He sat at the dining table with a nervous expression on his face. Ella took the chair opposite and stared at him until he lowered his gaze to the polished timber. She thought of the killers who took pains to insinuate themselves into police investigations, to get involved in searches, to miraculously locate the body. To find the car. To talk to possible witnesses before she did.

'Do you know why we're here?' she said.

'As part of the investigation, I assume.'

'And can you tell me why you're here?' She tried to keep her anger controlled.

'Aimee's a friend of Stacey's. I wanted to know if she'd heard from her. I thought if she had, I could let you know. She hadn't, but she rang her other two friends and told them what was happening and they came over, but they haven't heard from her either.'

At the end of the table Murray clicked his pen and made a note. Rowan glanced his way.

'Did it ever occur to you,' Ella said, 'that it might be important that we speak to these people for ourselves?'

'I knew you would eventually, but I thought in the meantime it would help.'

Did you just. She said, 'Tell me again how you came to recognise Stacey's car.'

'I noticed the paramedic sticker, then the numberplate. I see the car pretty often. I know what it looks like.'

Murray made another note.

'How close are you and Stacey?' Ella asked.

'We're friends, as I said earlier. Is this really helping, going over and over the same stuff?'

'Have you had an affair with her?' Ella asked.

'What? No!'

Murray marked his notebook again.

'How did you two meet?' Ella said.

'I told you, at work,' Rowan said. 'We were partnered together and became friends. As I've said numerous times now.'

'Then what?'

'Then what what? I don't know what you're expecting me to say.'

'When did you meet?'

'I told you before. Eight or nine years ago.'

'And you introduced her to James.'

'Again like I said before, I was friends with him already. We had a party at our place. They both came and they hit it off.'

'Were you jealous?' Murray asked.

'Are you kidding? I was married. They were – they are – my friends. I was delighted for them.'

'Do you ever see her outside work?'

'Now and then. Sometimes she comes to Playland with Em and me. Occasionally we have dinner at their place, or they come to ours.'

'When was the last time that happened?' Ella said. 'The dinner?'

Rowan frowned. 'It'd have to be a few months.'

'Why so long?'

He shrugged. 'I don't know.'

'Who stopped inviting who?' Murray asked.

Rowan paused. 'They did. I think. Or we both did. I don't know. Life's been busy.'

Murray wrote something else.

'What are you writing?' Rowan asked.

Ella said, 'How do you and James get on?'

'Fine. Why?'

'He ever have a problem with you and Stacey working together?'

'What? Did he say that?'

'I'm just asking a question,' Ella said.

'If he did, he never said so to me. And Stacey never told me either. It's a ridiculous idea, anyway.'

'All right,' Ella said. 'You happened to notice her car, you happened to glance inside it. You're talking to her friends before we do. Is there a reason you're so intent on helping us find her?'

'I'm her friend,' he said. 'Isn't that enough?'

Ella waited.

'Look,' he said. 'If you really must know, I have a son who's semi-missing. So a sign that something might've happened to someone I care about gets my attention. Okay?'

'I've never heard of someone being semi-missing,' Ella said.

'He left home five years ago and I haven't spoken to him since. But he sends postcards now and again, from different places in western New South Wales, so I know he's okay, but I've never been able to get in touch with him.'

'What's his name?' she asked.

'Angus. He's twenty-four.'

Ella wondered if this was some kind of convenient cover, an effort to mask his attempts at involvement in the case. She'd look into it later, but right now they had to get on with the case.

'That's all for now. Ask Ms Russell to come in now, and don't leave until we've spoken to you again.' That should keep him stewing in his juices.

Aimee Russell hurried in. 'So there's no news? You really don't know what's happened to her?'

'We're trying to put that together,' Ella said. 'Can we start with your full name and date of birth, please?'

When they had all her particulars, Ella said, 'When did you last have any contact with Stacey?'

'On Friday.' Aimee described how she'd rung her to go out for a coffee, but Stacey had said she was busy.

'Doing what?' Murray asked.

'She didn't say.'

'How did she sound?' Ella asked.

'A bit flat, like she was tired.'

'Did that seem strange?'

Aimee nodded. 'She's usually pretty perky unless she's coming off nights, and I know she wasn't that day. You can hear her smile when she answers the phone, that sort of thing.'

'And on Friday she wasn't smiling?' Murray said.

'Definitely not.'

'Did she ever confide in you?' Ella asked.

'She'd talk sometimes about work things – a sad case, a tough one – but she didn't talk much about personal stuff. If we were out as a group and someone started bitching about their husband or whatever, she didn't really say anything. The times when she did mention James it was pretty surface stuff: he was busy at work, that sort of thing. Never any detail about issues or sex or anything.'

'Do you know him well?' Ella said.

'Not really. He seems an okay guy, though when we were out he'd often text or call and ask her something, and it was always something that I'd think could've waited, like "do we have plans on the weekend?" or "did you buy any parmesan?". I asked her once whether he was suspicious of what she was up to, but she brushed it off. It always struck me as strange, though.'

'Did she ever give an indication that she was annoyed or upset about him doing that?' Murray asked.

'No,' Aimee said. 'She'd just answer him then go on with the conversation.'

'Did he do or say any other odd things?' Ella said.

Aimee thought. 'He was always up when I dropped her home, no matter how late it was. He'd open the door and wait for her to come in. But they don't have kids, so he probably doesn't need sleep as much as my husband does.'

'About kids,' Ella said. 'They're not having any?'

'When Charlotte was born, Stacey told me she'd like to, but that was three years ago and she's never said it again since, and when I asked her she said no.' As if on cue, a little girl came into the room and leaned on her mother's leg.

'I'm hungry,' she said.

Aimee looked at Ella and Murray. 'Are we finished?

'Almost,' Ella said. 'Did you ever get the idea that Stacey might be seeing or interested in someone else?'

'I'd be very surprised. If she was, she was hiding it well.'

'With some people you can tell when they're holding something back,' Murray said. 'You can tell if they're not being completely straight. Did she ever give you that feeling?'

'She can be quiet,' Aimee said. 'When she'd talk about those sad jobs, she'd say so much then trail off, but we all work with dying patients at some time so stuff doesn't need to be spelled out. But I didn't feel like she was hiding anything big, and I sort of thought that with her husband there just wasn't much to bitch about. Because she'd talk about her sister Marie pretty freely.'

'They don't get on?' Murray said.

'They do mostly, but apparently Marie sometimes has this bossy big sister thing going on and it bugs the hell out of Stacey.' Charlotte whined, and Aimee rubbed her back.

'Bossy how?' Ella asked.

'Well, one time she said that she was talking to Paris, her niece, Marie's daughter, about some problem with Paris's boyfriend. Marie told Stacey later she should keep out of it, that she couldn't possibly understand and help when she wasn't a mother herself. Stacey was really riled up. She said it was about relationships, not whether you were a parent. I said maybe Marie was jealous that Paris had talked to Stacey about it instead of her, but she didn't want to talk about it any more.'

'What else did they fight about?' Ella asked.

'That's the only thing that stands out. Claire and Vicky might remember more, though.' She gestured towards the lounge room as she spoke.

'The third woman out there,' Ella said. 'Who is she?'

64

'Her name's Imogen. She came here with Rowan. Was it okay that he was asking questions? I did say that I felt I should be talking to you instead.'

'That would have been better,' Ella said. 'How well do you know him?'

'Not very well. I see him around the hospital sometimes, but I was surprised when he turned up this morning. He and Stacey came here once in the ambulance, dropping off flowers after I'd had Charlotte, but it's a wonder he remembered where I live.'

Ella and Murray exchanged a glance.

'How did he seem when he was talking about Stacey?' Ella asked.

'Anxious and worried. I understood why he wanted to help.'

'Did you ever have reason to think there might be something going on between them?' Murray said.

Aimee shook her head, as Charlotte pulled on her arm. 'No. They seem like they get on well, and Stacey's said she has fun when she works with him, but from what I can see it's the same when she works with anyone else.'

Ella thanked her and gave her a card with the usual instructions, then asked her to send in Imogen.

'I don't know Stacey,' the woman said as soon as she sat down. She was around forty, round faced, short chestnut hair.

'Let's start with some personal details,' Murray said.

Once that was done, Ella said, 'I'm curious how she came up in conversation between you and Rowan.'

'We met for coffee,' she said. 'I know his son's girlfriend. She thought we'd get along and she arranged for us to meet up.'

'You mean you've only just met him today?' Murray said.

'Two hours ago,' Imogen said. 'He apologised for being distracted and said a friend of his was missing. He talked about what had happened and said he wished he could do something, like ask her friends if they'd seen her. I came with him.'

'Not the turn of events you'd expect on a blind date,' Ella said. 'How was he when he was talking about her?'

'Concerned, worried, upset. I'd thought he seemed distant because he didn't really want to be there, but then it made sense.'

They let her go, then interviewed Stacey's other friends. Claire Comber was a thin woman of thirty-nine who blinked back tears and crossed and recrossed her jeans-clad legs. She was a paramedic who'd worked with Stacey on and off over the past few years. 'I can't understand why this would happen. Stacey's the best.'

She couldn't recollect any stories of trouble with anyone, no hints that Stacey was hiding anything or seeing anyone behind James's back.

'James is a sweetheart,' she said. 'Keeps in touch, lets her know where he is. He calls the station sometimes when she's on duty, pretends he's Control and tries to give us ridiculous jobs.'

Ella resisted the urge to glance at Murray.

Vicky Page, a surgical nurse, forty-one, was deep-voiced and serious with dark circles under her eyes and long black hair in a plait.

'James is the one to look at,' she said as soon as she'd sat down.

'Why do you say that?' Ella asked.

'Because the first time I met him I shook his hand and knew he would cause her trouble. I'm a little bit psychic and I'm hardly ever wrong on these things.'

'Right,' Ella said. 'Has Stacey ever confided in you about problems she was having?'

'No, but I know she's unhappy in her marriage. I've been divorced three times, so between that and being psychic I can tell what's going on.'

'What's going on?'

'She's not happy. He doesn't treat her well. It looks fine on the outside but it's not.'

'Have you ever talked to Stacey about it?' Murray asked.

'I've tried a couple of times, but she's not ready yet,' Vicky said. 'She will be, one day. Meantime I make sure I'm there for her.'

'How do you do that?' Murray asked.

'Call her up, see if she needs a chat. Meet up for coffee. Plan a movie night. The little things can really help.'

'Have you ever seen signs that James was violent?' Ella said.

'I don't think he is. I've never read that in her stress levels.'

'Were you aware of times she was stressed because she wasn't getting along with anyone else?' Murray asked.

'Not so much,' Vicky said. 'Her personality type means she gets on with people.'

'Not so much,' Ella repeated. 'You mean sometimes?'

'No. More like not at all.'

Ella wanted to bang her own head on the table.

Murray must have felt the same, because he said, 'Is there anything else, anything at all you can tell us about her that might help us work out what's happened?'

'Give me a moment.' Vicky sank her chin into her neck and breathed deeply. 'No. Nothing's coming to me.'

Ella slapped her card on the table and stood up. 'Call us if you do happen to remember something.'

'There is one thing,' Vicky said.

Ella and Murray turned back from the doorway.

'It's important for you to look after yourself now.'

'Thank you,' Murray said. 'We will.'

'Not you,' Vicky said, and pointed at Ella. 'You.'

'What do you mean?' Ella asked.

'Just what I said.'

Ella gave up and went out. *Nutters – they were everywhere.*

Aimee, Rowan, Imogen and Claire were waiting in the lounge room.

'No more investigating,' Ella said to Rowan. 'You think of anything, you call us.'

He nodded, but seemed unperturbed.

'Thanks for your help,' Murray said to the group, then he and Ella walked outside.

It was starting to rain as they got into the car.

'Why'd she say that to you?' Murray said. 'I'm the one getting married in four days. I'm the one with the pre-wedding nerves, the one who needs to stay healthy.'

'Forget the crazy,' Ella said. 'Aimee said James calls Stacey when they're out and waits at the door when she gets home, and Claire said he calls the station. That's bordering on possessive, if you ask me.'

'I wait up for Natasha if she goes out, and I call her sometimes too,' Murray said. 'You're saying I'm possessive?'

'You're still in the honeymoon phase. They've been married for years. They'd be over that.'

'Only five.'

Ella ignored him and started the car. 'James was eyeing off Rowan and had asked Paris about him and Stacey; Rowan found her car and is snooping; what comes next?'

'Let's see who's home at Rowan's house,' Murray said.

★

After the police had left, Paris tried to talk to her mother, but Marie said she felt dizzy again and had to lie down, alone, in her room with the door shut.

Paris showered in a daze, then pulled on her pyjamas and climbed into her own bed. She lay there now, still awake, the quilt pulled up over her head though she could hear her mother up again and moving about.

She felt strange about telling the detective of James's phone call. It hadn't seemed right that he asked her about Stacey and Rowan, but there was no reason not to answer. And then he'd laughed and made her feel pathetic, as if she wasn't old enough to get the joke and never would be. So it felt right to tell her, but the gleam in her eyes made Paris think she'd just confirmed something the detective had suspected, and if she suspected that James or Rowan or both were somehow involved in whatever had happened to Stacey . . . It was incomprehensible. These were men she knew and trusted, even if she didn't exactly delight in their company. And tomorrow she was due back on shift with Rowan, with this in her mind on top of what'd happened last week.

They'd been finishing a nightshift on Thursday morning, and between her tiredness and the general difficulties she'd been having she forgot to replace an empty oxygen cylinder. Rowan was furious, and went on and on about the importance of oxygen and of replacing what you used before getting into 'how many times do I have to tell you?'. She'd stood with tears in her eyes and tried to apologise, but he'd shook his head and told her to go home and think hard about whether she was right for the job. She'd gone into the locker room and that's where Stacey found her, sobbing, when she'd come in for her shift ten minutes later. Stacey had comforted her, blamed the whole thing on nightshift and fatigue, and sent her home with money for a fancy coffee on the way and a promise to call later and check in. Rowan's car had still been on the station when Paris had left but she hadn't seen him, thank goodness, and when Stacey rang that afternoon she'd said she'd talked to him about it, he'd felt bad about getting angry, and everything was fine.

Problem was, everything wasn't fine.

She'd realised as a child that there was something wrong with her mind. It had started when she was still at school: after every exam she'd gone over and over it in her head, trying to think where she'd gone wrong, what she should've done better. She knew that everyone did that a little bit, but usually by the same afternoon or at most the next day they seemed to be over it. She would still be obsessing weeks later, and it was exhausting. It got worse after her dad died, then again in Years Eleven and Twelve, then had gone off the scale during her paramedic training. She'd done well – she always did well, coming at or close to the top of the class in most things – but it was like she couldn't trust herself, and always felt certain she'd done it all wrong. Since being on the road, the fear had developed a new dimension: she didn't trust her training and her knowledge, she was frightened of missing something important in the patient, and most of all she was terrified that this something would slyly worsen, she would fail to notice, and the patient would die right there in front of her.

Then Rowan said she might not be right for the job, and she realised that if he could see it, she had to admit it to herself. But being a paramedic had been her goal since Stacey had come to her house in her new uniform, first week on the job, full of stories about the people she met and the lives she saved. Paris had sat close by her, taking it all in, and thinking – she couldn't deny it – that someone in just such a uniform had been at her father's crash. That maybe one day she could go to something like that and this time save the person, and the life of some kid would always be the better for it.

The one thing that kept her going over the past six weeks was Stacey. She'd been a rock, talking her through the problems, reminding her how much she did know, saying that it was hard for a patient to secretly die when you were actually looking at them. She made Paris feel like perhaps she could do it; and perhaps she could make Stacey proud of her too. But now she was missing, and there was blood in her car.

Paris knew now what pools of blood looked like, smelled like. The thought of someone hurting Stacey, of some wound in her flesh like the wounds she'd seen – deep lacerations spilling yellowish fat, exposed red meat like steak, the white flash of bone . . . Who would do that to her, and why? She felt sick in every way. Her heart was cold in her chest, her stomach all clenched up. Her skin and her joints hurt like she had a fever.

And the fear of going to work tomorrow and not having Stacey there on belay froze her solid.

She peered with one eye at her phone, resting on the pillow beside her. She'd voicemailed her boyfriend, Liam, but in his job as a technician building medical equipment they had to leave their phones in their lockers. He wouldn't get the message for another couple of hours.

She called him again, needing to hear his voice even just in his message, and left a long rambly one of her own.

Her mother opened the door without knocking. 'Who're you talking to?'

'Liam.' Paris hung up and tucked the phone under her pillow.

'Why are you in bed? You're not on nights tonight.'

'I feel awful.'

'You look okay.' Still in the doorway, Marie looked critically around the room. 'Looks like time for a tidy-up.'

'I need all those books,' Paris said. 'Have you heard anything from the police?'

'Not yet.'

'I can't stand to think of her out there somewhere.'

'Then don't. Think about something else.' Marie nudged one of the books with her foot. 'Think about whether you need this badly enough to keep it on the floor.'

Paris felt tears coming. 'Do you think James did something to her?'

'Don't be ridiculous.'

'In the news it's always the husband, they always find out later he was behind it.'

'I've known James most of my life, and he wouldn't have done anything,' Marie said. 'Crying's not going to help her either.'

Paris wiped her face on the sheet. 'You knew him when you were kids, then when he met her. That's not most of your life.'

71

'I know him,' her mother said. 'He wouldn't hurt a fly.'

'I feel sick.' Paris buried herself under the quilt.

'You're fine. Come out from under there.'

Paris didn't answer.

'You need to get up and do something,' Marie said, 'like I do. I'm going to see James soon and make sure he's okay. I'll probably stay and cook dinner. You've got to keep moving. Find something to do. Activity's good for the soul.'

Paris looked out. 'You want me to go with you?' She didn't know which answer she wanted.

Marie shook her head. 'James needs to keep his spirits up. You'd walk in the door and collapse in a sobbing heap. You'd bring us all down.'

'You collapsed in front of the cops,' Paris said.

'That was shock and a whole different thing. You of all people should know that.'

Paris went back under the quilt.

'Well, if that's your response,' Marie said. 'I'm going now, so you'll have to sort your own dinner. I don't know when I'll be back.'

'I need a hug,' Paris said.

There was no answer.

She said it again, louder, then looked over the quilt. The door was open, the doorway empty. Her mother had walked away.

SEVEN

Imogen accepted another cup of coffee, so Rowan had one too, and Charlotte jumped around the room while everyone talked about the police and the investigation and what could have happened, and wasn't it terrible. And it was terrible, that was the thing: it was terrible, but it made Rowan feel even worse to sit around and chatter rather than get out and do something about it. The police had been clear that they didn't want his help, and maybe it did make him look odd to be involved, but this was what you did for your friends. He let the conversation wash around him and looked out the window. It was raining. Stacey hated working in the rain. He wondered if she was out in it now.

Finally they were done. Vicky left, then Claire, then he and Imogen went out and got into his car. He backed out of Aimee's driveway, waved at her in her doorway, and headed back towards the cafe and Imogen's car. The rain drummed on the car roof, and the tyres of cars going the other way hissed on the road. The car smelled of damp carpet and apple and one of the wipers squeaked. Rowan's head hurt.

Imogen was silent. Her hands were between her knees, her gaze out the windscreen.

He cleared his throat. 'I'm sorry about all that. I didn't mean for us to stay so long. I didn't think you'd get interviewed by the police too.'

'I don't mind.'

He glanced at her but couldn't tell if she meant it. He fixed his grip at ten to two and stared at the car in front, the tail-lights smearing red in the rain on the glass.

'I haven't been out with anyone for a long time,' Imogen said. 'I didn't know what it would be like. I was worried it would be boring. So at least it wasn't that.'

'True,' he said. 'Still, I am sorry.'

'Forget it.' She smiled at him, then placed her hand on his thigh, squeezed. 'You know something? There's nobody home at my place.'

He didn't know where to look. 'School will be out.'

'They both work,' she said. 'They won't be home until six. Maybe even later.'

'Oh,' he said.

She slid her hand higher. He could feel her nails through the denim of his jeans, digging in ever so slightly.

He coughed. 'I don't know. Stacey, I mean.'

'You're afraid you're too distracted? You don't need to do any of the work. I promise.'

'Doesn't seem right,' he croaked.

She raised her hand an inch off his leg. 'Seriously?'

He shrugged, eyes still front.

She shifted, her back against her door, both her hands in her own lap. 'Well. Okay. That's okay.'

'I'm sorry.'

'No need to be sorry,' she said. 'Life rolls along.'

They travelled the rest of the way to the cafe in what felt to him like an embarrassed silence. The rain was still falling when he pulled up next to her car. 'Thanks again,' he said.

'Anytime.' She leaned over with a smile and tweaked his earlobe, then got out.

Rowan scraped his teeth over his lower lip, listening but not looking as she started her car and drove off. At the last second he glanced over to see her wave at him, her hand out the window in the rain.

'Bye,' he said.

The rain grew heavier, pounding the car, and Rowan thought of Stacey.

★

Murray called Dennis and exchanged updates while Ella drove to Rowan Wylie's house in Homebush.

'No sign of her,' Murray relayed to Ella when he'd hung up. 'No Jane Does fitting her description at any hospital. There's some progress with tracking the cyclist, but they're nowhere close to an ID yet. There's no activity from Stacey's phone. James has called it a few times but not had an answer. And James, Rowan, Marie and Bill Willetts don't have records.'

'That only means they've never been caught,' she said.

The Wylie house stood on a quiet street and looked tired and in need of a spruce-up. The garden beds along the front contained as many weeds as they did agapanthus, which were themselves brown in spots and limp. The paint on the front doorframe was cracked, and a line of ants marched up the wall and into a crack between the house and the roof overhang. The windows in the upper storey looked like mournful eyes.

The woman who answered Murray's knock was in her late teens. She was round-faced and red-cheeked, wearing a sundress that was tight under the arms, and she bounced a little girl with bare feet on her hip. Emelia, Ella remembered.

'Rowan's not home right now. I'm his son's girlfriend.'

'Can we talk to you for a few minutes?' Ella said.

'Sure. Come in. We'll have to go in the backyard though. Emelia was just about to get in the sandpit and she'll go nuts if I tell her no now.'

Out the back they sat at a worn timber picnic table. The child jumped with both feet into a plastic clam-shell of yellow sand, her eyes on the grown-ups, making sure they were watching. It hadn't rained here yet, but grey clouds were turning darker overhead and thunder rumbled in the distance.

'Your name's Megan, correct?' Ella said.

'Yep. Last name's Wilkinson,' Megan said. 'I guess you're here about Stacey?'

Ella nodded. 'Do you know her?'

'We've met a few times. She's a nice lady. She sent this really cute little pink teddy bear when Emelia was born.'

'How about her husband, James?' Murray asked.

'He's a great guy. You know Simon works for him? A while back I was sick and couldn't look after Emelia, and Rowan was on shift so couldn't help, and James gave Simon time off to look after us both. And he's getting us an apartment too. This friend of his has one to rent, and James has told him to give it to us.' She beamed.

'That's great,' Murray said.

Emelia threw handfuls of sand onto the grass.

'Don't do that, sweetie,' Megan said. 'It really is. He doesn't have to help us out, but he is, you know? It's nice. It makes you realise there are nice people in the world.'

'When did you last see or talk to Stacey?' Ella asked.

'I couldn't even remember,' Megan said. 'At least a month ago? Something like that.'

'And James?'

'Wednesday last week. Em and I went to have lunch with Simon, and saw James in the shop. We all said hi and just chatted a bit, you know, then we went for lunch.'

'At McDonald's!' Emelia shouted.

'That's right,' Megan said. 'What a great memory you have.'

The kid kicked sand into the air with glee. The wind blew it back onto her legs.

Ella said, 'Were you home on Sunday?'

Megan nodded. 'Yep. Simon was in Melbourne with James at that conference, so it was me, Emelia and Rowan. In the morning we all went for a walk, but the rest of the time we were right here.'

'Rowan didn't go out at all?' Murray said. 'Not for petrol or the paper or anything?'

Megan shook her head. 'He fell asleep in front of the football on TV. I was studying – I'm doing this part-time course in graphic design – and I sat out here with my stuff and Emelia did her usual Emelia things. She likes dinosaurs. She builds them houses in the sand.' She glanced around. 'Honey, what did I just say about throwing that out?'

Ella thought over what Rowan had told her. 'How long have you lived here?'

'Almost three years. My parents threw me out when I got pregnant, when Simon was in Year Twelve and I was in Year Ten. Rowan and Jennifer weren't thrilled but when Simon told them how pissed my parents were, they said I could move in here. Jennifer was sick, you know, she had cancer, and it was really tough sometimes. We didn't always get along, but I saw them cry, I mean really sob, when Em was born. They both hugged me and told me how happy they were that I was there.' She sniffed and screwed up her nose and looked away. 'Jennifer died when Em was six weeks old. Sometimes I felt like I loved her more than I did my real mum. We sent her and my dad a card, like a baby birth announcement thing with a pretty photo and all that. Simon said he thought they'd send it back unopened. They didn't, but they never replied, or rang us or anything.' She pulled at the fabric in her armpit. 'So, yeah. I've been here a while.'

'Has Rowan been seeing anyone since Jennifer died?' Ella asked.

'Like a girlfriend? Only today. I set him up with a lady I know from my design course, she was an accountant or something but now she's really into design. They're out this afternoon.

He wasn't going to go when he found out about Stacey, he said it felt wrong. But I said wouldn't Stacey want him to go?'

'Is that how you found out about her? When Rowan told you?' Ella said.

'No, Simon rang before Rowan got home with Em. Rowan seemed upset, like not crying or anything, but just kind of stunned. Shocked. I made him a cup of tea.'

'What did he say about her?' Ella asked.

'Well, nothing really. I tried to prompt him, so he'd know I was there to listen if he like needed to talk, but he changed the subject.'

'To what?'

'To ask how college was, to say how happy he was that me and Simon and Em live here. That he's proud of us.' She blushed a little and turned away to look at Emelia.

Murray said, 'So apart from this date today, he's never gone out with anyone else?'

'Nope. Simon and I joke with him about it, but I guess he just hasn't been ready. Like we've kinda nagged him for a while, and I told him about my friend Imogen ages ago, but he only just said yes recently.'

Ella said, 'Is Simon an only child?'

'No, he's got an older brother called Angus. Nobody knows where he is though. He sends these postcards like once or twice a year. Always from somewhere different out in the country.'

'Does Rowan keep them?' Ella said.

'Yep. They're on the fridge.'

They followed her inside the house to the kitchen. She took a postcard from the front of the fridge and handed it to them, then lifted a thin rubber-banded collection from the top. The most recent was from Broken Hill, showing old buildings in the town, and scrawled across the back in tall leaning capitals were the words, *A quick hello from me. Angus.* Ella saw it was postmarked the third of March. A month ago.

Murray looked through the others. 'Hay, Albury, Deniliquin, Cobar, Bourke and Nyngan.' He turned them over and Ella saw similar brief messages all in the same handwriting.

'A couple of times Rowan called the cops out there, asking if anyone knew him and that sort of thing,' Megan said. 'But nobody ever knew anything. He keeps these here, and I guess he figures that one day Angus'll come back, or at least ring up or something.'

'He's sending them roughly every six months,' Murray said.

'Yep, but never for anyone's birthday or Christmas or anything,' Megan said. 'They're just kind of random.'

In the garden, Emelia tripped over the edge of the clamshell, fell onto the grass and burst into tears. Megan hurried out to her, leaving Ella and Murray in the kitchen.

'So,' Murray said, 'Rowan has an alibi.'

'From a family member who owes him,' Ella said.

Murray put the postcards back on top of the fridge. 'I thought you were going for James.'

'I have an open and inclusive policy,' she said. 'I suspect everybody.'

★

It was drizzling in Parramatta and the late afternoon sky was low and grey when Ella and Murray stepped out of the lift onto the Homicide office floor. Ella's mobile rang and she couldn't help but smile when she saw Callum's name on the screen.

'Let me guess who that is,' Murray said. 'Ella and Callum, sitting in a tree —'

She went to punch him in the arm but he ducked away laughing. She scowled at him as she answered the phone, 'Hey you.'

'Hey you yourself,' Callum said. 'Can you talk?'

'For a minute.' She waved the grinning Murray on. 'Thanks for the info this morning.'

'Any time. What happened?'

'A woman's missing. We found the blood in her car.'

'It's been hours,' he said. 'She'll be lucky to still be alive.'

'And we've got no strong leads yet.' She rubbed her eyes with one hand. 'How's your day? Did you finish golf before it rained?'

'Never made it. Mum called up in a state. She's decided to sell the house. I've been here all day helping her sort through stuff.'

'Just like that?' Ella said.

'She says it's been coming for a while, because of the mortgage and the legal bills. I'm not sure whether she'll really go through with it, but she had me buy a stack of boxes for when she starts packing.'

Ella felt a jab of guilt. No, not guilt – it wasn't her fault that twenty-four years ago Callum's father, Alistair McLennan, had murdered Callum's cousin, his own nephew. Despite Alistair's full confession, Callum's mother, Genevieve, had trouble believing her husband was guilty, preferring to blame Ella and her solving of the cold case for the life sentence Alistair had received and the situation she now found herself in – losing friends, broke, and unable to get work as a medical receptionist because people recognised her surname, or so she said.

Six months ago Alistair had been stabbed by another inmate, and it had seemed like the death knell for Callum and Ella's relationship, but he'd recovered and so had they. Things had been good lately, steady and comfortable and happy, just how a relationship should be. It was sadness Ella felt now, for Callum who was stuck in the middle.

'I'm sorry,' she said.

'Ah, well, the place is too big for her anyway.'

Ella had a sudden thought. 'She's not angling to move in with you, is she?'

'Don't even joke,' he said. 'That is not going to happen.'

She smiled.

'But listen, I can't get away this evening,' he said. 'She's all over the place emotionally and it doesn't feel right to leave.'

'It's fine,' Ella said. 'I don't know what's going to happen here anyway. If we find something we could be here all night.'

'Phew,' he said. 'I've heard that bad things can happen when a guy stands up a lady.'

'And every one of those rumours is true.'

'I bet.' There was a smile in his voice. 'I promise I'll get free for the dinner tomorrow night.'

Ella groaned. 'Do you have to? I've been praying for a reason to cancel. I thought this might be it.'

'What Aunt Adelina wants, Aunt Adelina shall have,' Callum said.

Ella's father's sister had been nagging Ella and her parents about meeting Callum for months. Years, actually – the two, or was it three years? – since they'd started their on-again, off-again relationship. Suspecting that Adelina planned to interrogate him on marriage and babies, Ella had put it off for as long as possible, but last time she and Callum had been at her parents' the three of them had gone ahead and arranged it all, right there in front of her at the dinner table.

'It'll be fine,' he said.

'Don't say I didn't warn you.'

She heard his mother call out in the background, the usual harsh tone in her voice.

'I'm being summoned,' he said. 'I'd better go.'

'Good luck,' she said.

'You too, sweetie,' he said. 'Bye.'

She went smiling into the office, and found Murray on his phone at his computer. The screen showed Saturday's weather forecast.

'Five per cent chance is nothing,' he was saying. 'It's the closest thing to zero there is. Yes, I'm looking at it now. It says westerly winds. That means any clouds will go out to sea and it'll be a beautiful day.' He glanced around at Ella. 'Honey,

I have to go. It'll be fine. I'll call you when we finish, okay? Love you too.'

'Trouble in paradise?' Ella said when he'd hung up.

She thought he might joke about Natasha freaking out, but he didn't seem to hear her. 'Five per cent really is nothing, don't you think? Not even a shower.' He chewed his lip as he stared at the screen. 'The marquee's not big enough to fit everyone in if it pours.'

'It won't,' she said. 'Five per cent. They shouldn't even have put it on there.'

He looked at her with hope in his eyes. 'You think?'

'For sure.' She clapped him on the shoulder, feeling like he was her young excited brother. 'It's going to be great. Callum and I can't wait.'

★

In the fifteen minutes before the meeting, Ella put Adelina and Callum and the whole family dinner/marriage and baby question out of her head, and called the lab to learn that the blood in Stacey's car had been typed as AB positive, the same as Stacey's and only two per cent of the population, and that two head hairs found stuck in the spatters had been confirmed under microscope as matching the ones collected from the hairbrush they'd bagged at her home. Comparing the DNA of the hair and blood would take time, but Ella had a deep leaden feeling about what the result would be.

She called Computer Crime to be told that Elizabeth Libke was off today but back tomorrow morning. She put down the phone and told Murray, who nodded and hammered on at his reports. Rain streaked the windows and the office grew noisy with arriving detectives, bringing with them the smell of damp clothing and sweat and hours spent in their cars and walking and talking to people, and getting nowhere.

Maybe thinking about the dinner wasn't so bad after all.

What bothered her wasn't the actual topic – marriage and kids weren't offensive ideas, per se – but the way Adelina pushed it. It was like you were nothing if you didn't get all that shit locked in and tied down. Especially as a woman. Adelina frequently lamented her own lack of children, and how 'it makes me feel empty, in here', said mournfully as she touched first her abdomen then her chest over her heart. She'd look at Ella and her ringless fingers with sorrow, and more than once Ella had overheard her asking her parents what was going on between her and Callum, whether it was proper and serious or not. No doubt tomorrow night she'd be asking that same question of Callum himself. The scenario made the back of Ella's neck uncomfortably hot.

'It's time,' Murray said, and she was glad to get up.

In the meeting room, the atmosphere had a different tension to the usual. Homicides carried with them the concern that the killer might get away or might kill again before justice could be done, but here – at least until Stacey's body was found – they had a chance to save her. Then Ella thought about what Callum had said earlier about the effects of the blood loss, and wondered whether Stacey was conscious, whether she was even still alive.

Their boss, Dennis Orchard, came in and closed the door. 'Marconi, Shakespeare?'

Ella and Murray took the floor. She looked at the solemn faces around the table and had a strange moment of deja vu, a feeling that somehow most of her days had been spent right in this spot, describing the terrible end of someone's life and the beginning of the path to getting them justice. Even when they achieved that, the person was still gone, the terrible end had still happened, and tomorrow she would be standing here again, talking about someone else, then someone else, then someone else. This time, would things be different? She felt tense, breathless, dizzy, then Murray cleared his throat and she came back to herself with a jolt.

'Stacey Caroline Durham is thirty-nine years old, married, and works as a paramedic,' she said, seeing their gazes move to the enlarged photo on the whiteboard behind her. 'She was last seen yesterday afternoon by a neighbour between five and five thirty, driving away from her home alone and looking cheerful. Her car was found this morning by a work colleague, Rowan Wylie, parked in a light industrial estate in Homebush. It was locked, and approximately one to two litres of blood was found inside.'

Murray handed out photos of the inside of the car, showing the location and spread of the bloodstain. Detectives studied it with grim faces.

'Stacey Durham's husband, James, was away from Friday until this morning at a conference in Melbourne,' Murray said. 'He was seen by a neighbour to leave his home on Friday afternoon, and travelled with an employee, Simon Wylie, who is Rowan's son. Their flights have been confirmed with the airlines, and their attendance at the conference by the hotel.' Dennis had told them before the meeting began. 'They returned to Sydney this morning. Durham states he last spoke to Stacey yesterday at about 4 pm. He said she told him she was tired, that she planned an early night. He texted her this morning and got no reply, but that's apparently not abnormal. He went directly from the airport to his work, a computer shop in Strathfield, then Rowan Wylie called him about the car.'

'Rowan Wylie was taking his granddaughter to a play centre when he claims to have noticed Stacey's car and felt curious enough to look inside,' Ella said. 'He and James Durham have been friends for ten years, and he has worked with Stacey for eight. He introduced them to each other. Rowan's current work trainee is Stacey's niece, Paris Kennedy. When interviewing Rowan I got the impression that he has some kind of attachment to Stacey, and Paris Kennedy told me that James had asked her once if she thought there was anything going on between the two.' She described James glancing over at Rowan as well, and Aimee Russell and Claire Comber's descriptions of James calling Stacey often. She then went over Marie Kennedy's behaviour and her phone conversation with Stacey at half past three Sunday afternoon about plans for Paris's twenty-first. 'Marie said Stacey sounded fine.'

Murray said, 'The Computer Crime section received an anonymous tip three months ago alleging that James Durham was defrauding his clients. An investigation revealed no wrong-doing and the matter was closed, but we've yet to speak to the investigating officer to find out further details.'

Ella said, 'At ten thirty this morning, when we were speaking to James at his house, he received a text message sent from Stacey's mobile. The text read,' she checked her notebook to make sure she got it right, '*You know what this is about and you won't see her again if you don't do the right thing.* I sent back a text asking who it was, and the reply said, *You know what this is about. It's time to tell the truth.* I then identified myself and asked where Stacey was. The sender said, *James knows everything.* I asked them to explain what that meant. The reply was, *Tell him to tell the truth.* I asked again for an explanation but there was no reply. Phone tracking showed that the messages were sent from an area of about one square kilometre between Stanmore railway station and Parramatta Road, and ten kilometres from the last known location of Stacey's phone, Bicentennial Park in Homebush, at ten past six last night. The phone hasn't been switched on since. James Durham denies any knowledge of what's happened to Stacey, and said he has no idea what the texter is referring to, though he then linked it to the anony-mous tip himself, saying that it should've been investigated more thoroughly at the time.'

Detectives scribbled notes.

'The Durhams' house was distinctly clean and tidy,' Ella went on, 'but Stacey's sister, Marie, said neither Stacey nor James are particular clean freaks.' She described the notebook with the missing pages and the imprint that was being analysed at the lab, then how James's first response when Rowan Wylie called him about his wife was to phone the bank.

Murray said, 'He told us it was to see if any money was missing, if she'd perhaps been forced to withdraw a large amount, but his employee Simon Wylie said he also asked about putting a stop on the accounts.'

'Huh,' Sid Lawson said. 'As if he thinks someone might try to make her empty them?'

Murray nodded. 'That's what he said.'

Ella summarised their interviews with the Durhams' neighbours, mentioned the neighbour yet to be interviewed, and again talked about Stacey's friends, and how Rowan Wylie had beaten them to them.

'Sounds like he's at the heart of this thing,' Lawson said.

'He also has an alibi for Sunday evening,' Murray said. 'In addition, CCTV near the location where Stacey's car was found shows this.' He played the footage from the office supplies store and the detectives watched the car pull in and the driver get out, then ride away on the bike. 'We can't tell from this if the driver is male or female, but they're smaller than Wylie. Checks were made of other cameras in the area.'

Sid Lawson and Marion Pilsiger came to the front.

'Most of the CCTV cameras we checked didn't take in the road,' Pilsiger said, as Lawson inserted a USB drive and brought up the file. 'And most of the ones that did reach that far didn't show us anything more than what we've already got. But these bits came from a shop at the corner of the street, then a traffic camera around the corner.'

Lawson pressed play. The camera showed a view inside the shop and to the footpath and road beyond. The cyclist rode up and stopped, presumably at a red light. He or she put one foot on the ground and kept their head low as if aware that there might be a camera watching. A light-coloured sedan pulled up on the other side of the person but the angle of the shot meant that the driver couldn't be seen. Cars passed it going the other way, then the sedan's passenger window slid down and the cyclist's head turned towards it.

'They're talking?' Murray said.

The cyclist shook their head and looked at the ground, and after a moment the window went up again.

'Someone asking directions?' Wilson Turnbull said.

'Or could be an accomplice checking about any problems,' Lawson said.

Ella stared at the car. Light-coloured sedan, probably white to blend in with the thousands of other white cars on the road. Late-model Commodore by the look of it. Again, thousands out there.

The traffic light evidently changed and the cyclist moved off, the car following it off the screen. Ella leaned forward as if that would let her see more of it. 'You can't see the plate.'

'Not in that clip,' Lawson said.

The screen changed to show footage from higher up, from a traffic camera on a pole. The entire intersection was visible, and Ella watched the cyclist turn the corner while the light-coloured car went straight ahead. Its back was visible but the numberplate was hard to make out even when Lawson clicked pause.

He said, 'We've already sent it to the lab for cleaning up.'

'Starts with an M,' Murray said. 'Or is it an N?'

'Then we have this.' Lawson pressed play again.

The cyclist moved across the lower half of the screen and a small dark-coloured car swung around the corner behind it. As the cyclist rode around a parked car, the moving one almost hit them. The car swerved and the cyclist wobbled. The passenger window went down and a dark face appeared, shouting something back at the cyclist.

'Nice,' Murray said.

'Even nicer is that we've already traced that plate, because further down the road they went past a speed camera and got snapped,' Pilsiger said. 'Owner's name is Mackenzie Walker, female, aged nineteen, lives with her parents in Strathfield. We've called them but she's out, and they can't contact her because her mobile's been cut off for non-payment. We left a message.

'Using what we got from other cameras, we were able to trace the cyclist to where they turned off Underwood Street into Mason Park, which, coincidentally or not, adjoins Bicentennial Park.' She put up a photocopy of a map, and drew a line in thick red pen to show the route. 'There are a number of places where they could've left that park and we've been unable to find out which one they took, so don't know where they went after that. But from all the footage we managed to get this photo from one of the CCTV cameras which might be suitable to put out to the media.'

Ella studied the black and white image. The shot was taken from some distance away and from above, but the cyclist had turned his or her head, and you could see the side and part of the front view of the face. She held it at arm's length and squinted. It was hard to make out the features at first, but it was also probably – hopefully – clear enough that somebody might be struck by its familiarity and look twice. This was good. Between this and what they could hopefully get from Walker, this was really good.

'Plus we have the exact locations and times so can put out a call for anyone who noticed him or her,' Lawson was saying.

'Good job,' Dennis said. 'Show it to James Durham, and Stacey's friends and colleagues too. Get it out to the media as well.'

One by one, the other detectives got up and listed their day's activities. The people in the businesses around Playland had been interviewed but no one had seen anything. Requests had been put in for Stacey's and James's landline and mobile phone records, including checks on whether she'd made calls in the time between leaving home and when her car was left. The last location of her phone on Sunday night, at Bicentennial Park, wasn't able to be narrowed down to an area under twelve hundred square metres, and it took in a car park and multiple paths and park areas with no CCTV. The area in Stanmore, where this morning's text had been sent from, was no more useful. Information had been released to the media in the hope that somebody had noticed something strange, or even just seen Stacey there herself. Her bank account had last been used three days before, when she'd got a hundred and fifty dollars cash out when buying eighty dollars of groceries – an amount that wasn't unusual for her, Turnbull reported. Most of Stacey's work colleagues had been interviewed and so far none had any ideas about what might've happened.

'Okay,' Dennis said. 'Leads going in different directions, and the clock is ticking. Some of you will be back in the morning, some will stay on tonight. We've got traces on both the Durhams' home line and their mobiles. We're monitoring her Facebook page, and also one that her friend Aimee Russell's set up asking people to help find her. Check in with the hospitals again, ask about any Jane Does, dead or alive. Talk to Mackenzie Walker. We need to keep going on both the cyclist going out and the car coming in. Stacey was seen leaving her house in Haberfield between five and five thirty, then the car was left in Homebush at six forty-two. It's only a ten to fifteen-minute drive, so what else happened in that time? Where did Stacey go when she left home? What happened then, and where? How and where did the cyclist get the car? Get the photo of the cyclist and one of the car to the media – someone might've noticed it on the way, might've seen the driver. Find out about that bike; those folding things can't be too common. Can we trace it? And get the pic of Stacey herself to anyone who doesn't have it yet. Someone must've seen her, must've seen something out of the ordinary if it was an abduction.' He looked around at them. The leaden feeling in Ella's chest grew heavier. 'It can't be so easy to spirit a woman off the streets of Sydney without a single person noticing anything.'

EIGHT

Rowan drained the water from the saucepan and started to mash the potatoes. A car door slammed out the front and Emelia bolted past him. 'Daddy!' Rowan heard Simon come in, heard Emelia's squeal as he swung her into the air and Megan telling him how the detectives had talked to her. He sliced a chunk of butter into the pan and kept mashing.

'Hi,' Simon said behind him, Emelia giggling upside down in his arms. 'Anything I can do?'

'Nope,' Rowan said. 'Almost done.'

Simon put Emelia down and steered her towards the doorway. 'Go get your ball and we'll have a kick outside after tea.'

Emelia ran off. Rowan poured milk into the potatoes.

Simon came to lean against the bench beside him. 'Smells great. I'm starving.'

'How's James?' Rowan asked.

'A walking disaster zone. The cops came and searched the house, and took stuff for DNA matching, and he was crying, then angry, then just staring at the walls. I didn't feel safe to leave until Marie turned up. She said she'd look after him, but when I said goodbye to him he was just sitting there on the lounge, holding a photo of the two of them, and he just nodded without looking up. Poor guy.'

Rowan scraped the mash off the sides of the saucepan and rapped the masher clean. 'The police didn't give him any new information? Progress reports, anything like that?'

'Not while I was there.'

'You'd think they'd know something by now.'

'I guess it takes a while,' Simon said. He hesitated. 'Megan said she told you about the flat.'

Rowan nodded. 'It sounds good.'

'Dad.'

Rowan elbowed him. 'It does. It's great that you and Meegs want to get out there on your own.'

'I was going to ease into the subject,' Simon said. 'I mean, you haven't been alone since like forever.'

'I'm a grown-up.' Rowan got out the plates. 'I'll survive.'

'I know, but . . .'

'But what?'

'It's not just that we're moving out. Mum's gone, and everything.'

'You think the realisation will finally hit me?' he said. 'Grab the cutlery. I know Mum's gone, mate. I know it every day. I'm okay.'

He took the tray of sausages from the oven where they'd been keeping warm and forked them onto the plates, then scooped carrots and beans from the steamer.

Simon went to the foot of the stairs and called Emelia and Megan, then came back. 'You'll be rattling around here like a bean in a barrel when we're gone.'

'I'll be fine.'

'If you sold, you could afford a unit at the beach,' Simon said. 'You and Mum always –'

'I won't be selling.' Rowan put the plates on the table.

'I'm just saying if.'

Rowan shook his head. 'Not going to happen.'

Emelia came running into the room and climbed up onto her chair. Megan followed. Since Jennifer died they no longer used the big table in the dining room but sat here in the kitchen instead.

'Yum,' Emelia said.

'Put the ball on the floor and don't talk with your mouth full,' Megan said, cutting up her sausages.

'Oh,' Simon said. 'How was the date?'

'It wasn't a date,' Rowan said.

'And it was a bust,' Megan said. 'They ended up at a friend of Stacey's talking to the cops again.'

Simon said, 'You know how to impress them.'

'Can we talk about something else?' Rowan said. He'd already told everything to Megan, at her insistence.

'Imogen texted me and said she had a good time anyway,' Megan said to Simon.

'That sounds promising,' he said.

'I'm sure she's very nice,' Rowan said. 'But I'm quite content on my own.'

Megan and Simon exchanged a glance, then Emelia coughed up a hunk of sausage and dropped her fork on the floor.

'You have to chew it more,' Megan said.

'Want to go out and kick the ball.'

'Not until after tea.'

When they'd finished eating, Rowan volunteered to go and play with Emelia if Megan and Simon cleared up.

'That sounds fair,' Simon said.

Emelia giggled and tugged Rowan to his feet. Outside, the air was fresh, the evening cool and smelling of rain on grass. Emelia kicked the ball straight into the shrubbery, then scrambled in to get it. Rowan put his hands in his pockets and looked at the fading sky, thinking about Stacey.

★

Paris pulled up outside the house in Lidcombe where Liam lived with his mother and baby sister. He'd called after work and listened to her cry, then invited her for dinner, and she'd got dressed and into the car quicker than she'd thought was possible.

His mother, Abby, opened the door and hugged her. 'I'm so sorry about Stacey.'

'Thank you,' Paris said. Abby always smelled like clean warm laundry and her arms felt nice around you. Paris liked that she hugged both hello and goodbye.

Liam looked up from feeding Lucy in her high chair. 'Hi, babe.'

Lucy babbled through smeared mashed peas and carrots. Paris kissed them both as Abby brought in plates of roast chicken and vegetables.

'How are you?' Abby asked when they sat down.

Paris felt her gaze look deep inside her. *She really sees me.* 'I'm petrified. The police said there was blood everywhere.'

'People can be tougher than you think,' Abby said. 'And from what I remember of Stacey at school, she was tough with a capital T. Hard to imagine that would've changed.'

'I know, but it's so scary to think of her out there some-where,' Paris said. 'I mean, who did it? Who's got her? What are they doing to her?'

Abby squeezed her hand. 'How about your mum? How's she doing?'

'Maaaarvellously,' Liam said under his breath.

'That's not nice,' Abby said.

'You've only met her once, for five minutes,' he said. 'Just wait.'

'She's okay,' Paris said. 'She fainted when the police were there.'

'For real, or like last time?' Liam said.

'It was over when I got there, so it's hard to say.'

'I bet I could say,' Liam said.

Abby frowned at him.

'Okay, enough, I get it,' he said, with a sideways look at Paris that made her smile.

Half an hour later, Lucy was bathed and in her cot, and Paris snuggled next to Liam on the lounge.

He kissed the top of her head. 'Going okay?'

'Going better.' He was warm, and his arm felt like a big safe wing wrapped around her. If she could stay here forever she'd be fine.

Abby brought in a cup of tea and sat in the recliner. 'Viewing options?'

Liam flicked through the channels with the remote. 'More free channels than ever and it's still all crap. Shopping? Ugh.'

'Stop there,' Abby said. 'Doco on castles.'

'No way.' Liam kept pressing buttons. 'Here we go. *Law & Order.*'

Abby said, 'That mightn't be a good choice.'

'Huh?' Liam's eyes were on the screen.

'Because there's a bit too much crime drama happening right here, don't you think?' she said. 'Liam?'

'I'm okay with it,' Paris said. 'Really.'

'Nothing bad in the castle doco,' Abby said. 'A very safe space.'

'Really,' Paris said again. '*Law & Order*'s fine with me.'

'Sweet,' Liam said, settling in.

Paris was all right for a while, then a woman was abducted and it looked like she was going to be murdered, and she found herself on her feet.

Abby looked at her, concern in her eyes.

'Bathroom,' Paris said by way of explanation.

In the hall she heard Abby tell Liam to change the channel, then she was out of hearing and locking the bathroom door with sweaty hands. She wasn't okay at all. She sat on the closed toilet lid and gripped her knees. Stacey was tough. She would've put up a fight with whoever took her, but it would've been a canny fight: she would've thought about what was best, how to keep safest for longest and all that. So the presence of blood was bad, and so much of it was worse, but Stacey knew how to stop bleeding and how to make sure – as best she could – that she didn't go into shock. If anyone could survive this, it was her.

Paris still felt sick though. And she remembered things. Like waking up after having her tonsils out at age eleven, not long after her dad had died, and Stacey not only being beside the bed, because her mother had had to work, but rubbing Paris's back when she threw up from the anaesthetic, stroking her hair as she fell asleep. Stacey at her Year Twelve presentation night, smiling with more pride and love than Marie seemed able to muster.

There was a tap on the door. 'Paris?' Abby said.

Paris stood up and flushed, then washed her hands. 'I'm all right,' she said when she opened the door.

'He's changing the channel.'

'He doesn't have to.'

'Yes, he does.'

Down the hall Lucy started to cry.

'Can I go to her?' Paris asked.

'Well, sure,' Abby said. 'If you want. Don't pick her up, just rub her back and say shhh.'

Lucy's room was dim, a ladybird nightlight under the cot glowing gently. The baby was pushing herself up on her arms and wailing. Paris stroked her head and down her back, then patted her thickly nappied bottom. Lucy put her face back on the sheet and turned her head from side to side.

'Shhh,' Paris said. 'Shhh.'

Lucy quietened and closed her eyes. Paris kept rubbing her back, then, as Lucy's breathing deepened, she stroked her little legs, her fine brown hair. Paris's vision blurred with tears, and she pressed her forehead hard against the cot railing.

★

Ella and Murray were two of six detectives who'd stayed back after the meeting and now they were headed for the Strathfield home of Mackenzie Walker. She lived with her parents in a cream stucco house on a tree-lined street near Santa Sabina College. The evening air smelled like roast chicken and baked vegetables when Ella and Murray climbed from their car, and Ella's stomach growled.

'We could've got something on the way if you weren't in such a hurry,' Murray said.

Ella pointed to the red Hyundai with P-plates parked on the brick driveway. 'But isn't it a good thing that I was?'

The front garden was lush, with a trickling water feature and ferns that were still wet from the afternoon's rain. Ella followed the brick path to find that behind a heavy security screen the front door was open. She heard heated conversation, and pressed the brass buzzer with anticipation.

The woman who came to the door looked harried, with a dent between her eyes from frowning. 'Yes? Oh,' she said, on seeing their badges.

'Detectives Ella Marconi and Murray Shakespeare,' Ella said. 'Mrs Walker? Is Mackenzie home?'

'Yes.' She unlatched the screen and opened it. Her face was made-up, and she wore cut-off jeans with deliberately frayed edges, blingy sandals and an expensive-looking white V-neck T-shirt that set off her tan. There were two silver rings on her right hand and three on her left, including a big engagement rock. 'Please come in. We were just discussing the fact that you might be dropping around.'

She led them into the living room, where a girl in her late teens sat cross-legged in a pink velvet armchair.

'Feet off the lounge,' her mother hissed. 'How many times –?'

The girl dropped her feet to the floor but didn't unfold her arms. She glanced at Ella and Murray, then picked up her phone and looked at the screen. She wore red Vans with no socks, slashed dark jeans that rode high over her ankles and a ripped black T-shirt.

'Mackenzie,' Ella said. 'So that's your car in the driveway?'

The girl didn't look up. 'Yep.' Her black and purple hair hung over her face like a curtain.

Ella sat down opposite her. 'Been for a drive today?'

'So?'

'You almost hit a cyclist.'

'Mackenzie,' her mother said.

'Alison,' Mackenzie retorted in the same tone. 'It was only almost.' She looked at Ella. 'And it was their fault. I hope they told you that.'

Ella noted the pronoun. 'How about you put down the phone and tell us what happened.'

Mackenzie glanced at the phone's screen again, then placed it on the arm of the chair. 'I was driving, I turned a corner, this idiot rode out into my way. I had to swerve. I was practically on the wrong side of the road. I could've been killed.'

Alison Walker snorted.

'Then what?' Murray asked.

'Then what what? I drove on in a sedate manner to my destination.'

'Except for the less-sedate moment when you got done by a speed camera,' he said.

Ella saw anger flash across Mackenzie's face.

'Really, Mackenzie?' Alison said.

Mackenzie shrugged, regathering her dismissive air. 'Everyone knows those things are just about revenue raising.'

'What was your destination?' Ella asked.

'KFC.'

'Did you see the cyclist again?'

'Nup.'

'What about your friend?'

'What friend?'

'The one in the passenger seat of your car,' Ella said.

'I was on my own.' She said it bluntly, with force.

Oho, Ella thought.

'It better not have been that Oliver boy,' Alison said.

'His name's Olivier,' Mackenzie said. 'And I just told you I was on my own.'

Murray stood up. 'Mrs Walker, any chance of a cup of tea?'

Once they were out of the room, Ella said, 'You've got three seconds to tell me the truth.'

Mackenzie scowled. 'What makes you so sure I'm not?'

'I saw his face in a CCTV photo,' Ella said. 'One.'

'Cops fake CCTV all the time, everyone knows that,' Mackenzie said. 'And I'm not a child you can use a count-down on. I hope you're not expecting me to crack like some toddler.'

'Two.'

'I mean, what did the idiot say? Nothing actually happened. I know my rights. There's no law against shouting when someone does something stupid like that.'

'A woman could be dead,' Ella said.

'No way did we hurt anyone.'

Ella smiled at her. 'We?'

'Oh, fucking – all right. But we didn't do anything wrong. Olivier just yelled. You better not tell my mother about this.'

'Was the cyclist a man or a woman?'

'You just said a woman.'

'That's someone else. Which was it?'

'I don't know. I didn't see.'

'Olivier didn't say? Didn't sit back and say "stupid bastard" or anything?'

She thought a minute. 'I don't think so.'

'What's Olivier's last name and address?'

'He'll have the shits if you lot turn up at his house. Plus his mum hates me even more than mine hates him.'

'Your mum's going to come in at any moment. You want me to keep asking?'

Mackenzie moaned into her hands, then gave a name and address in Abbotsford.

Ella got out her card. 'You remember any little thing about that cyclist, give me a call.'

'Can you get me out of that speeding fine?'

'Not my department, sorry.'

Mackenzie stuck the card into her pocket. 'Why am I not surprised.'

Murray and Alison Walker came back in with a tray of tea things, Alison saying, 'A job is what she needs.'

'I have a job,' Mackenzie said to Ella.

'Part-time at Coles is not what I'm talking about,' Alison said. 'A career. Is it hard to get into the police?'

'Like I'm too dumb to do anything better,' Mackenzie said.

'No offence taken,' Ella said.

'Milk? I hope skim's okay. It's all we drink. Sweetener?' Alison said. 'Was she any help at all?'

'She was fine,' Ella said. 'Thanks for the tea, but we have to get going.'

Outside, the air was cool, the trees motionless, and bats crossed the darkening sky. As Ella and Murray got in the car, she told him what Mackenzie had said.

He started the engine. 'One day someone's going to realise what we're up to with that tea thing and refuse.'

A

They talked to Olivier Tarlington while he fixed a bike on the lawn at the back of his parents' house. Moths flew at the floodlight over the back door, and the place was close enough to Hen and Chicken Bay that Ella could smell the mud exposed by the low tide and hear the clink of the cabling on the masts of the moored yachts out on the water. Her home was across the river in Putney, probably five minutes away if she was a crow.

'I don't really remember what I said.' Olivier spun the pedals of the bike.

Ella grabbed the tyre to stop it. 'Would a trip down to the station help?'

'You can't make me go,' he said. 'If my mum and dad were here you wouldn't be talking to me at all.'

'Lucky us,' Murray said.

Olivier pinched a mosquito off the back of his neck and flicked it onto the grass. His dark skin seemed to absorb the light. 'Mackenzie said you lied to her, said that some chick was dead to make her talk.'

'I said might be dead,' Ella replied. 'And it's true. We think the person you shouted at knows something important.'

'And you need my help to find them.'

'Yes.'

He spun the pedals again, then stopped them and fiddled with the chain. He wiped the grease onto his jeans. 'It was a chick.'

'You're sure?' Murray said.

He nodded. 'I yelled at her. I said she was a stupid dumb c-word and she should get the f-word off the road.'

Ella didn't smile at his propriety. 'How close were you?'

'I guess as far away as that fence.'

Ella looked. Five metres, maybe less. 'How clearly did you see her face?'

'Like looking at you,' he said.

'Can you describe her?' Murray said.

'All you whities look the same to me,' he said. 'Joking. She was kinda pale, like not super-tanned. Her face was thin. I think her hair was sort of light brown – she had a helmet on but there was a bit poking out at the front – and also her eyebrows weren't either really dark or really pale, so yeah, I'd be saying light brown.'

'Age?' Ella said.

'Pretty old. Forty or fifty.'

'Anything else stand out? Tattoos, jewellery, clothes?'

He thought for a moment, turning a pedal in his hand. 'Dark clothes, I think. Nothing really jumps out. I don't remember any tatts or anything.'

Ella took the photos of Stacey and of the cyclist from her jacket pocket. She showed him Stacey first. 'Is that her?'

He looked then shook his head. 'Nope.'

'You're sure?' Murray said.

'Completely.'

'What about this?' She held out the picture of the cyclist. It was the still shot that showed part of the face.

'Yeah, that's her. Same black helmet and everything.'

'Do you remember anything about the bike?' Murray asked.

'The wheels were little,' Olivier said. 'And it seemed tall and wobbly. I thought she was going to fall off.'

'Because you yelled at her?'

'No, we were still behind her then. We came around the corner and she was wobbling out to go around the car. That's why we had to swerve.'

'Wobbling as if she wasn't used to it?' Ella said.

'Yeah, maybe.'

'How did she react when you shouted?'

'She just looked at me. Maybe she didn't hear it over the music. We had it up pretty loud.'

'Mackenzie said she didn't hear what you yelled,' Ella said.

'She wouldn't have. It was that loud.'

Made sense, Ella thought.

'So you think she had something to do with what happened to that lady you mentioned?' Olivier asked.

'We're not sure yet,' Ella said. 'Why doesn't Mackenzie's mother like you?'

'She found pot in Mac's room and Mac told her it was mine.'

'And why doesn't your mum like her?'

'She found pot in my room and I told her it was Mac's.'

He grinned, then added quickly, 'But neither of us smoke it any more so there's no point rousting us or anything.'

'So were you really going to KFC yesterday?' Murray said.

Olivier nodded. 'I swear.'

'You swear,' Ella said. She got out her card. 'Thanks for your help, and if you remember anything else about the woman, or her bike, give us a call.'

NINE

Ella and Murray went back to the office, updated their reports, then headed home. Ella walked in her front door at nine thirty and put the kettle on with a sigh. The night was cool and quiet, a relief after the busyness of the day. Finding out that the cyclist was a woman was great, but it hadn't brought them any closer to working out who exactly she was or where Stacey might be. And the whole thing with James and Rowan bugged her.

The kettle whistled. She made a cup of tea and took it and her mobile out to the plastic outdoor setting in her backyard. The sky had cleared. She dried a chair with a rag, then sat down.

Was James genuinely suspicious of Rowan when he asked Paris about him and Stacey, or was he joking, as he'd said? And it could simply be chance that Rowan had found her car, but when combined with his actions in going to see her friends, particularly when they weren't also his friends (and who remembered an address after going there once three years ago?), it didn't really look like it. Then there was Marie and whatever weird thing she had going on, and Willetts from

103

over the road, and the anonymous complaint about James's computer shop.

She drew in a breath, held it, then let it slowly out. She needed to sleep tonight, and wrestling with the case more than necessary wasn't going to help. She shook her shoulders and looked around the dim yard. The grass was getting long; time to borrow her father's mower again. Franco used to come around and do it himself, putting the mower in the boot for the short drive from Chullora, then pottering around the yard humming, but he'd become frailer in the last year or so and she'd taken to bringing the mower over herself. Franco often came too, and so did her mother, Netta, the two of them trying to talk to her over the mower's roar, then sitting down together for lunch at the end. That made her think about tomorrow's dinner again.

She stretched her neck to work out the kinks, had a sip of tea, then called Callum.

'Hi,' he answered in a whisper after the first ring.

'You're still there? How's it going?'

'You can probably imagine. How about you? Did you find her?'

'Not yet.' The words were hollow.

'Do they know yet if the blood is hers?'

'The DNA's not back yet, but it's the same type. The hairs we found match hers too.'

'I'm sorry,' he said.

'Me too,' she said. 'Listen. Assuming she's still alive, how would she be?' She couldn't not ask.

'Depends. If the bleeding was stopped by someone putting firm pressure on the wound, either with their hand or with a decent pad and bandage, but she's had no treatment, like IV fluid replacement, she'll be weak, faint, prone to passing out if she stands or perhaps even if she sits up. She might be vomiting, her heart rate and breathing would rise, her blood pressure would fall, she'd be pale and sweaty and probably quite anxious.

If the wound was left alone, just allowed to keep bleeding with no treatment whatsoever, she would experience all these things more and more until she got to the point where she'd pass out even while lying flat, and then at some point, I'm sorry to say, she would die.'

Ella couldn't find anything to say.

'But look,' he said, 'even the dimmest dimwit knows enough to stop bleeding. And whoever took her must've done so for a reason. She has to be more use to them alive than dead, otherwise they would've killed her straight away. Wouldn't they?'

'Probably,' she said after a moment.

'So she's more than likely not feeling great, but not getting worse either. She's probably too weak to make an escape from wherever they have her, but given a few days' rest and food and water, she might be able to think about it.'

'If she's not tied up,' Ella said. 'If she's not behind locked doors.'

They were silent, then he said, 'So, tomorrow night. I'll pick you up on my way through?'

'I wanted to talk to you about that.'

'It'll be okay,' he said.

'You don't know what Adelina's like. She'll grill you like you're dinner. She'll ask whatever's on her mind, no matter how personal.'

'I'll be brave if you'll hold my hand.'

She laughed but felt no better. 'I'm serious.'

'I'm serious too,' he said. 'Hold my hand and it'll be okay.'

She closed her eyes. Maybe there'd be a break in the case; maybe she'd have to work back and dinner could be cancelled.

'I promise,' Callum was saying.

'Okay.' She heard him fight back a yawn. 'Guess I'd better let you go.'

'In a sec,' he said. 'I saw you on the news tonight, standing near the car.'

'I hope I looked more intelligent than I feel.'

'You looked perfect,' he said. 'Absolutely perfect.'

She smiled.

★

Rowan wiped down the sink and benches, listening to Megan and Simon dealing with Emelia's usual bedtime shenanigans upstairs. It was dark outside, and he couldn't see past his reflection in the kitchen window. The knock at the front door startled him. He opened it to find James standing there, red-eyed, rumpled and blinking in the porch light.

'Rowan,' he said, and Rowan smelled beer on his breath. 'Can I come in?'

They sat at the kitchen table. Emelia's crying rang through the house.

'Poor little thing,' James said.

Rowan closed the door to shut out the sound, and got James a glass of water.

'Sorry for just dropping by,' he said. 'I've been out driving. Looking, I guess. Though I don't even know where to start.' He gripped the glass in both hands. 'How could someone do this? Take her away like this?'

'I don't know,' Rowan said.

'The cops asked me about business competitors, and about that complaint.' James's face was oily and greenish in the fluorescent light. 'And that made me think of the conference, hundreds of computer people schmoozing, and all that time was one of them behind it? Was one of them watching me and knowing what was happening to Stace? Was he even talking to me, shaking my hand? Looking me in the eye like he was my friend while he was betraying me?'

'Are they certain it's that?'

'No, they're not certain, but what else could it be? Now whoever's got her is sending these text messages about telling the truth, about doing the right thing if I want to see her again. If it's some crazy patient she looked after, why would he blame me?'

'To throw off the police?' Rowan said.

'But how would the crazy even know about the complaint?' He got up to pace. Rowan could hear him grinding his teeth. 'All that blood, Rowan. How can she survive that?'

'It's possible,' Rowan said. 'The human body –'

'And the car being there,' James went on. 'Why was the car there? Why *there*? And you noticed it. Why you?' He turned to face him. 'Why you?'

'Coincidence is a weird thing,' Rowan found himself saying. 'It looks like it means something when it doesn't.'

James's gaze was hard. 'You'd tell me if you knew where she was. Right?'

'Of course I would. You know that.' Rowan could feel himself reddening. 'You know me. I'm your friend. I want her home safe as much as you do.'

'You wouldn't lie to me, would you?' James took a step towards him. The water slopped out of the glass in his shaking hand. 'You wouldn't have anything to do with this, would you?'

'James,' Rowan said. 'I'm your friend. I'm telling you the truth. I don't know where Stacey is or what's happened. I swear on my sons' lives.'

James stared at him a moment longer then blinked as if waking up, and glanced at the ceiling, through which Emelia's muffled cries still came. 'Of course. I'm sorry. I don't know where my head's at. I can't think straight.' He turned to the sink and the glass slipped in his hand.

Rowan heard it break then saw blood drip to the floor. 'Jesus, did you just cut yourself?'

'It's just a graze.' James squeezed his finger. Blood trickled across his palm.

'I'll get the first-aid kit.' Rowan hurried to the bathroom and grabbed the kit from under the sink. Back in the kitchen, he made James sit down at the table then looked at his hand. The cut was small, on the side of his index finger, and steadily oozed blood. It didn't need stitches.

'I can't even concentrate enough not to hurt myself,' James said, as Rowan applied Steri-strips. 'I'm so sorry for what I said.'

'Forget it.' Rowan covered the wound with a dressing and taped it into place. 'With what you're going through it's completely understandable.'

The door opened and Simon and Megan came in. Megan went to James and hugged him.

'We thought we heard voices. How are you?' she said. 'I'm so sorry about Stacey. The police were here this afternoon asking me stuff about her. They're really serious about it. What'd you do to your hand?'

'What stuff?' James said.

'Just about her and Rowan and our family, about how well I know you and her, stuff like that,' Megan said.

'Covering all the bases,' Rowan said. 'Thorough.'

James nodded. 'Yes. Well, it's good to have friends like you guys at a time like this.' He took Simon's outstretched hand.

'Whatever we can do,' Simon said.

James wiped his eyes. 'Thank you.'

Megan ran the tap to wash the blood down the sink. 'James, I got paid today, so we finally have the bond money.' Her voice was bright with excitement. 'We're ready to go whenever your friend is.'

But Rowan could see that James wasn't really listening. 'There's no rush,' he said.

'Well –' Megan began.

'Another time,' Rowan said.

James leaned against the bench, his hands gripping the edge of the sink behind him, his eyes haunted. 'What if I never see her again?'

*

After a night of bad dreams about Stacey being lost and hurt, and about patients with symptoms she couldn't understand no matter how hard she tried, Paris had a headache when she headed to The Rocks ambulance station early in the morning. She wanted to get in before Rowan, wanted to be checking the ambulance when he arrived, was determined to show him that she had a handle on everything. But when she walked up the driveway, she saw his car was already there.

He was standing in the lounge with Joe and Mick, the pair bleary-eyed from nightshift, watching the morning newsreader talk about Stacey's disappearance. There was footage of her car being taken away from the Playland car park on a flatbed truck and of police going in and out of nearby businesses, then a photo of Stacey and James on a beach, then one of her smiling that Paris recognised as having been taken at one of the family barbecues; she could even make out her mother's arm in the background.

The report was the same rehashing she'd seen before she left home, when her mother had been slumped on the lounge in her dressing gown, cup of coffee going cold in her hand.

'You're not going to work?' Paris had asked her.

'I've taken leave,' Marie had retorted. 'Yours isn't the only job that can look after its staff.'

Paris had let that slide. 'How was James?'

When Marie had come home at ten the night before, Paris had still been awake and feeling a little better after her evening with Liam and Abby and Lucy, but she hadn't called out.

'How do you think?' Marie said.

Paris had turned away at the hostility in her voice, and wondered now if Marie was still on the lounge watching the TV.

'Hey,' Joe said, seeing her in the doorway. 'We didn't know if you'd be in today. Are you okay?'

'Okay enough,' Paris said.

Rowan glanced at her, then back at the TV. It was impossible to tell whether the cops had told him what she'd said about James's question. The idea that he might think she'd taken it seriously, that she'd imagined he and Stacey might've got together, made her feel awkward. She left the room and got her bag from her locker. She opened their ambulance and switched on the internal fluorescent lights, then climbed into the back. Six weeks down and the truck was more familiar but still not the 'home' that Stacey had once described it as. Paris got out the checklist Rowan made her keep in her bag. He'd declared on her first day that by the third week she should know how to check the equipment without it, but when she didn't, and after she twice forgot to check and restock the oxygen masks and once left a different empty cylinder unchanged, he'd photo-copied the form and thrust it into her hand. 'I sign here,' he'd said, pointing to the box at the bottom of the columns, the words *when you do it right* left unsaid. She wondered if there'd be changes after last week's cylinder episode, whether he'd present her with another checklist or maybe insist on watching as she worked. *Not that you don't deserve it*, she thought.

He came out as she was repacking the intubation kit. She put it away and made sure he saw her ticking the form.

'Going all right?' he said.

'Yep.'

He opened the linen locker then closed it. 'How's your mum?'

'She's okay.'

'She go in to work?'

Paris shook her head. 'She's taken some time off.'

Rowan sat on the end of the stretcher. She felt his eyes on her as she checked the drug box. She counted ampoules of local anaesthetic with focused zeal.

He said, 'You know you can take compassionate leave. If you want.'

'I know.' But here was better than home, and in some way it felt important to keep going.

'Paris,' Rowan said, but the ringing of the station phone cut him off.

Mick answered it in the muster room, listened, then came outside. 'Collapse in Alfred Street Macca's.'

'We're on it,' Rowan said.

Paris closed up the back, then got in the passenger side and clipped in her seatbelt. Rowan started the engine. Other students from her class were already driving, she'd seen them around the city, but Rowan hadn't said anything about when she might start. She pulled on latex gloves as Rowan hit the lights and siren, and let out a secret breath, preparing for what was coming.

'What do we do first?' Rowan said.

'Check for danger. Check patient's response, and their airway, breathing and circulation.'

'Good. Then what?'

They flew past cars, shops, pedestrians. The reflection of the blue and red beacons flashed in the windows. Up ahead, people were waiting for them, listening for the sound of the siren, maybe doing CPR, maybe not doing CPR when they should, maybe glancing sideways at a moaning drunk – you never knew what you were going to with a collapse call. They would all stare at her and Rowan as they marched in with all their gear and took charge. Her heart skipped a beat. She pressed her fingers to her throat. If she had a heart attack of her own she wouldn't have to look after anyone else.

Rowan glanced over at her. 'Okay?'

'Yep.' She faked a problem with her uniform collar. How idiotic to think such things, to be such a baby. She'd trained for this, and even in just six weeks on the road she'd seen a lot. Chances were this would be a drunk or a drug overdose, and she knew what to do with either. In theory, at least. She snugged her gloves a little tighter.

'Then what?' Rowan asked again.

'Treat specific conditions.'

'Give me some examples.'

They were approaching the McDonald's now, siren still wailing, tourists looking their way, and, oh god, there was a staff member standing on the street waving at them.

'Examples,' Rowan repeated.

She couldn't think. She grasped the seatbelt, ready to release the clip and get out. There was a system: the treating officer took the Oxy-Viva and went in first, the driver followed with the drug box and monitor/defibrillator. She'd sling the Viva over her shoulder and walk in like she knew exactly what she was doing. She wouldn't have that frightened look on her face, and she wouldn't turn back to make sure that Rowan was close behind. Her voice wouldn't shake when she asked the right questions of the patient and the bystanders, they wouldn't glance at her then give the answers to Rowan instead, and she wouldn't then sit in the back of the ambulance beside the stretchered patient on the way to hospital wondering what the hell to say.

The waver met her at the door. He was young, maybe seventeen, and trembling. 'She looks really bad.'

She hoisted the Viva a little higher and nodded. She heard Rowan shut the ambulance door. 'Where is she?' Strong confident tone. So far so good.

'This way.'

She followed him inside. The aircon was cold, the air smelled of frying, the people eating hotcakes and McMuffins watched her walk by. Two young female staff members knelt either side of a twentyish woman who lay propped against the counter. Against the centre of the counter, with lines of people continuing to order food on either side, and the eaters all watching with interest.

Paris ran through the procedure in her head. Danger: everything looks safe. Response: the woman was conscious, looking at her from frightened eyes. Airway, breathing and circulation: her skin was pale, she was visibly sweaty, and she was breathing quickly. So, all reasonable, but not as good as they should be. No visible wounds, no blood on the floor. Okay.

The patient and the two women were looking at her. She could feel the audience behind her too. *Get a grip!*

She put down the Viva and smiled at the patient. 'Hello. My name's Paris. What happened?' Good. Good start. Strong start.

'She passed out,' one of the staffers said.

'Uh-huh. Do you remember that?'

'Not really,' the patient said. 'I remember feeling really dizzy, and like I couldn't really breathe, then I woke up here on the floor.'

'So you felt dizzy, then you passed out.' Trying to think of the possible causes for such a scenario, Paris unzipped the Viva. She saw the sphygmo. Yes. Check the blood pressure.

'She just folded up and collapsed,' the other staff member said. She squeezed the patient's hand. 'She was out for a minute or so.'

'I'm just going to take your blood pressure.' Paris knelt beside the woman, then made herself move closer. During training they'd gone on and on about assessing patients with touch, feeling for deformity and tenderness and what-have-you, but never once mentioned how hard it was to overcome a lifetime of respect for personal space and get right up close to a stranger. She gingerly wrapped the cuff around the woman's clammy arm and inflated it.

Beside her, one hand on the monitor, Rowan cleared his throat.

'Oh,' she said. 'Monitor, please.'

He unpacked the leads and attached dots to the ends, then smiled at the patient. 'Hi, I'm Rowan. What's your name?'

'Robyn,' she said.

Of course, of course, ask their name. How had she forgotten that? Heat crept up the back of her neck as she stared at the sphygmo dial.

'One hundred,' she said, so Rowan would know.

'Diastolic?' he said.

Shit. She took out her stethoscope, pressed the bell to Robyn's arm and inflated the cuff again.

'Do you have any medical problems?' Rowan asked Robyn as he ran off a strip of ECG.

'I've been a bit sick lately,' she said. 'The doctor said it's a virus. That's all though.'

'One hundred on sixty-five,' Paris said.

Rowan nodded and held out the ECG. She took it and studied it. She could feel them all waiting. The lines on the paper blurred. *What the fuck came next?*

'Are you still short of breath?' Rowan asked Robyn.

'A bit,' she said. 'Not a lot though.'

Double shit. Paris pulled out the sats monitor and clipped the probe on Robyn's finger, then hooked up an oxygen mask.

'Ninety-four on room air, ninety-six on O_2,' she said to Rowan.

But he was still waiting. They were all waiting. She felt like everyone in the place was looking at her, could see the panicked sweat breaking out on her body, the frenzied unspooling in her head. She grasped wildly for a question. 'Are you, uh, allergic to anything?'

Robyn shook her head.

Paris gave her a big smile. 'That's great.'

And it was, but now what? She couldn't think. There was some mnemonic about what to ask; she knew it started with allergies, but what came next? The harder she tried to recall it, the blanker her mind became. The only thing she knew for sure was that they were all looking at her and she was failing again. There was no way around it. She was going to have to hand over to Rowan. The embarrassment and humiliation brought a lump to her throat as she looked up at him.

'How about you get out the glucometer,' he said. 'Robyn, are you on any medication?'

Medication, of course. That was what came next. And her blood sugar had to be checked because she'd passed out. In a hot cloud of shame Paris took out the little machine and turned it on. What the fuck was wrong with her? How come she could remember all this only after it was pointed out to her? She'd come top of her class, she was going to be a bright shining star. And look, Rowan was talking to Robyn like they were old mates at the same time as he assessed her properly – yet another thing she'd forgotten to do – and now he'd found a swelling on her head from when she'd collapsed.

Paris gritted her teeth and glared down at her hands. *Dreams do come true.*

TEN

The morning homicide meeting was short, its purpose to get everyone up to speed as quickly as possible on what had been learned overnight then out on the streets working. Tired after a bad sleep during which she'd dreamed about blood trails and bodies facedown in overgrown ditches, Ella gave them the news that the cyclist was a woman, then relayed the rest of what Olivier Tarlington had told them. Detective Danni Yong reported on the continued lack of matching Jane Does in the state hospital system, then went on to information that had come in via the Crimestoppers hotline. Most of it was the usual irrelevant stuff – calls about people in racing outfits on racing bikes weaving through traffic, mentions of homeless people with bleeding feet in the CBD, allegations about various men in a number of areas of the city who either didn't answer their phones or behaved oddly on Sunday night. None of the names had criminal records or ties to Stacey or James Durham, but they'd been logged anyway. Aadil Hossain said nothing helpful had come up on the Facebook pages, and no ransom or other suspicious calls had been received at the Durham house or on James's mobile. Stacey's had not been turned on.

Dennis assigned the day's tasks with the precision and seriousness of a general going to war, and the detectives nodded while taking notes as if to do the things separately would waste time. They were keen to get going, to find the woman whose picture smiled down on them from the whiteboard. Ella thought of the bodies she'd seen in her dream and wondered if Stacey Durham was lying somewhere like one of them.

★

Ella's and Murray's first stop was Computer Crime, where they found Elizabeth Libke at her desk, fingers flying over the keyboard. She was a bone-thin woman in her thirties, with pink-framed glasses and pale hair in an angular bob. She sat back in her chair and listened to them.

'James Durham,' she said thoughtfully.

'Owns a little computer shop in Strathfield,' Ella said. 'The tip was apparently about some scam or other. You told him he was in the clear.'

Libke leaned forward to type. She read down the screen. 'Ah, yes. Mr Outraged. Wanted the whole cavalry looking into who'd made the complaint and wasn't happy when I failed to oblige.'

'Do you get lots of cases like that?' Murray asked.

'I've got so many going on I don't have time to scratch myself,' she said. 'Anonymous tips are often efforts to piss someone off, to harass someone. It was lucky that one even got that much attention.'

'What did you do with it?' Ella asked.

Libke looked at the screen again. 'Durham has no record, no issues with ASIC or anything, no credit problem, no traffic offences. I had a talk to him, he gave me access to his computers, I ran a few checks and nothing came up.'

'How many computers does he have?' Ella said.

'His personal laptop, two networked desktops at the shop and one at home.'

'Did you meet his wife?'

'No. Does she work there?'

'No, but she has a laptop too.'

'I had no reason to go into her stuff.' Libke shrugged. 'Like I said, most anonymous tips are pointless. Shit-stirring.'

'What did the tip actually say?' Ella asked.

Libke clicked the mouse button. 'It was a typed letter, addressed to this section, claiming that James Durham of Durham Computers was defrauding his customers.'

'That's it?' Murray said. 'No details?'

'No, and that's another reason we didn't take it too seriously. None of his customers had made complaints. I even contacted a few at random. Some said they'd lost money from their bank accounts being hacked before they'd had him come to get rid of malware and install antivirus software, but otherwise there'd been no problems.'

Ella said, 'Did he appear to have any thoughts about who was behind it?'

'No, and I pushed him on it but he seemed clueless.' Her phone started to ring. 'Is that everything?'

'Thanks,' Ella said.

Going down in the lift, Murray said, 'Sounds pretty weak and generic for a complaint. Hard to imagine it could be related.'

Ella nodded. 'It's a big leap for someone to go from that to abducting his wife.' It didn't mean they wouldn't keep it in mind, though.

Her mobile rang as they crossed the car park, and she sighed when she saw the screen. 'Hi Mum.'

'Don't sound so happy,' Netta said. She talked too loudly on the phone and Ella had to hold it away from her ear. 'Now I know you're busy, but your father said I should check what kind of dessert Callum likes.'

'Whatever,' Ella said. 'He's not fussy.'

'You got that right,' Murray muttered, ducking out of reach.

'He must have some kind of preference,' Netta said. 'What about –'

'Anything is fine,' Ella said. 'I'm on a case, Mum.'

'We know. We saw you on the news. Adelina rang and said you look too thin.'

They were still hours from dinner, and it had started already. 'I have to go.'

'Make sure you call if you're going to be late.'

'Bye,' Ella said, and hung up.

'Trouble in paradise?' Murray said.

'Smartarse,' she said. 'Get in the car.'

★

Paris knew from her fellow trainees that usually when the senior officer took over the treating of the patient, he or she continued looking after them in the back of the ambulance on the way to hospital while the trainee drove. Rowan hadn't done that so far in their partnership, and he didn't do it today either, instead motioning for her to climb up after they'd loaded Robyn in, giving her instructions to check the blood pressure again, run another strip from the monitor, and fill in as much of the case sheet as she could.

Paris sat beside Robyn, her face hot, as Rowan shut the back door and got behind the wheel.

Robyn smiled at her. 'New at this, are you?'

Paris nodded. 'A few weeks.'

'You must see some terrible things.' Robyn said it with the usual upwards inflection at the end, almost a question but not quite, the speaker hoping to prompt a graphic telling of those terrible things.

'All part of the job.' She saw Rowan glance at her in the rear-view and took out the sphygmo. 'Time to check your blood pressure again.'

At the hospital, Rowan gave the handover to the triage

nurse. Once Robyn was off the stretcher and walking to the waiting room, Paris wheeled the stretcher back outside.

Rowan followed, the case sheet folder in his hand. 'Feel like a chat?'

'I don't know,' she said. 'Do I?'

He sat on the ambulance's back step and motioned for her to join him, but she stayed standing. She looked at the passing traffic, at the blue sky, the pigeons flapping overhead.

'Do you want to tell me what's going on?' he said.

'I can't stop thinking about Aunt Stacey.'

'That's understandable.'

'I wonder if she's okay, who hurt her, who's got her,' Paris said. 'Why did it happen?'

'That's what the police are trying to find out,' Rowan said.

'Thirty-seven,' the controller called.

Paris hurried to answer. Another job meant another chance to do better, as well as another chance to fail, but it stopped the questions and meant her fear was still a secret.

★

Ella and Murray pulled up outside Durham Computers. It was the middle business of a row of five, with a half-empty parking area and a garden bed dotted with straggly geraniums separating it from the street. Ella looked at the other businesses as she crossed the asphalt. An accountant, a bicycle shop, an aquarium store and a dentist's office. There were no CCTV bubbles attached to the awning that ran the length of the building, and the paintwork on the frontage was in need of a fresh coat.

A buzzer sounded when they pushed open the computer store door, and a young man with an angular face and black-framed glasses emerged from a back room.

'Detectives Ella Marconi and Murray Shakespeare.' She showed her badge. 'Is James here?'

'He's just gone to the bank. He said you might be coming by. I'm Nick Henry.' He extended his hand over the counter. His palm was soft, his grip firm. 'Do you have any news about Stacey?'

'Is Simon working today too?' Murray asked.

'He's on a call-out. So there's no news?'

'Not yet.'

'That's a pity.'

The lenses of his glasses caught the light and Ella couldn't see his eyes. She said, 'How long have you worked for James?'

'Bit over a year.'

'So you were here when the anonymous complaint was made?'

'Yep. James was mega-pissed. The cops found nothing though.'

'What's your job?' Murray asked.

'Computer repair mostly. Sometimes we build new systems for people, but usually we're fixing things.'

'Busy?' Ella said.

He nodded. 'We do heaps of call-outs to people's houses, because so many of them can't do the most basic things, let alone fix the big ones. We go there and help them, fix the problem, then show them what not to do next time, what to look out for.'

'Like viruses?' Murray said.

He nodded. 'Spyware, Trojan horses, worms, keystroke loggers, blended threats, adware, rootkits. You name it, really.'

'Huh,' Murray said.

Ella knew he had no real clue what the man was talking about. She said, 'Do you know Stacey?'

'A little,' Nick said. 'She comes in to have lunch with James sometimes. I haven't really talked to her much more than saying hi, how are you, though.'

'When did you see her last?'

'Monday last week,' he said. 'She came in for lunch with James, while her car was getting serviced or something. Then she seemed to change her mind and went to the dentist instead.'

'Instead of lunch?' Ella said.

Nick Henry nodded. 'I thought it was weird too.'

'What happened, exactly?' Murray asked.

'She came in and went out the back where James was working.' Henry motioned towards the rear office. 'I was here with a customer, so I don't know precisely what happened, but I could hear them talking and then suddenly she came out and went outside. James followed in a bit of a rush, then a few minutes later he came back and said she was at the dentist, and he wasn't going out for lunch after all.'

Ella said, 'Did you get the impression they were arguing?'

'It did seem a bit like they were keeping their voices down, like it was softer than if James is on the phone, for instance, but apart from that I couldn't tell you anything about it.'

'Were you here when she came back?'

'No, James sent me for my own lunch break, and later I said was she okay and he said yeah, she'd come back and gone to get her car and go home.'

Ella looked at Murray, then at her watch. 'How far is the bank where James's gone?'

'Not far. He should be back any minute.'

'I'm going to the bike shop,' she said to Murray, and went out.

The bike shop smelled of new plastic and oil. A man straightened behind the counter as she approached, one hand at the small of his back. He was in his late fifties, grey hair shaggy on the collar of his polo shirt, a friendly smile on his face.

'Hi, I'm Mike. Can I help you choose a bike?'

Ella showed her badge, then tilted her head towards the computer shop. 'I'm investigating a situation involving your neighbour here,' she said, being deliberately vague to see what he would say.

'Has there been a robbery?'

'Do they happen often along here?'

'The aquarium got held up once, this kid waving a knife and demanding turtles, but when Dale said he had none the kid walked out. He was still standing outside when the cops arrived. On drugs apparently.'

'Uh-huh,' Ella said. 'Do you know the computer shop staff?'

'Vaguely. James is the owner, and Nick and Simon work for him. Simon's been in here to fix my computer. I know he has a little girl. He's going to buy her first bike here when she's a bit older.' He smiled.

'That's all you know?'

He nodded.

'James's wife is missing,' Ella said, watching his face.

'Oh no. That's terrible.' Dismay, alarm. 'That's just awful.'

'It was on the news last night. You didn't see it?'

'I don't watch TV,' he said. 'Except the Tour.'

'Have you ever met her?'

He shook his head. 'Can't say I've ever even heard her name.'

Ella took out the photo of Stacey and showed him.

'Don't recognise her, sorry.'

'Has there been any trouble around here recently?'

'Nope.'

'Anyone hanging about, watching the shop? Anything out of the ordinary?'

'Not a thing,' he said. 'And I'd notice. I'm always in the window, keeping the dust off the bikes. People want to see them shiny when they walk in.'

'Anyone come in asking questions?'

'Only you,' he said, then smiled as if worried he'd offended her.

She smiled back. 'Do you know the people who work in the other businesses along here?'

'Well, I know Dale with the aquarium store, and Chris does my taxes, and Zaina who works reception at the dentist's there. Did her a good deal on a Schwinn Cruiser a while back.'

'Uh-huh,' Ella said. She looked around. 'Do you sell bikes that fold up?'

'I don't,' he said. 'Had a couple in stock once and they took forever to sell. I can order one in if need be though.'

She held out the photo of the cyclist. 'Do you happen to know what kind of bike this is?'

He took it and squinted at it. 'Well, it's a folding one – you can see that by the long stem and post, and the smallish wheels.' He looked at her. 'The stem holds up the handlebars, the post holds up the seat.'

'Gotcha,' Ella said.

'But I can't say what make it is, or what model, sorry. There are shops in the city that might know, shops that stock them and sell them in decent numbers.'

'Thanks.' Detectives Paul Li and Sylvie Catt were already doing that, armed with a USB containing footage of the unfolding as well as photos.

'I can tell you a couple of things though,' he said. 'The seat's too high – see how the rider's having to touch the ground with their toes?'

Ella looked. 'In other footage you can see her wobbling.'

'That makes sense. If the seat's too high the balance is affected.'

'Does the seat get moved every time you unfold the bike?'

'Depends on the model. But owners would generally know how high to put their seat before they get on.'

'So this mightn't be her bike,' Ella said.

'Quite possibly not.'

Confirmation. Excellent.

'Thanks for your help.' Ella placed her card on the counter. 'Please give me a call if something does crop up, or if you happen to remember or see anything odd.'

'I will,' he said.

The young woman in the aquarium knew nothing about the guys in the computer shop and had seen nothing strange in the street; and the dentist was closed due to illness according to a sign on the door. Ella wrote down the dentist's name.

The accountant was on the phone in his shabby one-room office. Seeing Ella's badge, he covered the mouthpiece long enough to tell her that he did the books and taxes for the bike shop and the aquarium store, but not for the dentist or the computer shop, and he knew none of the people who worked in either.

'Thanks,' Ella said.

Mike was standing by the door of the bike shop as she came past. 'Get what you were looking for?'

'Not exactly,' she said. 'You said you sold a bike to the dentist's receptionist. Do you keep records of sales? Would you have her surname or phone number or address?'

'Somewhere.' He glanced over his shoulder into the depths of the shop. 'I do keep all that stuff but it's in a real jumble. Paperwork's not my strong point.'

It probably didn't matter; they'd get the dentist's address and go there first anyway. But still. 'If you have time to find it, I'd be grateful,' she said.

'I'll see what I can do.'

At the computer shop, she could see through the glass doors that Murray was still talking to Nick. She leaned inside. 'Not back yet?'

Murray shook his head.

She stepped back out and rang Dennis. 'Any news?'

'Not on this end,' he said. 'You?'

'Nope. James is at the bank apparently. We're waiting in the shop.' She told him what the neighbouring business people had said. 'And can you run a name? Jonathon Dimitri. A dentist, two doors from James but closed today.'

'Let's have a look,' Dennis said, typing. 'No record, lives in Campsie. Want the address?'

'Please.' She scribbled down the details he gave her. 'We'll nip over later.'

'Keep in touch.'

She hung up and went into the shop. Nick was talking about wi-fi hotspots.

Ella looked at her watch. 'Didn't you say James wouldn't be long?'

'Usually he isn't.'

'Does he drive there or walk?'

'Depends.'

'On what?' Ella said, trying to hide her exasperation.

'If it's a nice day, if he wants to stretch his legs, if there's a lot of work on.'

'And today?'

Nick peered out the front window. 'I can't see his car. I guess he drove.'

'Where is the bank?' Murray said.

He gave them directions. 'But I'm sure he'll be here any minute. If you go, you'll probably pass him coming back.'

'That's a chance we'll take,' Ella said.

The drive through the morning sunlight took a few minutes, and Ella kept her eyes on the oncoming traffic but didn't spot him. 'How long've we been waiting?'

'He could be talking to them about Stacey's accounts,' Murray said.

Inside the bank, two elderly women stood waiting to be served, and one middle-aged man was talking to a teller.

Ella went to the enquiries window and showed her badge. 'Do you know James Durham?'

The woman nodded. 'Yes.'

'Has he been in this morning?' Murray asked.

'No, he hasn't.'

'Are you sure?' Ella said.

The woman nodded again. 'I've been right here since nine, when we opened, and he always makes a point of saying hi.

126

Is this about his wife? Have you found her? I saw it on the news last night. It's just awful.'

'Thanks for your time,' Murray said, as Ella stepped away, her notebook out, looking for then dialling James's mobile.

'*Hi, this is James Durham of Durham Computers. I'm sorry I can't take your call right now. Please leave me a message, or contact the shop on the following number.*'

She hung up. 'Voicemail.' She followed Murray back onto the street, where they looked in both directions.

'Perhaps he couldn't handle being at work,' Murray said. 'He's gone home to hide.'

'I'll call his landline while you drive us there,' Ella said.

Murray pulled back onto the street and headed east with the traffic.

The landline rang out, so Ella called Dennis and updated him. 'I'm thinking perhaps we put out an alert on his car?'

'He's probably ignoring the phone and trying to get some rest,' Dennis said.

'But why didn't he tell his staff that's what he was doing? Why say you'll be back soon then take off?'

'Grief, worry, fear. You want me to go on? Knock on his door then call me back.'

Ella ended the call but kept her phone close. She'd keep trying James. She didn't like the thought that he was out there somewhere, doing who knew what.

'Can I say something?' Murray said.

'I have a feeling you're going to.'

'I agree that we need to check out the husband first, but you seem awfully focused.'

'I think he knows more than he's letting on,' she said. 'What I don't know is whether that means he's involved, or he thinks he knows who is.'

'You're so suspicious,' Murray said.

'That's because I'm dealing with suspects. It's right there in their name. And you said yourself, the husband gets looked at first.'

'Looked at, not set on fire by a magnifying glass like an ant. You wait. We'll get to the house and he'll be tucked up in bed trying to get some sleep.'

She wanted to say something about how his wedding didn't mean he could be the defender of husbands everywhere, but settled with making a scornful noise. 'Just drive.'

★

Rowan had worked with plenty of trainees over the years, but never one like Paris. Everyone started off full of nerves, though some were arrogant as well; and it was his job to build them up – and let the arrogant ones stumble too, just a little. You got them on the right track and set them off with a good start, then hoped they did all right on their own. It was like pushing a kid on a boogie board onto a wave. But Paris was different. Six weeks in and she seemed more nervous, not less. She shook when talking to patients. Her voice trembled. She couldn't remember what to do, not even the first steps. It was agonising to witness, and looked bad to the patient and family and bystanders.

Last week, he'd lost his temper and yelled at her in frustration. He knew he should be above that – he was the trainer so he was supposed to keep his cool – and Stacey had told him so in no uncertain terms when Paris had left. He'd still been angry then though, and so they'd argued . . . and now she was missing, and he'd thought Paris would take some time off, but here she was, more burdened, shutdown and frightened than ever.

He looked across at her in the passenger seat, her gaze out the windscreen. After the controller had given them this job, a transfer from Bankstown Hospital to St Vincent's, he'd tried to talk to her again, about the work, about Stacey, about anything at all, but she'd responded each time with mumbles and one-word answers. It felt like he was prodding her with a stick, hurting her to try to make her talk, and eventually he'd given up.

He thought, not for the first time, that the problem might be him. He figured he had two options: sort it out, as difficult as that may be; or ask for her to be assigned to someone else. He'd never done that before, and it felt like failure to even be thinking of it, but this might simply be one of those situations where two people were never going to get along.

He cleared his throat. 'Would you rather work with another trainer?'

She looked around. 'You don't want to work with me any more?'

'It's not about me,' he said. 'It's about what's best for you.'

She said nothing.

He said, 'They told us once in training school that people learn in different ways, and when they teach, their instinct is to teach in a way that matches that. So maybe I teach and you learn in opposite ways. Because this doesn't look like it's working, and I don't understand why.' He paused. 'Do you?'

She hesitated, bit her lip, and seemed to him like she was finally going to speak, then the controller called.

'Thirty-seven, what's your location?'

Paris grabbed the microphone. 'Thirty-seven's on the Hume Highway in Burwood.'

'Perfect, Thirty-seven,' the controller said, 'Head to Burwood Road at Enfield for a two-car MVA, possible code nine.'

'Thirty-seven's on the case.' There was a tremor in her voice. She rehooked the mike.

'See, that was good,' Rowan said. 'Not all six-week trainees can say where they are without having to check.'

She pulled gloves from her pocket, and did he see a tiny smile? 'Thank you.'

He smiled back at her and reached for the lights and siren switches. Maybe things would be okay.

ELEVEN

Ella and Murray reached the Durhams' house to find a silver Toyota parked in the driveway.

'Told you,' Murray said.

'That's not his.' Ella went back through her notebook. 'He drives a black Holden Cruze. This belongs to Marie Kennedy.'

'Oh,' Murray said. 'Huh.'

They knocked on the front door. The dog barked and someone shushed it. Ella heard the locks turn, then Marie looked out.

'Have you found her?' she asked.

'Not yet, I'm afraid,' Ella said. 'Is James here?'

'No, he isn't.'

'May we come in?'

'Certainly.'

Once inside, Ella could see her better. Her eyes were red and puffy, her skin grey with exhaustion. 'Are you all right?'

'You looking at me and asking me that feels like deja vu all over again.' Marie sat on the lounge and tucked her feet beneath her. The dog jumped up next to her. 'I came to see how James was doing, then let myself in. I can't believe she's out there somewhere and nobody can find her. I'm so frightened for her.' She wiped her eyes.

'You have a key?' Ella said.

'I know where they keep the spare.'

'Has James been here?' Murray asked. 'Or have you spoken to him on the phone?'

'I haven't seen him this morning; I assume he's at work,' she said. 'I called his mobile but it went to voicemail.'

'Did you come to talk to him about anything in particular?' Murray asked.

'Just to offer a bit of moral support. And get some for myself, I suppose. I thought I might cook something to go in the freezer too, but I haven't collected myself enough to start yet. I've taken some time off work, and Paris is on duty, so rather than hang about at home I thought I'd come here.'

'Where do you work?' Murray said.

'At a physiotherapist in Bankstown.'

Ella nodded. 'Excuse me a minute. I have to make a call.' She went into the hall and as she pressed to ring Dennis, she heard Murray say, 'Have you had any new thoughts about what might've happened?'

'Orchard,' Dennis answered.

'He's not here now and he hasn't been here all morning.' She lowered her voice. 'So Marie Kennedy tells us. She came over and let herself in.'

'To do what?'

'Wander about and cry by the looks of it,' Ella said. 'Is his phone visible?'

'No. It's turned off.'

Ella's radar went nuts. 'Why would he do that unless he knows we're keeping an eye on him and decided to hide?'

'Or his battery went flat,' Dennis said.

Yeah, right, Ella thought. 'So the alert?'

'Is being put into place now,' Dennis said.

Back in the lounge room, Marie was talking about the trouble she'd had getting to sleep and the dreams that swamped her when she did. 'I kept seeing this man with no face. When I'm awake, I can't imagine who would want to hurt her, and it's as if the same happens when I'm asleep.'

Ella scribbled a note about James's phone being off and handed it to Murray. 'Marie,' she said, 'is there anywhere James might go if he wanted to get away from people? Somewhere special to him, or to him and Stacey perhaps?'

'Nowhere springs to mind.'

'Where they honeymooned maybe?' Murray said, stuffing the note in his pocket.

'They went to Bora Bora. The place they liked best was here. This house.' She looked around sadly.

Ella took out the photo of the cyclist. 'Does this person look at all familiar?'

Marie studied it. 'Where was this taken?'

'It came up in the investigation,' Ella said.

'Is this who took Stacey?'

'We don't know. Do you recognise her?'

Her knuckles white, Marie stared at the picture as if she could leap in and throttle the woman. 'I don't know who this is,' she said finally.

Murray said, 'Nothing about it that's familiar? Person, bike, helmet?'

'None.' She held it out as if she couldn't stand to look any longer. 'James told me that someone texted and said he knew what it was about. Is that true?'

'Someone did say that, yes,' Ella said.

'Is James behind what's happened?' Her eyes were intense, her jaw tight.

'We don't know.'

'She's my sister,' she said. 'Tell me the truth.'

'I am,' Ella said. 'We honestly don't know.'

It was so frustratingly true. They finished up and left her

there, twisting her hands on the lounge, the dog still sitting patiently beside her.

At the car Murray said, 'Why would James turn off his phone?'

'More importantly,' Ella said, 'where is he, and what's he doing there?' The idea that he was sneaking around drove her up the wall, but until they got a lead on his location, they had to keep going. Jonathon Dimitri, dentist, was next on their list.

★

Paris squeezed the side of her seat, out of Rowan's view, as he drove them to the accident. His voice sounded like it was coming down a long tunnel as he asked her about potential hazards – power lines down, fuel leaks, and other cars crashing into them because the drivers were gawking – and reminded her about response, airway, breathing and circulation. She tried to focus, but what if the wreck was so bad she couldn't get to the trapped person? What if there was more than one code nine?

The cars in front pulled out of their way, a bunch of kids on the footpath waved and smiled, the gardens flashed green as Rowan accelerated. She was breathing too fast. She took in and held a breath, but it made the pounding of her heart reverberate in her chest even more. She didn't even have Stacey to talk to when it was all over.

The traffic grew clogged, and Rowan cut onto the wrong side of the road. There it was. Two cars, a T-bone collision by the looks of it, someone failed to give way. A woman in her fifties in a flowered dress stood in the road screaming. Paris couldn't see into the cars.

She picked up the mike with a trembling hand. 'Thirty-seven's on scene, will report shortly.'

'Copy, Thirty-seven.'

She got out. Sunlight glinted off the shattered glass on the asphalt and crunched underfoot. The Oxy-Viva hung over her shoulder, the thick padded strap reassuring in her hand. The woman was still screaming. A couple of bystanders tried to catch her hands to stop her tearing at her hair. Holy crap. What could make someone do that?

Calm. You can handle this. Just stay calm.

'Who was in the cars?' she found herself saying.

A man raised his hand and pointed to the car with damage to the front. 'I was driving this. I'm okay. She was driving that.'

Paris looked at the car with the crumpled rear passenger-side door.

'She just pulled out, right through the give way,' the man was saying. 'I was only doing fifty but I had nowhere to go.'

Paris could see a shape inside the car, beyond the shattered window in the back passenger seat, unmoving. She realised the woman was not just screaming but screaming words. 'Nicholas! Nicholas! Nicholas!'

Rowan was at the car, opening the back door on the driver's side, leaning in to the motionless child. Paris took a step closer and saw that he was blond-haired and about nine. His eyes were closed, his head back against the seat, his throat thin and pale and defenceless. The crushed door pinned him to the seat.

'Nicholas! Nicholas!' The woman screamed and sobbed and fought off the bystanders. She fell on her knees and howled. The sound and all its horror and despair struck Paris like a slap.

'Paris,' Rowan said, but she was already walking towards the woman.

The woman looked up at her, face haggard with grief, tears like rivers. 'He's dead. I killed him.' She grasped Paris's arm with icy-cold hands. 'I killed my own grandson.'

Paris crouched and hugged her. The woman clutched her like she was drowning. Paris had a pain in her chest and a lump swelling in her throat and she felt the woman's sobs against her neck, the sweaty anguish and wretchedness of her shaking body. She felt for her beyond words, but she also felt in that moment that this was what she wanted to do: provide comfort, even if it was just a hug in the terrible hell of a grandmother's guilt and loss.

Someone tapped her on the shoulder. She turned her head to see a bystander as he bent close to her ear. 'Your colleague said to come back because the boy's not dead.'

Shame swamped her. She tried to look back at the car but the woman wouldn't let her go. She pried the woman's fingers off and tried to direct her grip onto the bystander, tried to get away without saying anything. She didn't trust herself to speak, because what if she told her he wasn't dead and then later he did die?

The woman clung on. There was no other way.

'I need to go and look after him,' Paris said.

'He's dead, he's dead.'

'He's not,' Paris said. 'I need to go and help take care of him.'

The woman looked at her, shock and fear and hope in her eyes. Paris pulled free of her grip and hurried back to the car, feeling the eyes of the growing crowd, embarrassed to face Rowan in the car.

She reached the window. 'I'm so sorry.'

'Later,' Rowan said tightly. 'He's only pinned by the legs. If we push the seat cushion down we can get him out.'

Paris leaned in. The boy was still unconscious, but Rowan had fitted a cervical collar to protect his neck. He wore a robot T-shirt and red shorts, and cubes of shattered safety glass dotted his lap and chest. Rowan had put an oxygen mask on him, the sphygmo was wrapped around his thin right arm, and monitoring leads snaked from under his shirt to the monitor propped in the front seat.

'Press,' Rowan said.

Paris pushed down on the seat. The boy's legs were narrow, his knees exposed below his shorts, one bruised and oozing blood onto the back of her gloves.

Rowan worked to get his hands under the deformity in the door. 'A bit more.'

Paris forced the cushion down hard. Rowan eased the boy's legs out and free. He palpated them for evidence of fractures. 'Go get the spineboard and stretcher.'

'And tell Control we don't need Rescue?'

'I've already done it.' The rebuke in his voice was clear.

She hurried to the ambulance and pulled out the stretcher, then laid the spineboard on top. In the time it took her to hug that woman and get stupidly, idiotically, ludicrously proud of herself, Rowan had done so much. In addition, she was the treating officer and she'd walked right past a trapped and unconscious child to his screaming relative. How many times had they gone over that in school? It was the quiet ones you needed to check; by their noise, the others were demonstrating how good their airway and breathing were. For fuck's sake. For fucking fuck's sake.

She positioned the stretcher beside the driver's side of the car, then leaned in behind Rowan. 'What else?'

'Move the front seats as far forward as they'll go, then have the board ready,' he said.

The child was semiconscious and moaning, the woman sobbing in a police officer's arms on the footpath in front of a fascinated crowd. Paris knelt on the driver's seat and pulled the mechanism under the passenger seat, heaving it forward, then did the same on the driver's side. Her hands shook and her arms felt weak. She got the board and leaned it against the car, then saw another ambulance pulling up. She didn't recognise either officer.

They came over and glanced at her, standing there not knowing what to do with her gloved hands, then bent to the car. Rowan issued a list of instructions that Paris couldn't quite hear. The crowd craned their necks as the other officers moved, one into the front seat, the other squeezing in beside Rowan.

'Board,' Rowan said, and Paris fed it between Rowan and the other officer and felt one of them take hold.

She supported the end while they manoeuvred it into position, changing their stances so they could place it flat on the seat. The one in the front had jammed herself between the front seats, her hips holding her there so she had both arms free to help lift the crying boy. Paris stood with her hands on the board, envious of the way they worked.

'One, two, three,' Rowan said, and she felt the board dip under the child's weight. He was still crying, and his grand-mother was calling his name again.

People in the crowd murmured and took photos with their phones. Fire officers stood by with a charged hose. The air smelled of hot metal and oil and asphalt. She looked at her hands gripping the end of the board and wondered if this was the last case she'd do.

Rowan pointed Paris to the resus seat in the ambulance. It was at the head of the stretcher and out of the way. She got in and sat down, feeling small and stupid. The backup crew loaded the stretcher and Rowan climbed in alongside it, making sure the IV line and oxygen tubing didn't tangle, talking to Nicholas like everything was fine.

Nicholas was properly awake now, but still crying. 'Where's Nanna?' he hiccuped.

'She's fine,' Rowan said, 'she's right outside. She's going to follow us to hospital in the other ambulance.' As he talked he reconnected the monitor leads, ran a strip, checked the blood pressure. 'You are looking fine, my man. How do you feel?'

'My head hurts.'

'Yep, you've got a bit of a bump there. Do you know where you are?'

'In an ambulance.'

'Ten out of ten,' Rowan said. 'Do you remember what happened?'

'I remember we were in the car, but I don't know what happened then.'

'That's okay. Can you tell me where you were going?'

'To the shops,' he said.

'Goodo. And here's a tough one: do you know what day it is?'

'It's Tuesday.'

'Brilliant. High five.'

They slapped hands. Paris looked out the side window. Where did you get this ease with strangers? And now Rowan was starting on the case sheet, asking Nicholas his date of birth and whether he took any medicine, checking his pupils again, asking whether he liked his teacher at school. How did you become that person?

*

At the hospital, Paris stood around as they unloaded, watched the other officer help the still-shaking grandma out of his ambulance and then the tearful kissing of the grandson's face, and tagged along as the pair were taken inside. She hoped she might be able to help transfer the kid onto the hospital bed, but ended up somehow elbowed out by a couple of burly wardsmen and took it as a sign to drift back outside.

She climbed into the empty ambulance. It was so spacious when the stretcher was out. The sun lit the tinted side window and the white plastic of the side lockers was smooth and shiny. She started cleaning up, looping the monitoring leads and packing them into their pouch, replacing the oxygen mask in the Viva and turning off the cylinder after checking that it was still over half-full, restocking the drug box with the IV pump set and fluid bag and making sure there were enough cannulae, swabs and tape.

'Paris,' a female voice said, and she turned to see a woman at the open back door. She was in her late forties, her dark hair pulled back in a smooth bun, her uniform neatly pressed, and her epaulettes bearing both the paramedic supervisor and area superintendent markings. Paris's stomach fell.

'I'm Kathryn Beattie,' the woman said. 'Mind hopping out so we can have a chat?'

★

Blocks of units lined the street in Campsie where Jonathon Dimitri lived. Music poured from a dozen different places, including open garages and doors. Electrician, locksmith and plasterer's vans were parked fifty metres away outside a building with smoke stains on the wall above a broken ground-floor window. Leafy trees shaded the long grass on the nature strips from the midday sun, clean washing hung on racks on balconies, and three grinning children under five rolled on plastic tricycles along the footpath followed by a man in dark sunglasses who talked in another language on a mobile. As he passed their car he removed the phone from his ear long enough to shout, 'Jasvinder, not so fast!'

Dimitri's block was set back from its neighbours. Ella and Murray crossed the concrete forecourt and followed the path down the side. The entry door was held open by a brick, and they went in and climbed to the third floor, past doors behind which babies cried and TVs blared. Someone was cooking marinated meat, and Murray said, 'I'm hungry.'

Ella knocked on the door to unit nine. She waited a minute, raising her eyebrows at Murray, then knocked again.

'Not home,' Murray said.

'The sign on the surgery said closed due to illness. He shouldn't be out if he's sick.' She tested the knob but it was locked.

'Who are you, his employer?' Murray started back down the stairs. 'He's probably taken his girlfriend away for a few days and didn't want to say that to his patients.'

Ella leaned close to the peephole, hoping to see a change in light and dark that would indicate movement, but saw nothing. She crossed the landing and knocked on the neighbour's door.

'Who is it?' The woman sounded nervous.

Ella smiled at the peephole. 'Detective Ella Marconi, New South Wales Police.' She held her badge up, then smiled again. 'May I talk to you for a moment?'

'Is something wrong?'

'I'd just like to ask a couple of questions about your neighbour in unit nine. Can you open the door, please?'

A moment's hesitation, then the lock turned and the door opened. The security chain was still in place, and the woman who peered through the gap had frightened eyes. She looked at Ella, then past her to Murray, standing at the top of the stairs.

Ella smiled at her again. 'Do you know your neighbour?' She pointed over her shoulder.

'Only a little,' the woman said. She looked about thirty, and wore a bright blue hijab. To Ella's inaccurate ear she sounded Russian. 'We say hello. His name is John. He said he is a dentist and will check my family's teeth if we like him to.'

'Does he live alone?'

'Yes,' she said. 'Or I should say he has done so as long as I have known him, that is six months that we've lived here ourselves. But he has a girlfriend, I think. I don't know her name but I have seen her a few times in the last few weeks.' She blushed.

'When did you see John last?'

'On Friday afternoon, maybe five o'clock. He was cleaning his car in the space at the back, and we said hello. But I have been working, so maybe he's here and I didn't see.'

'Cleaning the inside or outside of his car?'

'Both,' she said. 'The outside was wet, and he had the little hand machine.' She made vacuuming motions.

'Thank you,' Ella said. 'I appreciate your help.'

The woman looked past her at Murray again, nodded, and closed the door.

'What'd she say?' Murray asked. 'I couldn't hear.'

'She saw him cleaning his car inside and out late Friday arvo.' Ella started down the stairs. 'And she's seen a girlfriend visiting the last few weeks.'

'I told you. He's gone for a long and dirty weekend.'

Ella didn't answer. At the car she googled the bike shop on her phone and rang the number.

'Mike's Bikes, this is Mike,' a gruff voice answered.

'This is Detective Marconi,' she said. 'We spoke earlier. I was wondering whether you'd been able to find Zaina's details?'

'I'm still looking, I'm afraid. Some of the paperwork's at home, it could be there, I just don't know.'

'Can you remember her last name, or anything about where she lives?'

'It's a foreign-type surname, but I can't recall it,' he said. 'I'm sorry. I'll keep looking and trying.'

'Please call as soon as you know,' she said.

★

Rowan stood inside the glass doors of the Emergency Department, watching Kathryn Beattie talk to Paris. Paris's head was down, her back against the wall, and she scraped at the bricks with the heel of one boot. He felt a tug inside. He wasn't sure if he'd done the right thing. At the time he'd thought he had no option, but now that he wasn't so angry he thought maybe he did. She wasn't the first to be drawn to a screaming uninjured person, and she wouldn't be the last. It was why they talked specifically about that during training.

Wayne Loftus came up behind him with the stretcher. 'She lost it big-time, huh?'

'She was okay.'

'Mate, I heard what you said on the air.'

'Her aunt's missing,' Rowan said. 'None of us would be at our best in those circumstances.'

'"You need a supervisor at the hospital because Officer Kennedy might need to sign off"? There's only one thing that means.'

Rowan rounded on him. 'Yeah, that she might need to sign off, and someone has to run her home.'

Wayne grinned and shrugged. 'Hey, whatever. You were there.'

'Exactly,' Rowan said. 'So don't say anything to her, all right?'

Wayne hit the button to open the doors and wheeled the stretcher outside without answering. After a moment's hesitation, Rowan followed.

TWELVE

Paris listened to Kathryn Beattie talk and watched Rowan from the corner of her eye. He emerged from the hospital doors without looking her way, said something to the officer with the stretcher, and then climbed into the back of the ambulance, out of her sight. In there he'd be able to hear what Beattie was saying.

'Do you follow me?' Beattie said.

'Yes,' Paris answered, wanting to say, *Do you think I don't know what I did? Do you think I'm not reliving it in my head, over and over?*

'Okay then,' Beattie said. 'Did you drive to work this morning?'

'I caught the train.'

'So how about I run you home?' She gestured to her station wagon.

'My bag's in the ambulance,' Paris said.

Beattie said, 'I'll get it for you. Go hop in. I'll be just one minute.'

Paris got in the front seat of Beattie's superintendent car and clipped in her seatbelt. Through the closed window she watched Rowan climb out of the back of the ambulance and hand Beattie her bag. They stood talking and didn't look her way.

Paris folded her arms, tucked her ice-cold hands in her armpits. Beattie would take her home and round off her little chat with . . . what? *We'll empty your locker for you, we'll bring you your stuff and the forms to sign, you'll hand back your uniforms and get a fortnight's wages.*

Her sight blurred. Six weeks, and it was all over.

★

Ella rang Dennis to update him on their progress so far but he cut in before she could tell him anything.

'I was just about to call you. James has been found.'

'Where?'

'At The Gap.'

She caught her breath. 'He jumped?'

'No, no,' Dennis said. 'Officers on scene say he's come back inside the fence and is talking to them.'

Ella hung up and told Murray to step on it.

★

The whole trip to Padstow, Beattie talked about what made a good paramedic: compassion combined with an ability to keep cool.

'Mm,' Paris said, and nodded, because she knew that already, that's what she was trying to be. Her bag was on her lap, and underneath it she was pinching the backs of her hands, trying to gather her courage to ask what she really wanted to know. She had to: it was crazy to keep going like this.

'Make sense?' Beattie was saying.

Paris nodded. She took a deep breath. *Here goes nothing.* 'What if you're afraid?'

'Everyone's afraid. Left here?' Beattie turned the corner. 'You just have to put it out of your head.'

'I mean, really afraid.' How could she get it across to her?

'Think about something else. Think about the stuff you do know how to do. Or distract yourself in some other way. I knew a paramedic who sometimes felt faint around a lot of blood, and he'd do times tables in his head. You're at number ten, you said?'

'What if that doesn't work?' Paris said. *What if you can't think, can't breathe?*

'Then you try harder.' Beattie turned into Paris's driveway. 'Don't stress. It'll get better.' She smiled.

Like it was just that easy.

'Car Twelve,' the controller said on the radio.

'That's me,' Beattie said. She put out her hand to shake Paris's. 'I'm glad we had this talk.'

'What's going to happen?' Paris said.

'We'll let you know.' Beattie picked up the mike. 'Twelve's clear in Padstow and ready for details.'

'Stand by, Twelve,' the controller said.

Beattie said to Paris, 'It doesn't necessarily mean you'll be suspended or anything like that.'

Sacked, Paris thought. *The word is sacked.* She looked up at the house. At least her mother hadn't appeared. Hopefully she wasn't home.

'It might mean retraining,' Beattie said. 'Counselling perhaps.'

She smiled again, and it almost killed Paris to muster a tiny one in return.

'Thank you for the lift,' she whispered, and got out, just as her mother's car turned into the driveway behind Beattie's.

Marie opened her driver's door. 'What's happened?'

'Nothing,' Paris said. 'You have to move. She needs to go.'

'But what's the matter? Why are you home?'

Paris could see that Beattie was annoyed and felt the hot

145

rush of embarrassment on top of everything else. 'Just back out so she can go!'

'There's no need to yell.' Marie slammed the door and backed onto the street.

Beattie reversed past her, then waved to Paris through the passenger window as she drove off.

'What was all that about?' Marie said when she'd parked her car.

'Nothing.'

'They got you on some funny shift now, ends in the early afternoon? They drive you home at the end because you're so special?'

'Ha ha.' *I will not cry.*

'I'm just teasing.' Marie looped her arm around her waist. 'Come inside. Sit down. Have you had lunch? I haven't. We'll eat and you can tell me what's happened.' She shut the front door behind them. 'Was work too much because of Aunt Stacey?'

'I'm not hungry.' Paris hated this fake interest, the smarmy voice that always accompanied it. 'Have the police been in touch? Is there any news?'

'Nothing.' Marie opened the fridge. 'What do you feel like?'

The emotions boiled up. 'You don't even care.'

'Of course I do.'

'No, you don't. Look at you. Making lunch like nothing's wrong.'

The relationship between her mother and Stacey hadn't been good. Over the years Paris had heard arguments, some more heated than others. Plus there'd always been an undercurrent of . . . she wasn't sure what it was. Resentment? Jealousy? She hardly remembered her grandparents, but her mother had hinted often enough that she felt Stacey was always seen as the special one.

'We need to keep our strength up,' Marie said. 'Surely they taught you that at your sainted paramedic school? Care for the ones who care. Is that why they brought you home? Because you're too stressed over your aunt to work?'

'No,' Paris said.

'Why then?'

'None of your business.'

Marie raised her eyebrows, then looked into the fridge again. 'So what does "paramedic supervisor" mean?'

Of course. She'd seen it on the car.

'Exactly what it sounds like,' Paris said.

'Whenever I've had to deal with supervisors it's because I did something wrong,' her mother said.

'The ambulance service is different.'

'So I have been told.' She said it leisurely, each word precise, her eyes on Paris's. 'How lucky are you, working in such a great organisation?'

★

Old South Head Road at The Gap was all but blocked off by media and police vehicles, and Murray squeezed the car half onto the footpath. The sun was shining and seagulls whined as they hovered in the breeze above the cliff edge. The Gap was a notorious suicide spot and Murray nudged her as they crossed the road. 'Ever done one here?'

'Ages ago,' she said. She'd been in the job just a couple of years but remembered the sight of the body on the wave-wet rocks like she was looking at it now. A nineteen-year-old man. She and her partner had had to tell his parents. 'You?'

'Same.'

They didn't say anything more but approached the news crews and uniformed police gathered on the wide path that led along the cliff. Durham stood in the centre of the group, addressing the cameras.

'– and yes, I came here out of despair, out of fear that I will never see my wife, Stacey, again.' He held up a photo, crumpled as if he'd been scrunching it in a damp hand. 'But the response of ordinary people who persuaded me back over the fence, the police who arrived to help, the paramedics who made sure I was okay, and now the news people here, have made me feel that there is hope, that someone must have seen something, and that someone just needs to look at Stacey's photo again and take a moment to think.' He paused and stared down the barrel of the closest camera. 'If you're the person who has my wife, please return her to me. I love her more than anything in this world. I'm lost without her, and so is her family. Even her dog, Gomez, is affected. He won't eat, he's practically pining away. Stacey's a wonderful woman and we all need her home.'

'Smart,' Murray said in her ear. 'Humanise her in the eyes of the abductor.'

Ella knew the tactic, but something about James's tone made her doubt his reasons. The feeling made her wonder if Murray was right, if she was too suspicious.

'I'm putting together a reward, so please get in touch. Tell me what you know. Help me find my beloved wife.' James held the photo forward as if to make the cameras focus in on it, but Ella guessed they'd be getting close-ups of the tears in his eyes instead.

There was a silence in which she could hear the crash of the surf against the rocks at the bottom of the cliff, then journalists started asking questions.

'How much will the reward be?'

'I'm still working that out,' James replied. 'But I'm aiming for fifty thousand.'

'That'll bring the nutters out of the woodwork,' Murray murmured.

'Has the blood in the car been confirmed as your wife's?'

'I'm still waiting to hear about that from the police,' he said.

'Do you think your wife's disappearance has anything to do with the murder of two paramedics last year?'

'I don't see how or why, seeing as the man who did that died,' James answered.

Ella felt her ears go red. She'd been the one who shot and killed the man as he was trying to strangle his final victim.

'What if it's a copycat?' someone said.

'The police haven't suggested that to me,' James said.

'Do you know the latest on the investigation?'

'Do the police have any leads at all?'

Before James could answer, someone recognised Ella and Murray. 'Detectives, can we get a statement, please?'

The camera lights were bright in her face.

'We have nothing to say at this time,' Ella said. 'Our concern here is to look after Mr Durham. Feel free to call the Homicide office in Parramatta.' Where they'd get nothing but the latest media release and perhaps a heads-up on a press conference.

The journos turned back to James and fired off more questions, but Ella pushed through and grasped his arm. He was trembling, and said, 'I need to get out of here.'

The tremble felt real, not faked, and almost against her will her attitude towards him relaxed a bit.

'No more questions,' she said loudly, as Murray went to James's other side, and between them they walked him down the stairs and across the street to their car.

He climbed in the back and put his head in his hands.

Ella got in the front and turned in the seat to look at him. 'Are you okay?'

He sat back, rubbing his face. 'Give me a minute and I'll be all right.'

'Do you need to go to hospital?' Murray asked.

James shook his head.

'We've been worried about you,' Ella said. 'We were waiting at the shop but you never came back from the bank.'

'I headed that way, then I got another text, the same as the others: *Tell the truth. You know what this is about.* I texted back, but they just said the same thing again. *You know what this is about.*

149

Tell the truth. You know what this is about. That and the grief and worry and everything were too much. I drove past the bank and kept going.'

'How did you end up here?' Murray asked.

'Stacey used to live near here,' he said. 'She loves the beach. I guess I thought that if I came to the place she loves, where she used to live, I could maybe, I don't know, have a revelation or something, work out what it is that I'm supposed to know. But it didn't help.'

'Where did she live?' Ella asked.

He gave them an address off Campbell Parade in Bondi. 'She always talks about how she could hear the surf when it was up, how she could smell the salt in the air.' His stare out the window was distant. 'One day we'll retire to the beach. I always promised her that. That we'd go back.'

Ella said, 'Why did you turn off your phone?'

'I couldn't stand the messages. I hate that they have the power. I hate that all they say is that one thing over and over, that they won't explain or give any more information. I mean, what am I supposed to do with that? How can I confess or make it right or whatever it is they want when I don't even know what they're talking about?'

'Would you turn it on now, please?'

He took his phone out of his pocket and pressed buttons. Ella heard the chimes of multiple messages. He studied the screen. 'Three from her phone. Same as before. Plus some missed calls.'

'May I see?'

He handed it over. She scrolled through the list of callers. Marie, the shop, her own number and that of the office. The messages sent from Stacey's phone were the same as the one James had described. They were spaced between thirty and forty-five minutes apart, and the last one had arrived more than an hour ago. She got out her notebook and wrote down the exact times, then gave the phone back.

'So you drove past the bank then over here to Bondi,' she said. 'Which way did you come?'

'The normal way,' he said. 'Through the city.'

'Took a while, did it? We were at the shop soon after nine and Nick Henry said you'd just left.'

'Traffic was bad, but I also sat at the beach for a while.'

'Which one?'

'Bondi. And walked along the streets. Walked past her old place. Walked in a daze, if I'm honest. I'd keep sort of waking up and not know where I was or how I'd got there.'

'But you still found your way back to your car?'

'Fortunately.'

She took the CCTV picture of the cyclist out of her jacket pocket. 'Does this person look familiar?'

He stared at it. 'This is the same person who rode away from her car, right? I still don't recognise them, and I don't understand any of this. Why would anyone take her? Why would anyone keep saying I know why when I don't?' He looked up. 'Do you think they've mistaken me for someone else?'

'Unlikely,' Ella said. 'They must know your name and Stacey's, and assuming she can talk to them, I'd imagine they would find out pretty quickly if she was the wrong person.'

'Assuming,' he said.

'I'm sure she can,' Ella said. 'I'm sure she's doing fine. Going by what we've learned about her, she sounds like one tough lady.'

'She is,' he said.

She studied him. He was calm now, the photo in his hand, his eyes on the camera guys filming the curious onlookers, the fence and the rocks below The Gap, while the uniformed constables looked on.

'I'll be back in a minute,' she said to Murray.

The constables were both taller than her, and stood with their hands tucked into their utility belts.

'Do you think he was seriously planning to jump?' Ella asked, looking up at them.

The senior constable shrugged. 'Some would say if they're serious they just do it.'

His face was peeling from old sunburn, and he looked hot and annoyed. The journos came closer, trying to listen in.

'He was back over the fence by the time we got here,' the younger officer said. She had a square face and a nice smile. 'Couple of bystanders were talking to him. They've gone now, but they said he climbed over right in front of them and was sobbing loudly. They called out, begging him to come back, and he talked about his wife and how upset he was, and then maybe four, five minutes later he climbed back.'

'Did he talk to you at all?' Ella asked. 'Tell you where he's been for the last few hours, anything like that?'

'Between bouts of sobbing he said he'd been driving around because she used to live near here,' the senior said. 'Then the media turned up and he was all theirs.'

'Thanks.' Ella headed back towards the car.

One of the journalists stepped into her path with a smile. 'Detective Marconi, I'm Rachel Nisbet. Has there been any progress in finding Stacey Durham?'

'No comment,' Ella said, moving past her.

Nisbet touched her arm. 'I saw you go red when the death of the paramedic killer was mentioned. Being the cause of four deaths in five years must take a toll.'

Ella stopped and looked at her. She was all ready to be filmed, in a tight black skirt and jacket and with her blonde hair tied up in a smooth bun. She was young and didn't know when to stop talking.

'I know they were all necessary,' Nisbet said hurriedly, 'all justified. Investigated and ticked off. But I'm talking personally. How it feels. I've been following your career for some time and I know you'd make an excellent subject for a feature article. The girl behind the gun. Girl cop takes on all the bad guys. That sort of thing.'

'Girl?' Ella said.

'It carries a certain jaunty ring.'

'I don't think so.' Ella turned to leave. Her phone rang and she answered. 'Marconi.'

'Perhaps you could think about it?' Nisbet called behind her.

'This is Mike from the bike shop,' the male voice said. 'I found Zaina's information. Have you a pen?'

Finally. 'Go ahead,' Ella said.

When she hung up she hurried back to the car. James sat slumped in the back seat and Murray stood by the open front door. 'Anything?' he said over the roof.

'Tell you in a minute. How about here?'

'Nope.' Murray made a locking gesture over his lips.

She put out her hand for the keys, got behind the wheel and started the car. Murray got quickly in too.

'Where are we going?' James said.

'I thought we'd drop you back to your car,' she said. 'Where is it?'

'Back down the road a bit.'

She did a U-turn and started driving. 'By the way, you didn't answer my question yesterday.'

'Which one?'

'About whether the business is in financial trouble.'

'No, it's not, and I'm as offended by the suggestion today as I was yesterday.'

'What suggestion is that?'

'That I did something to her for money.'

'I was only asking about the business,' Ella said blandly.

'And only an idiot wouldn't be able to see the subtext.' His voice rose. 'I'm a victim here. My wife's missing.'

'We know.' She pulled up beside his car, put on her hazard lights and looked at him in the mirror. 'Please don't turn your phone off again.'

He got out without another word and slammed the door.

'Right,' she said to Murray, when James was in his car and they were moving off, 'if you were serious about jumping, would you climb the fence right in front of a couple of bystanders and started sobbing loudly?'

'That's what he did?'

'A better way to draw attention to yourself does not exist.' Ella braked at a light. 'So whether he did or didn't send this morning's texts himself, which we can't really know because he conveniently turned his own phone off, he could've been doing anything in the past couple of hours. Disposing of the body. Dealing with the accomplice, whoever was on the bike, seeing as he knew we got their picture yesterday and would soon be finding out more.'

Murray frowned. 'Then even the anonymous complaint could be a fake. Making it look like he has some rival out there, someone who wants to hurt him. Trying to throw us off his scent for when his wife eventually disappeared.'

'Trying,' Ella said darkly. Her phone rang. It was the office, and she put it on speaker. 'Marconi.'

'It's Elizabeth Libke. I'm still working on James's computers, but I did find something on Stacey's Facebook page. She has a hundred and thirty friends, and I went through her profile to check for people who'd asked to be her friends but she hadn't allowed, or who'd sent her odd messages, or who'd she defriended or blocked – anything that might suggest either stalkerish behaviour or a falling out. There were no abusive messages, but I found three people who had been her friends in the past year but aren't any longer. Got a pen?'

'Certainly do,' Murray said.

'Christine Lamarr is a paramedic based in the inner west, and her boyfriend, George Tsu, also a paramedic, works with Stacey. Stacey defriended her six weeks ago. Neither Lamarr nor Tsu have a record, and they live in Lilyfield.'

She gave them the address. Ella recognised the street, just off Lilyfield Road.

'The second is Abby Watmough,' Libke went on. 'She friended Stacey after their high school reunion last year. Abby doesn't post often, just a pic now and again of her baby, but Stacey defriended her about four months ago. No record, lives in Lidcombe.'

Murray scribbled down the street and number.

Libke said, 'The third and final person is Steve Lynch, who Stacey friended after some posts about the reunion, but who she defriended a couple of weeks ago. They'd liked and commented on a few of each other's posts – he runs a dog training school at Dural and the posts were dog-related – then she deleted him.'

'She wasn't just having some sort of friend cull?' Ella said.

'Nope. That's all there's been in the last year, and they're spaced out. A cull tends to take out lots of people at once.'

'Is James on Facebook?' Murray asked.

'Yes, in a manner of speaking,' Libke said. 'He has a personal page, because you need one in order to set up a business page, but it's got no photo, no details except the link to the shop page, no friends, nothing. The posts on the shop page are all about computers: warnings about the latest viruses, software deals, the odd customer testimonial. That's all I've got for now.'

'Thanks,' Ella said.

Libke hung up, and Ella told Murray about the information she got from Mike about the dentist's receptionist.

'Excellent,' he said. 'Berala's near Lidcombe. We can go Lilyfield, Berala, Lidcombe, then Dural. Roadtrip it.'

Ella didn't answer, thinking about the pieces of the puzzle and how they fitted together.

THIRTEEN

A young woman was washing her car in the driveway of the house where Lamarr and Tsu lived. Ella glanced at her as she and Murray walked past, then saw an ambulance sticker through the suds on the back window.

'Are you Christine Lamarr?' she said.

The woman was about twenty-five, lean and tense, with skull earrings, black hair in a looped ponytail, and veins standing out on her arms. Water and suds had splashed across her black T-shirt and jeans, and her feet were bare on the wet concrete. 'Who's asking?'

They showed their badges. 'Detectives Marconi and Shakespeare,' Ella said. 'Got a minute to talk?'

Lamarr shrugged. 'Sure.' She dunked a sponge into a bucket, then stood on her toes and scrubbed at the car's roof.

'You know Stacey Durham?' Ella said.

'I do.'

'How well?' Murray asked.

'Well enough.'

Ella said, 'How about you face us when you're speaking to us?'

Lamarr threw the sponge in the bucket with a splash. 'I have to get this done. I've got a hair appointment in half an hour.'

'Did you and Stacey have a falling out recently?' Ella said.

Lamarr rolled her eyes. 'A falling out? How quaint. She's a bitch and I hate her. So I'd say it's more than a falling out.'

'And yet you were once friends on Facebook,' Ella said.

'Yeah well, live and learn.'

'What happened?' Murray asked.

'She couldn't keep her hands to herself, that's what happened. She worked a nightshift with George and came onto him. A married older woman. It's disgusting.'

'When was that?'

'Three weeks ago, give or take.'

'How did you find out?' Murray asked. 'Did George tell you?'

'He didn't have to. I saw it myself. I dropped into the station and there she was, grabbing hold of him. I walked in and she leapt up, all red in the face, and rushed into the bathroom. I yelled and said she'd better come out and face me, but she wouldn't. Then they got a job and George said I had to leave so they could go to work.'

'What did he say about it?'

'That she was upset, and he'd hugged her to comfort her. That's not what it looked like though, and if that's all it was why'd she run away?'

'Did she look upset?' Ella asked.

'All I saw was the bright red. In my book, there's only one thing that means.' She picked up the sponge and slapped it on the car's boot. Suds flew.

'Did you try to talk to her about it any time later?' Murray asked.

'I would if I'd seen her, and I will when I do.'

'You know she's missing?' Ella said.

'Yep.'

'Any idea about what might've happened?'

'Nope, and you must be hard up for leads if you're asking me.'

Murray said, 'Is George home?'

'Nope. He's working. Overtime shift at Penrith.'

'So he'll be back tonight,' Ella said. 'Thanks for the chat.'

They were pulling away from the kerb when her mobile rang. She didn't recognise the number. 'Marconi.'

'Vicky Page, nurse and psychic,' the voice boomed. 'I saw something.'

Ella put her on speaker. 'What did you see?'

'Stacey's in a small room. There's no door. It's been built specially for her. She's weak, and she's crying.'

'She's still alive then,' Murray said to the phone.

'Oh yes, and she's determined to stay that way,' Vicky said.

'Any idea where this room is?' Ella asked.

'Not yet.'

'Well, is it in this city?'

'I can't tell.'

Useless, Ella thought. 'Let us know when you can, won't you?'

'Of course,' Vicky said. 'I hope you're looking after yourself?'

Ella rolled her eyes at Murray. 'Thanks for your call,' she said, and hung up.

★

The Berala house of Zaina Khan, dentist's receptionist, was small and built of fibro with a low porch railing and sagging gutters. Two narrow paths of concrete formed a driveway on which sat a primer-patched white Holden Gemini. Pots along the porch wall held clumps of bright green aloe vera plants, and inside a screen door with the same metal scrolling as the porch railing the front door was open. Someone in the house was whistling.

Ella tapped on the screen's frame.

'Come on in, ya scrag,' a voice called.

'Ms Khan? New South Wales Police.'

'Oh, shit.' A young woman hurried up the hallway, her cheeks red. 'Sorry. I thought you were my friend.'

'It's no problem.' Ella showed her badge. 'Detectives Marconi and Shakespeare. Can we come in for a moment, please?'

The woman opened the door. 'Is something wrong? Has something happened?'

'We just need to ask you a few questions,' Murray said. 'Can you tell us where you work?'

'Sure. I do reception and admin at a dental surgery in Strathfield.' She stood in the hallway, hands clasped at her waist, her face anxious. She wore a short denim skirt and a pink collared shirt, and pink slippers with kawaii kittens on the toes.

'Who else works there with you?' Ella asked.

'Just the dentist, Jon Dimitri. He's the owner as well.'

'Is he supposed to be working today?'

She shook her head. 'He took a few days off. We're open again tomorrow.'

Ella said, 'Do you know where he's gone?'

'Not exactly, but he mentioned camping.'

'Do you know if he was going alone or with someone?'

She grinned. 'He's got a new girlfriend, so I'm guessing he's not out there alone.'

'Do you know her name?'

'Her first name's Cynthia, but I don't know her last. He's talked about her and she's rung, but I've never met her.'

'When was the last time you saw or spoke to him?' Ella said.

'Last Friday. He finished with a patient about four, then we cleaned up, and he told me to put the sign on the door about him being sick. He said that was better than just saying

159

the place was closed.' She looked at them. 'Has something happened to him?'

'Not as far as we know,' Ella said. 'Have you met the people who work in the neighbouring businesses?'

'I know Mike, at the bike shop. And I met another a week ago, Stacey Durham. I remember because I had to ask how to spell her last name. She was from the computer place.'

Ella resisted the urge to glance at Murray. *She remembered without prompting.* 'What happened?'

'She came in asking if the dentist was busy, if she could get an appointment straight away,' she said. 'I told her he was available, and then this guy came in from outside and said something to her like "How'd you go?" and she said she was going in now. The guy looked a bit surprised. Jon took her through – I think she only got a cleaning. Jon said something afterwards like she didn't even really need that.'

'Who was the guy?' Murray asked.

'I assumed he was her husband or whatever from the way they talked to each other. He left when she went in the back.'

'Did they seem cheerful, or stressed, or angry or annoyed?' Ella asked.

'The woman seemed a bit uptight, but lots of people are dental-phobic,' Zaina said. 'The guy was a bit gruff, I suppose. I had to answer the phone, so I didn't focus on them too much.'

'What day was that?' Ella asked.

'Monday last week.'

'Had you ever seen either of them before, or since?'

'No,' Zaina said.

'Do you watch the news?'

'Sometimes. Not regularly or anything.'

Ella took out the picture of Stacey Durham. 'Was this the woman you talked to?'

'That's her. Definitely. I remember because she has nice teeth and really nice hair.'

Ella looked at Murray. 'Get Dennis to email over one of James.'

He nodded and stepped outside.

'What's this all about?' Zaina asked.

'Stacey's missing,' Ella said. 'Her husband, James, owns the computer store.'

'Holy crap. What happened?'

'We don't know. Has there ever been any trouble along the shops there? Anyone hanging around, vandalism, anything out of the usual?'

'Not since I've been there. Far as I know, the only excitement was when some guy held up the aquarium for turtles, yonks ago.'

Outside, Murray's phone beeped, and he came in and showed the screen to Zaina.

She nodded. 'That's the guy who came in after the woman. They look like they matched. Both so nice-looking.'

Ella tried to think it through. Stacey had come in about seeing the dentist immediately, quickly followed by James. Was she trying to get away from him? 'Did it seem like Jon and Stacey knew each other?' she asked.

'No. He came out and introduced himself and shook her hand. That's when she mentioned the computer shop. I think the guy introduced himself too, but the phone rang again and I had to answer it so I didn't hear what he said.'

'And afterwards, did Jon say anything about her?'

'Only about her not really needing a clean. Then another patient came in, and we didn't talk about her again.'

Ella heard a car stop out the front.

Zaina looked out the door. 'It's my friend.'

'Do you have Jon's mobile number?' Ella asked.

'Sure.' Zaina fetched her mobile and read out the number.

Ella wrote it down, then got out her card. 'If you remember anything else, can you give us a call? Anything odd about that day, or something strange you noticed around the shops there.'

'Homicide,' Zaina read from the card. 'You think the woman's dead?'

Ella said, 'We really hope not.'

★

Ella called Jonathon Dimitri's mobile while Murray drove them to Lidcombe to see Stacey's old schoolfriend Abby Watmough. Dimitri didn't answer, and Ella left a message asking him to call as soon as he could.

Watmough lived in a shambling house set back from the road, with cream cladding on the walls and a huge frangipani tree that was just starting to drop its leaves into the front gutters.

Ella knocked. The woman who answered looked about forty, with brown hair in a short ponytail and a slender build in a Sydney Swans T-shirt and denim shorts. She held a screeching baby in a green Bonds suit and wore an annoyed expression.

'Didn't you see the sticker? It says do not knock.' She started to push the door shut with her bare foot, but Ella held up her badge.

'Abby Watmough? Can we come in and talk?'

'Has something happened?'

'We just need to ask you a few questions,' Murray said.

The living room furniture was practical and homely, like Ikea but one rung down. Abby Watmough sat on the edge of the lounge and patted the crying baby's back.

'Sorry if I was rude there. We get the religions here constantly. They just ignore the sticker. It's insane.'

'It's all right.' Murray nodded at the baby. 'Girl or boy?'

'Girl,' she said. 'Lucy. Silly Lucy to be crying, aren't you, huh? It's okay. It's all right.' She dotted kisses over the baby's head.

Ella watched, thinking of the woman on the bike in the CCTV images. Abby Watmough looked similar — as much as any woman with lightish-brown hair and a slim build would.

She cleared her throat. 'Do you know Stacey Durham?'

'Yes,' Abby said. 'A little. I know she's been missing too. I saw it on the news. Have you found her?'

'Not yet,' Ella said. 'How do you know her?'

'We went to the same high school. We weren't friends then, and only met at a school reunion late last year, where we realised that my son, Liam, is going out with her niece, Paris.'

'What?' Ella said.

'I was surprised too,' Abby said. 'Small world, isn't it?'

Discomfitingly small, Ella thought. 'How did that come up?'

'She said she was a paramedic, and I said my son's girlfriend Paris had been accepted to start training as one too. Stacey's ears pricked up at the name, and bingo.'

Murray said, 'You were friends with her on Facebook.'

'Were?' Abby said.

'She unfriended you a couple of months ago,' he said.

'Huh. Shows how much attention I pay to it.'

'Was there some reason she did that?' Ella asked.

'Not that I know of. As I said, I wasn't even aware that she had.'

'No argument or anything?'

She shook her head. 'At the reunion, everyone was saying they were going to friend everyone and keep in touch properly. Those sort of good intentions never last long in my experience. I hardly ever get on Facebook, and she probably decided to delete people like me who never post.'

'Do you own a bike?' Ella asked.

Abby looked puzzled. 'A motorbike?'

'Pushbike.'

'No. Why?'

Ella didn't answer that. 'Where do you work?'

'In the public service. Department of Health admin. But I'm on maternity leave right now.'

'Is your husband home?'

'Partner. We split up. He thought he was up for being a daddy, but after the birth he changed his mind. He's working in the mines in WA. Liam moved back home to help out.'

'Sounds like a good kid,' Murray said.

Abby nodded. 'He is.'

Ella took out the CCTV photo of the cyclist and unfolded it. 'Do you recognise this person?'

She studied it. 'No. Should I?'

'You don't think it looks a little like you?'

'I suppose so, a bit. But as I said I don't own a bike. Or helmet, or clothes like that, for that matter.'

'Where were you on Sunday evening?' Ella asked.

'Here with Lucy.'

'Was Liam home?' Murray asked.

'No. He plays indoor cricket and soccer. He had a couple of games in a row, then stayed to umpire.'

'Was anyone else here?' Ella asked.

'Nope. Just Lucy and me. Why?'

'Just checking.' Ella took the photo back. 'Thanks for your help.'

Abby saw them out, the baby dozing in her arms.

'That all sounded reasonable enough,' Murray said as they walked down the drive to their car.

Ella looked back at the house. 'The Paris link is weird though.'

'Life is stranger than fiction,' Murray said, taking out his phone to call Dennis. He put him on loudspeaker and gave him a quick summary while Ella mused on the coincidence.

'I have news,' Dennis said when Murray had finished. 'The lab worked out two things. Firstly, the DNA matches – it's definitely her blood in the car.'

Ella and Murray didn't speak for a moment, then Ella said, 'What else?'

'They worked out what was written in the notebook you found.'

'And?'

'You'd better come see for yourselves.'

★

In the office, Dennis held out the fax from the lab.

'I'm so scared. Will he go to jail for this? How much time do you do for fraud?' Ella read out, then looked up. 'It's her handwriting?'

'The lab says it matches the samples from the calendar you sent in,' Dennis said.

'Can we be sure she's referring to James?' Murray asked.

'Who else would she refer to as "he"?' Ella said.

'Whoever she wrote about on the previous pages,' Murray replied. 'The pages we don't have.'

'But would she be scared about a friend or colleague facing jail?'

'Wouldn't you?' Murray said.

'In case it is him,' Dennis said, 'we need to know more about James's business. I've got Elizabeth Libke coming in from Computer Crime to help. When she gets here, which should be any minute, give her the run-down.'

Ella and Murray went up the corridor to their desks.

'Let's assume it's James,' Ella said. 'He's doing something that could land him in jail. She's found out about it. What does he do?'

'Seems too obvious,' Murray said.

'Most crime is. Love, hate, money, revenge. He could be angry at her. He could be worried she's going to reveal something, either deliberately or accidentally, and he'll lose his money and end up in the slammer.'

'But she hadn't said anything so far, so why would she now? Why hurt or kill her now?'

'That anonymous complaint – what if that made her realise that something was going on? What if she asked him about it, or found out it was true, and now he's done something to her to shut her up? To protect whatever fraud thing he's running?'

'Libke checked him out though,' Murray said.

'But how well?'

'Well enough,' a voice said behind them.

Ella glanced around to see Elizabeth Libke pulling up a chair. 'I meant that he might be hiding stuff somewhere else,' she said. 'On another computer or something. You said yourself you just had a chat and checked a couple of things.' Her cheeks were warm.

Libke opened a manila folder on her knee. 'I'm guessing you want the layperson's version?' Her voice was cool.

Ella listened as she ran through the steps of what she'd checked, then said, 'Dennis told you about the imprint in the notebook?'

Libke nodded.

'Are there other ways to commit fraud than the ways you looked at?'

'Of course,' Libke said. 'But the note didn't say specifically it was about computers.'

'No, but if it's James she's referring to, that's got to be pretty much a given, don't you think?'

'I was wondering,' Murray said, 'if we shouldn't map out our next steps? We could take a couple of approaches, one being that it's James, the other that it's someone else, and start from there.'

Ella sat back in her chair.

Murray said, 'Elizabeth, say James is hiding stuff, is there a way you can go deeper and find out?'

She nodded. 'It'll take time, but sure.'

'Goodo. And Ella and I will do the less technical stuff. Talk to James again, interview the shop staff –'

Ella's phone buzzed with a text. She looked at the screen. 'It's from Stacey's phone.' She opened the message. '*Time is running out. James knows why. He must tell the truth*,' she read.

Murray hurried off to alert Dennis.

Libke said, 'Has that happened before?'

Ella shook her head as she typed her reply. *This is Detective Marconi. Who are you?*

Dennis and Murray came in as the answer arrived, Dennis with his phone to his ear.

Ella read out the reply. *'James knows who we are. When he admits what he's done, he'll see his wife again.'*

Tell me what he's done and I can help, she sent back.

'Phone's in Westmead,' Dennis said.

They waited in a tense group, but there was no answer. Ella, her hands trembling a little, pressed to call the number, but it went straight to voicemail.

'Switched off,' Dennis said, and ended his own call.

FOURTEEN

Paris sat on her bed, flipping through her textbooks and remembering the day she'd got them, how exciting and full of potential they – and she – had been. Stacey had picked them up for her from the paramedic shop at Rozelle HQ and brought them over, walking into the house with the pile up on one hand like she was a fancy waiter, a bottle of champagne behind her back and a grin from ear to ear.

They'd clinked glasses at the kitchen bench, just the two of them, the new-paper-and-ink smell filling the room, and Stacey had talked about the camaraderie of the job, the friends you made, the satisfaction you got, as well as the abuse you copped at random times for random things.

'Seriously,' she'd said, 'the other day I had the nicest-looking old lady try to punch me and then call me a –'

'Thank you,' Marie had interrupted, coming into the room. 'There's no need for that kind of language.'

'You don't know what I was going to say,' Stacey had said.

'And if she called you anything other than a competent professional I don't need to know.' Marie had poured herself a glass of champagne. 'Just because you work in a job where that sort of thing happens doesn't mean you need to bring it in here.'

'I've heard you swear like a sailor,' Stacey said.

Marie fixed her with a glare. 'I'm trying to raise my daughter to be a polite and well-mannered young lady.'

'She is,' Stacey said.

'And while she's under my roof she'll behave in the way I want,' Marie said, as if Stacey hadn't spoken, then she'd marched out of the room.

Paris and Stacey had kept talking, trying to get the mood back, but it was wrecked. Paris had felt resentment then, and sitting on her bed now she felt it steam up again. That had been her champagne, her moment. Why couldn't her mother support her? Or if she couldn't manage that, for whatever-the-hell reason, just leave her be?

There was a knock at the front door.

'Can you get that?' her mother called.

Paris let the book fall shut and went to open the door. Rowan Wylie stood there, the ambulance on the street behind him.

He smiled at her. 'Hi.'

She put her hands in her pockets. 'Hello.'

'Can I come in for a minute?'

She shrugged and stepped back. He walked in past her, the portable radio crackling on his hip, and she pushed the door shut with her foot. They stood there in the hallway looking at each other. She wasn't going to invite him further in, she wasn't going to ask if he wanted to sit down. He could say whatever he'd come here to say – sorry, if he had any conscience at all – then he could get the hell out.

'Well,' he began, then Marie appeared.

'Rowan! Come in! Sit down! Paris, don't just stand there like a fool, show him into the lounge room. Can I get you a coffee? It's so nice to see you again. How have you been?'

Paris wanted to crawl back to her room. He'd better not

go into the details of today, she thought; he'd better not let on how badly she'd been doing. She followed them into the lounge and watched Rowan stand there awkwardly while her mother flitted around him.

'I'm all right,' he said. 'Thank you anyway.'

Marie squeezed his arm. 'Then have a seat. How are you? How is work? Poor Paris had to come home early. Wasn't feeling well, apparently.'

'That's why I'm here, to see how she is.'

Paris tried to shake her head at him unobtrusively, to tell him not to say another word, but he was looking at her mother.

'Has there been any news about Stacey?' he asked.

'No, nothing,' Marie said. 'I don't know what the police are doing. How could someone disappear and nobody saw anything? It's hard to believe.'

'Have you spoken to James?'

'Briefly. He's very upset and frustrated, as you can imagine.'

Rowan nodded, then glanced at Paris. She looked at her feet. *Here it comes.*

He said, 'I wanted to let you know that because of the situation with Stacey and everything, it's been decided that you'll work as the third officer for a while.'

Paris looked up.

'Starting tomorrow,' he said. 'You can hang back and watch a bit. It'll take the pressure off you. The other officer is Wayne Loftus, I don't know if you've met him? He helped us at the crash today. Anyway, it'll make things easier for you.'

'I thought I was, uh, that I wouldn't be able to go back for a while,' she said. 'I thought I was out. For now, I mean.'

'How very generous,' Marie said. 'They'll change everything just for her? How marvellous.'

Paris ignored her. The relief that she was still in, that she might still be able to pull herself together, was enormous.

'Thank you,' she told Rowan.

'We look after our people,' he said.

'Marvellous,' Marie repeated.

Marie saw him out and waved as he drove off, then turned to Paris. 'What's going on?'

'What do you mean?'

'Him coming over here like that. He could've texted. He could've not told you at all. You'd find out soon enough, when you went back to work.'

Paris blinked. 'Why does that make you so mad?'

'Because I'm your mother and I should know what's going on in your life.'

'You do,' Paris said. 'I'm new in my job, my aunt's missing. Isn't that enough?'

'Are you seeing him?'

'What?' Paris couldn't believe it. 'Are you kidding me? He's older than you!'

Marie's jaw was tight. 'I know something's going on. What else am I supposed to think?'

'You're insane.'

'How dare you —'

'How dare you,' Paris shot back. 'You've seriously lost it.'

'My sister's missing,' Marie wailed.

Paris had had enough. She stalked into her bedroom and flung the door shut. She would put her headphones on and turn the music up loud, and she would study. She would get better at the job, and she would save up, and she would move out of here as soon as she could, and she would never ever come back.

★

Ella and Murray grabbed a late lunch to eat in the car on the way from the office towards James's house, where they planned to talk to him about the dentist visit, the imprint in the notebook, and the texts. Going through Silverwater, however, they came across a recent accident, and had to tend to the shaken drivers and direct traffic until the paramedics and uniforms turned up and took over.

They reached James's place to find Marie's silver Toyota in the driveway again.

'Interesting,' Murray said as they got out.

'Keep it quiet,' Ella said.

'You want to sneak up on them?'

'Sneak has bad connotations,' she said. 'I simply want to be quiet.'

'That dog'll spot you,' he whispered behind her.

She'd deal with that if it happened.

She tried to cross the lawn silently but without looking like she was creeping. She made it to the patio, expecting barking to erupt from somewhere within the house, but all was silent. She got to the lounge room window and looked in, not really expecting to find anything, but instead seeing James sitting on the lounge with his head in his hands and Marie next to him, stroking his head, a smile on her face.

Then Murray stumbled up the step, the dog leapt barking from behind the lounge where he'd apparently been sleeping, and James and Marie looked up at her.

She waved. 'Hello.'

James looked hopeful, and hurried to the door to let them in. Marie looked murderous.

'Have you found her?' James said.

Marie joined them in the hallway, her handbag already on her shoulder. 'Is there news?'

'Not yet, sorry,' Ella said. Marie had reshaped her expression into one of worry. She was really something.

Murray said, 'We have some more questions for James.'

'For people who are supposed to be looking, you spend a lot of time talking,' Marie said.

Murray smiled at her. 'It can seem that way, but we're only part of the team working on your sister's case. There are many others out there.'

'I guess I'd better get out of your hair, then.' Marie kissed James on the cheek. 'Try not to worry. They'll find her.'

Ella followed her outside. Marie was fast and was almost at her car already.

'Just a moment,' Ella said. 'I have a question or two.'

'Or three, I'm guessing.' Marie smiled widely.

Ella didn't smile back. 'How are you coping? No more faints?'

'Not so far.'

'Have you had any texts or calls from your sister's number?'

'Not a thing,' Marie said.

'What were you and James talking about?'

'Stacey, of course. Where she might be, who did this to her. I asked him straight out if he knew more than he was letting on, if he knew what the texts were about. He was adamant that he didn't.'

There was something frenzied in her voice. Ella said, 'And what about you?'

'I believe him,' Marie said.

'Do you know anything about the texts?'

'Of course not. How would I?'

'Do you know anything about the complaint that was made about James some time back?'

'Only what Stacey told me,' she said. 'That someone claimed he was defrauding his customers.'

'What did she think about that?' Ella asked.

'She said James was angry and upset.'

'But what did *she* think about it?'

Marie hesitated. 'She didn't say.'

'Did you ask her directly if she thought it was true?'

'No.'

'Did you yourself think it could be true?'

'No,' she said again. 'Stacey said James told her someone was trying to cause trouble, and it wasn't true, and if he ever figured out who it was he'd make them pay.'

'Did Stacey ever tell you that he figured it out?'

Marie shook her head. 'After the police said they couldn't find anything, we never talked about it again.'

Ella nodded and glanced at Willetts' house across the street. 'Was Stacey happy?'

'James would know that better than me.'

'Not necessarily.'

'We weren't the kind of sisters to share confidences,' Marie said. 'She seemed happy, I can say that much.'

'Did the two of you argue?'

'Now and again. Like any siblings.'

'What about?'

'What about?' Marie said. 'What do any sisters argue about? What do you and your siblings argue about?'

'I'm an only child,' Ella said.

'Well,' Marie said. 'We argued about the usual petty things.'

'Like what?'

Marie opened the car and dropped her handbag in. 'This is more than two questions.'

'More than three even,' Ella said. 'What did you argue about?'

'Petty things,' Marie said again. 'Like who brought the wine last time, like whether we should've got red or white.' She closed the door and walked away from the detective, around to the driver's side. 'Please find her.'

'We're doing our best, but it doesn't help when people won't tell us what they know,' Ella said. 'Why are you in such a hurry to leave?'

'Because I have a daughter who needs looking after,' Marie said haughtily. 'Do you have children?'

'No, I don't.'

'Then you can't know what it's like when your child needs you.' Marie got in and slammed the door, then cranked the engine and roared off down the street.

Ella watched her go, certain Marie was glancing anxiously

in her rear-view and wanting her to know she was onto her. *I've seen the relationship you have with your daughter, and if she ever needs anyone I really doubt it's you.*

When the car turned out of sight she headed back to the house.

In the lounge room James was talking to Murray about computer fraud. When she came in, Murray said, 'But that's not what we came to talk to you about.'

Ella took the fax from her pocket. James unfolded and read it. 'What is it?'

'It was written in the notebook we found in Stacey's bedside table.' Ella sat down opposite him. 'The page and some before it had been torn out, but the imprint of those words was left.'

He looked at it again.

'We know it's Stacey's handwriting,' Murray said. 'Do you have any thoughts about what she's saying?'

'My guess is that she wrote it when the complaint thing was happening,' he said. 'At the start she was frightened and worried that someone hadn't only contacted the police but also set me up, so that when the police did their checking there'd be something to find.'

'Does she often write down her feelings?' Ella asked. 'Does she keep a diary or journal?'

'No, she doesn't do it regularly or anything like that. But occasionally if she's done a tough case at work she'll write it down, then burn the pages. She said it was freeing. She might've done that here. Once the police said there was nothing to the complaint, she might've torn out the pages and burned them.'

Murray said, 'Wouldn't she have told you?'

'Not necessarily. She works shifts so she's here alone a lot. We don't give each other the full run-down of our days.'

Ella nodded. 'She went to the dentist on Monday, correct?'

'Yeah, she did. The plan was that she'd have lunch with me while her car was having a service, and then when she came in she said she had a toothache and wanted it seen to, so went to the dentist a few shops down.'

'Is that her usual dentist?' Murray asked.

'No, we go to one in Five Dock. I said why didn't she call him and go in there later, but she said she wanted it seen immediately, she didn't want it to get worse.'

It sounded weird to Ella. She said, 'You followed her in there.'

'If he couldn't see her then I was going to drive her to Five Dock. But he said he could.' James shrugged. 'How often does that happen?'

'What did she say the dentist said about her toothache?'

'That everything looked okay, it was probably stress from work, causing tension in her jaw.'

Zaina Khan had told them Dimitri said she asked for a clean, though she hadn't needed it. 'Had you been arguing that morning?'

'No,' James said. 'Why on earth would you think that?'

She'd wait until they found Dimitri and found out more about what went on in that room. 'Have you had more texts from her phone?'

'Not since the ones that arrived when we were at The Gap,' he said. 'And I've been good and kept my phone turned on since.'

'Did you send anything yourself?' Murray said.

'Just one. I told them to give me my wife back or I would hunt them down.'

'When was that?' Ella asked.

'An hour or so ago.'

'Why then?'

'Because I was here, alone, angry and fed up. I couldn't stop thinking about it. It didn't help when they didn't reply.'

'I got a message,' Ella said.

'What? When? What did it say?'

She handed over her phone.

James scrolled through the messages. 'More of the same shit. I don't know what they expect me to do. I don't know who they are or what they think I've done. How can I admit to anything?' He thrust the phone back at her. 'I'm starting to think she's dead and they're playing us for time, that eventually they'll say they killed her because I didn't confess, when really she's been dead all along.'

'You can't think like that,' Murray said. 'You have to keep hoping.'

Ella was surprised by the heat in his tone. She said to James, 'Are you absolutely certain that there's nothing you haven't told us?'

'Are you serious? My wife's out there somewhere, at best she's injured, at worst she's dead, and you think I've somehow overlooked something important?'

'I'm not saying you've done it deliberately. I'm saying you should take time and think. It could be something small. It could be something you haven't considered.'

'I've considered everything,' he said. 'I never stop considering everything. Whatever's happened to her has nothing to do with me.'

★

Ella drove back towards the office, Murray biting his thumbnail in the passenger seat. The late afternoon sun was low and orange in the city's haze, harsh even through sunglasses, and Ella had to sit her straightest to keep the visor shading her eyes.

She said, 'I've never heard you say that hope thing before.'

'Really.'

'Nope. Never.' She glanced over at him. 'You feel sorry for him?'

'You don't?'

'He's suspect number one.'

Murray lifted a piece of nail from his tongue, lowered the window an inch and flicked it out into the breeze. 'Or he's a victim whose beloved wife is missing.'

Beloved. It sounded corny coming from his mouth. She blamed the wedding.

'Don't you think it's odd that he actually said she might be dead?' she said. 'Most people hang on to hope until confronted with the actual body.'

'Everyone reacts differently.'

'Only to a degree. Going big picture, most people react the same way, and there's something off with how he's behaving.'

'Can't you give the poor guy a break?'

'Poor guy?' she said heatedly. 'What is it about him that's sucked you in? Do you see you and Natasha in the posh photo of them rugged up and laughing on the beach? You see yourselves with the nice house, the scrappy yet lovable dog, the super-happy marriage?'

'So what if I do? Jesus, Ella, not everybody's relationship turns automatically to shit.'

She bit down on her first reply and instead said, 'He's a suspect.'

'Or he's a man whose wife is missing and injured, and who might die.'

They didn't speak for the rest of the trip. Fantastic, she thought. This then dinner with Adelina. What an awesome end to the day.

At the office, Murray stormed off to the bathroom and Ella stalked to her desk. She found two messages waiting for her. One was from Rachel Nisbet saying it was important; the other from a Senior Constable Anne Percy at Broken Hill.

She picked up the phone and dialled.

'Yeah,' Percy said. 'I saw your email about Angus Wylie and called straight away.'

'So you know him?'

'Not exactly,' Percy said. 'He comes and goes, works for various people, doing odd jobs and so on. I've talked to him a couple of times: once he was a witness after a fight in a caravan park where he was living; another time he helped out at a truck crash, fetching and carrying for the Rescue people.'

'So he's never caused a problem?'

'Not for us. He seems a nice guy.'

'Is he at the caravan park now?' Ella asked.

'I don't think so. I haven't seen him for quite a few months. That's a little odd, come to think of it. I'll scout past there and check. Are you after him for any particular reason?'

'I've come into contact with his family in a case,' Ella said. 'It'd be nice to be able to tell them he's okay. If he wants them to be told, of course.'

'Let me look around,' Percy said. 'I'll be in touch.'

Ella hung up. Detectives were gathering, queuing for coffee in the little kitchen, their voices echoing off the tiles and hard floor. She had a few minutes still, and dialled the number that Rachel Nisbet had left.

'Detective,' Nisbet said. 'Thank you so much for calling me back.'

'I'm assuming this isn't about your interview idea,' Ella said. *It better not be.*

'Far from it,' Nisbet said. 'I wanted to let you know that I overheard someone at the station talking about the call we received telling us that James Durham was at The Gap. Usually we find out about that type of thing via the police scanner, so this was unusual. I managed to get a look at the message and apparently the male caller said, "James Durham is going to jump off The Gap". It struck me as odd that the caller would recognise him, even allowing for the fact that he was on the news last night, and equally odd was the choice of words. It seems to me that someone would be more likely to say "is threatening to", or perhaps even "looks like he might", because they wouldn't want to think the person would really do it. Which made me think that perhaps the caller wanted it to sound drastic so we'd all hurry down there.' She took a quick breath. 'Also, the phone number was still in the system, so I called it, and the person who answered said I'd rung a public phone box near The Gap. And then I called in a couple of favours with people at other stations and got them to check, and they all said they got the same message and from the same number.'

'Hmm,' Ella said, thinking about who might benefit from a media scrum, and why.

'So I hope that's helpful,' Nisbet said.

'Possibly,' Ella said. 'Thank you for letting me know.'

'You're welcome. And if you do ever change your mind about the interview, I'm always here.'

Ella put the phone down and leaned back in her chair.

Murray came back and sat at his desk. 'You look weird. Who was that?'

She told him what Nisbet had said.

'Semantics,' he said, opening the weather forecast webpage.

'But she's right,' Ella said. 'A bystander wouldn't say "is going to jump". And why specify who it was? A bystander wouldn't be thinking about that either.'

'So you're saying what?'

'That it was James himself who called the media.'

'Yeah, well, probably to get his face on the news.' Murray frowned at the monitor. 'Ten per cent chance of rain now on Saturday. Man.'

'It doesn't bother you that he might've played us all?' she said.

'He's desperate,' Murray said. 'Why can't you put yourself in his shoes for a second?'

'Why can't you take yourself out of them?' she snapped. 'And stop thinking about your wedding and concentrate on your job instead?'

He looked at her. 'That's a really harsh thing to say.'

'You know what I mean,' she said. 'Just . . . hang on, sit down and let's talk about things. Don't go. Let's talk about the Facebook friends again.'

But he'd already walked away.

FIFTEEN

In the meeting Ella sat with her arms folded four seats from Murray, listening to detectives list off the day's activities. It was demoralising. Around and around the investigation went, and what did they really know? There was no news on what had happened at that park in Homebush, nothing new from Stacey's friends, nothing nothing nothing. Plus the dinner was looming, and she kept checking her phone in her pocket, hoping Callum would call and have to cancel, that things were crazy at the hospital and he just couldn't get away. But he didn't.

She and Murray gave their report, listing the details of James going missing then to The Gap; the information about the Facebook friends, including what George Tsu was supposed to have done with Stacey and that he was yet to be interviewed; the texts that Ella had received; the strange behaviour of Marie; Stacey's visit to the dentist and their inability so far to locate him. They sat down again, then Sylvie Catt and Paul Li stood up.

'The make and model of the folding bike has been identified,' Sylvie said, 'but it's unfortunately one of around a thousand that was sold either online or by one of two hundred and sixty stockists in the country.'

'If we could get a serial number we might be able to trace the buyer, but right now we're at a dead-end,' Paul said. 'But we've asked the local stations in the area around Homebush, where the bike was last seen, to let us know if one is found, dumped in a canal or whatever. Even if the cyclist wiped the bike down, there's always the chance of a print surviving under the seat.'

'Wouldn't that be awesome?' Sid Lawson murmured in Ella's ear.

She smiled and nodded. His eyes were as bright as ever, enthusiasm and energy coming off him in waves. She felt old and jaded next to him, and as the meeting wrapped up and Dennis assigned tasks, including for a nightshift team to find and talk to George Tsu, all she could think was that now she had the family dinner to face.

★

Aunt Adelina must have been watching from the window, because she opened the door before Ella and Callum had climbed the first step to her parents' lit-up verandah.

'Welcome,' she crowed.

Ella wanted to say it wasn't her house to welcome people into, but didn't.

Callum shook her hand. 'It's nice to meet you at last.'

'It's nice to meet *you*.' She made him walk first down the hall, and whispered loudly to Ella, 'He smells good.'

Ella wanted even more badly to call the whole thing off.

In the kitchen, Netta was poking the contents of a big pot on the stove with a wooden spoon while Franco looked on. The air was warm and smelled of cooked meat.

'Osso bucco,' Netta said, after they'd all hugged and kissed.

'Wonderful,' Callum said.

'I set the table,' Franco said. 'Flowers and everything. Come and see.'

The two couples sat on the long sides, Aunt Adelina at the end. She looked like the queen up there, Ella thought, in the perfect position to pontificate both left and right.

The conversation started gently enough, with Netta asking Callum about his work, then skipped to Ella's work, then missing people.

'Like that ship, the *Marie Claire*,' Franco said.

'It's the *Mary Celeste*,' Adelina said.

'Or the Bermuda Triangle,' Franco went on, unperturbed.

'At least the woman has no children,' Adelina said. 'Terrible thing for little children to lose their mummy.' She filled her mouth with meat, chewed and swallowed, then looked at Callum. 'You're wanting children, I hope?'

'Adelina,' Netta said.

Adelina said, 'Ella's not getting any younger.'

'Ade,' Franco said. 'Leave the kids alone.'

'It's all right.' Callum squeezed Ella's furiously jiggling knee under the table. 'You never know what the future will hold.'

Adelina frowned. 'Is that a yes or a no?'

'It's an appropriate answer to a personal question,' Ella said.

'There's no need to be huffy,' Adelina said. 'This is my family. You're my niece. Nothing wrong with a fond curiosity. Callum, would you marry in a church, and if so, which kind?'

'How's your dinner, Callum?' Netta asked. 'Would you like some more?'

'Just a little would be lovely, thank you.' He pressed his thigh against Ella's.

'Do you know, Callum,' Adelina went on, 'my husband and I couldn't have children. We tried, oh my, did we try. It just didn't happen for us. I hope our problem was with him and not me. Less chance of something being wrong with Ella that way. With the genes. Well, you know how it works, you're the doctor.' She gave him a big toothy grin.

'Adelina,' Franco said, 'come into the kitchen and help me with dessert.'

'But we're not finished here yet.'

'It needs turning.'

'Pudding doesn't need turning.'

He grasped her arm. 'Come on.'

When they were out of the room, Netta shook her head in apology. 'She's getting old. She gets focused on ideas and won't let them go.'

'It's not age. She's always been like that,' Ella said.

'It's fine,' Callum said.

It wasn't to Ella. She just wanted to be left alone, for them both to be left alone.

The phone rang in the hall. 'Excuse me,' Netta said, and went to answer it.

Ella pressed her forehead against Callum's shoulder. 'Didn't I tell you?'

'Don't stress about it.' He cupped the back of her neck, his fingers light on her skin. 'You have to put up with more from my family then I ever do from yours.'

She breathed him in. He did smell good. He felt good too, the muscles of his arm, the cloth of his shirt in gentle folds against her cheek.

Netta cleared her throat in the doorway. 'Callum, your mother's on the phone.'

Ella sat up. He took his mobile from his pocket and looked at it. 'Eight missed calls. I put it on silent.'

'You'd better see if she's okay,' Ella said.

He kissed the top of her head as he got up. Netta sat down opposite Ella and they smiled at each other.

'He's really very nice,' Netta said.

'You said that last time we were here for dinner.'

'Well, he is.'

In the kitchen, Franco and Adelina bickered over the pudding. Ella could just make out the low tone of Callum's voice underneath.

She said to her mother, 'Did she say what she wanted?'

'No, but she didn't sound happy.'

'She knew we were coming here,' Ella said. 'She must've looked you up in the phone book when he didn't answer.'

They sat listening. Ella wished Adelina would shut up about the consistency of the damn sauce.

'He really cares about you,' Netta said.

Ella looked at her, feeling suddenly, scarily, close to tears. It was true, he did. And she really cared about him. This is actual love, she suddenly thought. This is what it felt like: she was frightened over their future because of his mother, but there was no doubt in her heart about what she wanted. Not a single scrap. *I want him.* And I want him forever.

The realisation took her breath away.

Callum came back. 'She said someone broke into her house.'

'Oh no,' Netta said.

'She was asleep and didn't hear anything, but she's terrified they might come back.'

It sounded like a doubtful story to Ella, and she read the same thought in Callum's eyes.

'I'd better go,' he said.

'But the pudding's ready,' Adelina said behind him.

'Sorry.' He held out his hand to Ella.

She took it, but said, 'Is this a good idea?'

'She says her house was broken into,' he said. 'The police should attend.'

★

Ella had never been to the McLennan family home. It was a tall two-storey house in Carlingford, with lights blazing from every window. Callum knocked and a moment later his mother, Genevieve, opened the door.

She glared straight past him at Ella. 'Look who's here.'

'You said someone broke in,' Callum said.

'Someone did.'

She walked into the living room. Callum went after her, glancing back at Ella, who hesitated for a second before following. Cushions had been tossed from the matching leather lounges onto the floor. The glass doors on a hutch stood open, and a couple of wine glasses lay broken and trodden into the carpet. A painting had been pulled from the wall and thrown across the room, the hook torn out of the plaster. A TV lay face down on its cabinet, the stereo speakers either side up-ended.

'Is anything missing?' Ella said.

Genevieve shook a cigarette from a packet and lit it without answering.

'She asked you if anything was missing,' Callum said. 'And since when do you smoke?'

'Nothing's missing. This is what they do.'

'What who does?'

'The people who are trying to drive me out.' She held the cigarette between two rigid fingers and gestured with them at the damage.

'How'd they get in?' he asked.

'How should I know?'

Ella said to Callum, 'I'll have a look around.'

Genevieve tossed her head. 'That's right, go and snoop.'

Ella went into the kitchen. Nothing was destroyed or disturbed. The glass in the windows was unbroken, the doorframe unsplintered, the lock sound. Same in the formal dining room next to it. Family photos hung on the wall and Ella looked at them as she passed. Callum as a teen, his proud parents. Alistair had once been broad and muscular, a far cry from the shrunken man she'd seen in court. Genevieve's smile had been lovely.

'I don't like her being in my house,' she heard Genevieve say.

'Mum –'

'Don't you *Mum* me,' she snapped. 'She's ruined this family. Why do you insist on seeing her? Are you trying to hurt me? Because it's working.'

'Mum, you need to stop this –'

'Because she can hear me? I'm well aware of that, and I do not care.'

'No, because who I choose to see is none of your business, and because I won't let you talk about her like that.'

Her back straight, Ella walked past them to check the lock on the front door. It too was intact.

'No sign of forced entry, no damage anywhere else,' she said to Callum.

He looked at his mother. 'How'd they get in?'

'So maybe I left the front door unlocked.' She ashed her cigarette forcefully in a saucer. 'It's no surprise. There's so much on my mind, and I'm here alone, having to deal with it all by myself.'

Callum and Ella didn't look at each other, but she knew this was what he'd expected, and the same went for her. On the drive over, they'd talked about everything else: her work, his work, Adelina (though not the questions themselves; she didn't know what she'd say if he brought those up), osso bucco. He'd had to stop for petrol, and she'd pondered while alone in the car what would happen when they reached this moment, when it was obvious that the break-in was a ploy to draw him back.

She picked up the painting and leaned it face out against the wall. Inside the elaborate frame, three brown cows stood in a meadow. Genevieve muttered something, as if Ella was checking its value, planning to spirit it away.

'Well,' Callum said, 'things don't look too bad. So we'll get on, shall we?'

'What?' Genevieve said.

'You're safe, the doors are fine, nobody else can get in.' He put the lounge cushions in place. 'We'll have it tidy in two minutes, then we'll leave you to it.'

'I'm frightened,' Genevieve said. 'I'm just an old lady, all alone.'

'You're so much tougher than you think,' Callum said to her. 'I've got Sunday free, so I'll patch the wall and rehang the painting then.' He and Ella lifted the TV up. The screen wasn't even cracked. 'Lock the doors after we go, and you'll be fine. People like that don't come back, do they, Ella?'

'No,' Ella said. 'They do not.'

Genevieve sucked a tooth. 'So you're going.'

'You don't need me.' Callum hugged her and kissed her cheek. 'I'll call you in the morning, okay?'

He and Ella stepped outside, and Genevieve slammed the door, turned the lock, and switched off the overhead light. Callum led Ella down the dark steps to the path.

'You don't think she'd hurt herself, do you?' Ella said.

'No. In her mind that's weak, and for all her "poor little me" act she'd never want to be that.' He started the car. 'It's after nine. What do you want to do? Go back for pudding?'

'Not really. You?'

'No.'

She put her hand on his leg. 'How about you take me home?'

'Oh, Miz Marconi, what are you doing? I'm just an innocent boy –'

She squeezed his thigh. 'Drive.'

In bed his skin seemed softer than ever before, his muscles firmer, his arms more enveloping as he cradled her to him. His breath was warm on her lips. She ran her hands down his sides, pulled his leg over hers and squeezed him to her.

'I love you,' she said.

'I love you too.'

They'd said it before, but it somehow never meant as much as it did right now.

SIXTEEN

Paris was wary when she walked into the station the next morning. Rowan had said the other officer had been at yesterday's crash, which meant he'd know exactly how badly she'd stuffed up. There were guys in the job who'd go hard at you, guys who'd bring up something like that every chance they got. Well, she probably deserved it.

After the slightly awkward introductions, Rowan sat at the desk to finish paperwork and Wayne Loftus followed Paris to the ambulance. He stood at the back door, watching while she went through her checklist.

'I'm sorry about your aunt,' he said.

'She's not dead,' Paris said.

'Sorry she's missing. Sorry whatever's happened.' He hitched his belt up with his thumbs. 'I worked with her a couple of times. Good operator. Switched on.'

It was the highest praise one officer could give another. Paris thought back to her first day on the road, when she'd imagined her trainer saying that about her.

'I hear you've been having some problems,' Wayne said.

'My aunt's on my mind.'

'Before that, I mean.'

She counted oxygen masks and ticked boxes.

'It's probably your expectations,' he said. 'I've seen it happen. People want to be perfect, and when they're not they can't handle it. Young girls especially.'

'Especially, huh?'

'Brought up to be Mummy and Daddy's little princess, to be perfect all the time. I have two girls, ten and nine, and I'm always saying to them, hey, life's not like that. You gotta roll with the punches.' He put on an accent. 'You gotta learn to deal.'

'My dad died in a truck crash when I was ten,' she said. 'My mum doesn't particularly like me. I know how to deal.'

The station phone rang. Paris saw Rowan answer it in the muster room, then write something down.

'Looks like we got a job,' Wayne said. 'That's your spot there.' He pointed to the resus seat at the head of the stretcher. 'Watch and learn, kiddo.'

'My name's Paris,' she said.

'Like the dude in the Trojan movie. Gotcha.'

Rowan came out with the keys. 'Man caught in a chair in Potts Point. Caller's in a state, so that's all we've got.'

'How do you get caught in a chair?' Wayne slammed the back door and the air pressure popped Paris's ears. He got in the passenger side, still talking, while Rowan climbed behind the wheel. 'I've been to kids with their heads stuck in the back of chairs, but never an adult. How could they not give more info? How do we know if we need Rescue?'

Paris clipped in her seatbelt and sat with her knees jammed against the head of the stretcher, watching out the back window as they drove out of the station. It felt odd to see the cars behind them instead of in front, and how people pulled in to follow, hoping for a clear run through traffic. The siren was as loud in here as in the front, and the ambulance rocked and swayed as Rowan braked and cornered. She breathed deeply, tried to be cool.

At the address, Wayne opened the side door and pulled out the Oxy-Viva. 'Bring the first-aid kit and drug box,' he said to her as she clambered out. 'When you don't know what you're going to, you gotta be prepared for everything.'

The cream brick of the ageing apartment building was stained by water below each balcony, and equally ageing residents peered over the railings to see what was going on. A woman Paris guessed was in her seventies stood in the open front door, her blue dress soaked, her hands shaking as she gestured for them to hurry.

'Hello there,' Wayne said. 'How are you? What's happened?'

'He's stuck, oh, it's terrible how he's stuck.'

'Your husband, is it?' Wayne said, but she herded them into the lift and pressed the button and started to cry.

'Your husband?' he said again as the lift wheezed upwards. 'How is he stuck?'

'Oh, it's awful, it's terrible.' She wiped her eyes with a crumpled tissue.

'What kind of chair is it?' Wayne said. He whispered to Paris, 'Sometimes you have to change your approach.'

'He screamed with the pain, I didn't know what to do.'

The lift shuddered to a stop and the doors opened on a hallway with grimy walls. The woman hurried out, her slippers scuffing the thin brown carpet, and Wayne muttered, 'Sometimes even then you don't get a straight answer,' as he and Paris and Rowan followed.

The door to the apartment was propped open by a chair. The air inside smelled of cats, and Paris heard at least one scratching at a closed door as they went along a gloomy corridor.

At the end, the woman tapped on a half-closed door and pushed it open. 'Arnold? They're here. Go on in. I can't look.'

Paris saw the glaring light of a fluorescent bar, tiles with dirty grout, threadbare towels on sagging racks. In the shower, an elderly man sat on a plastic chair with a dressing gown draped over his shoulders and across his thighs and a look of intense pain on his face.

'Mate.' Wayne put down the Viva. 'What's happened?'

'The chair's got me,' Arnold croaked. He gripped the chair's arms so tightly the veins on his wrists stood out. 'Got me by the knackers.'

'Ouch,' Wayne said. 'Okay then. Let's have a little look.' He crouched and lifted the dressing gown. 'Aha. Right. I see.' He lowered the gown and turned to Paris. 'The chair's got those gaps in the seat, you know the type, an inch or so wide, so you can leave the chair in the garden and the rain can go through. And his package has slipped right down one of those gaps.'

He clapped his hand on Arnold's shoulder. 'How'd it happen? Hot shower, the plastic legs give way a bit, something like that? You try to stand up and can't?'

Arnold nodded. His face was red, his bushy eyebrows and wet hair white. He blinked at them. 'Not a girl. I don't want a girl looking.'

'Don't worry about her,' Wayne said. 'She's one hundred per cent professional and specially trained in matters like these.' He checked under the gown again. 'Looking a bit swollen and chafed there, but I think we can manage without Rescue. You got some pain? Yeah, not surprised. Allergic to anything? Okay. Let's check your blood pressure, and we'll give you something for the pain, then let's see if between us we can't push the chair down and set this nice gent free.'

He gave the sphygmo to Paris, and she stepped gingerly onto the wet tiles beside Arnold's chair. 'Hello,' she said, then groped around for something else to say. 'We'll have you feeling better in no time.'

Arnold looked like he didn't believe her. He'd bitten his lip so hard he'd bruised it, and his clammy skin gave off a sharp vinegary smell that mixed badly with the dank odour rising from the drain. She moved the dressing gown back from his shoulder, wrapped the cuff around his bicep and inflated it. He looked like he'd once been big and strong, but age had turned him flabby on a shrinking frame.

'One-forty,' she said.

'All good,' Wayne said. He was inspecting Arnold's forearms. 'You don't have anything in the way of veins here, so Rowan's going to give you this stuff – it's called fentanyl, and you just snort it up your nose – for your pain, and then we're going to get you out of there.'

A black cat ran into the room, saw them, and shot back out.

Rowan gave the drug to Arnold, and in a couple of minutes he'd started to relax a little.

'Pain easing?' Wayne said.

'It's a bit better.'

'Good, good. Now Rowan and Paris are going to stand either side of you and press down on the arms of the chair when I say, all right? And . . .' He raised the gown and took another look. 'I might soap things up a bit, make it a bit easier. That okay?'

'Anything to get out of here.'

Wayne soaped his gloves into a foamy lather at the sink, then crouched in the cubicle and reached under the chair. 'Okay, just a little bit here, excuse my cold hands.'

Arnold flinched and shivered, and Rowan squeezed his shoulder.

'That should do it,' Wayne said. 'All righty, girls and boys, take your positions. Arnold, you have to let go there. Put your hands on my shoulders instead if you need to grab onto something.'

Arnold released his grip on the chair's arms and Paris and Rowan took hold of one each, their palms hard against the surface.

'One, two, three, and push.'

Paris pressed down, leaning into it with her back. On the other side Rowan did the same. The chair legs skidded out and stopped, then skidded further. Arnold gasped. Wayne reached under the chair again.

'Little bit more,' he said.

Paris pushed down and felt the legs give way again. She pictured the plastic gap widening. She heard a slippery sucking sound and Arnold yelped and half-stood as the chair released him, his hands grabbing hers and Rowan's, his legs shaking as they took his weight. The dressing gown slipped off him onto the floor. His sagging back was fish-belly pale and dotted with fleshy moles, his drooping buttocks marked with red lines from the chair.

He shuddered. 'Oh god, oh god.' He clutched at the shower wall, at Wayne's shoulder again.

Paris let go of the chair and grasped his arm. Rowan kicked the chair aside, and Wayne put his arm under Arnold's and around his back. Arnold clung to them and burst into tears.

Wayne wrapped Arnold's bruised and swollen scrotum in a towel-covered icepack, then they took him and his twitching wife to Sydney Hospital. Afterwards, Wayne stood filling in the case sheet and talking while Paris put clean sheets on the stretcher. She didn't know how to take him. His idiotic yap about expectations had her assuming he was one of those loud-mouth guys who didn't really care, but the way he'd managed Arnold made her think otherwise.

'See now, that was a good job,' Wayne said. 'We worked as a team, everything went smoothly, the patient's nuts were saved. Who could ask for more?'

Rowan came out of the Emergency Department and helped Paris tuck in the sheets.

'I was just saying how well that job went,' Wayne said to him. 'I mean, it's not like I want to rub soap over some old guy's ballbag, but when the job goes well you can't help but feel good. Am I right or am I right?'

'He said to say thank you,' Rowan told Paris.

'And that's nice too,' Wayne said. 'Some of 'em forget the

social niceties. So it was a good job all round.' He finished the case sheet. 'And you did well, Paree. Nice and calm, did as you were told. Didn't lose it for a second. Team player.' He bumped her shoulder with the side of his fist. 'Props, man.'

'Thanks,' she said, but it came out funny and she hoped he didn't think she was being sarcastic.

He glanced at her, then at Rowan, who was walking away, back into the hospital.

'I know kids like you,' he said. 'Playing it too cool for school, but underneath you're all quivering and soft, afraid of being kicked. Life's given you a hard shell, man, but times like this you need to open it up a little. I can see in your eyes how much you want to be good at the job. Why don't you let people help you?'

Paris didn't know what to say, where to look. If that was true, then . . .

'Thirty-seven,' Control called over the radio. 'Can you clear?'

'Rock'n'roll,' Wayne said, scrambling to answer. 'Thirty-seven's ready to go.'

'Thanks, Thirty-seven. Got a female with some issue we can't quite work out.' He gave them an address in Woolloomooloo.

'Thirty-seven's on the case,' Wayne said.

Paris got into her seat in the back, glad to be away from his gaze. Rowan ran out to close the rear doors, and swung up behind the wheel.

★

The morning meeting over, Ella and Murray got into their car in a somewhat tense silence and headed through the sunshine to Dural, where they planned to speak to Steve Lynch, the third person Stacey had defriended on Facebook. Other detectives were following up with the lab about the numberplate of the car whose driver appeared to speak to the cyclist at the lights; with a couple of Crimestoppers calls that had come in overnight, about someone dumping a bike in the Parramatta River and about what may have been a domestic in a car that vaguely matched Stacey's; with trying to find anyone who'd seen or heard anything in the area around Bicentennial Park where Stacey's phone had been turned off, and in the areas where the later messages had been logged. Dennis was chasing up the requests for the Durhams' phone records; and Elizabeth Libke was continuing her close examination of James Durham's computers, both the machine and laptop they'd collected from his home and the one in his shop. One good thing: George Tsu had been interviewed last night and had told the detectives that he and Stacey had gone to a miscarriage, and Stacey had broken down in tears afterwards. The parents had been hysterical with grief and Tsu said he himself had had a hard time keeping it together. The hug was friendly, collegial, and he said they'd both needed it, never mind what Lamarr thought she saw and accused them of.

Feeling good about last night, if less so about the case, Ella had smiled at Murray a couple of times and got nothing in return. Now, as he drove, she said, 'I'm sorry about yesterday.'

'Uh-huh.' Murray didn't look over.

'It was mean, and hurtful. I'm glad you're excited about the wedding. I think it's really great.'

He nodded, his eyes on the road.

She tried to sound jaunty. 'What's the forecast saying today?'

'Back to five per cent.'

'Good as nothing,' she said. 'It'll be great.'

He braked at a red light, and scratched his chin.

Ella touched his arm. 'I truly am sorry.'

He hesitated, then looked at her. 'You really think it won't rain?'

'It wouldn't dare.' She smiled.

★

They found Steve Lynch hosing out a dog run. The grass on his whole property was mown down close, the wire in the fences taut, the paint on the weatherboard house and garage and sheds fresh and neat. His dog training business had been registered at this location for ten years, with no complaints made against it, and he had no criminal record.

He straightened and clicked the hose trigger off. 'This is private property.'

'We knocked at the house but there was no answer.' Ella held up her badge. 'Got a moment?'

He gave the wet concrete a final squirt, then stepped out of the pen. It was empty, but the three next to it held five Alsatians between them. They sat silently on the drying floors, yellow eyes watching.

'They're quiet,' Murray commented.

'Well-trained.' Steve Lynch tucked his blue workshirt into his waistband with the flats of his hands. His Blundstones and trouser cuffs were wet. 'What can I do for you?'

'Do you know Stacey Durham?' Ella asked.

He thought for a moment. 'Can't say I do.'

'You were Facebook friends.'

He shrugged. 'I have about nine hundred. I don't know most of them.'

'She asked to be your friend after a discussion on the high school you apparently both attended,' Ella said. 'You commented on each other's posts about dogs a few times.'

'Oh,' he said. 'Scruffy dog? Wire-haired terrier cross-breed thing? Yeah, I remember now. She rang me, said did I remember her, apparently we went out once in Year Eight or something. I didn't remember her at all but kind of fudged along until she got to the point – that her dog sometimes plays up. Wanted some advice for free, like they always do.'

'Did you give it to her?'

'In a way. I asked about the home life. Basically the thing rules their roost – sleeps on the bed, jumps on the lounge, she lets it lick people. I said it'll never stop playing up while she spoils it like that, but once she gets some rules in place and is sticking to them she can bring it out here and I'll help her re-educate it. She said she'd let me know. I never heard from her again.'

'In fact she unfriended you,' Murray said.

He shrugged again. 'Eight hundred and ninety-nine more where she came from.'

One of the Alsatians made a sound deep in its throat. He looked over and the sound stopped.

'Did you ever call her back?' Ella said.

'No reason to waste my time. It wasn't hard to work out that she had no interest in training the dog properly. Nor that she didn't want to pay for help to do it.'

'So you've had no contact apart from that conversation?'

'No,' he said. 'Nothing.'

'That guy's sitting on a goldmine,' Murray said as they drove back past the mansions and clear green swimming pools and clay tennis courts of Dural. 'Little business like that, he must've bought the place years ago when it was way cheaper. Or inherited it maybe.'

Ella was thinking about Stacey. 'Do you think we're going about this all wrong?'

'This is the road we came in on,' he said.

'I mean, are we missing something in the case?' she said. 'Something big.'

'Like what?'

'I don't know,' she said. 'All these threads, but it feels like they're leading in different directions.'

'Because most of them probably aren't relevant,' he said. 'You know how it is, you get to the end of a case and you can see how the important leads linked up, but meanwhile everything that you thought meant something along the way has disappeared from your mind. People defriend and refriend people all the time. We're more than likely just ticking boxes here.'

He was right. So much of a case was checking, rechecking, crossing off. She had to calm down.

Her mobile rang. It was Dennis, calling from the office.

'Have you finished there?' he asked.

'We just left,' she said.

'Good. The lab cleaned up the numberplate of the car seen next to the cyclist at the traffic lights, where it looked like the driver was talking to her, and we got a hit. Registered owner's name is Ross Hardy, thirty-eight years old, record as long as my arm. Burglary, drug and weapons offences, stolen cars and extortion. He lives at Pendle Hill. Lawson and Pilsiger are already headed there. Can you meet them nearby?'

Ella said, 'We're on our way.'

'And now we have a new thread to wonder about,' Murray said wryly.

★

Ella and Murray met Detectives Sid Lawson and Marion Pilsiger two streets away from Hardy's address. Lawson bounced on his toes, his eyes everywhere with excitement. Pilsiger handed them Hardy's picture, described his house and went through his history.

'And in the extortion,' she wound up, 'he sticky-taped a .22 bullet to a solicitor's front door. This guy had been doing some work for some friends of Hardy's on a business deal, and things went sour. Hardy's thumbprint was found on the base of the bullet. He said it was a set-up, but the solicitor had got threatening phone calls and drive-bys as well, and identified Hardy's voice and car. He was convicted and spent eighteen months inside. Been out almost a year now.'

He didn't sound like the brightest spark, and going by the photo – round head, deep-set eyes in sallow flesh, vacant expression and a mess of dark hair – he didn't look it either.

Ella said, 'Any links between him and the Durhams?'

'Not that we know of, but it's definitely his car in the CCTV, so we'll be approaching him initially as a witness,' Pilsiger said. 'We don't expect any issue, especially not with the four of us there. All good?'

They nodded. Ross Hardy's house stood in the middle of the street, a tidy red-brick one-storey with a double garage at one end and a curtained bay window at the other. A tightly pruned murraya hedge grew inside a picket fence along the front, and Ella and Murray stood back near it while Lawson and Pilsiger went up onto the verandah. The late morning sun was warm on Ella's shoulders and she could hear bees in the flowers. Lawson pressed the doorbell and stepped back, and she saw the curtain in the bay window twitch.

'Someone's home,' she called in a low voice.

Pilsiger hit the door with her fist. 'Ross Hardy, it's the police. Answer the door, please.'

No response.

Ella and Murray started moving in opposite directions, she aiming to go around past the bay window to the left side, he crossing the herringbone driveway to the right. She watched the other windows as she went across the grass, looking for movement, knowing the sheer white curtains would let someone inside see out without being seen.

The grass down the side of the house was sparse, the area shaded by the eaves and the paling fence. She moved carefully, silently, the beat of her heart in her ears and throat. She heard Pilsiger pound on the front door again, and then the click of a door opening at the back of the house. He'd come her way, she bet. He would've looked out the front and chosen to run against the woman. Thought it would be easier to get through. She stiffened her back, flexed her thigh muscles. Did he just.

He came her way at a run, empty-handed, looking back over his shoulder to where Murray was rounding the corner. 'Stop right there,' Murray shouted, and Hardy put on a burst of speed. He looked ahead and saw her waiting, and she saw him ball his fists, lower his shoulder and tuck in his head.

She stepped aside, braced herself against the corner of the house, and kicked him as hard as she could in the leg. He went down with a grunt, then tried to scramble up the fence. She grabbed the waistband of his shorts with one hand and the collar of his shirt with the other, yanking him down, then Murray was beside her, pulling out his cuffs.

'We only wanted to talk,' Ella said to Hardy. 'Why did you try to run?'

'Fuck you,' he spat.

Lawson ran up as they stepped back from the prone figure. 'I can't believe I missed it.'

They walked Hardy into the house to get his keys and wallet and phone, then out to the car. He was moaning about the colouring bruise on his leg. Lawson was stern-faced with pride as he gripped the cuffs. He and Pilsiger would take Hardy to the office for a formal interview.

Ella's phone rang. She didn't recognise the number. 'This is Marconi.'

'My name's Jonathon Dimitri,' a man said. 'You wanted to talk to me?'

SEVENTEEN

The Woolloomooloo street was tree-lined, the apartment building bright white with tinted glass lobby walls. Wayne pressed the intercom button for unit twenty-nine, and Paris heard the line open and a woman crying.

'Ambulance,' Wayne said, and the door clicked open.

They squeezed into the lift with their kits.

'Now,' Wayne said to Paris, his eyes on the rising numbers, 'sometimes women patients respond better to women officers. So if we think that might be the case here, we'll get you to step up, okay? Besides, it's good practice.'

She felt the familiar anxiety, the tightening in her throat, but said, 'Okay.'

The corridors were a far cry from those at Arnold's. The carpet was thick and soft under her boots, the wallpaper clean and new, gold stripes on a white background, and warm yellow light came from lamps in fancy sconces on the wall.

Wayne tapped on the door marked twenty-nine and a shaky tear-filled voice called that it was open. Inside the apartment, a woman of eighty or so sat huddled on the lounge, a red fleecy dressing gown pulled tight over pink dotted flannelette pyjamas, thick socks on her feet. Her hair was white and thin, her face red and marked from crying.

She looked up as they approached, despair in her eyes, and Wayne said gently, 'I'm Wayne, this is Rowan, and this here is Paris. She's going to talk to you, okay?'

He nudged her forward, taking the first-aid kit and drug box out of her hands.

Her heart beating high in her chest, Paris knelt by the lounge. 'I'm Paris.' *He already said that. Idiot.* 'What's your name?'

'Pamela Chapman.' She clutched the gown around her neck. The bones of her hands stood out like sticks, her worn gold wedding band hung loose on her finger, and her skin was dotted with liver spots.

Paris saw Rowan walk further into the apartment, checking the rooms. She said, 'Can you tell me what's happened, Mrs Chapman?'

The woman shut her eyes tight. Tiny veins stood out in her temples. 'It's my husband.'

'What's happened to him?' Paris asked.

'I can't find him.'

Rowan came back, shaking his head. There was nobody collapsed or dead here, at least.

'Does he live here?'

Pamela Chapman nodded

'When did you last see him?' Paris said, thinking of an excursion to the shops, an old man getting confused and wandering in the wrong direction.

'I don't remember.' Pamela Chapman pressed her hands to her face.

Paris glanced at Rowan and Wayne. Wayne made a 'keep going' gesture.

Okay, Paris thought. *All right. Let's do some stuff.* 'Mrs Chapman, while we talk about Mr Chapman, can I check your blood pressure?'

'It's probably high,' she said. 'I'm just so worried. What could have happened to him?'

Rowan handed Paris the sphygmo, and she wrapped the cuff around Mrs Chapman's thin upper arm. Her skin felt hot.

'How are you feeling yourself?' she asked as she inflated it.

'I'm just so worried.' Mrs Chapman grasped her hand. Her fingers were long and thin and feverish.

'You might have a temperature,' Paris said, for Rowan's and Wayne's benefit. 'Your blood pressure is fine at one-thirty, but your pulse is a little fast at one-ten. Do you take any tablets?'

'Oh, there's a whole box of them in there.' Mrs Chapman waved a hand behind her and Wayne went off to find them.

'What about Mr Chapman? Does he take any?' Paris said.

'He takes even more than I do. He's a sickly man, very sickly.'

Wayne might find a clue there, Paris thought. Were there medications for dementia? 'What's Mr Chapman's first name?'

'Roger,' she said.

Rowan bent to Paris's ear. 'There's no sign that anyone else lives here,' he murmured.

Paris looked at Mrs Chapman. Her eyes were fever-bright, and now that she'd stopped crying her face was pale with red spots high on each cheek. At school they kept saying 'looks sick, is sick', and Mrs Chapman looked sick. She smelled sick too; her breath was sour, her body odour stale, and now and again Paris caught a whiff of something else, something like urine but not quite. Heat radiated through her dressing gown, and her hand on Paris's knee was just about burning through her trousers.

'How about we take that gown off you?' Paris said. 'You might feel a bit better.'

'Oh no, no. I'm so cold.' She bunched it up around her neck.

Wayne came back with a plastic box full of medication packets. 'Cardiac, hypertension, anxiety and arthritis meds. Nothing under anyone else's name.'

There was something else they said at school, something about confusion in elderly people, women in particular. Confusion could be a sign of low or high blood sugar, so they'd have to check that, then Mrs Chapman shifted on the lounge and Paris caught the smell again and remembered.

'Mrs Chapman, does it burn when you go to the bathroom?'

Mrs Chapman glanced up at Rowan and Wayne, as if horrified to be speaking of such things in front of them. She leaned close to Paris and whispered, 'I don't like to go. It burns terribly.'

'I think you might have a urinary tract infection,' Paris said.

'Oh no,' Mrs Chapman said.

Out of her view, Wayne grinned and gave Paris a big thumbs up.

'It's nothing too bad,' Paris said. 'We'll take you to hospital and they'll give you some medication and you'll feel better in no time. Though first we're going to check your blood sugar, to make sure that's okay.' And there was still the question of Mr Chapman.

Rowan got out the glucometer. 'This would be easier if we take off your gown.'

It wasn't true, they only needed her finger, but it had the effect they wanted. Pamela Chapman let them ease the gown over her shoulders and off her arms. Paris could feel the heat of her fever even just sitting next to her.

'When was the last time you saw Mr Chapman?' she said.

'I'm not sure.' Mrs Chapman flinched as Rowan pricked her finger and collected a drop of blood. 'Oh, wait. Yes, that's right. He was at Hedgebrook.'

Paris didn't know what that was, but Wayne said, 'The nursing home?'

'Yes,' Mrs Chapman said. 'But they sent him home. He should be here.' She looked around the room, puzzled.

Wayne caught Paris's eye and held a hand to his ear, miming a phone call.

'How about I ring them?' Paris said.

Mrs Chapman squeezed her hand with her overheated fingers. 'Would you? There's a dear.'

Paris found a phone on the wall of the kitchen and a phone book tucked in a cabinet below. The earpiece of the phone was grimy and she held it clear of her head as she dialled.

'Hedgebrook Village, can I help you?'

'Hi,' Paris said. 'My name's Paris and I'm a paramedic with the New South Wales Ambulance Service. I'm with a Mrs Pamela Chapman who's concerned about the whereabouts of her husband, Roger, who may or may not be living there now?'

'I remember Roger. He died about eighteen months ago, I'm sorry to say. Brain cancer.'

'Oh,' Paris said. 'You're sure? There couldn't be two of them?'

'Mrs Chapman lives in Woolloomooloo, right?'

'Yes.'

'That's definitely him,' the voice said. 'Sorry.'

'No problems. Thank you.' Paris hung up. Mrs Chapman must know already, but now she was going to find out again. Paris hadn't yet had to tell someone that their loved one was dead, though Stacey had told her she'd be doing it pretty regularly. She hadn't looked forward to it then and she didn't now.

She walked back into the lounge room and whispered to Wayne, 'He's dead. A year and a half.'

He made a face. She looked down at Mrs Chapman, the grey skin of her scalp, her thin shoulders inside the pink pyjamas. Rowan was packing away the glucometer, so the reading was obviously fine, and he motioned that he'd go to bring up the stretcher.

'I'll help,' Wayne said, giving Paris a wink, and followed Rowan out.

Mrs Chapman looked up at her, hopeful. 'Was he there? Did you find him?'

Paris sat down and took Mrs Chapman's hand. How the hell was she going to do this? So much for Wayne helping her. She cleared her throat but the lump didn't go.

'I talked to Hedgebrook and they said he used to live there, but he died eighteen months ago. I'm very sorry.'

Pamela Chapman looked stunned. 'What?'

'He passed away eighteen months ago,' Paris said. 'He had cancer.'

'No,' Mrs Chapman said. 'Oh no. That can't be right. He was coming home. They were letting him come home.'

'I'm sorry,' Paris said. 'The nurse remembered him. She was sorry too.'

Mrs Chapman shook her head. 'There's been some mistake. He was sickly, but he wasn't dying.'

How awful, Paris thought, and how sad, to have to relearn of your husband's death, maybe only when you were sick and confused, or maybe over and over and over again. Mrs Chapman was crying again, clutching Paris's hand, rocking back and forth.

Paris put her arm around her. 'Do you have any family nearby?'

'The children are all at school,' she wept. 'They won't be home for hours.'

Paris guessed she was talking about her own children, and in her confused state thought she was way back in the past. 'What are their names?'

'Angela, she's the oldest, almost fourteen now, and then there's Geoffrey. He's eleven, and Lynn who's only eight.'

'Let me check something.' Paris eased out of her grip and went back to the phone. The writing on the card beside the preset buttons was faded but she could just make out the names. She picked up the handset and pressed the first.

'Hello?'

'Is that Angela Chapman?'

'Yes, it is.'

Paris explained who she was. 'I'm with your mother now, and she's quite confused, especially about your father.'

'Christ,' Angela said. 'This again? I live right downstairs. I'm on my way up.'

The phone went dead in Paris's hand.

On the lounge, Mrs Chapman was still rocking, still weeping.

Paris rubbed her back. 'Angela's on her way.'

'He's supposed to be coming home,' she said. 'Why won't they let him come home?'

The lift dinged and a middle-aged woman hurried in, shirt hanging out, her hair half-done, followed by Rowan and Wayne with the stretcher.

'Mum,' the woman said.

'Oh, Angela, hello,' Mrs Chapman said. 'Have you seen your father?'

'Dad's dead, Mum.' Angela sat down beside her. 'Remember? We were all there with him. We all said goodbye. Geoff sang at the funeral.'

'No, that was someone else's funeral,' Mrs Chapman said. 'Give me a minute and I'll remember their name. Very sad it was.'

Angela looked across her at Paris. 'She goes like this whenever she has a fever. Usually she's fully with it. I suspected yesterday that she was getting sick, and I even made an appointment with the doctor for this afternoon, but I think she'd be better off in hospital.' She smiled. 'Thanks for looking after her.'

Paris smiled back, and when Wayne leaned close to say, 'Good job,' she felt a little light go on inside her.

★

'Now that was something to write home about,' Wayne said.

Paris sat sideways in the resus seat in the back of the ambulance, looking through the cabin out the front windscreen.

Wayne twisted in his seat to see her face as he spoke. They'd delivered Mrs Chapman to hospital, and now were going to collect a man from his nursing home at Camden and transport him to RPA. Purple clouds gathered in the sky further west, and Paris kept her gaze on them as Wayne talked.

'You stayed calm, you did your job,' he was saying. 'You even diagnosed her, fer Chrissakes. We left you on your own and you handled it, man. That was awesome.'

'Thanks,' Paris said.

'As for what happened yesterday, well, you reacted as many trainees do, but you're only six weeks in,' he said. 'But at the same time, you're six weeks in. You follow?'

'Yes,' Paris said.

'A good paramedic keeps her cool, keeps her eyes open, doesn't let herself get caught up in the emotion.' Wayne widened his eyes, emphasising his words. 'Nobody's saying that it's easy. The best of us have trouble sometimes, a job gets through the armour for whatever reason and next thing you know you're fighting the feelings, but you hold it back until the job is done. You lock it away, keep it inside.' He put one fist inside the other and squeezed. 'Lock it up tight, see what I mean?'

Rowan glanced across at him but didn't speak.

'Nobody in the job ever wants to see a trainee kicked out,' Wayne said, 'Nobody wants you to fail. Quite the opposite in fact: everybody wants you to succeed. I heard you came top of your class, is that right?'

'Yes,' she said.

'Okay, that's great. You've got it all in your head, which is cool. But there's obviously something wrong between here and here.' He pointed at her head, then her hands. 'It's not abnormal to feel a disconnect between what you learned in school and what you actually do once you're on the road, but there's more going on here than that. Even allowing for the thing with Stacey, and let's face it that only began yesterday, yet it sounds like you've been having trouble for weeks. Am I right?' He didn't wait for her answer. 'I thought so. So let's talk about that. Nerves are normal, I might point out here. This job is a big responsibility.'

He looked happy to be lecturing. The clouds outside grew darker. But Paris felt like finally, maybe, things were coming together.

'It seems all dashing and glorious when you're on the outside,' he went on, 'but then you're in it, and you're the one walking into a scene with everyone looking at you to fix what's wrong, and that can be damn nerve-racking.'

Paris took a big breath. 'It scares me to walk in and have them looking.'

'It scares everyone at first,' Wayne said.

'And they don't stop looking,' Paris said. 'I feel their eyes on me and I think they can see how nervous I am and how much I don't know and when I stuff up. I'm frightened that I'm missing something major.'

'And then you can't think about anything else,' he said.

'Exactly.'

'But look how well you did today,' he said. 'We left you there, testing you out, and you did what you had to do.' He grinned. 'I said to Rowan in the lift on the way down, you just watch, she'll cope fine.'

Paris saw Rowan glance at her in the rear-view, and wondered what he'd said in return.

'You have a bad case of the nerves, there's no doubt about that,' Wayne said. 'But hey, we're all different, right? And some of the best paras around started off just the same. But the thing to remember is this. When people look at you, they don't see *you*. They see a uniform. You're a pair of hands and a smile and a uniform, that's all. You know a lot, and you have to let that knowledge kick in. You smile at them, act like you know what you're doing even when you don't, and let the uniform do the rest. *Capisce?*'

He grinned at her like that was all there was to it, and for the first time she felt maybe there was.

★

Jonathon Dimitri had been camping in a remote area of the Blue Mountains with his girlfriend, and had come back into range to find Ella's message on his phone.

'Thanks for coming in,' Ella said when he sat down in the interview room. In the room next door, Ross Hardy was being interviewed by Pilsiger and Lawson, with Dennis sitting in.

'It's no problem.' Dimitri was a neat and stocky man in his early thirties, dressed in jeans, hiking boots and a plaid shirt with the sleeves rolled up.

'How was the camping?' Murray asked.

'Cold actually.' Dimitri smiled. 'But good.'

'We want to talk to you about a patient you saw on Monday of last week,' Ella said. 'Stacey Durham.'

He looked puzzled for a moment, then nodded. 'From the computer shop.'

'That's her.' Ella waited for some comment about how he'd heard about her on the news, but none came. 'Do you remember much about her visit? Did she mention a toothache?'

'I remember that she didn't need to be there,' he said. 'One look in her mouth and that was clear. She said nothing about a toothache either. Most of the people I see are well overdue, some by years, but her teeth were in excellent shape. I told her that and she muttered something about wanting a clean anyway. So I did it.' He shrugged.

'Had you ever met her before?' Murray asked.

'No, never.'

'How about her husband?'

'Well, he came in with her that day and introduced himself, but I'd never met him before either.'

211

'Did you talk much?' Ella said.

'To him? No. That was really all we said, then I took Stacey through to the room.'

'Your receptionist Zaina Khan said they both seemed surprised in some way,' Murray said.

Dimitri nodded. 'They did. When Stacey was in the chair she said something about not expecting to get an appointment so soon.'

'What else did she say?' Ella asked.

'Well, at one point she actually cried a little.'

'In what context?' Murray asked.

'She told me about her previous dentist, said she was looking to go somewhere else and this was handy to the shop. I said, oh, do you work there too? And she said no, that she's a paramedic, and it's her husband's business. I was getting things ready for the cleaning at that point and when I looked back at her she'd started to cry a little bit. She apologised and I said it was all right, that many people have issues with dentists, but she said that wasn't it, that things had been bad and she didn't know what to do.'

'Meaning what?' Ella said. 'Did she elaborate?'

Dimitri shook his head. 'I asked her, I said, "what things?", but she wouldn't say. She wiped her eyes and said she was fine, and lay back in the chair.'

He had nothing more to add, and Murray took him out with the aim of checking the camping story with his girlfriend, who was waiting in the cafe downstairs. Ella went to see if Pilsiger and Lawson were done with Hardy next door. The room was empty, and she found Dennis in his office. She told him what Dimitri had said, then asked about Hardy.

'He said yes he was driving, and yes he talked to her,' Dennis said. 'Said that he asked if she knew of an ATM nearby, and she said no and looked away.'

'Did you believe him?' Ella asked.

'I think so. He had an ATM receipt in his wallet from

nearby just after that time, and he gave a description of the woman matching what we already have.'

'That could all have been orchestrated though. The woman's photo's been in the news, so he could've known he had to give us that much to sound convincing.'

'Even so,' Dennis said.

'And why'd he run?'

'Same story as with any criminal. If you don't know why the police are at your door, don't wait around to find out.'

Ella wasn't convinced. But what did they have? A missing woman who'd cried in front of a stranger because things were bad but never confided in her friends. Whose husband declared their love to be the greatest, who put on a show at The Gap but possibly wasn't even close to going over. Odd bits and pieces.

'Anyway,' Dennis said, 'where's Murray?'

He appeared at the door. 'Here. Dimitri's girlfriend backed him up.'

'Good,' Dennis said. 'Aslett at Scientific called before. He wants to show you something about the blood in the car.'

EIGHTEEN

The nursing-home patient was a wizened man of eighty-four. His name was Aloysius Leary, he had terminal cancer, and his family had arranged for him to be admitted to RPA for investigation by a top gastroenterologist for chronic stomach ulcers.

'Beats me why they insist on putting him through any more trouble and pain,' the nurse said out of his hearing as she handed over the paperwork.

'You can look after him, right?' Wayne said to Paris as they loaded the stretcher into the ambulance. 'You rocked it with Mrs Chapman, and he'll probably sleep the whole way.'

Whether he did or he didn't, Paris could manage. More than manage. She'd thought non stop about what Wayne had said, and things were going to be different from now on. She had the knowledge in her brain and the uniform on her back. She'd fake it until she made it.

'Absolutely,' she said.

They'd just driven out onto the street when the rain began. Rowan said something to her in the mirror but she couldn't hear over the water pelting the fibreglass roof. She unclipped her seatbelt and went forward to ask him to say it again.

'Long slow trip,' he said, gesturing at the windscreen, grey with sheeting rain, and the mass of tail-lights beyond. 'Make sure he's comfortable.'

'You'll do great,' Wayne said in the passenger seat.

She nodded and went back. The patient looked up at her as she sat down. 'How are you doing, Mr Leary?'

'What?'

She repeated it, louder, over the rain beating on the roof.

'Fine, thank you, I'm fine.'

His breath made her eyes water. He was shrunken from the cancer, his dentures loose in his mouth, his ribs under papery skin visible through the open neck of his pyjama shirt. His hands and wrists were big and bony and dark with bruises; his eyes deep and dark in his gaunt face.

'We might be travelling for a while,' she shouted. 'Are you comfortable?'

He nodded. 'Yes, yes.'

She smiled at him and he smiled back, then thunder cracked overhead and he started and reached out. She took his hand. He squeezed her fingers with his own, cool and dry. He seemed reluctant to let go, so she didn't pull away. He closed his eyes and she settled in her seat, the rain making it feel like the ambulance was a little universe of its own, a place where she had no concerns but to look after him. Life outside was invisible beyond the road spray and the rain running down the windows, and they were a small warm space moving smoothly through it.

Wayne was right, she thought. People didn't see her, they saw her uniform and assumed the person inside was capable. It was something to stand behind, something to draw on. She knew far from everything about the job, but she knew a lot, and if she could only keep her cool she *could* pull it all together.

She thought of Mrs Chapman and Arnold, and how she and Rowan and Wayne had been able to help them. She looked at Mr Leary sleeping, frail eyelids closed, his hand in hers. This was why she'd joined the job. She squeezed Mr Leary's hand out of love, but gently, so as not to wake him up, and felt her heart expand in her chest.

★

Paul Aslett had spent years squelching through blood at crime scenes of all kinds, but he always looked cheerful, as if he'd found a way to push the emotion of each scene out of his head while adding the specific details to his already encyclopaedic knowledge of spatter patterns.

He squatted by Stacey Durham's car. Ella and Murray looked over his shoulder at the web of string he'd constructed in the front passenger footwell.

'From the shape and size of a bloodstain we can work out where it originated, right?' Aslett said. 'The string leads back from the spatters, and where they meet is typically the point of impact on the body.'

Ella and Murray nodded. They'd heard and seen it before, but Aslett liked to explain.

'Here, things are a little different.' He pointed to the strings. 'You can see they come together at a couple of different points. Those points are low down, around the height a passenger's knees would be, but these didn't come from injuries to anyone's knees.'

Ella sometimes wished he'd just get on and tell them.

'In fact, it's probably best if I demonstrate. Step this way.' He headed for another car parked in the yard.

'He says that like he hadn't planned this all along,' Murray murmured to Ella as they followed.

Aslett got behind the wheel and they stood in the open door, watching as he leaned over the passenger seat.

'Imagine I have a bag of blood in my hands,' he said, then jerked his hands over the footwell, once, twice, then a third time down over the edge of the seat itself.

Ella stared. 'That's why there's no drag marks, no smears on the sill or anywhere else.'

Aslett nodded. 'I've seen a lot of scenes where people try to cover up what happened, think they can change how the blood looks, or move things or people around,' he said. 'A person who knows blood can recognise rubbish like that a mile off. There was no assault on anyone in that car. Whatever happened happened somewhere else, and the blood was put here later.'

Ella's mind was racing. 'When you say a bag, what do you mean?'

'It was something with a small opening. A bag or bottle, or a jar, say, with a wide neck, would result in much bigger spatters than these.'

'It had to be something the cyclist could put in her pocket,' Ella said. 'She wasn't carrying anything, and nothing was found in or around the car.'

'And that's what she was doing in those couple of minutes between parking and getting out,' Murray said. 'But why?'

'Transporting a container of blood is easier than transporting an injured or dead person,' Aslett said. 'If you get pulled over and the bag's hidden, nothing looks awry. And you can park the car, do your thing, then get out all calm and casual. Nobody would look at you twice.'

That was it, Ella thought. That was *it*.

'It had to be planned,' she said. 'To go to so much trouble, to collect blood in something and take the folding bike and do all of that – there has to be a purpose to all of it. Right? Everything is deliberate.'

Murray looked thoughtful. 'So even the dump site must've been chosen.'

Ella nodded. 'Because Rowan Wylie would see it.'

★

It rained all the way. The sound on the roof was hypnotic, and Paris wasn't surprised that Mr Leary stayed asleep. Rowan glanced at her in the mirror every now and again, and Wayne looked back a couple of times, and she gave them a thumbs up, and they smiled at her.

Rowan drove into RPA's ambulance bay, parked and turned off the engine. Paris squeezed Mr Leary's hand but he didn't respond. She squeezed harder, then prodded his shoulder. Mr Leary didn't move.

Wayne radioed Control that they were at their destination, and Paris pulled her hand free of Mr Leary's and touched his face, his chest, his neck. He looked exactly the same as before, but he was dead.

Rowan and Wayne got out of the ambulance and closed their doors, oblivious.

Paris was paralysed. To have someone die and not notice . . . there was no coming back from that. It wouldn't matter that he was so small and the blanket so big that she couldn't see his chest moving beneath it, nor that the colour of his lips and face hadn't changed. They were always banging on in school about cyanosis, how the lips especially would turn dark with a lack of oxygen, how dying/dead people went blueish-purple. Not that she'd seen any except the ones being autopsied when her class toured the morgue, and they'd all been cold from the fridge and pale like naked chicken. Mr Leary looked exactly the same as when they'd left the nursing home.

Rowan unlatched the back doors and swung them open. He glanced at Mr Leary, then at Paris. 'It's good he was able to sleep.'

She was frozen. She didn't know what to say or do.

Wayne smiled at her as he released the stretcher. 'Told you you'd rock it.'

Paris's ears thrummed, her skin prickled. Rowan and Wayne had both looked at him and not seen any cyanosis or whatever either, so that was something to point out later, right? Something in her favour? But still, when they did notice, it would mean that she hadn't.

'Rowan,' a woman said.

Paris saw the detectives who'd talked to her about Stacey. Marconi and Shakespeare.

'We need a chat, Rowan,' the male detective said.

'I'm a bit busy,' he said, pulling the stretcher out of the ambulance.

Now, do it now. Paris stumbled down the ambulance steps and grabbed Mr Leary's hand. She looked at his face. 'He's stopped breathing.'

'What?' Wayne said.

She pressed trembling fingers to his throat. 'He's just arrested.'

Rowan pushed in beside her to check for himself, then whirled and grabbed the handles. The doors to the Emergency Department were right there. 'Go,' he said.

'You don't want to –' *Monitor*, she was thinking. *Oxygen, defib, shock.*

'It'd only delay getting in there.' Wayne started chest compressions as they rushed inside, leaving the detectives in their wake.

'Got an arrest here,' Rowan shouted in the corridor.

'Into resus,' a nurse called back, and in seconds they were lifting Mr Leary across onto the clean white sheet of the bed in the resuscitation room. Staff hurried in, one grabbing a Laerdal bag and fitting the mask to Mr Leary's bony face, another tearing open his pyjama shirt to attach monitoring dots. Wayne kept on with the compressions.

'What's the story?' a male doctor said.

'Eighty-four-year-old man with CA, routine transfer for admission for consideration for GE exploratory,' Rowan rattled off. 'Uneventful trip until just now.' He elbowed Paris for the rest.

She cleared her throat. 'He said he felt fine when we left, then slept most of the way. As we got here he, ah, opened his eyes and looked around briefly, didn't seem upset or in pain or anything, then closed his eyes again, and then as we pulled out the stretcher I saw that he'd, um, stopped breathing.'

'Found to be in complete arrest,' Rowan continued. 'And as it happened right outside the doors we brought him straight in.'

The staff were busy and didn't acknowledge the story, but Paris guessed that was how they always worked, listening and doing at the same time. She watched Wayne compress Mr Leary's skinny exposed chest while the nurse at his head with the bag and mask timed her squeezes to inflate his lungs between them.

The male doctor looked at the screen, which showed the flat line of asystole. 'You said he's got cancer?'

'Bowel and lung,' Rowan said, handing over the letter that the nursing home RN had given them.

The doctor read through it and raised his eyebrows. 'All this and no DNR?'

'Apparently the family refused it.'

The doctor looked at the monitor again, then at Mr Leary's frail body on the bed and the nurses gathered around him, one about to cannulate his thin forearm, another drawing up drugs.

'Stop,' he said. 'The poor bugger's got terminal cancer. Let him go.'

The nurses put down the bag and mask, the needles and the drugs. Wayne stepped back and shook out his shoulders.

Paris welled up.

'Time of death four-oh-three pm,' the doctor said, and a nurse wrote it on a form, and another nurse unfolded a sheet and draped it over Mr Leary, his shape still clear under it, feet and knees and hips and nose, and Paris felt a tear overflow and run down her cheek, and she swiped at it, angry, embarrassed and sick with guilt.

'You okay?' Rowan said.

The doctor was looking now as well, and the nurses, and Wayne from the sink where he was washing his hands. Crying over some old man. They'd think she was ridiculous. A total newbie. Rowan walked towards her, and the doctor came over too. The ID clipped to his belt loop said his name was Callum McLennan.

'It's her first,' Rowan said, squeezing her shoulder.

The doctor smiled kindly. 'It was just his time.'

She shook her head. 'Five minutes ago I was holding his hand. I should've . . . he shouldn't, I mean . . .' She started to cry for real.

'He was old and he was sick,' the doctor said. 'He was on drugs for his pain. He spent the last minutes of his life with you holding his hand, and then he fell asleep and he didn't wake up. If there's a better way to go, I've never heard of it.'

'I should've done more.'

'It was just his time,' Wayne said.

She shook her head again. She couldn't explain herself. Her face was wet with tears and hot with shame. The nurses looked away and busied themselves with little jobs or left the room. Mr Leary lay motionless under his sheet.

'I'm sorry,' she said to him.

'There's no disgrace in being upset,' Rowan said.

'None at all,' the doctor said. 'It shows you have a heart.'

'Damn straight,' Wayne said.

The doctor smiled at her again, then a nurse called him to the phone.

'Let's go outside,' Rowan said.

He wheeled the stretcher and Paris followed, Wayne walking beside her. The detectives stood talking by the ambulance's open back doors and looked up as they came out.

Rowan turned away from them to face Paris. 'The first one is always a shock.'

She wiped her eyes. How much earlier could he have died? She was sure she'd seen him move, twitch a little, a couple of times during the trip. Maybe he really had only just gone right then, right as they were pulling into the hospital.

'Rowan,' Marconi said.

'Give us a minute,' he said. He looked into Paris's face. 'Take a big deep breath. This is the job. People die. We do what we can, but people still die.'

'Win some, lose some,' Wayne put in. 'Actually, win some, lose more. Most people who arrest don't come back, so don't feel bad. Like the doc said, that right there's a cool way to go.'

'Rowan,' Marconi said again.

Paris wanted to walk out into the last drops of rain and turn her face to the sky. Even if he couldn't have been saved, which probably nobody could know for certain, she surely had a duty to tell someone. It was the right thing to do. But what would that gain? She would be in trouble, could very well get the sack, and none of that would bring Mr Leary back. But that was a selfish way to think, and all about her own skin rather than what was right and wrong.

She needed to talk to somebody, but she couldn't tell Rowan and she couldn't tell Wayne. They wouldn't get it. Stacey would. She would listen and understand and know what was best.

But Stacey wasn't here.

The detectives had walked Rowan away and were talking to him with serious faces. Wayne was making up the stretcher and glancing her way with sympathetic eyes. Paris pressed her back to the wall and saw again Mr Leary under the white sheet, felt his thin hand in hers.

★

Ella had watched with sympathy the realisation that the old man had died, the reaction of Rowan and Paris and the other guy, and their later emergence with the empty stretcher from the hospital. Paris was visibly upset, and Ella heard Rowan say

222

it was her first. It wasn't hard for Ella to remember her own: a man who'd died in his house but hadn't been found for three weeks. This old man's way was better.

'Have you found Stacey?' Rowan said.

'No,' Murray said. 'But we need to ask you some more questions.'

When Ella judged that they'd moved out of the other officers' hearing, she said, 'How often do you go to Playland?'

'Every weekday that I'm off duty,' he said.

'Who knows about that?'

He blinked. 'I don't know. It's not a secret. I've probably mentioned it to a lot of people.'

'Who would know it for certain?' Murray asked.

'My son, Simon, his partner, Megan, people at work, the people at Playland.'

Ella said, 'People at work being . . .?'

'Paris, I guess, and Stacey, and a couple of the guys who take their kids there too. It's Emelia's favourite place, so like I said, I don't keep it secret that we go there a lot.'

'So Stacey would know,' Ella said.

He nodded.

'James too?'

'Most likely, from Stacey or from Simon or both. I might've said it to him too.'

'Would you notice Stacey's car wherever you happened to see it?' Ella said.

'Yes. It's distinctive. Haven't we done this before?'

'What made you go close and look in the window?'

'I told you all this. I hadn't seen it there before. I was walking right past it. I thought she might be around. I thought –'

Ella saw his gaze turn inwards as he stopped himself. 'You thought?'

'I thought we could have a coffee,' he said.

'Nothing wrong with coffee,' Ella said. 'Why did you hesitate before saying it?'

'Because you might think that she and I were seeing each other. Coffee makes it sound like we were.'

'Coffee can be just coffee,' Murray said.

'Well, coffee was the reason I was looking for her. I checked in the shops, then on the way back I glanced in her car. That's when I saw the blood.'

'Ah, yes, the blood,' Ella said. 'We learned something about that today. It didn't come directly from her body.'

'What? Where did it come from then?'

'It was thrown,' Murray said.

'Deliberately placed.' Ella watched Rowan closely. 'Tipped out. Squirted. The drops, the splashes, the pool: somebody made it look like that. Somebody spilled blood in Stacey's car from some kind of container.'

He looked stunned. 'What does that mean?'

'What do you think it means?' she said.

'How the hell should I know? You're supposed to be the experts.'

Paris and the other paramedic looked over.

'Calm down,' Ella said with no sympathy. 'Why don't you tell us the truth?'

'I am,' he said.

'I don't believe you. You weren't looking for her for coffee. What's really going on?'

'Thirty-seven,' a voice called from the ambulance radio.

The other paramedic answered, then Ella heard a message about a fractured leg and an address in Leichhardt.

'Rowan,' Ella said, 'if you care about her as a colleague and a friend, you'll tell us.'

'There's nothing to tell, and I have to go.'

She watched him walk away.

'You believe him?' Murray asked.

'No,' she said, as her mobile started to ring. She didn't recognise the number. 'Marconi.'

'This is Esther Cooper,' the woman's voice boomed. 'It might be nothing, but I saw something on TV once about baddies trying to clean up a crime scene with bleach, so I thought I should call. Is this a bad time?'

'Not at all,' Ella said.

'Well, I went to take James some tomatoes just now, out of the garden, you know, but he wasn't home, and Stacey's sister answered the door. She seemed a little odd, a little mystified by the tomatoes for some reason, but also I could see past her into the kitchen, and she had a bucket, and the floor was wet, and the smell of bleach was so strong it made my eyes water right there at the front door.'

NINETEEN

TELL THE TRUTH

The front door was open inside the screen at the Durham house, the smell of bleach as strong as Esther Cooper had described. Ella could see Marie on her haunches in the kitchen, back twisting, arms reaching, as she scrubbed the floor with a big sponge.

'You think she's been doing that since Cooper called? How long's it take?' Murray said.

'Depends what she's trying to hide.'

Ella knocked hard on the doorframe, and Marie straightened and looked around. She took her time pulling off rubber gloves and draping them over the side of the bucket before coming to the door.

'Is James home?' Ella said.

'No, he's not.'

'Do you know where he is?'

'At the shop, I presume.'

He wasn't. Ella had called his mobile on the drive over, and Nick Henry had answered to say that James had been in the shop earlier but forgot his phone when he left, and he didn't know where he'd gone.

'Mind if we come in?' she said.

Marie hesitated, then flicked the screen's latch. Ella and Murray moved past her and inside. Ella looked in the bucket. The water was brownish with no tinge of red. The sponge floated in it, and the two pink gloves hung over the side. The kitchen floor was wet and the odour of bleach was almost overpowering.

'Why such intense cleaning?'

'It relaxes me,' Marie said. 'Plus this way it'll be spick and span when Stacey comes home.'

'Uh-huh.' Ella glanced around. 'Where's the dog?'

'I don't know,' Marie said. 'I guess he ran away. Or was stolen.' She went to pick up the bucket, but Ella stopped her.

'No more cleaning,' she said.

'It's not your house,' Marie said.

'It's not yours either,' Murray said.

Ella said, 'Have a seat in the lounge room.'

Marie sucked her teeth for a moment, then went.

Crime Scene arrived quickly. The kitchen floor had dried, and they didn't look positive when Ella told them about the bleach, but said they'd check it all anyway. In the past, she'd seen blood found in cracks in places where a sponge just couldn't reach, and she was hopeful.

Murray took Marie outside and waited with her while Ella went to talk to Esther Cooper.

'Have you noticed Marie at the house a lot?' Ella asked.

'I've seen her car come and go,' Esther said. 'Though I'm not always sure if James is home.'

'Was this happening before Stacey went missing?'

Esther nodded. 'She's here fairly often. I'd say once a week?'

'Was she here on the weekend?'

'Not that I saw. I was out most of Saturday though, for a family get-together.'

Ella went back to the house. James was pulling up and she

and Murray met him on the lawn. Marie was sitting on the porch steps.

'Where have you been?' Ella asked him.

'Have you found her?' James looked at the police vehicles. 'What's going on?'

'No, they haven't found her. I was cleaning and they freaked out,' Marie called.

'Just running some tests,' Ella said to James. 'We've been trying to contact you.'

'I left my phone somewhere. Tests for what?'

'You left it at the shop,' Murray said. 'Where have you been?'

'Driving around, like yesterday. Tests for what?'

'Various things,' Ella said. 'I asked you to keep your phone with you.'

'I can't help it if I have too much on my mind and I forget something. Don't you have to ask my permission to do stuff in my house?'

'It's just part of the investigation,' Murray said.

Ella said, 'When did the dog go missing?'

James looked shocked. 'I didn't know he was.'

'I think he ran away,' Marie called.

'Oh my god,' James said.

'There's something else.' Ella drew him further away from Marie. 'Our blood expert said the blood in the car didn't come directly from Stacey.'

'What the hell does that mean? You said it was hers, that the DNA matched.'

'It is hers, but it was poured there,' Murray said.

James looked equal parts stunned and confused. 'I don't understand. How can that be? What does that mean?'

'We don't know,' Ella said. 'Do you?'

He stared at her, then his gaze wavered and he ran a hand across his forehead. 'I think I need to sit down.'

Murray helped him to the porch, where he sat next to

Marie and put his head in his hands. Ella noticed Bill Willetts watching from across the street. He didn't look away when she met his gaze, and, intrigued, she excused herself and crossed towards him.

'Mr Willetts,' she said.

'You lot again.' He pulled a dead leaf from a shrub by his patio. 'I see on the news you haven't found her.'

'Not yet,' Ella said. 'Have you had any revelations about what might've happened?'

'Not a one.'

'Seen that dog of hers today?'

'Nope. It's no surprise. He never walks it.'

'You didn't see it out on its own? Or anyone taking it?'

'No,' he said. 'You're tracking missing dogs now? Wish I had your job.'

'How about that woman?' Ella pointed to Marie. 'You see her there often?'

'Plenty. I guess she's some close friend or relative or something?'

'Was she here on Sunday?'

'No, but she was on Saturday. In the evening. Five-ish. Or closer to six. Ish.'

'How long did she stay?'

He shrugged. 'Forty minutes?'

'Was Stacey home then too?'

'Beats me,' he said.

'Well, did you see her open the door when the woman arrived? Or come out to see her off when she left?'

'The other day you insinuated that I was some sort of pervert for watching, and now you're annoyed because I didn't watch more? Jesus.'

'Okay,' she said. 'I'm just asking.'

He muttered something and patted his hair down at the back of his head. 'I saw the car pull up but didn't wait to see that woman go in. I saw her once at the window there in the living room, with the light on as it was getting dark. I heard the car door slam then the car leave. I didn't see Stacey at all.'

★

Paris was glad that Wayne and Rowan took charge at the fractured leg job, a man who'd fallen off the back of a delivery truck and lay gripping his thigh, moaning and pale, on the road. She was glad to fetch the splint, hold padding as instructed, take a couple of blood pressures when she was asked, and help lift him on the spineboard onto the stretcher. She was glad to sit huddled into herself in the resus seat while Wayne joked with the man on the way to hospital. And when they rolled him inside the Emergency Department, she was glad to go to the empty staff bathroom and lock herself in a cubicle and sit on the closed toilet lid with her shaking hands trapped between her knees.

Dead. Mr Leary was dead.

She took out her mobile and scrolled to Stacey's number. She pressed it hard to her ear as it rang, then heard Stacey's voice.

'*Stacey here. Leave your deets and I'll bell you back.*'

'It's me,' Paris whispered, fighting back tears. 'Something bad happened. A patient died and I don't think . . . I think I could've done more. I think it might've been my fault.' She wiped her eyes with the back of her wrist. 'I hope you'll hear this, and that we can talk about it one day. And I hope you come back soon.'

The end-of-message beep sounded, and she put her forehead in her hand.

★

Marie was still sitting on the porch steps, arms folded and face set, when Ella crossed back over from Willetts' house. James Durham was pacing the lawn.

Murray came to meet her at the kerb.

'Willetts said that Marie was here on Saturday night,' Ella told him.

'Hmm,' Murray said.

They approached Marie.

'What now?' she said.

'You were here Saturday evening,' Ella said.

'So?'

'You didn't mention that when we asked you when you'd last seen Stacey,' Murray said.

'I told you I talked to her on Sunday afternoon about Paris's birthday,' Marie said.

'And that you hadn't seen her since Wednesday.'

'Which is the truth.'

'She wasn't here on Saturday evening?'

'No.'

'Two questions,' Ella said. 'Where was she, and why did you stay for forty minutes when there was nobody home?'

'I don't know where she was,' Marie said. 'I stayed because I thought she might be home any minute. I made myself a cup of coffee and watched a bit of TV. I guess I lost track of the time. I didn't know it was that long.'

Ella glanced at Murray, then said, 'Did she come home?'

'Not before I left.'

'Do you often come into their house when nobody's home?'

'Just because you've seen me here twice since she went missing is nothing,' Marie said. 'James is my brother-in-law, so of course I'm going to be around to support him. Clean up a bit. Cook if he wants me to. Feed the dog. Wherever he's got to.'

'Did you try calling Stacey on Saturday night when you were here?' Murray asked.

'I tried once, but she didn't answer. I figured she'd be home when she was home.'

None of it added up for Ella. 'Why did you come over?'

'She's my sister. I didn't know I needed a reason.'

'For dinner? For a coffee? There must've been some impulse that made you decide to drive here.'

'For coffee then,' Marie said. 'Does that make it better if I say that?'

Ella stared at her. 'Your sister's missing.'

'I am aware.'

'Is there anything else you need to tell us?' Ella said. 'Any occasion when you've talked to her since Sunday night, or seen her, or anything that she told you before she went missing?' Murray touched her hand and she brought her voice down a notch. 'Anything at all that you can tell us about her, whether or not it seems relevant to you?'

'No,' Marie said. 'Nothing.'

Ella had to walk away. James was still pacing the grass, and she went past him to the front door and inside.

'Anything?' she said to the Crime Scene guys.

'Not so far.'

She stood in the lounge room, her arms folded, watching James. Murray joined her.

'Something funny's going on,' Ella said.

Murray nodded.

*

The Crime Scene officers were almost done with their so-far unsuccessful examination and Ella was considering the next step when two media vans pulled up on the street. James Durham went straight to them.

Ella said, 'Don't most victims' families shy away from the media? At least a little? And how did they know to come here?'

Murray shrugged. 'Neighbours. Probably Bill Willetts. Probably got them on speed dial.'

'Or James himself?'

'On what? His mobile's at the shop.'

Ella watched the camera operators setting up. She couldn't spot Rachel Nisbet. The journalist's card was in Ella's desk drawer back at the office.

She said to Murray, 'I feel like we're being played.'

★

Paris made it through the rest of the shift without falling apart, mostly because Wayne and Rowan let her be the gofer the whole time. She appreciated that, and told them so as they signed off at the station at the end of the day.

'Things'll be better next time,' Wayne said. 'First death's always the worst, no matter how it happens.'

Rowan walked her to her car. 'You're sure you're okay?'

'I think it was just that on top of Stacey.' She couldn't tell him the truth.

He nodded. 'It sometimes happens that way. One bad job on its own you can manage, but two or three and suddenly your defences fall apart.'

She got in her car and closed the door. When she lowered the window, he leaned his broad hands on the sill.

'Call me if you need to talk,' he said. 'About this or anything.'

'Thanks,' she said, not wanting to look into his eyes, afraid of what he might see in hers.

He tapped the roof and stepped back, and she drove off. She headed home on autopilot, seeing but not seeing the cars and trucks around her, the on and off of their brake lights. When she pulled into the driveway she sat for a moment after turning off the engine, thinking about dealing with her mother, how she'd say she wasn't hungry and had a headache and was going to bed. But when she went inside, she found the house empty, the car gone from the garage, no note anywhere about where she was or when she'd be back.

It was good, she told herself, but as she took off her uniform and went to step into the shower she changed her mind. She dressed quickly in jeans and a shirt and went back out to her car, and drove to Liam's house.

TWENTY

Ella and Murray sat in their car, doors closed and windows up, Ella's mobile on speaker, to consult with Dennis about Marie.

'What did you say she does for work?' he asked when Ella had finished her summary.

'She told us she's a physiotherapist, based in Bankstown,' Murray said.

'Drop past on your way back here for the meeting,' Dennis said. 'See what you can find out.'

Ella ended the call, then looked across the grass at where Marie leaned against her car, watching the Crime Scene officers pack up in the late afternoon sun.

'What time do physios shut?' Murray said.

'Get going,' she said, bringing Google up on her phone. 'I'll find out where exactly in Bankstown it is.'

The physiotherapist clinic was fronted by glass sliding doors, the lower halves frosted, the upper bearing bright icons of enfolding arms and smiling faces as well as a list of staff's names, of which Marie's was the fourth. Both doors were locked and the clinic was dark.

'Damn,' Murray said. 'I told you we should've phoned.'

'I want to see their faces when we say her name,' Ella said. Asking questions on the phone gave the callee a buffer, made them bolder. She didn't want anyone feeling bold when she talked to them. 'They open at eight in the morning. We'll come back then.'

★

Abby opened the door, jiggling Lucy on her hip. 'Paris, hi. Liam's not home.'

'I know,' Paris said. It was his snooker night. 'Can I talk to you?'

'Sure. Come on in. You okay? You look like you've had a rough day.'

The sympathy in her voice made Paris want to cry. She ducked her head and blinked hard as she walked past her.

'Have you had dinner?' Abby said. 'I bet you haven't. I've got some quiche here. I'll go warm it up. Mind holding Lucy?'

She put the baby in Paris's lap and went into the kitchen. Lucy reached for a soft toy octopus and Paris walked it up her leg then dived it under her arm. Lucy laughed soundlessly, toothless mouth wide open. Paris put her face to the baby's fine hair. Abby hummed in the kitchen, and the house was warm and calm, and Paris missed Stacey with an ache like a tumour eating away her heart.

'Here you go.' Abby brought in a plate of quiche and salad and exchanged it for the baby.

'Thank you,' Paris said. 'Thank you for letting me come in, too. It's been an awful day. Nobody's home at my place.' Not that that was a bad thing.

'Something bad happened?'

'A man died. My first one.' She looked down at her plate.

'That would be terrible,' Abby said.

236

'I feel like I should've done more. The others said that's normal, but I wish Stacey was here to talk to about it.'

Abby gave her a sympathetic look over Lucy's head. 'I bet wherever she is she's wishing she could talk to you too.'

Paris had to turn her face to her plate again. She broke off a piece of quiche with her fork but didn't lift it to her mouth. 'I'm scared for her.'

'I know, sweetie,' Abby said. 'I can see it in your eyes. It's a terrible thing. I saw your uncle on a news update, he looked just as upset. He said the dog's gone missing too.'

It felt like the last straw. Paris burst into tears.

Abby hugged her, and Paris pressed her face into her shoulder and cried.

'It's okay,' Abby murmured. 'Everything will be okay.'

★

Ella and Murray struggled through peak-hour traffic and reached the office to find the other detectives gathered watching the news. Ella saw James Durham, filmed earlier on his front lawn, talking about Stacey and how their beloved dog was missing too, 'no doubt run away to try to find her'. Marie was visible in the background on the steps, then Ella and Murray came into view. A cheer went up, and Murray bowed.

Ella went to her desk, chewing the inside of her lip. A note stuck to her monitor asked her to call Anne Percy at Broken Hill again, and a small sealed cardboard box sat beside her keyboard. Her name and the office address were printed across the top.

'Where'd this come from?' she asked.

Turnbull looked over. 'Courier brought it.'

'From who?'

'Beats me.' Turnbull picked it up and shook it.

'Don't. Jesus. It could be anything.'

'You think someone wants to blow you up?'

'You're sure someone doesn't?'

He put it down and slit the tape with a ballpoint.

'At least put gloves on,' Ella said.

He lifted the flap with the point of the pen, then poked aside some crumpled newspaper. 'Holy hell.'

'What is it?' She leaned in close to see.

'A toe,' Turnbull said.

'Are you serious?' Murray said from across the room.

'Come and look if you don't believe me,' Turnbull said.

Ella stared into the box as the other detectives crowded around. The toe lay in a nest of newspaper, the nail neat and polished light pink, the skin smooth and unblemished except for what looked like tiny needle marks along the incision. The cut end had been wiped clean of blood, and the whitish joint in the dark red flesh looked like a tiny version of something you might see in a butcher's shop.

'Gross,' Murray said.

'No way that's real,' Sid Lawson said.

'Does it smell?' someone asked.

'Is there a note?'

'How about some elbow room?' Ella said.

She took gloves from her pocket and pulled them on, then bent back the flaps of the lid using only the corners. The newspaper was that morning's, and letters on the page directly under the toe were circled. They looked random but Ella felt sure that when the page was smoothed out the message would become clear. Clearer.

Photos were taken, the toe was lifted with tweezers onto a sterile sheet, and the page of newspaper underneath was carefully unfurled. The circled letters went down the page. Ella scribbled them out on a notepad.

'Now do you believe James is not telling the truth?' she read out.

'Okay,' Dennis said. 'We need to check the box and paper for prints and any other evidence. I'll have the toe taken to the morgue tonight so it can be properly refrigerated, and Marconi and Shakespeare, tomorrow see what the doc says. Whatever there is to know from it, we need to know. Lawson and Pilsiger, you'll trace the box. Couriers keep records so go get them. Where was it lodged, when and who by. Everything.'

They nodded.

Dennis looked around at the group. 'Let's get this meeting started.'

★

Abby left Paris to finish her cold quiche and stare at a cooking show on TV while she put Lucy to bed.

She came back twenty minutes later looking concerned, mobile in her hand. 'A friend just texted. One of her kids is sick and she needs someone to watch the others while she takes him to the after-hours doctor. Would you mind babysitting until Liam or I get back? Please?'

'Sure,' Paris said.

'Lucy shouldn't wake up, but if she does just pat her like you did before,' Abby said. 'I shouldn't be too late, but after the day you've had, feel free to lie down in Liam's room if you want. Or have a bath, whatever you like.'

'Thanks.' Being here was better than her own house, either empty or with her mother there.

Abby smiled at her. 'I should be thanking you. Take it easy. Put your feet up. Have a rest.'

A few minutes later, she went out the door with her bag over her shoulder and her keys jangling in her hand. Silence crept over the house. Paris used the remote to change channels, then turned the TV off. She checked the locks on the doors, looked in on Lucy, who was sleeping adorably, then went into the bathroom.

The bathtub was big and white. She found some lavender bubble bath and soon lay deep in hot water and foam. Lucy's bath toys hung in a bag on the tiled wall and she took out a little yellow rubber boat and floated it on the surface. She didn't want to think about Mr Leary but she couldn't stop her mind going back to him. She nudged the boat with her fingertips and told herself again that it had been a good death, that going in your sleep was really the most that anyone could wish for, but still the thought that she should have realised earlier, that he somehow might have been saveable despite the terminal cancer, kept intruding. She'd been holding his hand, for god's sake. Shouldn't she have felt something? Or was it possible that he'd died at the exact second she'd let go? Or that he'd gone the instant she saw he wasn't breathing?

There was a creak in the hallway beyond the closed door. Paris froze. Another creak. She'd heard that before, when she'd been here on the loo and someone had walked past.

'Liam?' she said. He must have come home and seen her car and worked out where she was. 'Liam. Stop being funny and get in here.'

Silence, then another quiet creak.

Paris held her breath, her skin goosepimpling under the water.

'Mr Leary?' she whispered.

No answer. No creaks. She had the strange sense of someone standing just outside the door, deciding whether or not to come in. She stared at the handle, her armpits prickling. It didn't turn, and after a minute there was another creak, further away this time, and then another even more distant.

Paris slid silently out of the water. She dragged her jeans and shirt on over her wet skin. She crept to the door. Listened. No sound, not even from the baby's room.

She eased it open and peered through the crack. The hallway was empty, the light burning overhead, no sound, no shadows. But she couldn't shake the feeling that there was someone else in the house, holding their breath, waiting, and she looked back into the bathroom for something to use as a weapon.

TWENTY-ONE

Wilson Turnbull was talking about the non-folding bike they'd dragged out of the river, and Ella was thinking about the toe, when her phone buzzed with a text.

'It's from Stacey's phone,' she said.

The meeting fell silent.

'*That was a warning,*' she read out. '*James still isn't telling you the truth.*'

'Why do they always have to be so cryptic?' Murray said.

'*How. About. You. Tell. Me. Then.*' Ella spoke the words one by one as she typed them out, then sent the message. The reply came back, and she read it to the group. '*Find the truth, or ask him which part of her he wants next.*'

'Ugh,' someone said.

'*What is the truth?*' Ella sent back.

They waited, but there was no reply.

Ella looked at Dennis, who was on his own phone checking the triangulation. He hung up. 'Leichhardt, then it was turned off.'

'They never give us any information except to insist that James is lying,' Murray said.

'Maybe there isn't any to give,' Lawson said.

'Or maybe there is but they don't know what it is,' Pilsiger put in.

'Why kidnap a woman and say it's because of what her husband's done when you don't know it for sure?' Paul Li asked.

Dennis said, 'Perhaps they don't know the details.'

Ella said, 'Or perhaps the whole thing is just to jerk us around.'

She spent the remainder of the meeting with one eye on her phone, but nobody texted her. Afterwards, she went back to her desk, tired from the day and all the mental running around.

'Going out tonight?' Murray asked, collecting his things.

'Home to peace and quiet.' Her gaze kept wandering to the note stuck to her monitor. 'You?'

'Going over our vows and speeches and so on.' He pulled on his jacket. 'Afterwards I'm taking her out for a fancy dinner. Our last as an engaged couple. It's a surprise.'

'Sounds romantic,' she said.

He smiled. 'See you in the morning.'

'Bye.' She waited until he'd left, then dialled Percy's number.

'Hey there,' Anne Percy said. 'I found Angus Wylie.'

★

Paris whirled in fright at the sound of the key in the front door lock, then felt embarrassed when Abby stepped in and looked at her two-handed grip on the carving knife. 'Problem?'

'I was in the bath and thought I heard someone walking down the hall,' Paris said.

'Really?' Abby put down her keys and her bag.

'You know how the floor creaks there underfoot?' Paris went on. 'I've checked all over – Lucy hasn't woken up – but I still have this weird feeling that someone's here.'

'The resident ghost perhaps?'

'I'm not joking,' Paris said.

'Neither am I.' Abby headed for Lucy's room and peeked in. 'I've heard and felt things too. Sometimes I think I hear a cough or a sneeze.'

'Seriously?'

'Seriously.'

Paris couldn't help glancing over her shoulder.

'Nothing bad's ever happened,' Abby said. 'It feels creepy, but I tell myself it's whoever lived here before just coming to say hello.'

'That freaks me out.'

'It did me too at first,' Abby said. She lifted the knife from Paris's hand with a smile. In the kitchen, she replaced it in the drawer, then looked at the toilet brush on the floor.

'It was my first version of a weapon,' Paris said, and took it back to the bathroom.

'Have you heard from Liam?' Abby asked.

'I didn't call him. I thought I'd let him have a peaceful night without me hassling him.'

'Don't think like that. He's your boyfriend. If he was upset, you'd want to know, right? You have to hold him to the same standard, expect the same response. A relationship has two parts.'

'I know,' Paris said. 'I guess I meant I didn't feel like it.'

Abby smiled. 'Then that's fine.'

'How's your friend and her kid?'

'Oh, they're fine. It was no big deal in the end.' She stopped, tilting her head. 'Did you hear that?'

'No,' Paris said. The house was silent.

'There it was again.'

Paris couldn't hear a thing. She shook her head.

'The floor creaking again,' Abby said. 'Whoever it is just checking us out.'

The hair on the back of Paris's neck stood up. 'I think I'd better go home.'

'It's nothing to be scared of, but I understand.' Abby followed her to the door. 'You'll be okay? After your bad day, I mean?'

'I probably just need a good sleep,' Paris said. 'Thanks for dinner and everything.'

'Any time.' Abby hesitated. 'Your aunt's tough, you know. I'm sure she's fine.'

Paris nodded, then got in her car and headed home, apprehensive of what she'd find there but too unnerved to stay.

What she found was her mother watching herself on television. 'You're just in time, they're playing it again,' Marie said.

Paris saw footage of James standing outside his house, of her mother in the background looking serious.

'Have they found her?'

'No,' her mother said, eyes still on the screen.

Paris knew it was silly to think Marie might've asked her where she'd been, but she couldn't help it, and couldn't help be disappointed when she didn't. *When will I learn?* 'I'm going to bed.'

'Huh?' her mother said in a distracted way, but Paris shut her door and didn't reply.

*

Megan and Simon had gone for dinner at the local club, so Rowan was putting Emelia to bed. She fought the covers, screeched in his face, and tried to climb out of the cot.

'Bed time,' he said.

'No!'

'Yes. Lie down. Close your eyes.'

'Another story!'

'I told you we'd have three, and that's what we've had. It's time for sleep.'

Emelia shrieked. She was overtired. She'd almost dozed off while eating dinner, and now had dark circles under her eyes and a fevered wildness to her thrashing. She threw herself down in the cot with a wail. When she pressed her face into the pillow, he heard someone knocking at the front door.

'Go to sleep,' he said, and patted Emelia's heaving back. 'Close your eyes, go to sleep.'

She sat up and glared at him. 'No!'

The knock at the door came again. He looked down at Emelia, wild-eyed and furious, then kissed her on the head and walked away. 'Good night,' he said, and closed the door against her screams.

The noise followed him to the front door. It was dark outside now, and he switched on the porch light, then looked through the peephole to see the female detective standing there alone.

★

'Have you found her?'

'Sorry, no.' Ella looked past Rowan into the lamplit house. A child was screaming upstairs. 'Emelia?'

He nodded. 'What can I do for you?'

'I'd like to talk to you about a couple of things,' she said.

By the time they were sitting in the lounge, Emelia's cries had slowed and quietened. Rowan looked anxious. Nervy. Ella took note.

'So,' she said. 'Two things. Number one, this is Angus's phone number.'

She put a piece of paper on the coffee table between them. Rowan stared at it.

'He's currently living in a caravan park near Broken Hill. He's been moving around, doing labouring work, fruit-picking, whatever's happening. I found a police officer out there who recognised his name, and she tracked him down.'

Rowan moistened his lips. 'He's okay?'

'Apparently. The officer said he asked if you'd call him.'

Rowan looked away, his eyes shiny with tears.

'The second thing,' Ella said, 'is that I need you to tell me the truth. There's something we're missing in this case, and I can't put it together until I know the facts about what's going on.'

He didn't answer, but she saw his eyes go back to the piece of paper.

She said, 'At the hospital today you almost let something slip. I know you know something about what's going on, and I need to know what that is.'

He pressed his hands on his knees as if trying to dry damp palms. 'I don't know anything about what's going on now.'

She sensed a *but*. 'What did you almost say at the hospital?'

'You asked me why I noticed her car,' he said. 'I said I thought we could have coffee, but it wasn't just that.'

Now we're getting somewhere.

'I told you that I last saw her on Thursday morning, when I was finishing a shift and she was coming on.' He looked at the ceiling for a moment before going on. 'I didn't tell you that she and I had an argument then, and I made her cry.'

'What was the argument about?'

'Paris. I'd yelled at her for stuffing things up earlier in the week, and I guess she was upset but thought she was hiding it. That Thursday was the first time I'd seen Stacey since, and she waited until Paris had signed off and gone home, then pulled me aside for a chat.'

'What did she say?'

'That I was too hard on Paris, that everyone makes mistakes and I should encourage her instead of shouting at her. I said I encouraged her all the time, that was practically all I did. I said maybe she needed shouting at as a bit of a wake-up call. Stacey was defensive and protective. I tried to point that out, but she denied it and got angrier. I said she wouldn't feel that way if Paris was just some trainee and not her niece, and she denied that too. In the end I said she should be more professional, she

246

was acting more like Paris's mother than someone senior in the job, and she should think twice before coming to me about that sort of thing again.'

His eyes were distant and he looked like he was reliving the moment. Ella didn't speak.

'She burst into tears and ran into the women's locker room,' he said. 'I didn't try to talk to her or get her to come out. I was too angry. So I left, and we had no contact over the weekend. I thought about texting her, but to be honest I felt she should approach me. But by Monday I was regretting it all, and when I saw her car I thought we could have coffee together and talk, and I could say sorry.'

'Why didn't you tell us this before?'

'I was embarrassed and I couldn't see how it was relevant,' he said, looking ashamed.

'Why do you think she reacted that way?' Ella asked. 'Was it because you were arguing?'

He shook his head. 'I've seen her blue with the best of them. She's strong, she doesn't cry, she doesn't take a backward step if she thinks she's in the right. She thought that on Thursday too, I could see it in her eyes, so when she started crying I was completely stunned.'

Ella sat back. Stacey fell apart over Paris being reprimanded, over a young couple's miscarriage, and came close for no apparent reason at the dentist, yet she never mentioned any problem to her friends.

What was going on?

★

Rowan paced the lounge room, his mobile and the scrap of paper in his hand. Marconi had left five minutes before. Emelia was sound asleep, Simon and Megan were still out, and the house was quiet. He could feel his heart thudding against his ribs. Five years. Almost six. He tried to picture Angus's face with a few lines, skin tanned from the sun, a laconic smile. Five years.

His mobile buzzed and he jumped. Imogen, inviting him to brunch in the morning. He'd reply later. He picked up the paper, tapped out the numbers, and pressed to call. The phone rang in his ear.

'Hello?'

'Angus?'

'Dad, hey.'

Rowan squeezed his eyes shut. 'How are you?'

'Pretty good. How're you? And Mum?'

'I'm okay,' Rowan said. 'I'm good. I'm glad to hear your voice. We've missed you a lot.'

'I've missed you guys too. How's Simey?'

'He's great,' Rowan said. 'But, Angus, mate, listen. Your mum –'

'Is she there? Can you go on speaker? I've got some news to tell you both.'

'Your mum died,' Rowan said. 'She had cancer. It happened two years ago.'

Silence.

'I'm so sorry,' Rowan said. 'I wanted to tell you. I sent letters to the post offices in the places where your postcards came from, but they got returned.'

'I should've rung,' Angus said in a cracked voice.

'I'm sorry to tell you like this.' He heard a key in the front door, then Simon's and Megan's voices. He wiped his eyes quickly. 'Listen, Simon's just come home. Hold on.'

He switched the phone to speaker and motioned for them to join him.

'Sime?' Angus said.

'Angus? Holy shit!' Simon grabbed the phone. 'Where you been, man? I was afraid you were dead.'

'Yeah, right, and sending postcards from the grave.' Rowan could hear that he was pushing down the grief.

'Well, between each one,' Simon said. 'Hey, guess what? I'm a daddy.'

'Me too,' Angus said. 'A boy. Eight months. Toby.'

'Mine's two. Emelia. And this is my girlfriend, Megan.'

'Hi,' Megan said.

Rowan had to leave the room. His longing for Jen at that moment was as bad as it had ever been, and as his sons' happy voices rang out he stood in the kitchen wet-eyed and alone.

TWENTY-TWO

At the morgue the next morning Ella and Murray had to wait while one of the pathologists finished a post-mortem. They stood in the corridor, listening to water washing down the drains, the clatter of steel instruments, and someone whistling to a radio. Outside, it was a bright and sunny morning. Ella was always surprised when she left the morgue and found anything but rain and gloom.

'I talked to Rowan Wylie last night,' she told Murray, and filled him in about Rowan's son and what Rowan had said about arguing with Stacey.

'We should've been doing that together, this morning,' Murray said.

'I made an executive decision. Then I went home and tried to map it all out. There's something we can't see, I'm sure of it.'

'There's always something we can't see. Once we see it, the case is solved. Seriously though, you should've waited for me.'

She shrugged. 'How was the dinner?'

'Excellent. Nat was thrilled. Made her cry.'

'You two,' Ella said. 'And the forecast?'

'Steady at five.'

They grinned at each other.

The pathologist came out, safety glasses still in place, drying his hands with a paper towel. 'Right. You're here about the toe, correct?'

Ella nodded. The doctor said something to a tech, who fetched it and handed it over.

'Interesting.' The pathologist took it back inside the room and they followed.

Two naked bodies, both male, lay on the steel tables, one about twenty, the other much older with a grizzled beard. Gowned and goggled staff were stitching up their chests.

The pathologist held the bagged toe under a bright light, turning it this way and that. 'Hmm. Sent to you in the post, you said?'

'By courier, but to me, yes,' Ella said.

He looked at her over his glasses. 'Lucky you.'

'Yeah, you'd think it was her birthday,' Murray said.

The pathologist said, 'I'll need to examine it more closely to be more specific, but I can tell you a couple of things right now. First, it looks to me like the fifth, or little, toe of the left foot of a white adult female. Secondly, the cut is through the middle of the joint and quite precise. No obvious hacking, a neat slice: probably done with a scalpel or similar, and by someone who hasn't necessarily done it before but was reasonably confident about what they were doing. Third, see these puncture marks here? They're caused by a fine-gauge needle, most likely a twenty-five, most likely for the purpose of delivering local anaesthetic. The spacing is slightly less than what a GP might use when preparing an area for an excision, so again, done by someone who hasn't necessarily done this before but is fairly confident. And who also wanted to make sure the tissue was, as far as possible, anaesthetised.'

'They'll cut off her toe but they don't want her to feel it?' Murray said. 'What sort of kidnappers are these?'

Ella was asking herself the same question.

★

Paris woke to the sound of knocking on her bedroom door.

'I'm sleeping,' she shouted.

'I need your help,' Marie said.

'I have nightshift tonight. I need to sleep.'

'Five minutes.'

Paris glared at the ceiling. 'For what?'

'To help me.'

She threw back the quilt and got up. If she refused, there'd be noise all day, but it'd been nice being asleep and not thinking about Mr Leary. She'd been so exhausted last night she hadn't even dreamed. Now she was awake, and it was all going around in her head again, and she'd be lucky to get back to sleep later at all, let alone into a deep and peaceful one.

She threw open the door. Her mother stood there, sipping coffee. Paris looked around. 'So what is it?'

'Lounge room.'

She went down to find one of the armchairs stuck in the doorway. 'Where in god's name are you moving it to now?'

'My room,' Marie said. 'I need a space of my own.'

'It's not going to fit.'

'I've already moved the bed over.'

'I mean through here.' Paris pushed at the chair. It didn't budge.

'It went in,' Marie said. 'It has to come out.'

'Yeah, well, Dad probably took the door off and used a couple of hefty mates,' Paris said.

Marie harrumphed. 'So take the door off if you're so smart.'

'I can't now you've jammed it in.' Paris climbed over the chair and tried to tug it free. 'Push, will you?'

Marie pushed while Paris pulled.

'How the hell did you get it in so tight?' Paris said, cheek on the upholstery.

'Don't damage the paint.'

Paris straightened. 'This isn't going to work. I'll get Liam to come around sometime and he can help.'

'It's not staying stuck here until then.'

'It's going to have to.'

'No,' Marie said. 'I got it this far on my own, so I can't see why between us we can't get it all the way.'

'It doesn't fit.'

'We just have to find the right angle.' Marie tugged. Her narrow hands looked as useless as paws on the chair's big rolled arm.

'This is insane,' Paris said. 'I'm going back to bed.'

'We can't just leave it. I can't live with this thing stuck here.'

'Should've thought of that before you started yet another pointless rearrange.' Paris climbed back over the chair. 'I mean, why can't you just sit on your bed?'

'It's called a parent's retreat,' Marie snapped. 'And I need one.'

'Retreat from what? The entire house is yours. You even come into my room whenever you like and without knocking.'

'Pay half the mortgage and then you get your own space.'

'I pay more than enough board for one little room.'

'Just help me,' Marie said.

'No. I need to go back to bed.'

'You just woke up.'

Paris laughed, a hollow sound. 'It's true what they told me when I joined the job. Only people who've worked nightshift understand not to disturb you in the day.'

'The job,' Marie said, mocking. 'You're all so precious.'

'Yeah, we are,' Paris sniped. 'We're family too. You know what they asked when I went to work yesterday morning? Whether I was okay. You haven't asked me that once.'

'You haven't asked me, and she's my sister,' Marie snapped.

'I have so. I asked you yesterday.' Paris wasn't certain she had. But she must have, surely.

'Would you just help me move this thing?' Marie said.

'If Dad and his mates got it in there, it's going to take more than you and me to get it out.'

'Your father had nothing to do with it. Left me to deal with it all. Went off working.'

'He did not,' Paris said.

'When we moved in here, you were seven and he was driving interstate,' Marie said. 'I packed the old house myself, moved it all over myself, and unpacked it, guess what, by myself.'

'So it wasn't Dad but a couple of removalists,' Paris said. 'Whatever.'

'Yes,' Marie went on, as if she hadn't spoken, 'because your sainted father had other priorities.'

'Oh, like paying the mortgage? Putting petrol in the car and food on the table?'

'Paying for your private school, more like,' Marie said. 'He could've worked locally, could've been around more, but he had to do long-haul. Had to make that bit more money just for the damned school fees.'

'Oh yeah, it's all my fault,' Paris said. 'It all comes down to me. I made him go out driving, I made him crash and die. Yeah, I did it. Blame me.'

Marie tugged at the chair without answering.

Paris stared at her. 'You do, don't you? You do blame me.'

'Don't be ridiculous,' Marie said. 'Talk about self-centred. Why's it always have to be about you? Your sleep. Your job. You think there's nobody else in the world? Only you, and what you think and feel?' She let go of the chair. 'Oh, forget it. Forget this whole thing. Don't bother getting Liam over. I'll deal with it, I'll manage by myself, just as I always do. By myself. Talk about being your father's daughter.'

Paris stormed into her room and slammed the door. She scowled at her bed. She'd never get to sleep now. Not here anyway.

She stuffed a clean uniform into a bag and stomped back out. 'Enjoy your retreat.'

'Where are you going?'

'What do you care?'

She got in her car and drove away, glancing back once and seeing that her mother was nowhere in sight.

★

A woman in a white polo shirt with a navy Alice band in her hair looked up over the physiotherapy clinic's desk and smiled. 'Good morning. How can I help you?'

Ella held up her badge. 'Detectives Marconi and Shakespeare, New South Wales Police. Is the owner or manager here?'

The woman's smile wavered. 'Just a moment.'

She disappeared down a corridor. Murray fiddled with a plastic spine on the desk and Ella tried to sort out her thoughts. The anaesthetised toe, the breaking down in tears, the text messages. She felt that they all added up to mean something, but she couldn't see what.

The woman came back with a sandy-haired man of about forty-five, wearing an identical white polo and navy pants.

He put out his hand. 'Gerald Bobbin, owner and physio. How can I help?'

His grip was firm, his skin soft. Behind his gold-framed glasses his eyes were nervous.

Ella said, 'Is there somewhere we can talk?'

Bobbin's office was neat and small. He sat behind his desk and clasped his hands on the top. Ella and Murray sat in the ergonomic chairs across from him.

'We have a couple of questions about Marie Kennedy,' Ella said.

'Oh,' he said. 'Ah. Because of what's happened to her sister?'

Ella noticed his tone. 'What is she like as an employee?'

'Fine,' he said, too quickly.

'There's some problem with her?'

'No. Not really.'

She and Murray waited.

Bobbin sighed and glanced out the window. 'Marie is an excellent physiotherapist, let me say that right upfront. But we did recently have an issue.'

'Regarding?' Murray said.

Bobbin blushed deep red. Ella could see the colour climb right up his scalp through his sandy hair.

'Marie made, uh, advances towards me,' he said.

'Unwelcome, I presume?' Murray said.

'Of course. And very firmly rejected. My wife, Neroli, on reception out there, can attest to that.'

'She saw it?' Ella asked.

'She walked in when Marie was, uh, touching my person.' The blush grew more intense.

'When was this?'

'A fortnight ago. Things have been awkward since, so in a way I was pleased when she asked to take leave. Not that I'm pleased about her sister, I didn't mean that. It's terrible. I hope you find her.'

Ella said, 'Did she say anything before you rebuffed her?'

'She said that, uh, she thought I was very handsome, and that she had certain feelings towards me that she felt it was time she acted upon.' He pushed his glasses further up his nose. Ella thought she detected a slight sheen of sweat. 'She said she was happy for it to be purely physical, that as physiotherapists we know the value of touch and that she was badly in need of some. She grabbed me by the, uh, in the region of my trousers, and that's when Neroli – thankfully – walked in.'

'Okay,' Ella said. 'And after?'

Bobbin shook his head. 'She was very quiet. I said that it was unacceptable, that I'm her employer and a very happily married man. She mumbled an apology and left, then came in the next day as if nothing was wrong.' He pushed his glasses up again.

'Have there ever been complaints from other staff, or clients?' Ella said.

'No, nothing. Thank goodness. Is this relevant to your case?'

'We were just after some background,' Ella said. 'Apart from that incident, have there been any other issues with Marie?'

'Personality-wise she can be intense, but I've always been satisfied with her work.' He blinked, owlish. 'How is she managing?'

'She's managing all right,' Ella said, thinking of how she was stroking James's hair. 'Thank you for your time.'

Outside, Murray said, 'Do you think Marie has motive?'

'She used to go out with James Durham, she's keen for male company, she doesn't seem a happy woman. But is that enough to want to hurt her sister? And then with all the texts and so on?' The knot of thoughts in Ella's mind was tighter than ever.

'Being a physio she'd know enough about anatomy to cut the toe off,' Murray said. 'And there's the weird bleach cleaning.'

'The toe was anaesthetised before it was cut off. If Marie wanted to hurt Stacey, why not make her suffer?'

'Maybe her target's someone else,' Murray said. 'Maybe she wants to hurt James.'

'Not judging by the look in her eyes when I interrupted them on the lounge.' Her phone rang in her pocket. She saw the office number on the screen and answered. 'Tell me you have something good.'

'The Durhams' other neighbours checked in,' Dennis said, 'They've been away, and called in this morning. They heard a loud argument Wednesday night last week in the Durham house. An argument bordering on screaming, and between two women.'

'Stacey and Marie, surely,' Ella said, excitement building. 'Time to bring her in for a formal interview?'

Dennis said, 'I've just sent someone to get her.'

★

Paris couldn't think where she was when she woke up, then remembered she'd knocked timidly on Abby's door to ask if she could sleep there for a couple of hours. She'd been welcomed and hugged, then got into Liam's rumpled bed and snuggled down with her head sandwiched between two pillows.

She didn't think she'd actually slept, dozed maybe, but not for long, and now she could smell baking. It could be good, helping out in the kitchen – it was easier to talk while your hands were busy, while your eyes were on a task.

'Well, hello,' Abby said, when Paris walked into the kitchen. 'You sure you got enough sleep?'

'I never sleep much before nights.'

The kitchen smelled of sweet biscuits and the oven warmed the air. Lucy kicked in a bouncer suspended from the doorway. Paris knelt by her and fingered her little hand. Lucy smiled, all gums. Abby rolled a wooden pin across a sheet of cinnamon-coloured dough, then pressed a star-shaped cutter into it.

'Can I help?' Paris asked.

'Sure.' She nodded to a bowl. 'Roll out that next batch.'

Paris washed, dried and floured her hands, and got stuck in. There was so much that she wanted to say, about her mother, about Stacey, about Mr Leary. About work. It made her head hurt. She didn't know where to begin.

'Any news on your aunt?' Abby said, as if sensing her problem.

'Not that I've heard.'

'How's your mum going?'

'Going's the right word.' The dough was warm and pliable in her hands. She pressed it down hard on the benchtop.

'She's out a lot?'

'Either that or giving me a hard time,' Paris said. 'She's constantly zipping off to James and Stacey's. I don't even know if he's home half the time she goes there. Then she comes back and hassles me about every little thing.'

'I guess she's worried about her,' Abby said.

Paris pressed the pin onto the dough and started rolling it out. 'We all are.'

Abby slid a tray of biscuits into the oven. 'I'm sure it'll all work out.'

Paris was surprised by the platitude, but before she could say anything the doorbell rang. Abby wiped her hands on a tea towel and went to answer.

Paris listened, and heard a familiar voice. She went to the doorway. 'Uncle James?'

'Oh, hi,' James said. He looked exhausted, dark stubble on his cheeks, his eyes tired. 'How are you, Paris?'

'Is there any news?'

'No. I'm just following up with the people Stacey knows, seeing if I can find out anything more.'

'Come on in,' Abby said.

He sat at the kitchen table. Abby made him a hot sweet tea and served it up with a plate of warm biscuits. Paris finished rolling and cutting her dough, then sat opposite him.

'How do I look?' he asked her. 'Like a zombie, right?'

'Not that bad.'

'I can't sleep,' he said. 'Your wife's missing, you can't sleep, this is how you look.'

'It must be terrible,' Abby said.

'It is. Horrendous.' He curled his hands around his cup. 'I'm sorry I haven't made an effort to meet you before now. You and Stacey went to school together, right?'

'Many years ago.'

'And met up at the reunion last year,' James said. 'I remember her coming home and saying what a small world it is, that the son of one of her old schoolfriends ends up with our niece.' He smiled at Paris.

Abby nodded. 'We had good intentions of staying in touch. I don't know what happened.'

'Time goes by, life goes on,' James said. He paused and stared at her. 'Huh. You looked really familiar there for a second.'

'Did I?' she said.

He nodded, wrinkling his forehead. 'I can't think from where though. Paris, we haven't all been at one of your mother's barbecues, have we?'

'No,' Paris said, confused.

'Wait,' James said, 'I know. I know where I've seen someone who looks like you. You're not going to believe it, and it's the strangest thing, but the cops showed me this picture of this person on CCTV, riding a pushbike, and it really could be you. Or you could be it, or whatever I'm trying to say.' He smiled. 'Like I said, strange, huh?'

'They showed me the same picture and asked me the same thing,' Abby said. 'I said sure we're alike, if you count two people who are white and of average height and build as being alike.'

Paris looked at James, puzzled. 'What are you saying?'

'Just how it's odd that this person looked like her,' he said. 'I mean, to the degree that I had this kind of deja vu moment sitting here.'

'Deja vu's an odd thing all right,' Abby said, and raised her cup to her lips.

'I guess so,' James said. 'May I use your bathroom?'

'It's along the hall,' Abby said.

He went out of the room.

'That was weird,' Paris said.

'Desperate people clutch at straws,' Abby said. 'They see things where there's nothing to be seen.'

'But it doesn't bother you, him saying that?'

Abby shrugged. 'Why would it?'

'Because he's sort of suggesting you had something to do with it, isn't he?'

'You're Stacey's niece. Does it bother you?'

'No, because I don't think it's true.'

'And that's why it doesn't bother me.'

Paris heard the toilet flush, then James came back in. He crouched in front of Lucy in her bouncer.

'Now here's a cheeky-looking youngster,' he said. 'I love babies. Any chance of a cuddle?'

'She's due for her nap soon,' Abby said. 'Cuddles from strangers get her too wound up to sleep.'

James reached out and tickled Lucy's chin. 'Well, maybe one day I won't be a stranger any more, will I, little darlin'?'

'Maybe you won't,' Abby said.

Paris looked from one to the other. She felt like there was a subtext here she couldn't read. She watched James say he better be going, and followed as Abby walked him to the door. There was a strange moment when they looked at each other, Abby inside the house and James out, then James walked off down the driveway without even saying goodbye to her.

Abby shut the door. She looked distracted.

'That was weird,' Paris said.

'Hm?' Abby didn't wait for an answer. 'I have to go out. I just remembered.'

'Do you want me to stay and mind Lucy? While she has her sleep?'

Abby focused on her. 'No, I'll take Lucy with me. She can nap in the car.'

Paris hesitated, then said, 'Can I come?'

A thought flashed behind Abby's eyes, then she said, 'Sure. Yes. Yes, of course you can come.'

TWENTY-THREE

'Did they find Marie?' Ella asked Dennis when they got back to the office.

He nodded. 'She's waiting in interview one.'

Ella was keen to talk to Marie, to dig a little deeper. In the same way that talking face to face was better than on the phone, talking in a stark interview room when the interviewee had come in through the busy office, seen everyone hard at work, and finally recognised themselves to be caught deep in the workings of an investigation could get results like nothing else. 'Let's do this.'

Marie Kennedy sat with her arms folded, the table in front of her bare. 'Have you found her?' she said the instant they walked in.

'Sorry, no,' Ella said. 'Can I get you a coffee? Water?'

'No, thank you.' Her voice was clipped, her face expressionless.

Ella and Murray sat side by side, Ella placing a manila folder on the table. The pages inside were blank, a wad pulled from the stores cupboard for effect, but Marie didn't even glance at it.

'We just spoke with your boss,' Ella said. 'Do you want to tell us what happened there?'

'No,' Marie said.

'It's no big drama,' Ella said. 'He was concerned, obviously, but there's no law against it.'

'Yes, it's a big joke to you, isn't it? Is this about Stacey or not? That's what I was told.'

'Have you heard from her?' Murray asked.

'No. Don't you think I would've said something?' Marie pulled a face. 'Look, if this isn't about Stacey, I have things to do.'

'Here's the thing,' Ella said. 'Your behaviour is far from what we'd expect from someone whose sister is missing with a lot of blood left behind. It's obvious that you know something, either about what's happened, or about what's really going on underneath what we can see. It's time to tell the truth.'

'It's "obvious"?' Marie glared. 'Because I haven't fallen in a heap you think I don't care about my sister and must've had something to do with it?'

'You have to admit your behaviour is unusual,' Murray said.

'Because I support my brother-in-law? Because I clean their house? You'd prefer he was alone and living in a pigsty?'

'Scrubbing with bleach for over half an hour is more than what most people would call cleaning,' he said.

'You people and your judgements,' Marie snapped. 'Have you had a sister go missing? Then how can you know how you'd react? Ridiculous to say something like that.'

She was building up a good head of steam. Ella was pleased. Angry people said stuff they didn't always intend to.

'Ridiculous,' Marie said again. 'A person can't be who she is, can't do what she needs to do to keep herself going and keep her own mental strength up, without the police immediately thinking she did it. Oh, she's not sobbing every minute of the day, she must be guilty. Oh, look at her, being strong for the people around her, she must have something to hide. In a situation like this someone has to stay strong, and here it's me. Nobody notices, they take it for granted, except of course you lot, who think I did something horrible to my own sister.'

'Who's taking you for granted?' Ella asked. 'James?'

'Of course not. How can he be expected to do anything but worry?'

'Paris?' Ella said.

Marie's jaw tightened. 'You've met her. She's a silly girl. She doesn't know how good she's got it.'

'She wouldn't understand how it feels to be missing a sister either,' Murray said.

'Exactly,' Marie said. 'It's all about her. She was upset this morning because I hadn't asked her how she was feeling. Ha.'

'You had an argument?' Ella asked, thinking ahead.

'Nothing unusual,' Marie said. 'She might not technically be a teenager any more but it'll be some time before she stops acting like one.'

Ella said, 'You argue with Stacey too, don't you?'

'You asked me that yesterday. Yes. Siblings do.'

'But you wouldn't tell me what you argue about.'

'Sibling issues. My goodness, is this what you do all day? Pester people with pointless questions?'

'I think you went to Stacey's house on Saturday night because you wanted to talk to her,' Ella said. 'I think the two of you had an argument during the week, it got out of hand and things were said, and you wanted to patch things up.'

Marie looked at her. 'That's what you think, is it?'

'It is,' Ella said.

'Well, more fool you. If anyone should apologise it's her. Not that she ever would, or ever has. Always the favourite, since the day she was born.'

Ella imagined four-year-old Marie, dismayed by the new baby and its noise and the way it sucked up attention. 'You weren't happy when she got together with James, when they got married, were you?'

'She didn't like him when we were going out,' Marie said. 'She used to laugh at his acne, hang around and be a pest. Then she turns up with him all handsome and with money and everything, and says to me, "Remember this face?" Like it's a joke that once he was with me and now he's with her.' Her hands were fists on the table top. 'The wedding was gorgeous. Paris was bridesmaid, lanky awkward teenager that she was. Stacey fussed and fussed over Paris's dress, told her how lovely she looked and everything. I tried to tell her it's not the wedding that counts, it's the marriage afterwards. She said yeah yeah, like she knew it all already. Like because my husband was dead and hers was brand new, she had it better than me. And she did. She does.'

Ella saw it all in a flash. 'That should be your life.'

'Paul and I were going to sell the house and caravan around the country, settle in the place we liked best. The two of us. Paris accused me this morning of blaming her for his death, and I told her that was a stupid thing to say, but I do. God help me, I do. He was the one who wanted her in the first place, he insisted on the private school, he had to do the long-hauls that brought in the money. I said we could get by and there was nothing wrong with public schools, but he insisted. For her. And now.' She spread her empty hands. 'Now what have I got?'

'Is that one of the issues you argued with Stacey about?' Ella said. 'That she has a husband and you don't?'

'She told me once that if I wasn't enough without a man, I'd never be enough with one. I know she was upset but I couldn't believe she could say that.'

'When was that, and why was she upset?' Murray asked.

'Two years ago. She'd had a miscarriage. It was very early. I was kind, but I said these things were usually for the best, and she still had James, that she was lucky really.'

Ella thought Marie had been lucky not to get a punch in the mouth.

265

'She said she thought James had caused the miscarriage,' Marie went on. 'I said he should get checked at the doctor's then, but she said it wasn't that. She said she'd told him about being pregnant and even though he'd said he was happy she didn't really think he was, and then after the miscarriage he hugged her and said now they could be normal again, just the two of them.'

'What did she think he'd done?' Ella asked.

'I don't know. I said it was silly to think that, and she started screaming at me and made me go home. We didn't talk about it again.'

'And that was two years ago.' Ella's mind was ticking. 'You were heard arguing at her house on Wednesday. What was that about?'

Marie huffed. 'I'd told her what had happened at work. It was stupid to say anything, but I did. We'd been talking about Paris's birthday, again, and quite frankly I was sick of the subject. I said, how about we talk like two grown-ups, talk about our lives or our jobs or whatever. She had this look on her face and said, with this attitude, okay then, how's your job? As if my job means nothing. And I felt like slapping her, and next thing I was telling her. She was all incredulous, but I could tell she was laughing inside, like I was pathetic and she was so great and had it all together. I said she didn't understand, she had a husband, she didn't know how it felt. To not have someone there. You miss the physical contact, arms around you, the flesh and muscles and the bones underneath.' She looked at the table. 'It's hard to explain. She didn't even try to understand. She had this look on her face and was saying, but you have Paris, you have Paris. I said kids weren't all they're cracked up to be. She said how could I say such a thing, that didn't I think kids were the reason we're all alive? And I was so angry about everything that I said that same thing back to her: that if a person wasn't enough without a child, they'd never be enough with one.' She wiped her eyes. 'I guess by that time we were yelling, but she suddenly burst into tears. I was so angry over the whole situation that I got up and left.'

It was eerily close to Rowan's description of his argument with Stacey and her reaction then. Ella frowned, thinking it through.

'Where was James when all this was going on?' Murray was saying.

'He was working late or something, I don't know.' Marie rubbed her face.

'When did you next speak to her?'

'Friday she sent me a text, said we could talk about the party on the weekend maybe? I said yes, that'd be great. I dropped in on Saturday but she wasn't home and didn't reply to my text. Then we talked Sunday afternoon as if nothing had happened. That's what happens when we argue – after a couple of days things blow over.'

A thought dawned out of the blue in Ella's mind, and she gripped Murray's arm. 'We have to talk to Callum.'

★

Rowan got to the cafe before Imogen this time, and had just sat down when she came in. 'It's great to see you.'

She smiled. 'It's great to see you too.'

They hugged, and it felt good. They sat down and started talking. It was easy this time, and Rowan found himself telling her about the detective's visit and his phone call to Angus.

'So did Angus say why he went, or why he stayed away?' she asked.

'He told Simon that at first he simply wanted to go, wanted to be out on his own with no family connections,' Rowan said. 'But he felt a bit bad because he knew we'd worry, so he sent the postcards to let us know he was okay. He said he never thought that we mightn't be. And since his son was born he's been feeling like getting in touch, so when the police officer turned up he said all right, we could call.'

'And now you're a grandfather of two,' Imogen said.

He showed her the photo that Angus had texted him last night, the round sleeping face, the shock of dark hair. 'He's got Emelia's mouth.'

'Listen to you.' She grinned at him.

The waitress came over and they ordered, then Rowan put his phone down.

'How about Stacey?' Imogen asked. 'Has there been any news there?'

'Nothing,' he said.

'I saw her husband on the news again last night, talking about how now their dog's run away too. He looks devastated about the whole thing. Have you talked to him much?'

'Not really,' Rowan said. 'He doesn't answer the phone. I've left a couple of messages, and he's called me back once. It's taken over his life.'

'Understandable.'

'Of course.'

The waitress brought their food and coffee. Rowan picked up his cutlery, then his phone rang. The screen said the number was blocked. He hesitated.

Imogen said, 'I don't mind if you answer.'

He picked it up. 'This is Rowan.'

'It's me,' Stacey whispered. 'Can you talk?'

Rowan struggled to speak. 'Are you okay?'

'I'm all right. I only have a minute. Listen.'

'Where are you? Everyone's worried sick.'

'You have to listen,' she said. 'Gomez didn't run away. He'll be at a pound somewhere. He might look different. You have to find him.'

'What?' Rowan said. Imogen was staring at him.

'Keep him at your place. It's the only way he'll be safe.'

'What's going on?'

'Please, just do it.' Her whisper was urgent. 'I don't have much time. Please find him.'

'But —'

'Say you will. Promise me.'

'The police are looking for you. All that blood –'

'Promise,' she hissed.

'I promise,' he said. 'But you need to tell the police where you are. Or tell me and I'll tell them.'

'No. You can't let anyone know I called. If it gets out –' There was a sound in her background. 'I have to go. Don't tell anyone.'

The line went dead. Rowan lowered the phone to the table, his gaze on his plate.

'Who was that?' Imogen asked.

Stacey had said not to tell anyone. She'd sounded frightened. He thought over what he'd said, what Imogen had heard.

He raised his eyes to hers. 'I can't tell you.'

She frowned. 'From what you said –'

'I know, but I was asked not to tell anyone.'

Imogen's frown deepened. 'She asked you that? Why?'

Rowan poked the congealed egg with his fork, then laid it down. 'I have to go.'

'Where?'

'To find a dog.'

Imogen looked at him for a moment. 'Can I come?'

★

Rowan had never thought about how many council pounds were dotted across the city. He started with the one closest to Stacey and James's house in Haberfield, then worked his way outwards, using Google Maps on his phone to guide him. At each, he asked about a small wire-haired dog, mostly brown, with dark eyes and a black nose, who'd come in yesterday or today. He'd seen a couple that barked and jumped at the wire in their pens just like Gomez would but were distinctly not him.

In the car heading to the next place, Imogen said, 'So you won't tell me, but I bet I can guess.'

He didn't look over, didn't say anything. Regretted, not for the first time, bringing her along. Why hadn't he just said no? He was so weak.

'Stacey asked you to find her dog, the one that her husband talked about on the news,' Imogen said. 'That's right, isn't it?'

'I was asked not to say,' he said, matter-of-fact.

'How come she can call you but not call the police?'

He turned on the radio. John Farnham filled the car briefly before Imogen reached over and turned it off.

'It makes you look dodgy,' she said.

'I'm not.'

'They already think you're up to something.'

'I'm not,' he said again.

'Don't you think you should tell them she rang you? I mean, what do you think is going on with her? How can she ask you to find her dog, but she can't tell you where she is or how to find her? It makes no sense.'

'She asked me to get her dog, and that's what I'm doing.'

'But what if that was a coded message or something? What if she was told by whoever's got her that she could ask you to find the dog but nothing else, but really she wants you to tell the cops?'

'You didn't hear her voice. It was like she only had a minute before someone came into the room.'

'But if she had access to a phone for just a minute, why not call the cops?'

'Look,' Rowan said, 'I don't know, okay? I don't know what's going on. And because of that, I'm going to do what she asked me, and that's to find the dog and not tell anyone.'

'You just told me.'

He turned sharply into the RSPCA car park and hit the brakes, pulled out his wallet and dropped a twenty in her lap. 'Get yourself a taxi back to the cafe if you disagree so much with what I'm doing.' He yanked the keys from the ignition and strode across the concrete to the front door without looking back.

★

270

The dog that jumped against the wire had clipped patches between areas of straggly hair, and his long eyebrows were gone, but Rowan said, 'It's him.'

'You're sure?' said the girl.

'Definitely.' Rowan squatted and put his fingers through the wire and the dog went into an ecstasy of wagging and leaping circles. 'Do you know how he got here?'

'A guy brought him in as a stray yesterday. Poor pup was unconscious, and the guy said he'd found him on the side of the road and thought he might've been hit by a car.'

'His hair was already like this?'

'Yep, and smeared with mud as well.'

'And was he hurt?'

'Not at all. The vet discovered he'd been overdosed on Valium. We gave him oxygen and looked after him and he woke up hours later.' She opened the pen and Gomez leapt into Rowan's arms. 'There's a fee to get him out.'

He looked down at the dog's sheared-off eyebrows, at the roughly clipped patches on his body. 'Who was the guy?'

'No idea.'

'Don't people have to leave details or anything?'

'He did, but when we tried the mobile number he'd left it was disconnected.'

In the office, Rowan sat with Gomez tense with excitement on his lap while the girl filled out forms and crunched his credit card. He wondered if Imogen was still in his car, if she was right.

A bit more chat, a liver treat for Gomez, then Rowan was walking out with the dog cradled in his arms. Imogen was gone, his car left unlocked. He put the dog in the back seat and got behind the wheel, trying to think clearly, and failing.

TWENTY-FOUR

Callum said, 'It's nice of you to drop by, but I'm too busy to stop for lunch today.'

'I have a question.' Ella followed him into the consulting room. 'It's work-related.'

'Is it now?' He sat on the edge of the desk and smiled at her. 'Come and whisper your work-related question in my ear.'

'Murray's here too. Gone to the bathroom,' she said.

Murray appeared in the doorway, drying his hands with paper towel. 'What did he say?'

'I haven't asked yet,' Ella said. 'Could a person take a litre and a half of blood from their own body?'

Callum said, 'As in . . .'

'As in out of their vein or whatever. A person familiar with blood and needles. Let's say, a paramedic.'

'I would say yes, with conditions.'

'Those being?'

'Can they manage themselves so they don't lose more than that? Can they replace that fluid, and do it without losing consciousness?' Callum said. 'Am I right in who I think you're thinking about?'

'Most likely,' she said. 'Could that person do all of those things?'

'I would imagine so. It'd take a long time to get that much blood out though. As an example, the blood bank only takes four hundred or so millilitres at a time, less if you're small, and that takes maybe ten minutes. Plus it'd start to clot immediately.'

'And the clots would then dry?'

'That starts to happen straight away,' he said. 'On the surface at least. Obviously.'

Some of the blood in the car had been still semi-liquid, some of the clots still wet.

'How does the blood bank avoid clots?' she asked.

'The equipment's treated with a substance, usually citrate or heparin, that inhibits the clotting factors in the blood. Otherwise, as soon as the blood comes into contact with plastic, or air, or pretty much anything, whammo, clotting begins.'

Ella nodded. 'A test of the blood would show that up?'

'Yep,' he said.

She took out her notebook. 'Spell citrate and that other one for me.'

He did so. 'Also, once having taken that blood out, the person would probably need intravenous fluids.'

'Which a paramedic could give to him or herself?'

'Shouldn't be hard at all,' Callum said. 'They'd be anaemic though, and have to eat a lot of iron-rich food or take iron tablets if they can't get a blood transfusion.'

'Anaemia would show up in any subsequent blood test or in any body part, right?' Murray asked.

'Yes,' Callum said.

'Could a paramedic get access to citrate and heparin?' Ella asked.

He glanced out the door. 'Let's ask one.'

'Ask about local anaesthetic too, and a scalpel. And twenty-five-gauge needles.'

Callum disappeared for a minute, then returned with a lanky paramedic. The young man's hair was blond and spiked up, and the name on his badge said Grant.

'Just a couple of questions,' Callum said. 'Could a paramedic get access to local anaesthetic, a scalpel, IV fluids and a giving set, and citrate and/or heparin?'

Grant blinked. 'Well, local we have on station, so no problems there. Same with IV fluids and giving sets, and twenty-five-gauge needles and the small syringes we use with them.'

'Do you need to log those things when you take them?' Ella asked.

'Nope, they're just there. Take them whenever you need them. The scalpel, well, we don't stock or use them, but it'd be easy peasy to lift one from a hospital. Stores rooms are open all the time.'

'That's true,' Callum said.

'Citrate and heparin are more tricky,' Grant said. 'I don't know where heparin's kept, if you need the keys to get it or whatever. But there's a bit of citrate in the blue-top blood tubes, and tubes are everywhere in a hospital, so again if you really wanted to you could lift a couple pretty easily.' He screwed up his face. 'That sounds like I've thought about how to nick stuff, but really I haven't.'

A voice said something unintelligible over the radio on his belt, and he started. 'I gotta run.'

'The amount of citrate in the tubes he mentioned is tiny,' Callum said when he'd gone. 'Only enough to keep two mils or so from clotting. Heparin's stored in the drug cupboard and not necessarily under lock and key. You could get it if you knew what you wanted and chose your timing. It'd be easy enough to then inject it into the container, though the levels wouldn't be precise.'

'I don't think they'd need to be,' Ella said.

'Where do the local and the scalpel come in?'

'Someone couriered me a woman's little toe. There's a bunch of needle marks around the cut edge that the pathologist said are probably sites of local anaesthetic injection.'

'Wow,' Callum said.

'Yeah, you'd think it was her birthday,' Murray said.

'You're still trying with that one?' Ella said.

'I like it.'

'You asked about a paramedic,' Callum said. 'What are you thinking? That she's done all this herself?'

'Maybe. If you were a kidnapper and had to cut off part of someone's body and send it as a threat, you'd send an ear or a finger. Something highly visible in life that'd make it mean more. And would you fill the victim with local anaesthetic first? Plus you'd send it to the husband, along with your demands. Why send it to me? Why keep sending me text messages as well? If, on the other hand, you were doing it to yourself, you'd go for something you could manage pretty well without, something not so noticeable later in life. And you'd use plenty of local anaesthetic.'

Callum looked sceptical. 'But why do it at all? For police attention? Or because she's got a psych issue?'

'Or because she needs something and thinks I'm the only one who can give it to her,' Ella said.

'Like what?' Murray asked.

Ella said, 'Help.'

★

Ella called Dennis and explained everything then called the lab and asked for the tests on the blood and the toe to be done urgently. Added an extra one, knowing it sounded like an afterthought when really it wasn't.

'So you're thinking what, exactly?' Murray asked, but before she could explain, her mobile rang.

'This is Imogen Davidov,' a woman said, sounding

concerned. 'I'm a friend of Rowan Wylie's? You interviewed me on Monday?'

'Yes, I remember,' Ella said. 'What can I do for you?'

'Well, I had brunch with Rowan this morning, and during it he took a call that I am almost certain came from Stacey Durham.'

★

Rowan carried Gomez into the house, calling, 'I'm home.'

'You brought us a dog,' Megan said in the kitchen.

Emelia ran in from the backyard and squealed.

'Don't scare him,' Rowan said. 'We're just minding him for a bit.'

Emelia tried to pull Gomez out of Rowan's arms.

'Sit on the floor,' he said. She sat cross-legged, her arms out.

He crouched and let them look at each other, Gomez wagging so much his body shook, his tongue trying to reach Emelia's face. She was already giggling.

'No squealing,' Rowan said. 'Ready?'

She nodded, and he put Gomez into her lap. The dog jumped up on her straight away and she fell backwards laughing, the dog whining with delight in her arms.

'How about we go outside,' Megan said. As the pair chased each other on the grass, she added, 'Am I right in thinking I've met this dog before?'

Rowan knew she and Simon had been to a barbecue at James and Stacey's house. 'Probably.'

'Where did you find him?'

'At the RSPCA. Someone left him there unconscious.'

'How did you know to look?'

'Just a hunch,' he said.

Gomez raced in circles around Emelia, who ran after him laughing.

'It might be a problem when he has to go home,' Megan said.

There was a knock at the front door. Rowan looked through the back screen to the front, and saw the detectives.

★

The sun shone down from a cloudless sky as Ella watched Rowan's granddaughter play on the lawn with Gomez. The dog's hair had been cut off in patches, especially round his face, to the point where she wouldn't have recognised him. Further away, the little girl's mother pulled weeds from a vegetable patch, glancing their way as she tossed the weeds onto the lawn.

'So Imogen told you,' Rowan said.

'Yep,' Murray said. 'So now you'd better tell us.'

'I got a call asking me to go and find him.'

'From who?' Ella asked.

'I don't know.'

Ella looked at him. 'That's not what Imogen said.'

'She only heard my side of the conversation. It was a woman, but she was whispering, and she never gave her name.'

'Did you think it was Stacey?'

'I couldn't be sure.'

Ella gritted her teeth. 'This woman, whoever she was, asked you not to tell anyone that she'd called. But if it was anyone but Stacey, I don't think you'd be lying to us.'

He looked at the kid and the dog.

'Rowan,' Ella said.

'Yes,' he said. 'It was her. She asked me not to tell anyone. She said it couldn't get out. I asked her why she didn't call you, and that I could pass on information to you, but she said I couldn't tell anyone.'

'How did she sound?' Murray asked.

'In a hurry. It seemed like she had to get off the phone before somebody came into the room, something like that.

There was a noise in the background, and she said she had to go and hung up.'

They'd already checked, and knew that no call or text had come from Stacey's phone that morning.

'Did the number show on your screen?' Ella asked.

'It was blocked.' He took his phone out of his pocket and gave it to her.

'Did she sound sick or weak?' Murray said.

He shook his head. 'Anxious, and stressed, I guess.'

Ella scrolled through his phone to the last call received. Number blocked, as he'd said. But that only meant the number was hidden from the receiver; it was traceable once they got onto his provider.

She said, 'What do you think is going on with her?'

'How would I know?' he said.

'You must've been thinking about it. You must've wondered why she'd say not to tell anyone, why she'd call you about the dog but not say anything about how you could help her.'

He looked away at Emelia. 'I don't know why she'd do that. I asked her and she pretty much told me to shut up and listen. Made me promise her I'd get the dog.'

'But why?' Ella said. 'Why only that?'

'She loves him,' Rowan said. 'She loves that dog so much.'

'More than herself?' Murray asked.

Ella looked again at the dog on the grass. It was pouncing on the thrown weeds. Stacey was alive, and apparently well, or reasonably so, and . . . and what?

'Did the RSPCA people say how he got there?' she asked.

Rowan nodded. 'A man took him in unconscious yesterday, saying he'd found him like that by the side of the road. The RSPCA vet said he'd been drugged with Valium, and his hair was cut all ragged like this and he was covered in mud.'

Ella thought of the Valium in James and Stacey's bathroom cabinet.

'They tried to ring the man later but the phone number was

disconnected.' Rowan paused. 'Stacey told me Gomez might look different.'

'So she knew,' Murray said.

'She said "might",' Rowan said.

Ella shook her head. 'She knew.'

★

The RSPCA waiting room was busy with families clutching pet-carriers containing yowling cats, massive dogs that strained at their leads and barked like the hounds of hell, and a surly elderly man with a panicking canary in a cage in his arms. Ella and Murray had to wait while the girl at the desk helped a woman who had some creature scratching about in a cardboard box. Ella resisted the urge to push in, and had to fight not to pace the room as well. They were getting close now – she could just about smell it.

Finally the woman moved on and the girl smiled at them. Ella showed her badge and explained what they wanted.

'That was me,' the girl said. 'Hold on a sec.' She found someone to replace her at the desk, then took them through to an office that smelled like disinfectant. 'He said he found the dog on the side of the road and thought it was dead before he realised it was unconscious. When I tried to call the number he'd left so I could ask if he'd noticed if the dog had vomited, it was disconnected.'

'He left a name as well?' Ella said.

She nodded and turned to the computer on the desk, typing quickly. 'Barry Watson.'

Ella wrote it down, along with the number the girl read out. 'Did you think he was telling the truth?'

'I did at the time,' the girl said. 'I've seen people trying to surrender their pet by saying they found it, it's not theirs, but usually they seem either a bit upset or a bit shifty. He didn't seem like he was either. The other giveaway is that the animal clearly knows the person, though of course this dog was unconscious.'

'Of course,' Ella echoed. 'The dog had been given Valium, was that right?'

The girl nodded.

'Is dog Valium different to human Valium?' Murray asked. 'Could you tell which one he was given?'

The girl shook her head. 'It's the same drug called diazepam, but it wouldn't be given to a dog unless he was having seizures or something like that.'

Ella said, 'What did this man look like?'

'He was white and middle-aged,' the girl said. 'I didn't notice much else. I was more worried about the dog.'

'What kind of clothes was he wearing?' Murray asked.

She thought. 'It was a business-type shirt, white, I'm pretty sure, but without a tie. I remember because there was mud on the front from him carrying the dog. But I don't know what else he was wearing, like the kind of pants or shoes or whatever.'

'Did he have a beard or moustache?' Ella said.

'Not that I can remember.'

'You didn't notice any tattoos or anything else?'

'Sorry. Like I said, I'm always fixated on the animal.'

Murray got out the photo of James Durham. 'Was it this man?'

The girl took it. 'I don't know. Maybe.'

'You're not sure?'

'It's hard to say. Like I said, I was worried about the dog. It might be him, I don't know. Sorry.'

'Do you have CCTV here?'

'Yes, but it's broken at the moment. It's getting fixed tomorrow.'

Timing, Ella thought. 'Okay. Thanks for your help. Give us a call if you remember anything else, or if the man gets in touch.'

As they stood up, the girl said, 'Do you know how the dog's doing now?'

'He's perfectly fine,' Ella said.

The girl smiled.

TWENTY-FIVE

His phone by his elbow, Rowan watched Emelia and
Megan play with the dog. He'd texted Stacey and asked
her to get in touch but there'd been no reply. The detectives
hadn't said where they were going but they'd seemed pretty
certain that Stacey had known where Gomez would be, and
that meant . . . what? He wasn't sure. He couldn't tell. What
was going on? She was okay enough to call, but not tell him
anything. He was afraid that she somehow was in danger. And
he knew he should call James and tell him about the dog, but
he couldn't make himself do it.

'Hello hello?'

'Daddy!' Emelia leapt up and ran to the back door. 'Look!
I got a puppy!'

Simon came out of the house, followed by James. Rowan's
heart seized up for a second, then, trying to sound jovial, he
said, 'Poor Nick, all alone in the shop.'

James knelt by the excited dog and looked up at Rowan.
'Mate, I can't tell you how pleased I am that you found him.' He
rubbed the dog's head without taking his eyes from Rowan's
face. His smile was peculiar, more like a grimace, Rowan

thought. 'Who's a lucky dog, eh? Who's a lucky, lucky boy?'

Gomez rolled on his back and kicked his feet in the air. Emelia pulled his tail.

'Gentle,' Megan said.

'It was lucky,' Rowan said. 'I know how much he means to you both, and how losing him too was the last thing you needed. So I had a hunch and started checking at the pounds. And there he was.' The words felt dry as dust in his mouth.

James was still smiling at him. 'Thank the little birdies for hunches.'

'Mummy said gentle,' Simon told Emelia.

'I meant to ring and tell you,' Rowan said. 'But time sort of got away.'

'Oh, well,' James said, still looking at him. 'These things happen.'

Simon kissed the top of Megan's head. 'James said he's got something to tell us about the flat.'

Megan jumped up. 'It's really happening?'

'Well, it's not going to be the news you'd hoped for.' James got to his feet and faced them. 'I asked Simon to drive me here because I wanted to tell you too, Megan, personally, how sorry I am, but my friend's changed his mind and he's not going to rent it out after all.'

The disappointment on Megan's face sliced into Rowan's heart like a knife.

'We can't have it?' she said faintly.

'Sorry,' James said. 'I wish I'd known earlier, so you didn't get your hopes up.' He glanced at Rowan. 'It's a real pity.'

In a flash Rowan had the thought that the friend hadn't changed his mind at all, that James was doing this to get at him. Because he thought he had something to do with Stacey? Had he had Simon drive him over, planning to give them they keys or whatever, then changed his mind when he saw the dog?

He cleared his throat. 'The friend can't be persuaded?'

'I've tried myself,' James said. 'Again, I'm really sorry.'

To Rowan he didn't sound sorry at all. Megan started to cry, which made Emelia burst into tears. Simon hugged them both.

Rowan motioned James aside. 'You're certain there's nothing we can do?'

'What are you suggesting?' James's expression was cold. 'Have you had another hunch?'

'No, but.' He gestured at the little family. 'I can help out, if money's the problem.'

'It's not.' James reached out idly and brushed dog hair off Rowan's shirt. 'Are you sure you don't know where Stacey is?'

'I swear to you I don't.'

James's eyes bore into his.

Simon's mobile pinged. 'It's Nick, asking when we'll be back.'

'Then we better go.' James suddenly smiled and clapped Rowan on the shoulder. 'You okay to keep the dog for a bit, mate? He's not getting much attention at home at the moment and I'm sure he's lonely without Stacey around.'

Megan looked at Rowan. 'Emelia would love it.'

The prospect made Rowan uneasy, but he nodded.

'The puppy's staying!' Megan said to Emelia.

Emelia pressed her face forcefully into Gomez's hair. 'Puppy sleep in my bed tonight.'

'I don't think so,' Simon said. 'Bye Em, Daddy go work now.'

'Bye.' She didn't look up from the dog.

James smiled. 'Kid's got priorities.' He looked at Rowan. 'Keep me informed on the hunches, okay?' He winked and walked away, leaving Rowan cold.

★

The lab report came through and Ella punched Murray's shoulder. 'I knew it.'

284

'Ow.'

'Come on.'

In Dennis's office, she slapped the printout down on the desk.

He read it, then looked up. 'So what are you going to do?'

'Text her,' Ella said. 'See if she'll call me back.'

'We'll see where it locates to,' Dennis said.

She took out her mobile and typed: *I tested the blood for citrate and for hormones. I know what's going on.* Then she sat back to wait.

It rang ten minutes later. The screen said it was Stacey's number.

'This is Detective Ella Marconi,' she answered.

Nobody spoke, but she could hear breathing.

Murray stared at her. Dennis murmured into his landline and gave her a thumbs up that the location of the call was being traced.

She said, 'Stacey, I know what you're doing and I think I know why. I can help you, but you have to talk to me.'

A voice whispered, 'This isn't Stacey. This is a friend.'

Ella couldn't tell if the voice was male or female. She scribbled *friend* on a notepad on Dennis's desk. 'Let me help you both then.'

'You don't know enough yet,' came the whisper. 'James is still free.'

'We don't have anything on him,' Ella said.

'Look on the computers.'

'There's nothing there. We've pulled them apart. There's nothing to find.'

Silence.

'It could be on Stacey's laptop,' Ella said. 'If you can get that to us —'

'We've already looked,' the voice whispered.

'Things can be hidden,' Ella said. 'In ways that only an expert can find.'

No answer.

'You don't have to give it to me in person. Use a courier, like with the toe. We have people here –'

'No, no,' the whisperer cut in. 'He told Stacey he has friends there. He said he's helped with cases before, under-the-table stuff, hacking computers when there wasn't enough evidence for warrants to catch paedophiles and drug dealers. He said people owe him.'

'That doesn't happen,' Ella said, thinking of Libke. 'He was lying.'

'He knew you'd talked to me.'

Ella blinked at Murray and Dennis. 'Talked to you?' She thought back through the people they'd interviewed. 'What did he say?'

'He told me you'd asked me about her, said he was following up.'

'Where are you?'

'I'm sorry, but we can't trust anyone,' the caller whispered and hung up.

Ella lowered her phone. 'They don't trust us. They said James knew I'd talked to them.'

'How could James know that?' Murray said.

'That's the point. He apparently claimed to have helped officers hack into computers when they didn't have warrants to do so, and said they owed him. The friend believes someone is giving James information about what we're doing.' She looked at Dennis. 'Where did it triangulate to?'

'A brand new location. Ryde.'

'That's more than ten minutes' drive from any of the people we spoke to, isn't it?' Murray said.

'Only if you think they were at the same place as they were when we talked to them,' Ella said. 'There's Esther Cooper, Bill Willetts, Marie, Paris, the dentist, his receptionist, the jealous paramedic who was washing her car, the bike shop guy, the dog trainer, and the old schoolfriend.'

'And the angry guy in Padstow,' Murray said. 'The kids driving the car, the woman in the bank. Stacey's friends. Rowan and his daughter-in-law or whatever she is.'

Rowan, Ella thought. 'The caller was whispering, so I couldn't tell if it was male or female, and there was no background noise to give me any clues.'

'There was no ping from any phone towers between Ella's text and the call being made either,' Dennis said. 'That means they were already in Ryde when they turned the phone on.'

Murray frowned. 'Does anyone we've come across in the investigation have any links to that area?'

'None that I remember,' Ella said. With Ryde being so close to her home in Putney, she was sure she would've noticed.

'Okay,' Dennis said. 'Assuming the caller is telling the truth, that James did speak to them and did say he knew you'd spoken to them, and that it is someone you've talked to, who on that list would you pick as most likely?'

Ella thought for a moment. 'It's so hard to say. It seems odd that Marie or Paris would say that, but for the rest of them, where do you begin?'

'Go by location?' Murray said. 'The ex-schoolfriend, Abby Watmough, lives closest to here, and she has the extra link of her son going out with Paris. The shops are probably next. Although the dog guy bordered on uncooperative when we were at his place, so there's that to consider as well.'

Ella nodded. 'Let's just start.'

★

Rowan was in the kitchen, making a cup of coffee and trying to reason away the feeling that James was not who he seemed, when his mobile rang. He recognised Imogen's number and answered straight away. 'Hi.'

'I want to say sorry,' she said. 'I told the police that Stacey called you.'

'I know.'

'People might say it wasn't my place to do it, but I'd do it again, and you need to know that,' she said. 'But I just wanted to say sorry in case it hurt you. In case I hurt you.'

'It's okay. You were right. I should've told them.' He told her how the detectives had come around, how they'd talked.

'I'm glad it was okay.' She hesitated. 'So what are you up to this afternoon?'

'I'm taking Emelia to Playland later. Would you like to join us?'

'Sounds delightful,' she said, a smile in her voice. 'What time?'

★

Ella knocked on Abby Watmough's front door and listened. No answer, and no sound from inside.

Murray checked the windows. 'Locked up tight,' he said.

Ella knocked again, then hunted through her notebook for Watmough's mobile phone number. It went straight to voice-mail, and she left a message: just her name and the request that Watmough call her back.

Next stop was the computer shop. Nick Henry was at the counter with a plump middle-aged woman in too tight jeans and white high heels, and he glanced over her shoulder as Ella and Murray entered. 'And there's your receipt, and there's your bag,' he said.

Murray held the door for the woman. She thanked him and tottered out.

'Nick,' Ella said, 'is James here?'

'No. I haven't seen him today, and he hasn't rung to say if he's coming in.'

'Thanks,' Ella said.

In the bike shop, Mike was on his knees, his polo shirt tight across his shoulders as he fitted a wrench to a nut on a child's pink bike. The bike was upside down and the streamers on the ends of the handlebars lay on the painted concrete floor.

'I haven't talked to anyone about you coming to see me,' he said.

'You're certain?' Ella asked.

He nodded. 'Who would I tell? I live alone. Customers here don't need to know stuff like that. And I don't believe in gossip between neighbouring businesses.'

'Have people from the other shops been talking about it?' Murray asked.

'Oh, they talk and talk.' He stood up and exchanged the wrench for another. 'Nothing of any significance though, or I would've called you.' He pointed to Ella's business card taped to the wall. 'James never seemed that friendly, and people like to jump to conclusions and exercise hindsight at the same time. Though I'm sure you know that for yourselves.'

Ella nodded. 'Has James himself come in and talked to you?'

'No,' Mike said.

'Not once?'

'Not ever.'

She believed him. 'Thanks. If he does –'

He smiled and motioned with the wrench to her card. 'I know where you are.'

★

The sign on the dental surgery door declared it was open, and they went in to see an Asian man in his fifties paging anxiously through a *Woman's Day* in one of the four waiting chairs and Zaina Khan smiling at them from behind the front desk.

'Hello again,' she said.

Ella smiled back. 'Can we speak to Jonathon for a minute?'

'Should be fine, he's just setting up. Let me check.' She went out the back, then returned. 'He said you can go on through.'

The room smelled like every dentist's Ella had ever been in – cold, metal, disinfectant and nerves. Jonathon Dimitri was dressed in a white smock and laying out tools she didn't want to look at.

'We just need a moment,' Murray was saying. 'Have you spoken to anyone else about Stacey Durham since you talked to us?'

'I mentioned it to Zaina and to my girlfriend,' he said. 'But all I said was that I'd talked to you.'

'That's all?' Ella said.

Dimitri nodded.

Murray unfolded the photo of James Durham and held it out. 'Recognise him?'

'Yes, he's Stacey's husband, isn't he? He came in that day with her.'

'Have you seen him since?' Murray asked.

'Only on the news.'

'He hasn't come to talk to you, either here or anywhere else?' Ella asked.

'No. I've been meaning to pop into the shop and give him my best wishes, but I wasn't sure exactly what to say. I should do it anyway, I suppose.'

'Thanks for your time,' Ella said.

They went out the front and Dimitri called the anxious patient through. Ella waited until the surgery door was closed, then asked Zaina the same question about who she'd spoken to.

'My girlfriend who arrived when you were at my house, because she wanted to know what was going on,' Zaina said. 'I didn't give her details though. And then the husband, James. He came to my house last night.'

The hair on the back of Ella's neck started to rise. 'What did he say?'

'He told me who he was, though I'd already recognised him from the news and the photo you guys showed me. I could see in his face that he recognised me too. He said he was trying to remember something specific that Stacey had said when they were here. He said he felt like it was there in his head but he just couldn't catch it, and he thought I might be able to remember. I said I didn't remember anything except her asking about an appointment. He said he knew that much, he'd talked to you two about that, about what I told you and where I lived, but he thought she'd said something about where she had to go later that day.'

Ella thought about that. 'But you're sure she only talked about the appointment?'

'Absolutely.'

'How did he respond when you said that?'

'Okay. Just puzzled, like he was still trying to remember,' she said.

'Then what?' Murray asked.

'He asked to use the bathroom, and I said sure, then he came back out and said thanks and left.' She looked at their faces. 'That was okay that I talked to him, wasn't it? I figured, you know, he's the husband, and you guys told him you'd talked to me and everything, so it had to be fine.'

The front door opened and an elderly woman stumped in, a walking stick in one hand and a patent black handbag in the other. 'Toothache,' she barked. 'Need the dentist.'

'We'll get out of your hair,' Murray said to Zaina, and he and Ella walked outside.

On the footpath, Ella faced him. 'So James knew about Zaina, but not about the dentist or the bike guy.'

'Did you leave them out of your notes?'

'No, they're all there, all typed into the system.'

'Perhaps he hasn't got around to them yet.'

'I don't think that's it,' she said, hurrying to the car. 'Call Dennis, tell him we're going to Dural. And get him to send people to see the jealous paramedic and Esther Cooper and Willetts. Then call Watmough again.'

TWENTY-SIX

By the time they arrived at Steve Lynch's place in Dural, Murray had left another two messages on Abby Watmough's phone and had none back.

Steve Lynch was twisting a post-hole digger into the soil. He wore khaki shorts and the same grubby Blundstones, and his shirt hung over the gate. He glanced up but didn't stop working as they got out of the car.

'Mr Lynch,' Murray said.

'What now?'

'Can you stop for a moment?'

He heaved the digger out of the hole and knocked the compacted earth and stones out against a tree. His back was tanned, and sweat glistened along the hollow of his spine and in his chest hair when he faced them. Ella glanced past his house at the dog runs and saw the Alsatians sitting silently in a row behind the wire, watching.

'Been talking to anyone about our visit?' she said.

'Why? Was it a national secret?'

'Yes or no?'

He brushed dirt from his arm. 'Only the husband. What's

292

his name? James.'

'What happened?' Murray asked.

'He turned up here last night, said who he was, then started saying how he'd talked to you and knew you'd been here, and he wanted to follow up on something about Stacey. He started asking questions about what I remembered from the last time I saw her, and I thought that was odd because we'd only talked online and on the phone.'

'What did you tell him?' Ella asked.

'Just that,' he said. 'That I hadn't seen her, that she hadn't seemed real happy when I told her she was spoiling the dog, that that was ages ago and I hadn't so much as thought of her until the both of you turned up.'

'How did he react?'

'A bit annoyed, frankly. He asked a few more questions – was I sure I hadn't seen her, whatever – and I said I had stuff to do. He asked to use the loo before he left. I said there's a public one in the park down the road. He said he'd only be a minute, but I said no and told him to get on his way.'

'You didn't want him in your house?'

'I like my privacy.'

'Are you sure he was who he said he was?' Ella asked. 'Had you seen him on the news?'

'Nope. I don't see any reason why he'd lie. And he said you'd told him that you'd been here.'

Murray got out the photo of James Durham. 'Look anything like this?'

'Yep,' Lynch said. 'That's him. Same smarmy smile.'

Ella glanced at the silent dogs again, then at the house. 'Mind if I use your bathroom?'

'That's a joke, right?' Lynch said.

'Not even slightly.'

He put his hands on his hips. Dirt marked the creases in his knuckles and ringed his fingernails. 'Going to have a little snoop while you're in there?'

'Why? You hiding anything?'

He snorted air and looked across at his neighbour's property where a woman in a white dress was vacuuming leaves from a tennis court. 'Snoop away. What do I care?'

The inside of the house was cool and dim. The floor was polished timber, the walls white, the venetians on the windows turned to block the light but not the breeze. Ella looked into each room in turn: lounge with two armchairs, one pushed back and the other in front of the TV, under which a gaming console blinked green lights; two bedrooms, one Lynch's judging by the framed dog certificates and photos, the other spare, dust rising from the blue quilt when she touched it. A third room served as an office, with a desk and humming computer, more certificates and ribbons on the walls, and a filing cabinet containing training records. The bathroom was unrenovated, neat and plain. She flushed without using the toilet, washed her hands, then went into the kitchen at the back of the house. Plain brown Laminex, white bread in a bag on the bench, plate and cutlery in the sink. Out the window she could see the dogs staring back at her. Next to the runs stood a large corrugated-iron shed. Lynch had said to snoop away, so she opened the back door and went out.

The dogs didn't move, but as she drew nearer she became aware of a deep rumbling growl, a five-dog sound that seemed to start considerably lower than their throats. She walked past the pens, looking at them sideways. Their eyes were fixed, unblinking, on her, and the growl intensified. She fought the urge to run.

'Find anything yet?' Lynch called.

He and Murray were watching her from their spot near the gate. She raised a hand oh-so-casually and kept walking.

A padlock hung open through the hasp on the shed door. She removed it and pulled the door open. An ex-ambulance painted blue was parked in the centre, and she opened the back doors to see the space had been converted into a number of dog crates. A photo of a sitting Alsatian and Lynch's name and mobile phone number were plastered on both sides of the vehicle, and again in smaller font on the two front doors. Shovels, bags of fertiliser, containers of oil, a ride-on mower, lengths of timber, fence posts, bags of concrete and rolls of fencing wire took up the rest of the garage space.

She stepped out to an instant resumption of growling, rehooked the lock through the hasp, and walked back to the front gate.

'No bodies?' Lynch said. 'No missing women? How odd.'

Ella placed her card on the top of the post. 'Give us a call if James comes back.'

They got in the car and Ella started the engine, feeling Lynch's eyes on her.

'Call Dennis,' she said to Murray. 'See if he's found out yet where else James has been.'

She drove five minutes down the road, then pulled over.

'Okay, great,' Murray said into his phone. 'Thanks.' He hung up. 'Lamarr, the jealous paramedic, got a visit from James. Cooper and Willetts didn't. The Pendle Hill crim isn't home but one of the neighbours said that a man saying he was James had come to their door and asked if they knew anything about Stacey.'

Ella got out her notebook and looked back through it, working out the timeline, thinking over the steps. She said, 'James didn't go to the people we talked to, but the places we went.'

'I don't get it.'

'We went to Zaina Khan's house, to Steve Lynch's house, to Christine Lamarr's house. James went back to all of them.'

'We went to Dimitri's place too, but James didn't talk to him.'

'But when did we do that?'

Murray looked confused.

Her heart beating hard, Ella got out and climbed in the back, feeling in the pockets on the backs of the front seats, in the cup holders in the back doors, down the back of the seat itself. She felt something, pushed harder to grasp it.

'What are you doing?' Murray said.

She pulled out a plastic device as big as her thumb. 'He was sitting back here alone after The Gap. He's been tracking us. He talked to the neighbours as well because he couldn't tell exactly which house we'd gone to.'

'Because?'

'Because,' Ella said, 'he thinks we're going to find her, and he wants to find her first.'

★

On the drive back from Ryde, where Abby'd collected some things from a homewares store while Paris trotted Lucy around a nearby park in her stroller, Paris finally stopped thinking about working nightshift that night, poor dead Mr Leary and missing Stacey, and let herself imagine that she was part of this family. She couldn't decide the configuration though – whether Lucy, asleep in the back seat, was her little sister or cousin or niece, or whether Abby was her sister or aunt or her mother.

'What are you smiling at?' Abby said.

'Nothing.'

Abby smiled back.

Paris thought she heard a low vibration. She checked her own phone but she had no missed calls. 'Is your phone on silent?'

'No, why?'

'I heard something vibrate,' Paris said. 'Sounded like a missed call on a muted phone.'

'Wasn't mine.' Abby glanced in the mirror. 'Lucy, was it yours?' Lucy slept on. 'Guess not.'

When they pulled up in the driveway, Lucy woke and started to cry.

'Damn,' Abby said. 'I hoped she'd stay asleep. I'm going to have to keep driving. Or take her out in the stroller.'

'I could take her out,' Paris said.

'You really want to?'

'It's a nice afternoon.'

'Okay then. Why not? Thanks.'

Five minutes later, Lucy was strapped in and chewing a rusk, and Paris was proceeding down the footpath through the afternoon sunshine. Just like a big sister, she thought. Or an aunt. Or a mother herself.

She tried but failed to imagine her own mother ever having pushed her along the street like this, and decided, savings or no savings, it was definitely time to move out. She straightened her shoulders and lengthened her stride. She would find a sharehouse or something. Assuming that she kept her job, of course. She could scrape up her bond, she could manage rent too. And food and bills. She pictured a couple of friendly girls, other paramedics or nurses maybe, cops were good too, and they'd sit around and watch TV in the evenings and tell stories about their days. They'd share cooking and maybe the house was near a cool Thai place and maybe a funky pub, she'd always fancied having a local though she didn't drink much, and oh yeah with an awesome beer garden, not like something in an RSL, all white plastic chairs, but like one you'd see in ads for Melbourne, full of laughing happy people, a place where you'd make friends as easily as tripping over.

And the job would be okay too. Away from her mother she'd do better, and she'd get some counselling and sort out this frightened thing once and for all. She'd trust people and not be scared to tell them how she felt.

She smiled into the stroller and found that Lucy had fallen asleep, the rusk in one loose fist. She turned a corner and headed back, easing the stroller over bumps so as not to wake her.

As for Mr Leary . . . she would tell Rowan what happened. They would talk it over. If he wanted to report her, that was okay.

Coming back to the house, she crossed the street and levered the stroller up the kerb, then followed the path to the front door. It was closed. She turned the knob but found it locked.

She tapped on the frame. 'Abby?'

There was no answer.

The car was still in the driveway, so she hadn't driven anywhere. Paris went back to the street and looked both ways, thinking she might've wanted to catch up with them on their walk, but there was nobody in sight. Maybe she was in the bathroom.

Paris knocked on the door again. Lucy twitched in the stroller, her mouth open, her eyes closed. Paris heard a noise. Something – or someone – banging.

She pressed her ear to the door and heard it again. 'Abby?'

A cry.

The front door was solid, the lock firm. Paris grabbed the stroller and ran to the side of the house, fumbled the gate latch with clammy hands and got through. The back door was closed but unlocked, and she burst in, hefting the stroller in after her with Lucy jolted awake and wailing.

Abby lay covered in blood in the doorway to Lucy's room.

Paris dropped to her knees, hands shaking, heart racing. Abby gasped for air, blood on her lips, blood soaking through her shirt. Paris lifted the shirt and saw a gaping wound in the right side of her chest, a wound that leaked blood like a hose, that sucked inwards as Abby breathed in and closed off as she breathed out.

Panicked, Paris tried to think. *Cover the hole!*

She pressed the palm of her hand over it, sealing it off as best she could. The blood flowed between her fingers like hot oil. Abby grasped her wrist and stared into her eyes like she was dying.

Paris screamed for help.

★

Ella parked outside Abby Watmough's house and looked past Murray. 'Car's there anyway.'

'You hear something?' Murray said.

'Like what?'

The front door flew open and Paris burst out, blood on her hands, screaming like it was the end of the world. Ella ran across the lawn as Paris disappeared back inside. Whatever had happened had only just happened. The neighbours were just now starting to look out their windows and step out their doors.

'Help!' Paris screamed.

Ella went in with her hand on her weapon and Murray two steps behind. 'Police,' she shouted.

'Help! Help me!'

Ella followed the sound, and found Paris kneeling by a panting and blood-soaked Abby on the hall floor. The baby howled in her stroller nearby.

'Call an ambulance,' Paris said. Blood spotted her face and coated her hands, which were pressed to Abby's ribs. 'And get me some plastic wrap from the kitchen.'

Pulling out his phone, Murray dashed off.

'Help me sit her up straight,' Paris said. 'It'll make it easier for her to breathe.'

Ella crouched and between them they pulled Abby into a sitting position against the doorframe.

'James took Stacey,' Abby gasped, then coughed wetly.

'How long ago?' Ella said.

'Ten, fifteen minutes.' She sucked air.

'Okay,' Ella said, taking out her phone, pressing the button to dial the office. 'Did he do this to you?'

She nodded. 'Big knife.'

'Did he hurt your baby, or Stacey?'

Abby gave a half-shake of her head. 'Yelling about computer. Stacey hid it. In the roof.' She gripped Paris's wrist in her own blood-soaked hand and grimaced in pain.

299

'The baby and I were out,' Paris said.

'Orchard, Homicide,' Dennis answered.

'James has Stacey,' Ella said. 'He stabbed Abby Watmough and left ten or fifteen minutes ago. The laptop's apparently still here.'

'Okay,' he said. 'Alert's going out on his car now, and I'll get people on their way.'

Murray was back with the box of plastic wrap. 'Ambulance is coming.'

'Tear off a piece as big as my hand,' Paris barked.

Murray did so. 'What else can I do?'

'Unless you've got oxygen, nothing.'

Abby opened her eyes. 'You know Stacey's pregnant?' she gasped.

'Pregnant?' Paris said.

'Yes,' Ella said. 'Her sister told us she thought that James caused the miscarriage two years ago. Is that why she felt she had to disappear?'

Abby nodded. 'Protect herself and baby,' she puffed. 'I worked domestic violence. Know what it's like. Told her at reunion, and she told me. Offered to help. Made the room. Planned it all.'

'And the texts?' Murray said.

'Make you think James involved, not directly, but make you investigate him,' she gasped. 'He told Stacey once, getting more money than she could imagine. Laughed when she asked how. She knew. Bad stuff. Going on.'

'So she sent the anonymous complaint?' Ella said.

Abby nodded again. 'Didn't work. Had to do more. Then found she's pregnant. Not safe. Had to go. Blood to make it serious. Toe even more serious. Investigate harder. But he still found us.'

She closed her eyes, panting for breath. Her skin looked grey. Ella hoped it was the poor light.

'Don't talk any more,' Paris said. 'Just breathe. Breathe.'

Ella felt useless. 'Stacey's computer's in the roof?'

Abby gestured weakly to a corner in the hallway. Ella went around it, and in the ceiling between Abby's bedroom and that of her son saw an open manhole in the ceiling. A narrow ladder lowered from it to the floor, and around it lay a scattering of items, as if thrown down, including a folding bicycle.

'The bike,' she said to Murray.

Abby gasped something and Paris called out, 'It was her ex-partner's. He left it when he moved.'

Murray held up a dark long-sleeved shirt, dark pants, a cap and helmet. He went back to talk to Abby again, and Ella went up the ladder.

By the light of a fallen lamp, Ella could see the room in the roof was just long enough for the narrow overturned foam mattress, and almost as wide as the span of her arms. She could hear the murmur of voices downstairs. Boards that had been laid over the beams to form a floor had been kicked up and there were holes in the dusty cobwebbed insulation. A pedestal fan had been knocked onto its face but the blades continued to whir inside the protective cage. A pillow and rumpled sheets lay in a heap beside bottles of water and a scattering of apples, bananas and paperback novels. An empty bucket on its side in a corner smelled faintly of urine, and a plastic supermarket bag spilled a tangle of empty IV lines and fluid bags, bloody dressings, apple cores and banana skins, and a used scalpel and needles in a plastic lunchbox. The tops of the plasterboard walls had been torn down by someone with blood on their hands, and chunks flung all over the place. The roof space beyond was gloomy except for the occasional chink of light squeezing between the tiles.

Murray appeared in the manhole. 'Jesus.'

'He wanted that computer,' Ella said.

She looked over the broken walls. The insulation lay untouched. If a laptop had been thrown over, it wouldn't have gone far. She'd be able to see some kind of disturbance.

301

'Abby said Stacey told him she'd gotten rid of it before she came here,' Murray said. 'She tried to get him to believe that she thought he might be able to trace her if she used it.' He climbed up and balanced on the beams. 'He made her come up here while he searched. I guess if he'd had more time he would've torn the walls down completely.'

'He tore them enough to see it's not out there,' Ella said. 'We need to find it. With luck it'll give us some information about where he's taken her, as well as what he's been doing that he so badly needs to hide. Abby doesn't know where it could be?'

'Only that it has to be here somewhere. She said James pushed his way into the house and was hitting her, trying to make her give Stacey up, and she lied and said she didn't know what he was talking about, but when he stabbed her and she screamed, Stacey let down the ladder. James heard it and was waiting for her, so she couldn't have taken the laptop down into the house and hidden it before he saw her.'

'She couldn't have sneaked it down somehow?'

'Abby was adamant. It sounds like it all happened too quickly for that.' He pulled at the torn insulation, and dust rose into the air.

The plasterboard was dry in Ella's hands, snapping off in big pieces when she bent it. She wanted to see further into the roof. She could hear Paris talking to Abby downstairs, telling her to hang in there, but no sound from either Abby or Lucy. A siren approached in the distance.

'Hey,' Murray said, 'it's exactly like the psychic said. Small room, built for her, with no door.'

Ella snorted. 'Exactly like any captive's room on any crime show or movie in the last billion years.'

But he was eyeing her. 'So what did she mean when she told you to take care?'

'She meant for you to shut up,' Ella said. 'Why couldn't she tell us that Stacey was with a friend? Or that she was even here in Sydney? Or where the goddamn laptop is?'

'I suppose.' Murray stooped under the low angle of the roof at the front of the house. 'You can see the street from here.'

She crossed the beams and half-crouched beside him, the rough wood of the rafters catching her hair. She felt the day's warmth in the tiles on her face as she peered closely at the tiny gap. She could see their own car parked at the kerb. 'She would've seen James arrive.'

'And probably had a plan for the laptop then.' Murray looked around. He picked up the mattress and squeezed it, then the pillow.

Ella felt a breeze against her legs and knelt to see the second gap. Something had been pushed between the tiles, something that glinted. A wedding ring, she realised; only visible from up close. She worked it loose from the gap, then felt the tile above it shift. 'This one's loose.'

She wriggled it free and looked outside. There, propped in the gutter, wrapped in a plastic bag and hidden from the street by the top leaves of the frangipani, was a shiny pink laptop.

TWENTY-SEVEN

Paris felt like she was blathering, but Abby squeezed her arm periodically as if to say, *I'm still here.* Lucy sniffled in the stroller.

The siren drew closer.

'That's them,' Paris said. 'They're almost here. They'll come in like a herd of elephants, laden down with gear, and then it'll be action stations all around you.'

Under her compressing palms the plastic wrap was hot and slick with blood. Abby's breathing had evened and calmed a little, and the plastic meant that no more air was being drawn into her chest from the outside at least. Her skin was pale and clammy, her lips tinged with blue. Kneeling there in her blood, Paris realised what it meant to be able to give oxygen and IV fluids, to know backup was a radio call away, to have a sidekick to bring in the stretcher, and an ambulance in which to race to hospital.

'It'll get busy around you,' she went on, 'but don't be scared. They might put the siren on when they take you to hospital, but don't get scared by that either. This time of day, traffic's crapola and it's just to get them to move.'

She wanted to say, *It doesn't mean you're dying,* but wasn't sure she could make the words convincing. Abby opened her eyes and Paris saw that she knew the truth.

'Listen,' she said.

'Don't talk,' Paris said. 'Save that air.'

'It was Stacey in the hallway last night. When you were in the bath.' She closed her eyes. 'She wanted to talk, tell you everything's okay. That she loves you.'

Paris didn't know what to say. 'So you don't have a ghost?'

Abby smiled. 'No ghost.'

The siren stopped outside. Paris saw the ambulance through the open door, the paramedics grabbing their gear. 'Hang in there. You're going to be just fine.'

'Look after Lucy,' Abby whispered. 'Tell her and Liam I love them. I'll always love them.'

'You'll be telling them yourself after a bit of surgery,' Paris said. 'You're going to be fine.'

The paramedics came in, two women Paris had met before. 'Paris, right?' one said, and Paris nodded. 'What's happened?'

'This is Abby. She got stabbed in the right chest. It's a sucking chest wound, I've got plastic over it. The knife didn't come out her back, and she's not hurt anywhere else. Um, I don't have a watch but her pulse has been about a hundred to one-twenty, around there, and her resps were like about forty at the start and now down to thirty or so.' Now that help was here she could feel the tears and the shakes creeping up. 'She's lost all this blood, it's like, I don't know how much . . .'

'It's okay. You've done great.' The first paramedic put an oxygen mask on Abby's face. 'Hi, Abby. I'm Jo and this is Tia. This is oxygen to help you breathe. Tia's putting a tourniquet around your arm and she's going to pop in a little needle to give you some fluids. We'll check out this dressing on your side where Paris has done such a great job, and whizz you off to hospital. Are you allergic to anything? Do you take any medication?'

Abby shook her head twice.

'Great. Okay.' Jo listened to Abby's chest, then hung the stethoscope back around her neck. 'Keep the plastic in place there for me,' she said to Paris. 'The little one's okay? And you?'

'We're fine.' Paris felt the crack in her voice.

Abby's eyes were closed, her grip on Paris's arm loosening a little. Under Paris's hands her chest moved in and out as she breathed, but her skin felt cooler. She heard the detectives come down the ladder, then they appeared with a laptop.

'How's she doing?' Marconi asked.

Behind her, Shakespeare was taking the laptop into the kitchen and turning it on.

'Good,' Paris managed to say.

Jo held a clean wad of dressing in one gloved hand and an adhesive plastic-backed dressing in the other. 'When I say go, lift off and let's get this thing in place. Ready? Go.' Paris released the pressure on Abby's ribs. The paramedic removed the blood-coated plastic wrap and fixed the new dressing in place. She made sure the edges were stuck, and winked at Paris. 'You did good.'

'Abby,' Marconi said, 'was James here last night?'

Paris said, 'He was here earlier today. I was here too. He said Abby looked like the woman in the CCTV photo and was talking about how she and Stacey had met at the reunion.'

'Did he use the bathroom?' Marconi asked.

Paris nodded.

'Where is it?'

'Along there.'

Paris followed them. They opened the door to the bathroom and went in.

Marconi said to Shakespeare, 'He didn't hurt the others. He knew Stacey was here and not at the other houses. She only had that bucket up there, so she must've come down sometimes, to the toilet and shower. If he planted a bug here, he could've seen or heard her.'

Paris watched them inspect the walls, the architraves, and items on the bathroom shelves. Then Marconi stood under the fan vent and looked up. 'Murray.'

He went over, and she put a hand on his shoulder for balance and climbed onto the edge of the bath. She pressed her fingers into the grille of the vent and twisted. It came loose from the fitting, and Paris saw a tiny camera taped to the plastic cover.

'Bingo,' Marconi said.

★

By the time the ambulance left with a semiconscious Abby onboard, Liam and Paris following in Abby's car with Lucy strapped in the back, Crime Scene were working the hallway and the room in the roof and Elizabeth Libke was hunched over Stacey's laptop. Patrols were checking the Durham house and Marie's house, and were still searching for James's car.

Ella, feeling restless, fevered, watched Libke's fingers fly over the laptop's keys.

'There's definitely a partition here,' Libke said. 'He's set it up so if Stacey stumbled across it she'd think it was an ordinary error message.'

'And he never had to worry about anyone finding it because if she had a computer issue she'd get him to fix it,' Murray said.

Libke nodded. 'But if you know where to look, there's a password box.' The box appeared on the screen, the cursor flashing in the left side.

'Can you get around it?' Ella asked.

'Possibly. Though there's a chance he's programmed it to delete the files if I try, or if we attempt too many wrong passwords.'

Ella said, 'It could be our only chance to find out what he's been doing and where he's taken Stacey.'

★

Emelia clapped her hands as Rowan drove into the Playland car park. 'We here!'

'Yes, we are,' he said. He couldn't see Imogen's car, but they were a little early. He was looking forward to seeing her again.

'Guess what I doing first.'

'Going in the ballpit?'

He started to swing into the parking space, but the back door opened. James got in beside Emelia, a knife held low, and shut the door.

'Don't blow the horn, don't shout, don't do anything to alert anybody,' he said. 'If you love this kid like I love my wife, you'll put the car in reverse and drive out of here. Nod if you understand me.'

Mouth dry, blood screaming through his veins, Rowan nodded. In the mirror, he could see the tip of the knife pressing against Emelia's stomach, catching in the lace on the front of her dress.

'Don't hurt her,' he whispered.

'Do as I say and I won't need to.' James smiled down at Emelia. 'How's that puppy?'

But she was looking out the window as Rowan backed out of the space. 'Want to go in the ballpit!'

'It's okay, honey,' Rowan said.

He drove towards the street at a crawl, hoping to catch someone's eye, hoping someone would reverse out without looking and give him a reason to stop. In the mirror, James's eyes watched him, cold and hard, his free hand over the back of Emelia's car seat and his fingers twirling her curls. Emelia tried to move her head away but his hand followed. Rowan's heart twisted with fear.

'It's all right, sweetheart,' he managed to say.

Ahead, he saw Imogen's car turning in from the street. He willed her to recognise him, to notice. *See me. Look at me.*

The cars drew closer. He couldn't wave in case James saw. Imogen craned her neck, looking for him near the parked cars.

He slowed a fraction and stared at her face with all the intensity he could muster.

See me. See me.

And then he was past.

★

Detectives had gone to the Durhams' house then to Marie Kennedy's, but had found only Marie, who seemed genuinely stunned when they told her what had happened. Officers all across the city were looking for James's black Cruze. Ella paced in Abby Watmough's living room, wondering how Murray could sit still.

'That was easier than I thought,' Libke said at the table. 'He obviously never thought anyone other than Stacey would have serious access to her laptop.'

Ella looked over Libke's shoulder, but couldn't understand what was on the scrolling screens. 'Have you found any addresses?'

'Not so far.' She was still typing and reading as she talked. 'From what I can see, he's been running a few different Trojans and key loggers. A client would call him for an issue, say a virus or whatever, and he'd clean that off but hide the malware on their computer instead. This gave him access to things like their banking details, but he didn't use that – instead, he used their emails to send the malware on to their friends, often months down the track. Then he'd access the friends' banks and credit card details, and by keeping the value lowish – one to two thousand, say – when they discovered the problem and reported it to their bank, the bank would repay them and not put too much effort into tracing where the money had gone. Typically, scammers like him use VPN proxies, which means the IP address leads to a dead-end, often somewhere in Russia.'

'So nothing happens?' Murray said.

'We need to find Stacey,' Ella said.

'Nobody can keep up with it,' Libke said to Murray, her eyes still on the screen, 'and it's cheaper for the banks to deal with it that way than fix the system. They're in the business of making money, after all, so they'll take the cheapest option every time. Oh, this is interesting. An overseas account in the name of Stacey Jame – not Jane, not James – Durham. Stacey's a male name in the US, and Jame could be passed off as a misspelling of Jane or vice versa, so the gender could be explained either way. He's got half a million in that. And he's made a few drug purchases. Let's have a look. Prozac. For himself or her, I wonder? Viagra. Ha. Mifepristone.'

Ella googled it on her phone. 'For medical termination of pregnancy. Stacey was right.'

'The bastard,' Murray said.

Ella took a big breath. 'Still no addresses?'

'You'll be the first to know,' Libke said.

Ella went back to pacing, then her mobile rang. She grabbed it up. 'Marconi.'

'This is Imogen Davidov,' a woman said. 'I'm sorry to bother you, it might be nothing, but something strange has happened.'

'Like what?' Ella said.

'Rowan driving out of the Playland car park with Emelia in the back and James Durham beside her,' Davidov said. 'I almost missed them, and only saw the side of Rowan's face, but from what I could see, something's very wrong.'

'Got it,' Libke said behind her.

TWENTY-EIGHT

The address was a luxury apartment complex in Rhodes, with views of the city to the east and over the Parramatta River to the north.

'I'm talking to security there now,' Dennis said on speakerphone as Ella drove, her foot hard on the pedal. 'There's no answer in his apartment, but they're checking the car park for his car, and the CCTV as well.'

The sun was low and filled the car with an orange light. Ella could feel the tension in her jaw, her whole body. Cars were slow to move, not seeing her lights or hearing her siren until the last moment. 'He must've had a bug in Rowan's place too,' she said. 'To have heard him telling Imogen when he was going to Playland.' She braked hard and swerved around one inattentive driver and squeezed the wheel in frustration.

'You realise we're no good if we're dead,' Murray said.

At the address, a young Indian woman in black pants and jacket, a radio in her hand, waited on the footpath. A marked car pulled up right behind them.

'I'm Naseem Habib, duty security supervisor,' the woman told Ella and Murray. 'We didn't find Mr Durham's car, but in his space in the underground car park there's a blue Holden with a child seat in the back. I just spoke to your boss and gave him the numberplate. He said it belongs to a Mr Rowan Wylie.'

'The child seat's empty?' Ella said.

Habib nodded.

'Any blood in the car?'

'Not that is visible.'

'What sort of access is there to the apartment?'

'I'll show you.'

★

Rowan sat with his back against the wall and his arms tight around Emelia. She'd settled, thank goodness, and was playing with his keys. Her screaming had agitated James and that was the last thing in the world Rowan wanted.

'Just tell me the truth,' James said again. He knelt facing Stacey, who sat against the wall like Rowan, three metres further along.

When Rowan had been forced in here, Emelia wailing in James's arms as he held the knife to her chest, he'd initially felt relief at seeing Stacey, even though she was pale and bound and gagged, with a bandaged foot, and then terror at the entire situation. James had clearly lost it, and they were trapped in here with him.

'I have,' Stacey said. 'Rowan has nothing to do with it. I wanted him to save Gomez, that's all. I knew you wouldn't just dump him somewhere. I knew you'd want him to be adopted so he'd forget all about me.'

Rowan tried to catch her eye, but she didn't look his way. Around her lay strips of the duct tape James had torn from her mouth and her limbs. To Rowan it looked like he was hoping she might make a break for it so he'd have a reason to stab her.

'That's the truth,' she said to James, 'so you should let them go. This is just you and me.'

312

James dug the tip of the knife into the carpet. Rip, rip went the fibres on the blade. 'The thing is, I don't think that is the truth. So they can't go.'

Rowan went over the dimensions of the empty apartment once more. Three metres between him and Stacey. Four more to the glass sliding doors to the balcony, which were closed and latched. A metre on his other side to the island bench, and another two past there to the door. James had locked it and put on the security chain.

'It's the betrayal I can't stand,' James said.

'It's your baby, not his,' Stacey said.

James's mobile rang again. Rowan had heard sirens, guessed they were gathering outside somewhere. James had raised his head at the first one but hadn't reacted since.

'James,' he said.

'You shut up.'

Rowan rubbed his cheek on Emelia's hair. He couldn't see how this would end. A drawn-out hostage situation, with SWAT officers swinging onto the balcony and firing tear gas into the room? He'd already tried to suggest that Stacey could take Emelia and leave, and the two of them would talk it through, but James had told him, like just now, to shut up.

'I never cheated on you,' Stacey said. 'I asked him to find Gomez because he's my friend.'

'It doesn't make sense.' James ran the knifepoint back and forth, fraying up the carpet. 'You see how it doesn't make any sense?'

The phone rang again. The noise was harsh and Emelia started to cry.

'Shut her up,' James said.

'She's hungry and scared,' Rowan said. 'Is there any food in the cupboards?'

If James was annoyed enough by the sound to let him get up, he could rush the door. Let the cops in before James knew what was happening, before he could hurt Stacey.

'There's nothing,' James said.

'Let them go,' Stacey said. 'This is about us. They don't need to be here.'

'If you tell me the truth, you can all go,' James said.

'I am,' Stacey said.

Rowan shushed Emelia, nibbled her cheek with tiny kisses. She turned into his chest and put her hot arms around his neck.

'I gave you everything,' James said. 'I worked so hard.'

'Stealing other people's money,' Stacey said.

'You were going to get the life you always wanted – the island house, the walks at sunrise and sunset. We'd eat seafood every day and swim, and lie on the sand. We wouldn't have to work. We'd just be.'

'That's not the life I want at all.'

'It is. You told me on the honeymoon how much you wished you could stay there forever.'

'Something I said in the moment is not me stating my life's ambition. Honeymoons aren't reality. I want to work, I love my job. I want kids. I want my family around me. I've tried to tell you all this, but you don't hear me. I don't want to live on an island where it's just us, and I don't want anyone to lose their life savings because you're trying to give that to me.'

'Nobody lost their life savings,' he snapped. 'If it wasn't me, it would've been someone else. It happens all the time; the banks even factor it in. And it's not like I'm gambling or drinking it away.'

'That doesn't make it okay.'

Rowan wanted to tell Stacey not to provoke him, to say whatever he wanted to hear. If she really was pregnant, they both had children to get out alive.

Someone knocked at the door.

★

'James, it's Detective Marconi. Can you come to the door and talk to me, please?'

Ella waited. Either side of her, Murray and Sid Lawson and Marion Pilsiger and four uniformed officers waited. SWAT were on their way, and paramedics with their gear were gathering in the stairwell.

The third-floor apartment faced the river, so there was no view into the place. They'd gained access to the apartments either side, but there was no way to get from one balcony to the next without ropes. Nothing could be heard through the walls. Once SWAT got there with all their equipment, things would be different, but for now all they had were their voices.

'James, I just want to talk, and make sure everyone's okay. You don't even have to open the door.'

There was no response.

★

Rowan was sweating. Emelia was quiet, occupied with pulling all the cards and receipts out of his wallet, but James looked like he was getting angrier.

'If you're telling the truth,' he said to Stacey, when the voice outside stopped, 'that means you want to leave me.'

God, Rowan thought. *Say no. Say whatever he wants to hear. Just get us out of this room.*

'That's right,' Stacey said.

'But I gave you everything.'

'It's not about that. We want different things out of life. That's all.'

'That's all?' He dragged the blade across the carpet. 'You went off the pill. You put yourself in this situation. You made me do all this.'

'I fell pregnant when I was taking it,' she said. 'It happens, and it happened to us. I stopped taking it once I knew, but I didn't go behind your back.'

315

More knocking on the door. Emelia dropped the wallet and started to cry.

'Just shut up! Everyone shut up!' James shouted.

His voice rang off the walls of the empty apartment. Emelia cried harder. Rowan tried to muffle her face against him, but she fought to push him away. James screwed up his face and looked like he was about to scream.

'You know they'll kill you,' Stacey said through the noise. 'If you hurt us, you won't get out of here alive. So what are you going to do?'

'Shut up,' James said.

'They're all outside,' Stacey said. 'Probably about to come through those glass doors too.'

'Shut up, shut up.'

Rowan shook his head, trying to catch her eye.

'What did you think would happen?' she went on. 'We'd live happily ever after?'

'I thought you'd tell me the fucking truth,' he said.

'And then what? Huh?'

At the look on James's face, Rowan put Emelia on the floor and tried to tuck her behind him.

'We'd fix it and live happily ever after, just like you said.' James stood up. 'But now you say you want out. So where does that leave me?'

'In jail.' Stacey got awkwardly to her feet, pushing off the wall, hopping to keep the weight off her injured foot. 'And for even longer after this little stunt.'

Emelia wailed.

'Shut up!' James said.

'Hey,' Stacey said. 'Don't look at them, look at me. Your problem's with me, remember? Because you know what? I'm the one who sent the anonymous note to the cops. I knew you were up to something and I wanted them to find out.' She took a limping step sideways, towards the balcony. 'You let it slip, just like you let slip that you were glad when I lost the baby.'

Another step. Rowan realised she was drawing James's attention, drawing him away. The police were right at the door. If he could get to it and let them in quickly enough . . .

'I knew you'd guess I hadn't really been abducted,' she said. 'I knew that when Rowan saw the car he'd ring you, and you'd ring the bank. I knew what that would look like to the police. I knew you'd pull dramatic shit like going to The Gap.'

'Sit down,' James said.

'No.' She kept moving.

James looked from her to Rowan and back again. 'Sit the fuck down!'

'No.' She took another step, then stumbled and grabbed the handles of the sliding doors.

Before James could move, Rowan was on his feet, scooping Emelia up and running for the entry door. Emelia was screaming, and James was shouting, and Rowan scrabbled at the chain and turned the locks with slick fingers and a hammering heart.

'Go, go, go, go, go,' he found himself saying as he was bustled out and away, cops grabbing his arms and taking Emelia's screeching weight, while more cops poured inside.

★

Ella and Murray rushed in past Rowan and his wailing granddaughter with their weapons drawn. Stacey and James were fighting at the glass doors that led onto the balcony. They screamed at each other, and then the latch gave way and one of them, she couldn't tell who, shoved the door open. She saw the knife in James's hand, envisaged a close-up hostage situation, his back to the wall, the knife at Stacey's throat.

'Drop it,' she shouted.

He looked up.

'I told you,' Stacey said to him.

Ella saw in his eyes that he was trying to decide what to do. 'Just put it down. That's all you have to do. Let it go.'

He looked at her, a thought in his eyes that she couldn't read.

He let go of the knife. It fell with a clink on the balcony tiles. Ella started towards him, but he grabbed Stacey's arm and lunged for the wall. Stacey shoved him and threw herself on the balcony floor, and he lost his grip, then Ella saw him grasp the top of the wall as if to leap over.

She launched herself at him. Her hands slipped off his waist, off his jeans, as he went over the wall, then locked around one leg. He kicked, caught on top of the wall, and she stumbled against Stacey, who was trying to get up. Ella felt something tear loose in the old injury in her shoulder, then he kicked again, and as Murray came racing out to help, she lost her grip and James fell.

Murray ran for the door. 'He jumped. Send the paramedics down there.'

Ella looked over the wall. James lay on the grass, unmoving.

'Is he dead?' Stacey said in a small voice.

'I don't know.' Ella crouched beside her, her shoulder throbbing. 'Are you okay?'

In the fading light, Stacey looked ashen, even corpse-like. Her skin was cool and as dry as paper. She seemed hardly able to stay sitting upright.

'Get paramedics in here,' Ella shouted.

When they had her lying down, on oxygen, and were setting up to give her fluid, Ella stepped back, cradling her bad arm with her good.

'Hey, look,' Murray said. 'I bet that's what the psychic was warning you about. She knew that'd happen.'

'Don't be a moron. If she knew, why didn't she tell us the address instead? Then we could've been waiting for him.'

Murray shrugged. 'I'm just saying.'

She looked over the balcony wall again. James was moving

in the centre of a huddle of paramedics. One was trying to get him to lie still. Police were gathering, and she saw Detective Sid Lawson give her a huge and cheerful thumbs up. *We got him!*

'He's alive,' she said.

'Wet ground,' one of the paramedics on the balcony said. 'All that rain recently – makes for a soft landing.'

Ella saw James look up towards her.

'Tell her she'll have to visit me in jail,' he cried. 'She'll have to bring the kid and visit me whenever I want. I'm still alive, and I'm never going to die. She's mine forever.'

Stacey was crying. 'I know that's his voice, but what's he saying? I can't hear from down here.'

Ella shook her head. 'Nothing but nonsense.'

TWENTY-NINE

Saturday morning was clear and sunny. Callum brought Ella tea and toast in bed, and sat beside her to check her shoulder again.

'It's hard to drink when you're doing that,' she said as he rotated her arm in the air. 'Ouch.'

He pressed his fingers into the joint. 'Does that hurt?'

'A little.'

He moved to the old bullet and surgical scar. 'How about that?'

'Not so hard.'

He moved down her back, prodding the vertebrae and the muscles either side. 'Anywhere here?'

'No. Yes. Ow. There.'

'What about here?'

'No. All good.'

'Aaand here?'

'Thankfully that breast is fine,' she said. 'That one too.'

'Just making sure.' He sat back with a smile. 'You should get an X-ray though.'

'Monday,' she said.

'No, this morning. We'll go past RPA on the way to the wedding.'

She looked at the clock. 'You're joking.'

'Go as you are,' he said, and pulled back the covers. 'You look absolutely fine.'

★

There was no parking at RPA so Callum drove into the ambulance bay.

'This is silly. We'll be late,' Ella said. 'And you can't park here.'

'I'll run in with you and arrange it, then come back and move the car.'

She felt absurd hurrying through Emergency in her fancy blue dress, Callum smart in his suit and matching blue tie.

'Here we go,' he said. She followed him into radiology, where a smiling young woman greeted them. 'Penny, hi,' Callum said. 'This is my girlfriend, Ella. Previous shoulder injury from gunshot five years ago –'

'Six,' Ella put in.

'Six,' Callum said. 'Two days ago the same shoulder got wrenched in a fight with a bad guy. Some pain, decreased movement, tenderness in the area and into the thoracic spine. Should see him though: fractured T4, pelvis, looking at a long jail term once he's out of hospital. Reckon you could fit her in, please?'

'Not a problem,' Penny said. 'I've got a leg in the room, then I'll put her in after him.'

'Thanks so much.' Callum turned to Ella. 'If I can't find a park I'll just do laps, so text and I'll pick you up, okay?'

He dashed off. Penny pointed Ella to a chair and gave her a form to fill in. She felt ridiculous in her heels. It was cold in the radiology department and people kept looking in at her as they went by. She wrote out her details and looked at her watch.

'All done?' Penny took the form off her. 'You've ticked "not pregnant". You're sure?'

Ella let out a laugh.

'I'm serious,' Penny said. 'When was your last period?'

'Six weeks?' Ella said. 'Seven? Around there. But I've never been regular.'

Penny rummaged in a drawer, then handed her a pregnancy test kit. 'Bathroom's to the right.'

'Is this really necessary? It was nine weeks once, so six is nothing. And we're practically late for a wedding already.'

'The quicker you go,' Penny said. 'To the right. Pee on that stick.'

★

Twenty minutes later, she walked outside as Callum pulled up. 'Timing,' he said, as she got into the car. 'What did Penny say? Did she give you the films?'

Penny had practised with her until she could say two things. 'No fractures, and the films will be on your desk.'

'Great.' He checked for traffic and eased out. 'How's the pain? You're sure you don't want a sling?'

'I'm good.'

She stared out the window. She felt like she was standing on the edge of a chasm, and she knew she had to commit to the leap, but she was terrified of falling and never stopping. At the same time, a bright silver bubble rose in her chest.

She talked to herself the whole way to the park. *See that corner? You have to tell him before then.* The corner went past. *Those traffic lights. The following traffic lights. That roundabout. Before the next suburb. Before the* next *suburb.*

'You're sure you're okay?' Callum said.

She nodded.

'I know you didn't want to stop, but look, we're right on time.'

The street was lined with cars, the top of the marquee visible among the trees in the park.

'I'll drop you, then find a space and walk back,' Callum said.

'No. I'll walk with you.'

'The closest spot could be streets away.'

'Doesn't matter.'

They found a place to park, then started walking back. Callum took her hand. 'You're all clammy. You're sure it's not hurting?'

'No. I mean, yes. I'm sure.'

He looked into her face. 'You're pale too. What's wrong?'

How to say it? She felt tears rise.

'Ella.' He hugged her, kissed her. 'What's the matter?'

'The test,' she managed to croak.

'The X-ray?'

'The test they do before the X-ray.'

He stopped. 'The pregnancy test?'

She couldn't read his face through her tears. She felt full of both hope and fear.

'You're pregnant?' He held her arms, looked into her face, his grin huge and growing. 'Really? Truly?'

'Is this . . . I mean, I didn't know anything about it, I didn't intend for it or anything.' She wiped her eyes. 'And then there's the family, your mother, and your father, your mother's going to go nuts, and there's work and everything. It's so . . . It'll be so . . .'

'I can go part-time,' he said. 'I can work around your shifts. It'll be easy. It'll be great.'

She looked into his shining eyes. 'Is this what we want?'

'I do,' he said. 'I want you, and I want this.'

The silver bubble in her chest enveloped her heart.

'What do you want?' he said.

'The same,' she said. 'You and this.' They'd make it work, no matter what his mother said, no matter how they had to juggle work. And imagining her parents' delight made her cry all over again.

It was all going to work.

'Welcome!' said a man's voice.

Ella blinked and saw a tuxedo-clad Frank Shakespeare, Murray's father and retired Assistant Commissioner. He'd been her nemesis ever since he turned up in civvies at her crime scene and she'd told him to get the fuck out; and the relationship hadn't improved when on another occasion she'd mistaken him for a maintenance man and asked him to hurry up and fix the boiler.

Today, his face was flushed with pleasure, and he grasped her hand, then Callum's. 'Welcome! Come along in. They're about to begin.' He leaned close, as if to share a secret. 'It's a great day.'

Ella pulled Callum closer, and as she felt his smile against her cheek and his hand cup her belly, she blinked away her tears and said, 'A very great day indeed.'

ACKNOWLEDGEMENTS

Dear reader,
 This is the final book in the Ella Marconi series – for now, at least. The last eight years of writing about Ella and her police and paramedic friends and foes have been simultaneously marvellous and exhausting, and while I will miss her, I am relieved to be taking a break.

But, reader, what I will miss much more is the connection that the books and characters have built between us. Thank you for the support you've shown me, whether by reading the books, getting in touch to tell me how much you liked them, or talking about Ella in such a way that I know she's as alive in your head as she is in mine. It was you I thought about when I wrote, trying to work out what you imagined might come next and how I could turn that on its head to keep you reading, and the messages you sent about having to stay up all night to find out what happened made my day, every single time. So, thank you again.

Writing and publishing involves many people, and so thanks go to my agent Selwa Anthony, publisher Cate Paterson, editors Libby Turner and Nicola O'Shea, and publicist Charlotte Ree, as well as to everyone else in the Pan Macmillan family, past and present, who I've had the honour and pleasure of working with over the course of the series. I could not have wished for a better publishing experience, and I know how fortunate I am to be able to say that.

Thanks to my writer friends dotted all over the country. We've celebrated and commiserated over the years and I look forward to continuing that. Special thanks go to Graeme Hague who helped me get going, to my friends in the MPhil group (12 years since we started!), and particularly to dear Karen Brooks who is always there on the end of the phone, no matter what or when.

Thanks for answers (and stories) to Adam Asplin, Karen Davis, Alan Smith, and Mel Johnson.

Thanks to Rachel Nisbet, Sue Hickson, and Elizabeth Libke for their charitable donations and allowing me use of their names (or in Sue's case a combination of her grandchildrens' names, producing the inimitable Sid Lawson).

And thanks, lastly, to my family. You guys are the best, and you, Benette, are the bestest.

Cheers,

Katherine

Katherine Howell
Frantic

In one terrible moment, paramedic Sophie Phillips' life is
ripped apart – her police officer husband, Chris, is shot on their
doorstep and her ten-month-old son, Lachlan, is abducted
from his bed.

Suspicion surrounds Chris as he is tainted with police
corruption, but Sophie believes the attack is much more
personal, a consequence of her own actions.

While Chris is in hospital and the police, led by Detective Ella
Marconi, mobilise to find their colleague's child, Sophie's
desperation compels her to search for Lachlan herself. She
enlists her husband's partner, Angus Anderson, in the hunt for
her son, but will the history they share and her raw maternal
instinct lead to an even greater tragedy?

'Howell may have left the ambulance service but she can still
drive a narrative at full speed with the sirens blaring'
SYDNEY MORNING HERALD

'Compelling drama from the author whose career as an
ambulance officer gives the tale an
unnerving ring of truth'
WOMAN'S DAY

Katherine Howell
Cold Justice

The past haunts the present . . .

Nineteen years ago teenager Georgie Daniels stumbled across
the body of her classmate, Tim Pieters, hidden amongst
bushes. His family was devastated and the killer never found.

Now political pressure sees the murder investigation reopened
and Detective Ella Marconi assigned to the case. She tracks
down Georgie who is now a paramedic. She seems to be
telling the truth, so then why does Ella receive an anonymous
phone call insisting that Georgie knows more? And is it mere
coincidence that her ambulance partner, Freya, also went to
the same high school?

Meanwhile, Tim's mother suddenly turns her back on the
investigation yet his cousin, the MP whose influence reopened
the case, can't seem to do enough to help.

The more Ella digs into the past, the more the buried secrets
and lies are brought to light. Can she track down the killer
before more people are hurt?

'A murder, a secret and a detective who
won't let go – *Cold Justice* has pace,
precision and a wonderful sense of place.'
MICHAEL ROBOTHAM

'One of my favourite books of the year.
Katherine Howell has written a winner!'
TESS GERRITSEN

Katherine Howell
Web of Deceit

When paramedics Jane and Alex encounter a man refusing
to get out of his crashed car, with bystanders saying he
deliberately drove into a pole, it looks like a desperate cry for
help. His frantic claim that someone is out to get him adds to
their thinking that he is delusional.

Later that day he is found dead under a train in what might be
a suicide, but Jane is no longer so sure: she remembers the
raw terror in his eyes.

Detective Ella Marconi shares Jane's doubts, which are only
compounded when the case becomes increasingly tangled.
The victim's boss tries to commit suicide after being questioned,
a witness flees Ella's attempt to interview her, and then to
confuse matters further, a woman is beaten unconscious in
front of Jane's house and Alex's daughter goes missing.

Ella is at a loss to know how all these clues add up, and feels
the investigation is being held back by her budget-focused
boss. Then, just when she thinks she's closing in on the right
person, a shocking turn of events puts more people in danger
and might just see the killer slip through her hands.

Praise for Katherine Howell:

'Howell is good at panic and rush . . . at character and
dialogue . . . what she does best: relationships in all their
complexity . . . the real strength of this
always interesting series' Sue Turnbull,
SYDNEY MORNING HERALD

'Howell's books are always suspenseful
and her plots thicker than minestrone'
SATURDAY AGE

'Not to be read on public transport: you
might miss your stop' SUN-HERALD

Katherine Howell
Deserving Death

Detective Ella Marconi returns in this thrilling case, set against
the dangerous background of drug deals, police corruption and
deadly consequences.

Two paramedics murdered in a month. Coincidence, or the
work of a serial killer? Detective Ella Marconi isn't sure, but
goes hard after her key suspects, including police officer
John Morris. But each turn of the case throws up more
questions and entanglements, and Ella and her partner,
Detective Murray Shakespeare, fight to find the truth among
the lies.

Ella also struggles to balance work and her relationship with
Dr Callum McLennan – a relationship made more difficult by
the anniversary of his cousin's murder.

Meanwhile, Carly Martens – close friend of the second
victim – conducts her own investigation into the murders.
She's certain that fellow paramedic Tessa Kimball is hiding
something, and Carly's refusal to let it go puts her, Tessa, and
Ella into even more danger.

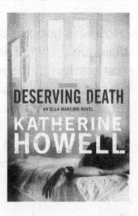